Praise for *That Certain Summer*

"The lives of these endearing characters intertwine over a summer and undergo change as Hannon has readers rooting for each one of them in this uplifting story about love and redemption."

—*Publishers Weekly*

"*That Certain Summer* is a story about . . . the courage to face one's darkest fears and the wonder of the human spirit. Irene Hannon knows the power of words and the miracle of faith."

—*New York Journal of Books*

"Beautiful storytelling and genuine, vulnerable, faithful characters are the strength of this story. This one simultaneously moves you to tears, makes you laugh, and leaves you speechless while warming your heart. A gem of a read."

—*RT Book Reviews*

"Hannon creates characters that we can both relate to and root for; we learn from their lives as we are also entertained—the true mark of an amazing summer read."

—*Hope for Women*

"A great weekend or rainy-day read, *That Certain Summer* will warm your heart and might even make you take a fresh look at some of the difficult relationships in your life."

—*USA Today's Happily Ever After* blog

Praise for *Vanished*

"An engaging, satisfying tale that will no doubt leave readers anxiously anticipating the next installment."

—*Publishers Weekly*

"This novel's fast-paced plot and compelling characters (including a surprisingly complex villain) make it an excellent suggestion for inspirational-fiction fans as well as readers who enjoy Mary Higgins Clark's subtly chilling brand of suspense."

—*Booklist*

"This fast-paced, suspenseful series debut novel is typical Hannon, a blend of action and romance, and is sure to please her fans."

—*Library Journal*

One Perfect Spring

Books by Irene Hannon

HEROES OF QUANTICO
Against All Odds
An Eye for an Eye
In Harm's Way

GUARDIANS OF JUSTICE
Fatal Judgment
Deadly Pursuit
Lethal Legacy

PRIVATE JUSTICE
Vanished
Trapped

That Certain Summer
One Perfect Spring

One Perfect Spring

Spring

A Novel

IRENE HANNON

Revell

a division of Baker Publishing Group
Grand Rapids, Michigan

© 2014 by Irene Hannon

Published by Revell
a division of Baker Publishing Group
P.O. Box 6287, Grand Rapids, MI 49516-6287
www.revellbooks.com

Printed in the United States of America

Library of Congress Cataloging-in-Publication Data
Hannon, Irene.
    One perfect spring : a novel / Irene Hannon.
        pages cm
    ISBN 978-0-8007-2267-8 (pbk.)
    1. Love-letters—Fiction. I. Title.
PS3558.A4793O54 2014
813'.54—dc23   2013049193

14 15 16 17 18 19 20   7 6 5 4 3 2 1

To my parents, James and Dorothy Hannon,
as they celebrate sixty years of marriage.

Thank you for your example of faithfulness and devotion,
for your unwavering support and encouragement,
and for your unconditional love.

You are—and always have been—
the wind beneath my wings.

I love you more than words can say.

Prologue

Dear Mr. McMillan,

My name is Haley Summers. I'm 11 years old.

I saw your pixture in the paper from when you gave money to the childrens hospital. My mom said you do a lot of nice things for people. So I wanted to ask if you could do something nice for our friend next door.

A long time ago, she had a baby. But he got adopted and she never saw him again. Now she's sad and wishes she could find him. Her name is Docter Chandler and her birthday is in May. She's going to be sixty and she's been real sick and this would cheer her up a lot.

She's a very nice lady. She teaches at a college and makes awesome cookies and gave me a present on my birthday last year. This year, I want to give _her_ a present.

I hope you can help me. Thank you very much

Haley

1

It was going to be another late night at the office.

Keith Watson rotated the kinks out of his neck, leaned back in his chair, and grimaced at the intimidating stack of solicitations on the corner of his desk.

Donations from the McMillan Charitable Foundation might produce positive PR for the company, but press coverage for events like that check presentation at the children's hospital always stirred up a plethora of do-gooders—and good-for-nothing handout seekers. If past experience was any indication, there'd only be one or two appeals here worth passing on to David McMillan for consideration.

Keith tipped his coffee mug toward him. Nothing but dregs—and it was too late in the day to brew a new pot.

Too bad.

He could use a caffeine infusion.

Resigned, he set the mug aside. Why couldn't his boss have given this ongoing task to someone else eight months ago instead of dumping it on his desk? Sorting through pleas for money wasn't the most productive use of an MBA/CPA's time—nor did it contribute to the construction company's bottom line. And David McMillan was all about the bottom line.

Or at least he used to be, back in the days when he took a hands-off approach to the foundation and delegated duties like this to the PR company they kept on retainer instead of to his executive assistant.

Who knew why he'd brought this job in-house?

Just one more thing that had changed in the past year.

Heaving a sigh, Keith tugged the stack toward him across the polished mahogany. If he wasn't heading out of town tomorrow, he could push the review off until the morning—but since he didn't have any big Friday night plans anyway, might as well wrap this up and be done with it.

Stomach growling, he checked his Rolex. Six o'clock. If he sped through the stack, he might be able to make it to his favorite Chinese takeout place before . . .

"I'm out of here." The administrative assistant he shared with David shrugged on her trench coat in the doorway to his office. "Do you need anything else?"

"I'm set—but why are you still hanging around? I thought Fridays were always date night with your husband?"

Robin made a face. "Not when you have two children who both decided to get the flu on the same day. John picked them up at school right after lunch. My evening will consist of forcing fluids and watching kids upchuck."

He winced. "That's almost worse than going through these solicitations. Almost."

"Trust me, it's worse. Besides, I spotted a couple of interesting requests in the stack that might keep you entertained."

"I'll bet." A bolt of lightning sliced through the dark clouds massed in the April sky outside his window, followed by a boom of thunder that rattled the glass. "But I doubt we'll ever top the guy who claimed he'd inherited a map from the Middle Ages that would lead to a trove of never-discovered paintings by Michelangelo."

Robin grinned. "Yeah. As I recall, he wanted the foundation to fund his trip to Europe so he could scavenge around. What an angle. But he did offer to split the proceeds with us."

"Right."

She finished buttoning her coat. "So once you dig out from that pile of letters, any exciting plans for the weekend?"

"Other than going to the regional builders association dinner in Des Moines tomorrow night and visiting our office building project in Cedar Rapids on Sunday?"

"Whoops. Forgot about that. Maybe you could take a comp day next week."

"There's too much to do here."

She shook her head. "You need to get a life."

"I have a life. One I happen to like very much."

"More's the pity. Remember, all work . . ."

"Tell that to David."

"He's been a lot better about that since his wife died. Too bad it took a tragedy to make him see the light." She sent him a pointed look.

He waved her out the door. "Go home and take care of your sick kids. Once I get through this pile, I'm out of here."

"Until some new, urgent email comes in. But hey . . . it's your life." Another crash of thunder boomed through the building, and she cringed, surveying the pelting rain. "Looks like I'll be taking my evening shower en route to my car."

"No umbrella?"

"Plenty of them. All in the coat closet in my foyer."

Keith pulled out the bottom drawer of his desk and retrieved a collapsible version. "Take mine. The rain may let up before I'm ready to leave."

Hesitating, she squinted out the window again. "I doubt this storm will end any time soon. You may need it."

"I'm parked near the door—and I can run fast."

"Sold." She took the umbrella. Tapped it against her hand. "Are you ever caught unprepared?"

"Not if I can help it."

"I wish some of your planning ability would rub off on me. Thanks for this"—she waved the umbrella at him—"and have a good trip to Iowa."

As she disappeared out the door, the office fell silent. The rest of the staff had probably headed out closer to five, anxious to prepare for family events or primp for dates or gather with friends at a happy hour after a long week of work.

For one tiny second, Keith felt a touch of jealousy—but he quashed it before it could take hold. He'd chosen to focus on his career instead of a social life, and he had no regrets.

Jobs were a lot more predictable than people.

Psyching himself up for the task at hand, he picked up the first solicitation and dug in.

Forty minutes later, surrendering to a yawn, he set a plea from a funds-strapped sailing club on top of the large reject pile and turned his attention to the last appeal. Handwritten by an eleven-year-old girl, it had a certain childish charm. But help a woman find a son she'd tossed aside years ago? That didn't even come close to meeting the parameters of the McMillan Charitable Foundation. While some of the requests had required a bit of thought, this was a no-brainer.

He added it to the reject pile, straightened the stack, then stood and stretched. A heaping plate of chicken broccoli with a side of egg rolls was sounding better by the minute.

Another crash of thunder shook the building, and he swiveled toward the window. Day had given way to night, and torrents of rain were slamming against the glass. So much for any hope the storm would let up. Par for the course this time of year in St. Louis, though.

His stomach growled again, spurring him into action. He picked up the large stack of rejects in one hand. With the other, he snagged the only two requests worthy of further evaluation. After depositing them on Robin's desk with a note to send the usual form letter to the rejects and pass the two possibilities on to David, he grabbed his computer and briefcase and headed for the exit.

At the main door, he paused to survey the sheets of rain pummeling the asphalt. Who would have guessed this morning's blue skies would turn gray? Strange how unsettled weather could sneak up on you. Might as well plunge in—and hope for the best.

What else could you do when you found yourself in the middle of a storm?

At the discreet knock on his half-closed door Monday morning, David McMillan tucked the sheet of paper in his hand under a report on the side of his desk. "Come in."

His executive assistant took a step into the office. "Robin said you wanted to see me as soon as I got in. Sorry I'm running a little late. My flight from Cedar Rapids had a weather delay last night and ended up being rescheduled until—"

"Keith." David held up his hand. "You've been with this company for eight years, and my assistant for the past three. I know your work ethic. Have a seat." He waved the younger man into the chair across from his desk. "How did the trip go?"

"Fine. The rubber-chicken dinner wasn't too exciting, but I made the circuit and spoke with the key players. I also took a quick look at the books in Cedar Rapids while I was there. Everything appears to be in order."

David studied the thirty-three-year-old go-getter across the expanse of burnished wood. Once upon a time—and for a very long time—that had been him. He'd wanted to get ahead, make a mark, create a security net for his family. And he'd succeeded beyond his wildest dreams. His wife and daughter had never lacked for any of the creature comforts.

But if he had it to do over . . . ?

He brushed that thought aside. It was too late for regrets. What was done was done. But perhaps he could keep another young man from making some of the same mistakes.

And the perfect opportunity had just dropped into his lap.

"Sounds like a worthwhile trip. I'm sorry it infringed on your weekend."

Keith shrugged. "I didn't have any plans that couldn't be changed."

"I bet your mother was disappointed when you didn't make it for Sunday dinner."

The other man shifted in his seat. "She understands my work can be demanding."

"Maybe you can drop in on her some night during the week."

David watched Keith squirm. Right about now, he was probably wishing he'd never mentioned his standing Sunday date with his widowed mother. When it came to his personal life, the man was as closemouthed as a savvy bass on a bad fishing day.

"Maybe."

But not likely. Keith always stayed at the office until seven or eight, and his mother lived in South County, a good forty minutes away.

David pulled the sheet of paper from beneath the report. "I found this on the floor next to Robin's chair this morning. One of the cleaning people must have knocked it off over the weekend. From the height of the stack on her desk, it appears quite a few people noticed that check-presentation photo in the paper." He handed the letter over. "Including a little girl."

His assistant spared the note no more than a quick glance. "I'll take care of this."

"That's exactly what I was going to suggest."

Keith sent him a wary look. "What I meant was, I'll make sure Robin sends the standard rejection letter."

"And what I meant was that you should follow up on it."

A couple of beats of silence passed before Keith responded. "This request is from an eleven-year-old. And it doesn't meet any of the foundation's parameters."

"I agree it's outside our charity's normal scope of activities. So it will require some personal involvement—and perhaps a private donation. But it sounds worthwhile. An ailing woman, a long-lost son, a little girl with a compassionate heart—a touching scenario, don't you think?"

A muscle twitched in Keith's jaw, but he remained silent.

David waited him out.

"I could make a phone call. Get a little more information." His tone was grudging, at best.

And David knew why.

Keith didn't consider this kind of assignment to be productive work.

But productivity was measured by goals—and while following up on the little girl's letter might not be productive in terms of Keith's goals, it dovetailed nicely with his own.

"An excellent start. Let me know what you find out and we'll go from there." He leaned forward and drew a pile of reports toward him. "I'd like to get a roundtable together this week with some of the foremen to vet the draft of our bid for that apartment complex rec center. Can you set it up, call in the right people?"

"Of course." Keith rose, scanned the girl's letter . . . hesitated.

The muscle flexed in his jaw again, but after a moment he continued toward the door.

Leaning back in his chair, David tapped a finger on the arm and watched his assistant exit. Keith was a good man—smart, capable, stellar work ethic, single-minded focus on the job at hand—all qualities that added up to a promising future. When Tom retired next year, it would be easy to slide Keith into the job of controller with nary a blip in operations.

In fact, that had been his plan for almost two years.

Now . . . he wasn't as certain.

David swiveled toward the credenza behind him. As always, Carol smiled back at him from the photo he'd snapped on their Mediterranean cruise three years ago. The one she'd insisted they take for their thirtieth anniversary, overriding his protests that things were too busy at work. They were always too busy, she'd claimed—and she'd been right. How many times through the years had he begged off family events with that excuse?

Too many.

Yet the light of love shone steady in her eyes despite her years of playing second fiddle to his work. Leaning against the railing of the ship, the blue sea behind her, she looked the picture of health and far younger than her fifty-seven summers.

Who could have guessed that one year later, she'd be dead?

His throat tightened, and a film of moisture blurred his vision.

So many missed opportunities to spend time with the woman he loved.

So many missed opportunities to attend Debbie's dance recitals and school plays and volleyball games.

So many missed chances to say "I love you" with attention and time as well as with words and material things.

He shifted his gaze toward the scene outside his window. After the long, cold winter, the tulips and forsythia bushes were finally in bloom. Carol had always called spring the season of hope; for him, it had always been the season of headaches, often filled with costly rain and mud delays.

But these days he chose hope over headaches.

If only Carol had been around to witness his transformation.

And if only Debbie had been receptive to it—not that he blamed her for her coolness. Why should she be grateful for the attention he lavished on his grandchildren when he'd had so little time for her during her own childhood?

He wasn't giving up, though—even if that meant he had to spend more time from now on building bridges instead of pouring concrete.

And along the way, perhaps he could help another young man learn that no matter what drives a person's ambition, in the end the only success that really matters can't be measured by a balance sheet.

Hefting two plastic sacks of groceries in one hand and her overstuffed tote bag in the other, Claire Summers limped from the driveway toward her front door.

What a day.

The odds had to be astronomical that two of her second graders would throw up, the class's pet gerbil would die, and she'd slip and twist her ankle in the grocery store parking lot—all in the space of eight hours.

Then again, when had the odds ever been in her favor?

"This smells really good, Mom."

She looked down at Haley prancing along beside her, the sack with golden arches cradled in her arms—and her spirits lifted.

Thank you, Lord, for a daughter whose sunny disposition and kind heart are a constant reminder that not all of my luck has been bad.

"Don't get used to it. You know how I feel about fast food." That last-resort meal option was reserved for only the toughest days—and today certainly qualified.

"I know, I know. Home cooked is healthier and more nutritious." Haley parroted her standard words back to her. "But I love French fries!"

Of course she did. What eleven-year-old didn't?

Claire stepped onto the porch of their bungalow, set her tote bag down, and rummaged in her pocket for her key. As soon as they finished dinner, she was going to have to check out the garage door that had refused to budge this morning. "I like them too—in moderation. A little bit goes a long way . . . like with Hershey kisses."

Haley scrunched up her face as she followed her through the door. "Yeah. I'll never eat a whole bag at once again. Throwing up all night was no fun."

"For me, either." Claire plunked the grocery bags on the kitchen counter and dropped her tote on the floor next to the small island. "Why don't you pour yourself a glass of milk while I get a—"

The phone rang, and she huffed out a breath. A survey or solicitation, most likely. Those calls always seemed to come at dinnertime.

She crossed to the counter. When an unfamiliar name blinked back at her from the digital display, she let the call roll to the answering machine.

While she filled a glass with ice and water from the fridge, the answering machine kicked in. "Please leave a message." A beep sounded.

Silence.

The corners of her lips tipped up. Her pithy greeting surprised a lot of people . . . but why say more? Everyone knew the drill by now. If a phone went unanswered, either no one was home or the machine was being used to screen calls. As for the ubiquitous beep—there wasn't a soul in the developed world who needed instructions for that.

In this case, either the person on the other end was still too taken aback to speak, or it had been an automated call that had disconnected when the machine answered.

As Claire slid into her chair at the table and picked up a fry, a male voice finally spoke.

"Good afternoon. This is Keith Watson with McMillan Construction. David McMillan received a letter from a Haley Summers at this address, and I'm trying to reach one of her parents. I'd appreciate a call at your earliest convenience."

As the man recited his number, Claire looked at her daughter.

The little girl's eyes were wide, her fries forgotten. "Wow! I wasn't even sure the letter would get to him."

"What letter?"

"The one I sent about Dr. Chandler." Her face lit up. "I bet he's going to help me!"

Claire pushed aside her burger and folded her hands on the table. "Haley . . . let's start at the beginning. Why did you write a letter to this company—and what does it have to do with Dr. Chandler?"

At her serious tone, the little girl's smile faded. "Am I in trouble?"

"I have no idea until you tell me what you did."

"I was just trying to give Dr. Chandler a really awesome birthday present."

"Her birthday isn't until May."

"I know, but it could take awhile to find her little boy."

Claire's heart stumbled. How in the world did her daughter know about Maureen's son? She'd only found out herself three weeks ago. Unless . . .

"Were you eavesdropping on our conversation?"

"No." Haley gave a vehement shake of her head. "But I heard

you talking about it when I got up to get a drink of water that night after we had pizza for dinner. Remember how pepperoni always makes me thirsty?"

"Yes. But you aren't supposed to listen in on private conversations."

"I didn't mean to. I was coming down the stairs, but I stopped when I heard Dr. Chandler crying. I've never heard her cry before." She poked a French fry into the ketchup but didn't eat it. "She sounded so sad about her lost baby. I went back upstairs without my water, but I couldn't go to sleep for a long time. I thought it might cheer her up if I could find him for her. Was that wrong?"

At the anxious question, Claire took a deep breath. Since the day she'd found an abandoned baby bird as a toddler, Haley had shown remarkable compassion for anyone—or anything—in need. It was a trait to be encouraged, not criticized . . . even if Claire still had no idea what the phone call from a construction company was all about. "It's never wrong to want to help people. But why did you send a letter to this David McMillan?"

"Remember that picture of him in the paper, at the children's hospital? You said he was giving them money because he liked to help people. I thought maybe he'd help me too. I wanted it to be a surprise, so I looked up the address of the company on your computer and asked Dr. Chandler for a stamp and sent him a letter."

Claire could conjure up only a vague recollection of their exchange about the newspaper photo. No surprise there, since her inquisitive daughter asked dozens of questions every day.

"Did I do a bad thing?"

At Haley's timid question, she reached across the table and patted her hand. "Your intentions were good, and I'm proud of you for wanting to help Dr. Chandler. But I'm sure Mr. McMillan won't have time for a project like this. People in big companies are very busy, and usually they do things that help a whole lot of people, not just one. Like the hospital donation."

"Then why would a man from that company call us?"

Because he had a soft heart? A nice thought—but she wasn't going to hold her breath. Most of the businesspeople she'd met weren't the softhearted type.

Especially one.

"Mom? Why would he call us?"

Forcing her taut lips to relax, she refocused on her daughter. "I don't know, but no matter what, Dr. Chandler shared that information with me in private—like a secret. I don't think she wants a lot of people to know about her son."

"Why not? And why did she give her baby to someone else, anyway?"

There were days when motherhood was easy and fun and the best job in the world.

This wasn't one of them.

How did you explain to an eleven-year-old who still went to bed with her Raggedy Ann doll that their single, fifty-nine-year-old art professor neighbor had had a one-night stand twenty-two years ago that resulted in a baby?

Claire smoothed out a paper napkin and chose her words with care. "She wasn't married, honey, and she wanted her baby to have a mother and a father."

Haley poked at another fry. "I don't have a father, and you kept me."

A steady ache began to throb in her temples. "I was married when you were born, and you were already five when we got divorced. So your dad was part of your life."

"Then how come I don't remember him?"

Because once the marriage ended, he hightailed it to the West Coast as fast as he could and never looked back. And he wasn't home much before that, either.

But she couldn't say that. *Wouldn't* say that. She wasn't going to demonize her ex-husband to their child—even if he deserved it.

"Like I've told you before, he had a busy job, and after he moved all the way across the country it was very hard for him to visit." Lightening her tone, she slid the fries closer to her daughter. "Now we better eat up or our dinner is going to get cold."

Haley opened her chicken nuggets. "So are you going to call that man back?"

"Yes. First thing tomorrow. But this is personal business for Dr. Chandler, so we have to let her handle it her own way and not interfere. Besides, her son is all grown up now. This happened a long time ago."

Haley issued a protracted sigh. "Okay." She popped a fry in her mouth and winced. "Eww! This is already cold."

"I'll put everything in the microwave for a minute." Claire gathered up the cardboard boxes, dispersed the food to plates, and set about rewarming their dinner.

"I wish I could remember my daddy."

Better that you don't.

But again, her spoken words were different. "You have pictures."

"That's not the same. And you never talk about him."

"We got divorced, honey. I don't have very happy memories."

"But you must have loved him in the beginning. You know, like in my storybooks."

Had she? Those early days seemed long ago now. She'd been young and foolish and far too susceptible to flattery and a roguish eye. Only in hindsight had she recognized the truth of her parents' assessment—her romance had been more about lust than love.

Another subject she wasn't ready to discuss with her daughter.

Hoping to divert further questions, she pulled Haley's dinner out of the microwave and set it in front of her. "Dive in."

Haley picked up a fry and took a tentative bite. "This is much better." The youngster began to eat with gusto.

A minute later, the microwave pinged again. Claire removed her own plate and joined Haley at the small table against the wall. In general, this one-on-one time with her daughter was a favorite part of her day.

Yet all at once, she found herself wishing things had worked out better for her in the romance department. That she'd had the kind of ending found in Haley's storybooks, where a couple rode off into the sunset and lived happily ever after. That she could warm up her disillusioned heart as easily as she'd warmed up their dinner.

A microwave for the heart.

Now there was a fanciful thought.

Pushing aside such whimsy, she picked up a fry, took a bite—and let out a yelp.

"What's wrong?" Haley sent her a startled look.

"Hot." She waved her hand in front of her mouth, then took a long swallow of cold water.

"Ouch." Haley gave her arm a commiserating pat. "I burned my tongue on one of those chocolate chip cookies you made last week, remember? You told me to let them cool, but they smelled so good I didn't want to wait."

"Uh-huh." She took another drink of water, every thought about microwaves for the heart vanishing.

Because when food—or hearts—got too warm, people could get burned.

Been there, done that, never going down that road again.

Love was a gamble . . . and she'd had her fill of losing.

2

. . . .

C. Summers.

As the name flashed on the digital display of his desk phone, Keith groaned. He'd half hoped Haley's parents would ignore his call.

But no—that would have been too easy.

Angling away from the first-quarter report on his laptop screen, he reached for the receiver. Might as well get this over with.

"Watson." The greeting came out more clipped than he intended.

"Mr. Watson, this is Claire Summers." The woman on the other end of the line didn't sound any too friendly, either. "You called last evening about the note my daughter sent to David McMillan."

"Yes. According to her letter, she saw Mr. McMillan making a donation to—"

"Haley explained it all to me last night."

At her interruption, he fell silent. Fine with him if she wanted to take charge of this conversation.

"I appreciate your follow-up, but I'm sure you have more

important business to take care of. Besides, while her intentions were admirable, Haley overstepped. This is a private matter for my neighbor, and the information Haley overheard was shared in confidence."

Despite the sarcasm underscoring the words *more important business*, some of the tension evaporated from his shoulders.

He was off the hook.

No reason not to be cordial now. "I understand. We certainly wouldn't want to invade anyone's privacy. I'll let Mr. McMillan know we touched base and that you thought it best to let the matter rest."

A couple of beats of silence ticked by.

"Out of curiosity . . . you weren't going to offer to help my daughter anyway, were you?"

He shifted, the leather creaking beneath his weight as he wrestled down the temptation to say no. "Mr. McMillan did ask me to look into the situation. He's a very compassionate man, and your daughter's letter touched him. If he could have helped with her request, I believe he would have."

"Interesting." Was that a hint of surprise in her inflection? "But I take it you would have had to do the grunt work."

"I'm his assistant."

"And this kind of task isn't your forte."

He frowned. Somehow the conversation had gotten off track—and he didn't like her condescending tone.

Before he could respond, she spoke again. "Please thank your boss on behalf of my daughter. Now I'll let you get back to your work."

With that, the line went dead.

He removed the receiver from his ear and stared at it.

Sheesh.

Had the woman gotten up on the wrong side of the bed—or was she just naturally ornery?

Whatever.

At least the problem was off his desk.

He dropped the receiver into the cradle and swiveled back to his computer. After opening a blank email, he began to type.

> David: I spoke with Haley Summers's mother, who said her neighbor shared the information about the child she gave up for adoption in confidence. She prefers we not intrude on this personal matter. I've assured her that wasn't our intent. When you get back to the office, I'm ready to discuss the agenda and the list of attendees for the bid meeting.

Keith spell-checked the document, tapped the send button, and blew out a relieved breath.

That was that.

As the kindergarten class took a bow, David joined the rest of the grandparents in a round of enthusiastic applause for the youngsters' spring theatrical effort.

"I wish Mom could have been here for this."

At Debbie's melancholy comment, he turned. In profile, his daughter bore such a striking resemblance to Carol at the same age that it paralyzed his lungs for a moment.

He swallowed, giving the applause a chance to die down. "I like to think she is in spirit."

"It's not the same." Debbie kept her focus on the small stage, watching the kindergarteners scramble down and head for their respective relatives.

"I'm here."

She ignored that, bending to give Grace a hug instead. "You were wonderful, sweetie! The best butterfly in the whole show!"

His granddaughter extricated herself and tucked her small hand in his. "Did you like it, Grampa?"

He lowered himself to her level. "I loved it. You were a beautiful butterfly. The prettiest one I've ever seen."

Glowing, she tilted up her chin to regard her mother. "Did Daddy come?"

"No, sweetie." Debbie's smile was strained around the edges. "Remember, he had to fly to New York this morning for a meeting. But I took a video with my phone, and we'll send it to him later."

The little girl's face fell. "I was hoping he might wait until after my show to leave."

"When you have a job, you have to go to meetings when the boss tells you to." Her accusatory gaze locked with his, her unspoken words hanging in the air between them.

But you were the boss while I was growing up. You made the schedules. You could have come to my special events.

There was no denying the truth—nor could he change the past. He could only do better in the future . . . if she'd let him.

Maybe someday she would, if he kept at it.

"Are you going to stay for our party, Grampa?"

"I wouldn't miss it."

"First I have to change out of my costume."

"I'll help you. We'll meet Grampa back in your classroom. Can you find your way?" Debbie took Grace's hand as she tossed the query to him.

"I remember from the party after the Christmas play."

"We'll see you there." Debbie led Grace off, the little girl's gossamer wings bobbing behind her.

As the rest of the grandparents began to stroll toward the hall, he pulled out his cell. It had vibrated half a dozen times since he'd arrived, but watching his granddaughter perform took precedence.

Joining the crowd moving toward the kindergarten classroom, he scrolled through the messages. There was nothing that couldn't wait, based on the subject lines. But when he saw "Letter/Meeting" in the header of Keith's email, he clicked it open.

Halfway through the message, he stopped walking while the crowd divided around him. The child's letter had seemed like a providential opportunity to involve his assistant in a hands-on people project that might open his eyes to the fact that there was more to life than numbers. Eight months of dealing with the donation requests for the charitable foundation certainly hadn't done the trick.

Now that appeared to be off the table.

Slipping the phone back on his belt, he ambled toward Grace's classroom, tuning out the chatter around him. Of course he could understand how this might be a private matter. And it was possible his plan was dead in the water.

Then again, maybe it wasn't—depending on what he discovered after he did a little investigating of his own.

"Does your ankle still hurt, Mom?"

Claire closed the car door, wincing as her forearm brushed against the edge. The bruise she'd gotten last night freeing the stuck garage door hurt a lot worse. "Not as much."

"What are we having for dinner?"

"Chicken."

Haley wrinkled her nose. "I had chicken last night."

"McNuggets are fried. Baked chicken tastes a lot different."

"Yeah, but I like fried better."

What kid didn't?

Claire unlocked the door that led from the garage to the

kitchen and gestured Haley inside. "I'm going to grab the mail while you put your school things away."

"Okay."

On her trek down the driveway to the box at the curb, she inspected the peeling surface and the gouges beneath her feet. The harsher-than-usual winter had done a number on the asphalt. No way could she put off a sealing job until next year.

Another unbudgeted expense to add to her growing list.

Worst of all, it would eat up the funds she'd earmarked for paint to brighten up the drab, coffee-colored walls in Haley's bedroom that had bothered her ever since they'd moved in last spring. A little girl deserved happy colors.

Maybe she should have made a more modest down payment and kept some discretionary funds on hand, instead of opting for a smaller monthly mortgage bill. But who knew the economy was going to tank and derail the ambitious schedule she'd set to rebuild her savings?

She toed off a loose piece of driveway coating. She could always seal it herself. How hard could it be?

Toying with that possibility, she pulled the mail from the box and riffled through it. A preponderance of bills, as usual. Looked like she was going to have to be a do-it-yourselfer for a long time to come—whether she wanted to or not.

But owning a house was a far better investment than paying rent. She was building equity, and that was a smart, logical thing to do.

She needed to keep reminding herself of that.

With a sigh, she glanced at Maureen's house and started back up the driveway. At some point she needed to let her neighbor know about Haley's letter, but there wasn't a whole lot of urgency. Maureen wouldn't hold Haley's unintended indiscretion against her, and as far as McMillan Construction was concerned, her daughter's note was surely in the dead letter file by now, no harm done.

31

When she entered the house, Haley was having an animated conversation on the phone—and it took Claire only a moment to identify the caller. The man who'd been her rock since the day she was born might live in South Carolina, but he made it his business to touch base at least twice a week. And his calls always brought an extra spark of animation to his granddaughter's face.

"Yeah! That would be fun! Mom just came in. I'll let you ask her." Haley held out the phone. "Cap wants to know if we can come visit this summer."

Claire gave her daughter's French braid a gentle tug. "We'll discuss it."

"That means no."

"It means maybe."

"Same thing." She huffed out a breath and put the phone back to her ear. "Make her say yes, okay, Cap?"

Whatever her father said generated a giggle from her daughter. "Yeah. Here she is."

"Start your homework while I talk to your grandfather."

"Oh, Mom! I just got home from school."

"Better to get it done right away. Then the whole rest of your evening will be free." Turning her back on Haley's grumbling, she wandered over to the window that looked into the backyard. "Hi, Dad. How's the fishing business?"

"Can't complain."

He never did. No matter what hand fate dealt him, he kept plugging along. But the languishing economy and consequential belt tightening must still be having an impact on his charter business, as it had for the past several years.

"Are you getting some bookings?"

"It's still early in the season."

That meant no. Or not enough.

Her stomach clenched. Worrying about her own finances was bad enough without adding her father's woes to the mix.

As if he'd read her mind, he spoke again. "I had a profitable job yesterday, though. A group of businessmen from Nashville wanted to try some inshore fishing. Came away with a nice catch of bass, trout, and mackerel. I'm hanging in, Claire. You don't need to worry about your old man. I have food to eat and a roof to sleep under and a fine boat to spend my days on in the sunshine and fresh air. What more could a man want? Now how are you and Haley doing?"

A section of sagging gutter caught her eye, and she leaned forward to examine it. When had that happened?

One more job to add to her to-do list.

"We're fine." She turned away from the window—but it was hard to escape reminders of the work that needed doing. A piece of peeling wallpaper near the ceiling fluttered in an air current, almost as if it was waving at her.

She'd gotten the house at a great price, though. All the fundamentals were sound, and the neighborhood was charming. With some judicious cosmetic work, the place would look good as new. She was fortunate to have found it.

For some reason, her usual mental pep talk didn't lift her spirits much tonight.

"So what do you think about heading my direction over the summer for a couple of weeks? I could take Haley out on the boat. She loved that the last time. And there's plenty of room at the house. It would just be a matter of gas money."

Except given the astronomical price of gas, that money could pay for some of the repairs she needed to do—or paint for Haley's room.

Still, summer visits were the only chance for Haley to see her grandfather. He couldn't afford to close up shop in the busy season, such as it was, and come to St. Louis. And the weather between St. Louis and the coast was dicey in the winter, when

Haley was off school for Christmas. As for spring break—it was hardly worth the long drive for such a short visit.

"I'll see if I can work it out, Dad. We'd both like to see you, but I'm trying to line up some tutoring jobs for the summer."

"Are things that tight, sweetie? I know it was a stretch for you to buy that house, even though it seemed like a great buy. But did you overextend?"

Maybe.

"No. We'll be fine. I'm just watching our pennies until I get a few cosmetic improvements taken care of."

"I wish I could help you out with those—and that I could have helped after the divorce too. But I can't seem to get much ahead with my cash reserves these days."

She knew all about the difficulties of saving despite the best of intentions—and it was worse for her dad. He might never complain about money, but her mother's extended battle with early-onset Alzheimer's had drained his savings. Insurance only paid for so much.

"I wouldn't have let you help back then, anyway. I got myself into that mess; I needed to get myself out." Haley looked over at her, a question in her eyes, and Claire lightened her tone. "As for coming out, I guarantee Haley will keep working on me. She's already giving me that 'please, can't we go?' look."

Claire hoped he got her message that youthful ears were listening and that a change of subject was in order.

He did—although the new topic wasn't much better.

"How's the social life?"

"About like yours." She moved over to the refrigerator and pulled out a package of chicken breasts.

"That bad, huh?"

"Not bad at all. Haley and I make a great team." She winked at her daughter, who grinned back.

"There's room on most teams for more than two people."

Odd that he'd bring this subject up when only yesterday she'd had that fleeting yearning for a touch of romance in her life.

"Not this one."

"You know, sweetie . . . not all men are like Brett. Take yours truly, for instance."

"Ah, but you're one in a million. I think God broke the mold after he made you."

"Not true. You're just not giving yourself a chance to do any fishing."

"That's your specialty."

"You spent enough time on the *Molly Sue* growing up to learn a thing or two. Fish in the right waters. Know what you're looking for. Throw back the ones that aren't worth keeping. It's a big ocean out there. I have to believe your social life would improve if you tossed in a line."

She propped the phone on her shoulder while she opened the package of chicken. "There are too many sharks in the sea for my taste—and I have other priorities these days. One of which is fixing dinner for a hungry little girl."

"Fine. I get the message. I guess you'll have to find your own way. But think about a trip out. I'm not getting any younger, you know."

Her heart skipped a beat, and she froze. "Is there something you're not telling me?"

"No." His voice was firm. "I'm hearty and hale and expect to be taking the *Molly Sue* out for a long time to come—but life has a way of throwing us curveballs. It's important to live each day and not put too much off until tomorrow."

He had a point. Everything might be fine today, but things could change overnight. Like they had with Mom—and Brett.

"I'll give it some serious consideration."

"You do that. And tell that granddaughter of mine to watch for a surprise in a couple of weeks."

More gifts he couldn't afford.

"You don't have to do that. We know you love us."

"Never hurts to demonstrate that once in a while in a concrete way. It's a grandfather's duty to spoil his grandchildren. Listen . . . if gas money is the issue about coming out, I can always—"

"No." The refusal came out more terse than she intended, and she softened her tone. "Thank you, but I'm not taking your money."

An annoyed grunt came over the line. "Are you ever going to outgrow that stubbornness?"

"Did you ever outgrow yours?"

"Point taken. I'll call again Friday night—unless you have a date."

"Dad . . ."

"I'll assume that's a no. Take care, sweetie. Love you."

"Love you too."

As Claire put the phone down, Haley rested her elbow on the table and propped her chin in her palm, her expression hopeful. "So do you think we can go visit Cap this summer?"

If she sealed the driveway and repaired the gutter herself, and if she bought the bedroom paint on sale—maybe.

"I hope so. We'll talk about it again in a few weeks, when school is winding down. In the meantime, focus on your home-work. What do you want to work on first?"

Haley withdrew a notebook from her backpack and flipped it open. "The paper I have to write for English."

"What's the topic?"

"It's supposed to be about a person you like a lot. I think I'll write about Dr. Chandler." Pencil poised over the lined sheet of paper, Haley tipped her head. "Do you think she'll ever find her son?"

Not based on what their neighbor had told her the night she'd broken down in this very kitchen.

No sense making Haley sad, however.

"That's hard to say. Tracking down children who've been adopted can be very difficult." She dipped the chicken in milk, then in bread crumbs, and placed the pieces in a baking pan.

"I bet Mr. McMillan could have found him. Are you sure Dr. Chandler wouldn't want him to try and help?"

"I'm sure." Claire opened the oven door and slid the chicken in. "But we'll think of something else nice to do for her birthday."

"It won't be the same."

Maybe not.

But even if she'd agreed to present David McMillan's offer to Maureen, there wasn't much chance the man would have succeeded in his quest. Why raise false hopes—and put her neighbor in the position of having to deal with that Keith Watson, who'd seemed annoyed by the whole affair?

It was better to let the matter rest.

And she had a feeling David McMillan's assistant would agree.

3

Maureen Chandler had cancer.

As the professor rose from behind her desk to greet him, David paused in the doorway, trying to mask his shock. This was definitely the woman he'd googled, even if her wavy, shoulder-length russet hair had been replaced by the kind of ultra-short spikes that spoke of chemotherapy treatments in the not-too-distant past.

"You must be David McMillan." She held out her hand.

He managed to get his feet moving and crossed to the desk. "Yes. It's nice to meet you."

Despite her slender build, her grip was firm. And that killer smile—it lit up the large, startlingly green eyes that matched the hue of her silky blouse.

"I must admit your phone call intrigued me." She extracted her hand from his with a gentle tug and gestured to the chair across from her desk. "How can I help you?"

He waited until she sat before taking his own seat. "First, thank you for seeing me on such short notice. I hope I'm not disrupting your schedule too much."

Once again, she gave him that megawatt smile—making him wish he'd ducked into the men's room at the office and dispensed with his five o'clock shadow.

"My schedule, such as it is, tends to be in a state of constant disruption. Students have a habit of dropping in unannounced, and I learned long ago to give their crises priority over my calendar. As a result, I'm always behind. That used to bother me, but if nothing else, my bout with cancer taught me not to sweat the small stuff. Although I do have to admit I miss my hair." An appealing dimple appeared in her cheek.

Amazing that the lady could joke about what surely had been a traumatic experience.

"So . . . what brings you to Manchester Christian today? I googled your company, and it's rare for me to be visited by anyone interested in buildings that date past 1400 AD."

At her prompt, he finally managed to transfer his gaze from her dimple to her eyes. They looked amused.

He cleared his throat. "That doesn't surprise me, since your specialty is sacred art during the latter part of the Middle Ages." Her eyebrows rose, and he hitched up one side of his mouth. "I did some googling too."

Rocking back in her chair, she rested her hands on the arms and crossed her legs as she waited for him to continue.

He had a feeling she had great legs.

Too bad they were hidden by her desk.

On the other hand, he didn't need any more distractions. He was here for one reason and one reason only—though having the chance to chat with a lovely woman was a definite bonus.

Gesturing toward the door behind him, he stood. "May I shut that? The matter I have to discuss is confidential."

Her expression went from curious to surprised, but she nodded.

After taking care of the door, he brought her up to speed on

Haley's letter, using his trademark cut-the-small-talk-and-get-to-the-point briefing style.

By the time he finished, distress etched her features and her posture had stiffened. "I had no idea Haley overheard the conversation I had with her mother."

"That's what Ms. Summers told my assistant. She said it was a private matter and asked us not to intervene."

"She's right." The professor linked her fingers into a tight knot. "Yet here you are."

"I have an ulterior motive."

She cocked her head. "I'm listening."

David studied her. This idea had been a gamble from the get-go, starting with his phone call to set up today's appointment. He was still gambling, still winging the whole thing, letting his instincts guide him. So far, that was working out. The professor was as cordial in person as she'd been on the phone, and his gut was telling him to proceed with his proposition.

On the other hand, he hadn't expected to feel this unsettling adolescent zing in her presence. He was sixty-four years old, for crying out loud. Shouldn't he be past all that stuff?

Apparently not—because when she leaned forward again, closing the distance between them to fold her hands on her desk and reveal a bare ring finger, another jolt of electricity zipped through him . . . followed by a rush of warmth.

Keep breathing, David. Do not *run your finger under your collar.*

"Let me back up a bit, if that's okay." Despite the high-voltage effect of her nearness—which seemed to be short-circuiting his brain cells . . . and perhaps his instincts—he tried to stay focused.

"Start wherever you like."

"Two years ago, I lost my wife to a brain aneurysm."

Shock flattened her features. "I'm so sorry."

He hadn't meant to begin with that piece of personal information—and he had no idea why he had.

However, now wasn't the time to analyze his motives.

"Thank you. There are days it's still hard for me to believe she's gone. But the whole experience was a huge wake-up call. During all the years of our marriage, I was a workaholic. Carol knew my background, understood what drove me, and she put up with it, God bless her."

He could read the question in her eyes, but he pushed on. No need to provide the sordid details of his past.

"It wasn't that I didn't love my family. I did—and I tried to demonstrate that by providing them with every possible material comfort. I achieved that goal . . . but along the way I missed a lot of the important moments in their lives, shortchanging both them and myself. Only in hindsight did I recognize a simple but profound truth—the things that matter most aren't things at all. Which brings me to my ulterior motive."

Maureen Chandler's demeanor had warmed while he spoke, and her shoulders were less taut.

All encouraging signs.

"My executive assistant, Keith Watson, reminds me of myself at his age. He's a go-getter who eats, breathes, and sleeps his job. I can't speak to his motivations, because he hasn't shared a great deal about his background, but I'd like to help him find some balance in life sooner than I did. To understand that worldly success and money in the bank don't take the place of loving relationships and memories in the heart."

The professor's expression was curious—and receptive. "A worthy objective. But how do I fit in?"

"Several months ago, I put Keith in charge of reviewing solicitations we receive for the company's charitable foundation. I thought it might give him a new perspective on life. Sad to say, that hasn't happened. Then I got Haley's letter, and I saw it as an opportunity to get him personally involved in a project."

"Put a face to a cause."

"Exactly."

She tapped her index finger against the desk. "I wouldn't think Haley's request would fit the parameters of a charitable foundation."

"It doesn't. But neither does it involve a donation. This will require more legwork than dollars. Keith is sharp, tenacious, and results-oriented—and he doesn't like to fail—so assuming you're still interested in locating the child you gave up, he might be your man."

Settling back in her chair again, she rested her elbows on the arms and steepled her fingers. "I'm very interested—but I've already exhausted every search avenue I could find, beginning with the private adoption agency I used. It went out of business many years ago, after a fire destroyed their offices . . . and their records. Then I listed myself with the state reunion registry in Massachusetts, where the adoption was finalized, in case my son was looking for me as well. I never heard anything. I also signed up with several online adoption database registers. Not so much as a query. I even hired a PI to dig deeper. He got nowhere. I'm not sure what else your assistant can do."

David frowned. Neither was he. Based on what little knowledge he had about adoption, it sounded as if the professor had conducted a thorough search.

But from his perspective, finding her son wasn't the only goal.

"I'm not certain Keith will succeed, either, but I still think he could profit from the journey—if you're willing to let him take a shot at it. Knowing his doggedness, I wouldn't be at all surprised if he comes up with a lead or two even your PI missed."

Brow furrowed, Maureen swiveled away to look out the window to her right. The late afternoon sunlight was merciless, highlighting the fine grooves at the corners of her eyes that spoke of both age and strain. Yet with her svelte figure and auburn hair—not to mention her limber, youthful grace—it was hard to believe she was fifty-nine.

At last she turned back to him. "I've kept the secret about my child for twenty-two years, Mr. McMillan. Only two very good friends knew about it, and both are dead. I shared it with my neighbor in a moment of weakness, the night I got the discouraging report from the PI. I'm not certain I want to risk anyone else finding out about this."

"We'd handle this with absolute discretion. I can assure you I won't say a word to anyone, and Keith is accustomed to dealing with sensitive and proprietary information. I trust him implicitly and feel confident you could do the same."

She let a few beats pass, then sighed. "I'm inclined to believe you. But I'm wondering if dredging up the past is a good idea after all."

"You must have felt differently when you began your quest."

A sad smile whispered at the corners of her mouth. "Going through surgery and chemotherapy and radiation tends to remind one life is fragile and that it's not wise to put off unfinished business until tomorrow."

"I understand. Losing someone you love can have the same effect."

"I'm sure it can." Her voice softened in sympathy. "And regrets can weigh on a person's soul. The truth is, while I've kept my son a secret for all these years, I've never made peace with my decision to give him up. I guess I hoped connecting with him might give me some closure. But perhaps that's selfish. Perhaps he's seen my listings and doesn't want anything to do with me."

He caught a sudden sheen in her eyes, but she blinked it away and leaned sideways to straighten an already aligned stack of papers on her desk.

"That may be true." He took his time responding, giving her a chance to regain her composure. "But I think your initial thought process was sound. Seeking closure—and making amends—is important. Perhaps for both parties."

She flicked him a questioning glance. "That sounds like the voice of experience."

"I have some fences to mend with my daughter for all the years I wasn't there for her while she was growing up. It's slow going, but I think it's worth the effort."

"Life is full of mistakes, I suppose—although some are far bigger than others." She sent him a direct look. "You must be curious about my background."

Yes, he was. A lauded professor at a respected Christian college who'd given up a baby no one knew about for adoption? There had to be an interesting story there.

However, it wasn't any of his business.

"I am. But what happened twenty-two years ago isn't relevant to my offer. One thing I've learned since my wife died is that it's important to focus less on the past and future and more on making certain today counts."

"A nice philosophy—though not easy to implement."

"I agree . . . and I'm not there yet. But I'm working on it."

She let out a slow breath. "I do appreciate what you're trying to do for your assistant. And selfish or not, I'd still like to find my son. Let me give our conversation some thought—and prayer."

"That's fair." David slid his card across her desk. "I have my cell with me at all times. Use that number—and don't hesitate to call as soon as you reach a decision. I'll keep the content of our conversation confidential and would ask you to do the same. I wouldn't want my assistant to think I'm meddling in his life . . . even if I am."

She flashed that dimple again. "All with the best intentions, though. And I won't say a word."

"Thank you. Now I'll let you get back to work."

As he rose, she came around the desk and extended her hand. "If nothing else, I enjoyed meeting you."

"Likewise." He took her hand, gave it a squeeze—and held on just a fraction too long, based on the slight parting of her lips. When he released it, she slipped both hands into the pockets of her slim, knee-length black skirt. "I'll be in touch."

Was it his imagination, or did a slight flush rise on her cheeks?

"I'll look forward to hearing from you."

She followed him to the door, and when she opened it, a college-age kid sitting in a chair in the hall looked up from the book he was reading.

"Are you waiting for me, Jarrod?"

"Yes." He closed the book and stood. "I know you're busy, but I'm having some trouble with a chapter in my thesis and I hoped you might have a minute to spare."

"Of course. Go on in." David moved aside as the student edged past them, and Maureen gave him one last smile. "Proof of what I told you earlier about my schedule being flexible. Can you find your way out?"

"Yes. Thanks."

She retreated to her office, and after following her progress for a moment, David turned away and retraced his route through the building, toward the parking lot.

All the while wishing he could have found some excuse to extend their conversation.

But that was nuts. His life was already complicated. He had a business to run, a daughter to win over, grandchildren to spoil, and an executive assistant to set straight. There was plenty on his plate already. Letting his head be turned by an attractive professor with a life-threatening disease a mere two years after he'd lost the woman he loved to another fatal condition wasn't the least bit smart.

He was old enough to know better.

So how come he suddenly felt like a besotted teenager?

Shaking his head, he slid behind the wheel of his Lexus. He might not have an answer to that question, but he knew one thing for sure.

The professor did, indeed, have great legs.

As the doorbell pealed, Claire set aside the red pen she was using to correct her second graders' spelling tests and rose from the kitchen table.

"Do you want me to get it, Mom?" Haley's hopeful voice wafted down the hall from her room.

Claire rolled her eyes. Any excuse to take a break from homework.

"No, I'm on my way. Keep working on that math and let me know when you're ready for me to check it."

A groan echoed from the recesses of Haley's room.

Lips twitching, Claire moved toward the peephole. She wasn't in the mood to listen to a salesperson's pitch or a Mormon missionary's proselytizing—and who else would come calling unannounced on a Thursday night?

But when she peered through the fish-eye lens, she found Maureen Chandler on the other side, a plate of cookies in hand.

Much better than what she'd expected, despite the sudden niggle of guilt that prodded her conscience. She should have spoken with her neighbor earlier in the week about Haley's letter, as a courtesy if nothing else.

Oh, well. No harm had been done, near as she could tell. Still, the unexpected visit gave her the perfect opportunity to put the whole thing to rest.

After sliding back the bolt and twisting the lock, she pulled the door open.

Maureen lifted the plate of cookies. "I come bearing gifts."

"I noticed through the peephole. Come in." She motioned her through. "But you didn't have to do that."

"I like to bake—and I know a little girl who's partial to these."

As if on cue, Haley poked her head into the tiny foyer. A grin split her face the instant she spied the plate of cookies. "Are those oatmeal?"

"Excellent guess. I hope you're not too full from dinner."

"I'm never too full for oatmeal cookies. Can I have some, Mom?"

"Yes, you *may*."

Haley acknowledged the correction with a long-suffering sigh, but it didn't dampen her enthusiasm as she reached for the plate. "Thank you, Dr. Chandler."

"My pleasure."

"Why don't you put a few on a plate and pour yourself a glass of milk? You can have your snack while you finish your homework."

Haley stared at her. "What about the no-food-in-my-bedroom rule?"

"We'll suspend it tonight."

"Awesome!"

While her daughter hurried to the kitchen, Claire motioned toward the rear of the house. "Will you stay and chat for a few minutes?"

"I'd enjoy that, thanks."

"Can I offer you some tea? Or there's plenty of soda in the fridge." Claire led the way. "We could have a drink and sample your cookies."

"I've done plenty of sampling already." Maureen patted her flat stomach. "I acquired this figure the hard way, and I intend to keep it. But why don't you have a few while I sip a cup of tea?"

"Well . . . since you're twisting my arm." Claire grinned and, with a gentle tug on Haley's braid, snagged one of the four cookies off her plate. "Let's start with three, young lady." Lifting the cookie to her nose, she closed her eyes and inhaled. "Mmm. I'd love to eat three myself, but this will have to suffice."

"You could afford to gain a few pounds."

Claire bit into the warm cookie before she responded to Maureen. "So could you." As far as she could tell, her neighbor hadn't regained much of the weight she'd lost during her chemotherapy treatments.

"I like my current weight—but I must admit I am eating more these days."

Milk in one hand, plate of cookies in the other, Haley retreated down the hall.

"Is your taste starting to come back?" Claire filled a mug with water, added a bag of Maureen's favorite herbal tea, and slid it in the microwave.

"Bit by bit, thank the Lord. That metallic flavor I had during treatment was *not* appetizing."

"I can only imagine." Claire motioned toward the stools on one side of the island. "Have a seat. The tea will be ready in a minute."

They chatted about their day while they waited for the tea to warm, but once Claire retrieved it and claimed her own stool, she got down to business.

"Maureen . . . there's something I need to tell you."

"This sounds serious." The older woman took a sip of tea, eyeing her.

"I hope you won't think it's *too* serious." Taking a deep breath, she plunged into her tale about Haley overhearing their confidential conversation and sending a letter to David McMillan, plus the subsequent call from the man's assistant. "I've been meaning to tell you about it since Monday, but the week got away from me. I explained to the assistant that it was a private matter and I believe he respected that, but I want to apologize for the breach in confidentiality."

Oddly enough, Maureen didn't seem in the least surprised—or upset—by the news of Haley's indiscretion. Nevertheless, Claire plowed ahead.

"All I can say in defense is that Haley meant well and I don't think the information she shared in her letter went any further."

"Actually . . . it did."

The bottom fell out of Claire's stomach.

Keith whatever-his-name-was had to be behind this. She should have known she couldn't trust McMillan's executive assistant. He'd answered the phone with a snotty attitude and hadn't mellowed much even after she'd told him he didn't have to bother with Haley's letter.

"I had a call—and a visit—from David McMillan."

Despite Maureen's mild tone, Claire closed her eyes.

It was even worse than she'd expected.

"Hey . . . it's okay."

At the touch on her arm, she peeked at her neighbor. Given how shattered the woman had been the night she'd tearfully shared the secret she'd guarded for more than two decades, why was she so calm and unruffled about strangers finding out such private information?

"How come it's okay?"

Maureen rested an elbow on the island, her expression thoughtful. "I'm not certain—except that David McMillan struck me as an honorable and discreet man who has the best intentions."

"I'm glad to hear that—but I'm still sorry about this."

"Don't be. Some good might come of it after all."

"How?"

"I'm thinking about letting his assistant look into the matter for me."

Claire gaped at her. "Are you serious?"

"Very. Mr. McMillan has high regard for this man's stick-to-it-iveness—as well as his discretion. He said his assistant is quite a go-getter."

"I can believe that." Her reply came out more terse than she intended.

Maureen gave her an appraising look. "From your tone, can I assume you weren't impressed with him?"

Claire handpicked her words. "We only had a brief conversation. He was very businesslike."

"So David McMillan said." There was an amused twinkle in Maureen's eyes.

What was with that?

Since she hadn't a clue about that answer, Claire asked another question.

"From what you told me that night a couple of weeks ago, you've already tried every avenue you could think of to locate your son. Why do you think this guy will do any better?"

"Maybe fresh eyes will see some important clue everyone else has missed."

"Even a PI?"

"One never knows."

Claire studied her friend. There was something Maureen wasn't telling her. Strange, considering how close they'd grown over the past few months, after she'd learned the older woman had no family to turn to for help during the roughest days of her treatment. How many stories and confidences had they shared over the bowls of homemade soup she'd carried next door when Maureen was too weak and sick to prepare—or care about—food? More than enough to cement a solid friendship.

Yet her neighbor was holding back now.

And Claire had a feeling no amount of digging was going to pry loose any more information.

Footsteps sounded in the hall, and a moment later Haley stuck her head in the kitchen.

"Can I have one more cookie, Mom?"

"How's the homework coming?"

"I'm almost done."

"You may have another cookie after you finish."

Her daughter let out an exaggerated sigh and started to turn away.

"Hey . . . how about one more thank-you?"

"Thank you again, Dr. Chandler. Those are the best oatmeal cookies in the whole world."

"I'm glad you like them. Now that I'm feeling better, I have a recipe for ginger cookies I think you'll like too."

"Epic! See you later."

As Haley retreated down the hall, Maureen rose. "I need to run along. I have a chapter of a thesis to review, and it appears you have a tableful of spelling tests to correct."

Claire trailed behind as her neighbor headed toward the front door. "So when are you going to decide whether to let this guy work on your project?"

"When God gives me the guidance I need."

"I hope your prayers produce clearer direction than mine do." A bitter thread wove through her words, and she pulled the front door open with more force than necessary.

"Sometimes it's hard to hear his voice and discern his direction—but that's a human failing, not a divine one."

Of course Maureen would say that. She was a professor at a Christian college. A faithful believer, albeit one with human failings. Yet despite her past trauma and the challenges of the last year, her belief in God's love and mercy had never wavered.

Claire tightened her grip on the edge of the door. "I wish my faith was as strong as yours."

"It could be, if you give it a chance. Just believe—and trust."

She shoved her free hand in the pocket of her jeans and clenched her fist. "I'm not great at trust."

Maureen touched her arm. "I know—and for sound reasons. Your husband failed you. But God never will."

Deep inside, she still believed that. But somehow she'd lost her connection with the almighty.

"Sometimes I wish I could talk to him, you know?" A touch of wistfulness crept into her voice.

"That's what prayer's all about."

"I mean talk as in a conversation."

Maureen smiled. "Did you ever see that old movie called *Oh, God?*"

"No."

"The script had some serious theological issues, but there's a great line at the end when the main character is talking to a physical manifestation of God. He asks if God will reappear in the future if he needs further guidance, and God—in the form of George Burns—says, 'You talk. I'll listen.' And the truth is, he does listen. He also answers our prayers, often in ways we least expect." Maureen leaned close and gave her a quick hug. "Now if I were you, I'd go have another one of those oatmeal cookies. An occasional treat is a great morale booster."

With a wave, she stepped through the door and crossed the lawn toward her house.

Claire watched until she disappeared onto her front porch, then slowly shut the door and wandered back into the kitchen. The plate of cookies beckoned, and for once she gave in to the temptation. Another hundred calories wasn't going to add an inch to her hips.

Chewing the cookie, she retook her place at the table. Maureen's story about the George Burns movie was cute—but she could sympathize with the main character. She might pay lip service to prayer for Haley's sake, but it felt dry and rote and very one-way. If God was listening, she hadn't seen any evidence of it.

Still, she hoped he gave Maureen the guidance she was seeking with her decision.

Because trusting in God was one thing. Trusting in men was another. And while Maureen had apparently gotten positive vibes from David McMillan, his assistant hadn't impressed Claire in the least.

She only hoped her friend wasn't about to make a mistake she'd live to regret.

4

. . . .

"Turn right."

Following the Yoda voice from *Star Wars* that he'd chosen for his GPS system, Keith swung onto Maureen Chandler's street and eased back on the gas pedal.

This was ridiculous.

Why in the world had David gone to see the professor after her neighbor asked them to drop the whole thing?

And why had Dr. Chandler insisted on meeting him before accepting his boss's offer of help?

Blood pressure spiking, he compressed his lips and flexed his fingers on the wheel. This assignment could have been handled with a few phone calls or emails. He needed facts, not small talk. And once he had those facts in hand, he'd organize, analyze, and act—just as he did with every assignment.

Not that there'd be much acting required in this case. Based on the information the woman had shared with David, she'd covered all the bases already. Dot a few i's, cross a few t's, he'd be done.

First, however, he had to get through this meeting.

Gritting his teeth, he increased his pressure on the gas pedal and accelerated slowly down the sidewalk-lined street of small but well-kept houses—the kind of neighborhood once favored by rising young professionals or retired couples who'd downsized.

But a lot of younger folks—like him—went the hassle-free condo route these days, while a lot of older people were choosing retirement communities for the same reason. Why bother with home maintenance chores if you didn't have to? Surely that woman on her hands and knees doing something to her driveway had better ways to spend a Saturday morning.

"You have arrived."

Still rolling, he verified the number on the mailbox. Yep. This was it.

"You have arrived. Powerful, you have become."

The Star Wars theme began to play.

"Yeah, yeah. I got it the first time, Yoda."

He flipped off the device as he pulled close to the curb, and the X-wing starfighter icon representing his car disappeared. After setting the brake, he checked the digital clock on the dashboard. Eight fifty-eight. Right on time.

Tucking the notebook he used for business meetings under his arm, he slid out of the car and turned to find the woman next door—the one who'd been working on her driveway—watching him.

The woman next door.

Maureen Chandler's neighbor.

His jaw dropped.

Could that stunning blonde be Haley Summers's snippy mother?

As she broke eye contact, stood, and walked toward her garage, he squinted at her mailbox. The number matched the return address on Haley's letter.

Huh.

Claire Summers wasn't at all what he'd expected.

For one thing, in her skinny jeans and a faded T-shirt that appeared to have shrunk a size or two, she didn't look old enough to have an eleven-year-old daughter. He'd have pegged her at twenty-four, twenty-five, tops.

And a blonde . . . for some reason he'd expected a brunette with a short, no-nonsense cut. Could that ripened-wheat color of her long hair be real—or was it bottled?

As for those soft curves . . .

Keith jerked his gaze away from her retreating figure. He wasn't here to ogle Dr. Chandler's neighbor. Nor was she likely to appreciate his perusal if she happened to glance over her shoulder. In fact, given her prickly attitude during their terse phone conversation, she might very well march over and whack him with the broom propped against her garage.

Time to get to work.

Keeping his attention fixed on Maureen Chandler's door, he strode up the walk, stepped onto the porch, and pressed the bell. He'd make this as quick as possible and then get on with his day. A couple of hours at the office to finish a report for David and review the latest numbers for the new project in Wentzville, an hour at the gym, a quick jog, and a cursory cleaning of his condo.

The perfect Saturday—except for this part.

At least it would be over soon.

And perhaps, if the fates were kind, the good professor would decide she didn't want to take advantage of David's offer after all.

One could hope, anyway.

Keith Watson didn't want to be here.

Tray of coffee and scones in hand, Maureen rejoined him in

the living room, where he was sitting stiffly on the edge of one of her wing chairs. She couldn't fault his manners. Even now, he stood to relieve her of the tray and settle it on the coffee table. Waited until she took her seat before sitting himself. Accepted a cup of coffee while politely declining a scone.

But she wasn't picking up a single positive vibe.

No wonder Claire hadn't been gung ho on the man.

Yet David McMillan had praised his sterling qualities.

It was an odd disconnect. Claire's instincts were sound. And despite their short acquaintance, she trusted David McMillan's too. Of course, he'd also known Keith a lot longer than Claire had.

Perhaps David's assistant was simply so business-focused he resented wasting time on a job with no bottom-line value. Or perhaps he'd had other things to do with his Saturday morning. Who could blame him for being unhappy about giving up his personal time for one of his boss's pet projects?

Better to reserve judgment until they had more of a chance to chat . . . the very purpose of the meeting she'd arranged by phone with David yesterday.

"I apologize again for intruding on your Saturday morning." She added a generous dash of cream to her coffee, softening the dark hue.

Keith left his java black and lifted his cup. "I'm used to working on weekends. It's not a problem."

"Well, I won't keep you long. I thought it might be best if we had a chance to get to know one another before I give your boss the green light on this project, since you and I will be working together."

He took a sip and waited her out, expression neutral, eyes guarded.

"So tell me a little about yourself." She leaned back and settled in.

A few beats of silence passed as he carefully set his cup back in its saucer. "What would you like to know?"

"Anything you'd care to share. Some background, perhaps."

He sat back in his chair too—more to put distance between them than to relax, she suspected.

Even though she'd left the request open-ended, it was clear he wasn't comfortable sharing information about himself. She could almost hear the rant running through his brain.

I didn't sign on for this. My personal life is none of this woman's business. She has a lot of nerve asking me questions. That's supposed to be my job.

Truth be told, he was right—and she'd respect his feelings if he gave voice to them.

But he didn't. And that told her a lot too. David had given him an assignment, and he was committed to carrying it out . . . even if some of the tasks were unpleasant.

"I was born and raised in St. Louis, so of course you'll want to know my high school." He managed a taut smile at the humorous reference only a St. Louisan would understand. No one in this town meant college when they asked what school you'd attended, as she'd learned years ago as a newcomer.

He provided that piece of information, then continued with his college and work history. It was a recitation of his resume and offered zero personal insights.

When he finished, she topped off her coffee and added some more cream. "You're quite accomplished for one so young. Any brothers or sisters?"

"No."

"Are your parents still living?"

"My mother is."

"Any other family?"

"No."

"Then we have a bit in common, except you're more fortunate than I am. You have a mother. My relatives are all gone. That's one of the reasons I'd like to find my son." She took a sip. "Since I've been asking all the questions up until now, why don't you take a turn?"

With the expression of a man who'd just been paroled, Keith picked up the leather notebook he'd set on the edge of the coffee table and put her through a quick quiz about all the steps she'd taken to find her son.

He didn't ask one personal question.

After jotting a final note, he closed the notebook. "I think that's all I need to get started."

She gestured toward his half-empty cup of coffee. "Would you like a refill?"

"No, thank you."

The man couldn't wait to escape.

When the silence lengthened, he twisted his wrist and looked at his watch. "Is there anything else we need to discuss?"

"You haven't asked about the circumstances of my son's birth—or why I gave him up for adoption."

He cleared his throat. "I don't need to know that."

"Need to know—or want to know?"

She had no idea what had prompted that question, and based on the slight flush creeping over his cheeks, it surprised him as much as her.

"I don't think it's any of my business."

His reply was similar to David's, but while his boss's had been couched in kindness, she was picking up an entirely different emotion from this young man. It was stronger than indifference, or even resentment about being tasked with an assignment he thought frivolous.

Was there a touch of hostility in his attitude?

Whatever it was, she didn't like it.

Rising, she set her coffee cup on the table and gestured toward the foyer. "I think we've covered everything for today. Let me show you out."

At the door, he offered her his card. "So shall I dig into this on Monday?"

"I'm going to give it a bit more thought. Please let your boss know I'll be in touch if I decide to proceed."

He hesitated, faint furrows creasing his brow. "I can spare a few more minutes if you'd like to talk further. Did you have any other questions for me?"

Plenty.

But he'd only offered to extend their visit because he was concerned she might give a negative report to his boss. He had to know he'd been less than friendly during their conversation.

Or did he?

She was beginning to get a handle on the problem David saw with his protégé. The man might be an ace with numbers, but he flunked empathy. There was nothing remotely warm and fuzzy about this guy.

"No. I think we covered enough ground today." She opened the door. "Thank you for stopping by. I hope you enjoy the rest of your day."

Left with no choice, he exited.

As she wandered back into the living room to tidy up, she fingered his card. She didn't doubt Keith Watson was a workaholic with a lot of smarts. He seemed intense and focused, and the questions he'd asked about her search had been astute. Given the assignment, he might very well turn up some piece of information she and her PI had missed.

But he didn't want to help her—and she had a feeling his aversion had nothing to do with wasting time on what he deemed a less-than-productive endeavor.

So what *did* it have to do with?

Maureen picked up his coffee, the blackness unredeemed by

the merest hint of cream. She had no clue about the answer to that question—but that young man was in need of . . . humanity . . . perspective . . . compassion . . . *something*.

And she did want to locate her son.

It didn't appear to be a match made in heaven. Yet having a resource drop in her lap out of the blue, after she'd more or less given up any hope of finding her child, was too providential to brush off.

So she'd sleep on it. Pray about it. Think it through from every direction.

And trust that if God wanted her to proceed, he'd provide the guidance she needed.

Arms aching, shoulder muscles screaming in protest, Claire tried again to heft the plastic drum of driveway sealer out of the trunk of her car.

It rose a mere inch.

She let it drop back in with a thud and planted her hands on her hips.

No wonder the guy at Home Depot had carried it to the checkout lane and loaded it in her car for her. The thing weighed a ton.

She glanced at the Hamilton house next door. Too bad Todd hadn't made a trip home from college this weekend. The strapping quarterback could have lifted the drum out of her trunk one-handed. But the street spot always claimed by his rattletrap Focus, just a few yards in front of where she'd parked her own car for the duration of the sealing job, was empty.

It was up to her—and today was the day. The forecast was for dry weather, and the driveway had been prepared. After spending her Friday night patching cracks and trimming the grass and weeds along the edges, and after rising at the crack of dawn to sweep the asphalt, clean the oil stains, and hose down the surface, she was getting this sucker done today.

Lips locked, she wiped her palms down her jeans, grabbed the handle, and pulled. All she had to do was get it on the ground. She could drag it from there.

Somehow she managed to maneuver the tub to the lip of the trunk. As it teetered on the edge, she gave one more yank, swinging around at the same time.

And ran into a brick wall.

As she staggered, an "oomph!" registered. Then two masculine arms encased in crisp, oxford-cloth sleeves shot out and grabbed the handle alongside hers.

By the time she regained her balance, the tub of sealer had been tugged from her grasp and set on the ground.

Steadying herself with a hand on the fender, she lifted her gaze.

It was the guy who'd gotten out of that red Infiniti sports car parked in front of Maureen's house.

She tried not to stare, but he was even better-looking up close than he'd been at a distance. Neatly trimmed dark brown hair, intense dark eyes . . . and tall. He topped her five-six by half a foot, minimum. As for the ease with which he'd handled the heavy drum—there were some serious muscles under that oxford cloth.

It figured that the one day a hot guy crossed her path, she'd skipped her morning makeup routine.

Good thing she wasn't in the market for male attention.

He took a step back and gestured toward the drum. "I saw you struggling as I got to my car and figured you could use a hand."

"Thanks. It was heavier than I thought."

"Why don't you tell me where you want it and I'll carry it for you?"

She rubbed her palms down her slacks again. Why were they sweating?

"I can manage from here, thanks. Getting it out of the trunk was the hard part. I just need to drag it up to the top of the driveway."

Instead of responding, he snagged the handle of the drum with one hand and started toward the garage.

Did the man not understand English?

She slammed the lid of her trunk and took off after him.

It was nice he was willing to lend a hand, but ignoring her wishes was demeaning. No more patronizing attitudes for her, thank you very much.

"Hey!"

He kept walking.

She picked up her pace. "Mister . . . I said I could handle it."

Three strides later, he plunked the drum of sealer at the top of the driveway and turned to her. "I know you did, but I was trying to save you a hernia." He gave her a sweeping appraisal. "This thing probably weighs half as much as you do."

Fifty-five pounds times two . . . he was darn close.

But that was beside the point.

"Look . . . I appreciate the gesture, but I'm used to doing things on my own."

He cast a quick glance at her bare left hand and frowned. "Are you going to seal this thing yourself?"

"Yes."

"It's hard, messy work."

"I'm not afraid of hard work, and I dressed for messy."

He gave her a quick head-to-toe scrutiny, then cleared his throat and surveyed the squeegee on a stick, off to the side. "Have you ever done this before?"

"No. However, I know how to follow directions—and the ones for this job aren't rocket science."

The house door inside the garage opened, and Haley stuck her head out. "Mom, can I watch the . . . oops. Sorry. I didn't know we had company."

"We don't. This . . . gentleman . . . helped me carry the driveway sealer up from the car."

"That was nice." She beamed at the man. "Mom's always trying to lift stuff that's too heavy, and she never lets me help. I'm Haley."

Usually her daughter's cheery disposition brought smiles to the faces of the people she encountered.

This guy's lips didn't budge.

Curious.

And what was with those stiff shoulders?

"Nice to meet you, Haley." Then he shifted his attention to her. "Claire Summers, I presume?"

She narrowed her eyes. "Yes. How did you know that?"

"I'm Keith Watson." He extended his hand. "David McMillan asked me to introduce myself if I got the chance while I was visiting Dr. Chandler."

Keith Watson—McMillan's executive assistant?

The guy with the attitude?

She gave him another once-over. Yeah, it fit. Preppy clothes, sporty car, expensive shoes, take-charge attitude.

Her assessment of him morphed from hot to hotshot in a heartbeat.

But ignoring his hand would be rude.

She gave it a quick squeeze and retracted her fingers.

Haley bounded down the two steps from the kitchen door and joined them, her eyes sparkling. "Are you going to help us with Dr. Chandler's birthday present?"

"We've made the offer. Now it's up to her. She and I met this morning to discuss it."

Since when had Maureen decided to move forward with this whole thing?

Apparently God had given her the guidance she'd been seeking sometime since Thursday night.

"This is so awesome!" Haley did a little happy dance and

clapped her hands. "Mom said a big company wouldn't help just one person, but I prayed and prayed—even harder than when I wanted a new bike last year. And this time God listened!"

"He always listens, honey." Claire repeated the same words Maureen had said to her two nights ago, wishing she had as much confidence in them as her neighbor did.

"Yes, but sometimes I think he's too busy with other stuff to answer."

Before Claire could respond, the phone trilled from inside the house and she gave Haley a gentle push toward the door. "That might be Cap."

"Okay." She called over her shoulder to Keith as she trotted toward the door, "Will you be back?"

"I have no idea."

"I hope so." With that, her daughter disappeared inside.

"I guess I'll be on my way." Keith inclined his head toward the tub of sealer. "Good luck with this."

"Thanks."

He flicked another glance at her bare left hand, so fast she'd have missed it if she hadn't been focused on those brown eyes.

"Look . . . isn't there someone who could help you with this? Even tipping a container that heavy can be tricky."

"No. There isn't." She lifted her chin a fraction. "And now I'm sure you have better things to do with your Saturday than talk about sealing a driveway."

A hint of pink colored his cheeks at her dismissive tone, and for a moment she was tempted to apologize . . . until anger sparked in his eyes and he gave a haughty nod.

"As a matter of fact, I do—and reviewing balance sheets will be far more pleasant."

He turned on his heel, stalked to his car, slammed the door behind him, and accelerated down the street without a backward look.

Well.

That had gone really well.

Claire shoved back a wisp of hair that had escaped from her haphazard ponytail and scowled after him.

What was it with that guy, anyway? Was it so hard to be civil?

Wait a minute—isn't that like the pot calling the kettle black?

At the reprimand from her conscience, Claire huffed out a breath. Okay, fine, she hadn't been Miss Congeniality, either. But she had her reasons. That guy might not have looked like Brett, but he was her ex-husband's clone in other ways—same arrogant, superior attitude; same fancy clothes and car; same ambitious leanings; same focus on business and balance sheets. And he might be the same in a lot of less pleasant ways too.

What was *his* excuse for being rude?

Maybe he has one too.

Maybe.

No matter. There wasn't much chance they'd be seeing a whole lot of each other, even if Maureen decided to continue with her quest.

As she began prying the lid off the drum of sealer, her daughter reappeared in the doorway. "Is that man gone?"

"Yes. Who was on the phone?"

"Somebody doing a survey. Is he coming back?"

"I don't think so." She lifted the lid and eyed the tarry gunk inside.

"We might see him again if Dr. Chandler decides to let him help her, though."

"It's possible."

"He was nice."

Nice? Claire retrieved the squeegee and set it on the asphalt beside her. What had her daughter seen that she'd missed? "How do you figure?"

"He helped you carry that stuff, didn't he?"

"That was a polite thing to do—but nice is different. He never even smiled."

"You don't smile much, either, and you're nice. Nice is different than happy, I guess."

At her daughter's matter-of-fact comment, Claire froze. She smiled a lot—didn't she?

Maybe not.

The worry and stress that came with single-handedly trying to keep her and Haley's lives on an even keel had robbed a lot of the joy from her days. Nor did her residual bitterness help—though until today she thought she'd dealt with most of the garbage from her past.

Given her reaction to Keith Watson, however, she might have to reexamine that conclusion.

"After I finish my homework, may I watch the DVD we got at the library?"

At the query, she refocused on her daughter. "Yes. I'll be out here awhile."

"Do you want me to help?"

"No, that's okay. No sense both of us getting dirty."

The door closed.

Bracing herself, Claire gripped the edge of the tub and tipped it forward. Sealer flowed out, splashing on the driveway and spattering her shoes and the legs of her jeans. She'd expected that. But she didn't expect the gunk to slosh backward when she lowered the tub to the asphalt too quickly. It rolled over the edge, coating not only her fingers but one of her shoes.

Meanwhile, rivulets of the stuff began flowing down the driveway.

She snatched up the squeegee to corral the liquid. Pull, don't push, according to the directions that came with the sealer. Establish a rhythm. Let gravity work in your favor.

It had all sounded so simple.

But as her shoulders began to ache, as more and more sealer found its way onto her clothes and into her cuticles, as the promised rhythm proved elusive, she resigned herself to the reality.

This job was a lot harder than she'd expected—just as Keith Watson had predicted.

She'd get through it, though. Claire Summers wasn't a quitter. She knew how to roll with the punches, to plow ahead when things got tough, to take responsibility for her own life and trust no one but herself.

Brett had taught her that.

And it was a lesson she didn't intend to forget.

5

. . . .

Keith wiped his forehead on the sleeve of his T-shirt, jockeyed
the lawn mower into its place in the garage, and joined his
mother in the kitchen.

She turned from the stove as he entered. "All done?"

"Yes. I can't believe the zoysia is green and growing already."

"Me, either, given the cold winter." She took the lid off a
pot, releasing an aroma that jump-started his salivary glands.

"Is that pot roast?" He crossed the room and leaned over
her shoulder.

"Your favorite."

"You shouldn't have gone to so much trouble."

"It's never trouble to do things for people you love." She
replaced the lid, wiped her hands on her apron, and rose on
tiptoe to give him a kiss on the cheek. "Why don't you clean
up and we'll have a catch-up session on the patio. I missed you
last Sunday."

"Trust me, I'd rather have been here than in Cedar Rapids. A
fast-food burger can't hold a candle to your cooking."

"So it was my food you missed, not me."

"You know better." He gave her a hug. "You're my favorite lady."

"I'm flattered—but I'm willing to cede that title to the right woman when she comes along. Any rivals on the horizon?"

For some reason, an image of Maureen Chandler's prickly neighbor flashed through his mind.

Weird.

"Trust me—your position is secure."

"Must be because you're not trying very hard to replace me."

"No time. Work keeps me too busy."

"Hmph. That's a convenient excuse, at any rate. Well, go freshen up. I'll meet you on the patio."

More than happy to end a conversation his mother had been initiating with increasing frequency, Keith hustled down the hall. It wasn't as if he'd written off marriage. But the professional women he met at business gatherings were as career oriented as he was and had no time to devote to developing a relationship, either. As for the women he met during his occasional happy hour forays—good for a few laughs, but not white-picket-fence material.

In the bathroom, he splashed water on his face and sudsed his hands, his mother's final comment replaying in his mind.

Was he using his busy career as an excuse to shy away from commitment?

It was possible.

Dealing with numbers was a lot more cut-and-dried than dealing with people.

Twisting off the faucet with more force than necessary, Keith studied the reflection in the mirror. A successful, fast-track businessman who had his act together stared back.

What a sham.

Peel away the façade, and that illusion would evaporate, leaving a driven man who'd been plagued as far back as he could remember with the need to prove himself—and his worth. A man who never felt quite good enough or secure enough or confident enough.

All because his birth mother hadn't wanted him.

How sad was that, after all these years?

Keith dried his hands, scrubbed the nubby towel over his damp face. There was no reason for his lingering feelings of inadequacy, for his fears of abandonment, for doling out trust in miserly increments. His adoptive parents had been wonderful—loving him unconditionally, sacrificing to give him the best possible education, putting him at the top of their priority list.

How many times had Dad come home after a long day at work and patiently walked him through his math homework or cheered from the stands at his basketball games? How many times had Mom shuttled him to extracurricular activities and sat with him after school, listening to the events of his day as he ate homemade cookies?

Carl and Alice Watson couldn't have done more for him.

Yet neither their loving care nor the counseling sessions they'd taken him to had been able to compensate for his first three traumatic years.

But he'd learned to suppress those memories, to relegate them to such a dark, remote corner of his mind that they rarely escaped to the light.

Tossing the towel over the bar, he frowned. So why was he thinking about that whole can of worms now?

Maureen Chandler.

As the woman's name flashed through his mind, giving him his answer, his mouth flattened into a hard line.

Dealing with her was dredging up all the old garbage.

One more reason to resent the assignment David had yoked him with for reasons known only to his boss.

Today, however, was not the time to hash all that out. Sunday afternoons were reserved for his mom.

She was waiting on the patio, as promised, the sun silvering her hair. At seventy-one, she was active and healthy, and there was no reason to think she wouldn't be around for many more years.

Yet he'd thought the same thing about his father until a stroke had taken him at seventy-three, just two years ago.

He needed to do his best not to miss any more Sunday visits, despite the demands of his work.

"Doesn't the lawn look pretty after it's been cut?" His mother took a sip of her iced tea. "But I'd be happy to pay someone to do it so you wouldn't have to bother."

"I don't mind." Keith dropped into a chair beside her and picked up the glass of tea she'd set at his place. "It gives me an excuse to visit."

"You don't need an excuse. You might live in a fancy condo now, but this will always be your home—until you create one of your own. So how was your week?"

"Busy."

"Tell me something I don't know. Anything out of the ordinary happen?"

He swirled the ice in his glass. In the distance, a cardinal trilled. A dog barked. The voices of children at play drifted through the quiet air.

All the comforting sounds of his childhood.

The snarl of tension in his shoulders relaxed.

"David gave me a rather unusual assignment."

The instant the words left his mouth, he regretted them. Why on earth had he brought that up, when the last thing he wanted to think about was Maureen Chandler's quest?

"Tell me about it."

Too late to backtrack now.

He gave her the condensed version, starting with Haley Summers's letter.

"That's a little out of left field for you." His mother sent him a keen look, the one she always wore while working a crossword or Sudoku puzzle—or trying to figure out what her son was up to.

"Very."

"So what's behind it?"

"I wish I knew."

"How do you feel about it?"

Trying to ignore the tension creeping back into his shoulders, he gave what he hoped came across as a nonchalant shrug. "David's the boss. He gives the orders. But it seems like a waste of time to me—and not the best use of company resources."

"I meant, how do you feel about it on a personal level?" She laid her hand over his, concern sculpting a few more lines into her face.

"It's not my favorite assignment." If he was lucky, she'd leave it at that.

"Can I ask you a question?"

So much for luck.

He braced. "Yeah. I guess."

"Do you know anything about the Missouri Social Services Adoption Information Registry?"

He blinked.

Where had *that* come from?

"No."

"It's a place where adult adoptees and biological parents can register if they'd like to make contact with each other. It's especially helpful in cases where the court adoption records are sealed."

"Why would I be interested in that?"

She traced the circle of condensation left on the table by her iced tea glass. "Your father and I often talked about whether it might be helpful for you to learn more about the circumstances of your birth. The early years of a child's life are so critical . . . we thought meeting your mother might offer some closure."

"You're my mother."

"Thank you for that." She patted his hand. "And you're as dear to me as any child your father and I might have conceived together. But we're all shaped by our backgrounds, and Carl and I always knew there were gaps we couldn't fill and hurts we couldn't heal, hard as we tried. I'm sorry for that."

Keith's throat tightened. All these years, and they'd never said a word about the burden of worry they bore or their own sense of inadequacy.

"Mom . . ." He took her hand. "You and Dad gave me more than I could ever deserve."

"But that's just it." She leaned toward him, earnest and intent. "You've always deserved more than you've allowed yourself to believe. That's what we couldn't overcome. And it's why we thought if you connected with your birth mother, learned the reasons she did what she did, you might be able to move past that. We tried to broach the subject after you became an adult, but you brushed us off."

If that conversation had occurred, he'd blocked it from memory. Why would he want to meet the woman who hadn't loved him enough to want to raise him, no matter the challenges she might face?

When the silence lengthened, his mother spoke again. "Have you met this woman your boss agreed to help?"

"Yes. Yesterday."

"What did you think of her?"

"She's pleasant. Very successful in her career. Not married."

"Why is she pursuing this so long after the fact?"

"She's got cancer, and she told David that was a wake-up call.

According to him, she claims if she had the decision to make over again, her choice might be different. Of course, that's easy to say in hindsight."

"Or from the perspective of age and experience. Perhaps she's learned a thing or two. Perhaps your birth mother has too."

They were back to that.

"I hope so, in both cases. But that doesn't change the past."

"Still, the timing of this assignment is odd. I've been thinking a lot about grandchildren lately—and all the reasons you work so hard to succeed but avoid serious relationships."

"Dr. Watson, psychologist." He softened the comment with a quick quirk of his lips.

"Hardly. Just a lot of decades living and learning and observing. You're old enough to know your own mind and make your own choices, but I wanted to throw the adoption registry idea out in case you decided investigating your own background might be worthwhile. Now let's go eat pot roast."

He followed her in, filling the water glasses and retrieving the butter and condiments by rote, as he'd done all the years the three of them had shared family meals in this homey kitchen.

His mother didn't bring up the subject again, chatting instead about the movie she'd seen with friends during the week and the new blankets-for-babies project at her church and her volunteer work at Missouri Botanical Garden.

But she'd planted an idea he couldn't pluck out. It followed him back to the sterile condo that possessed none of the charm of his childhood home and functioned more as a place to sleep than a place to live.

Nevertheless, he had no intention of following up on her suggestion. He didn't need to locate his birth mother to find closure on his early years. He just needed to get over them, forget about the past, refuse to let events from three decades ago have one iota of impact on his self-image or his life or the decisions he made now.

He tossed his car keys on the counter in the kitchen, got himself a drink of water—and stared at the half-empty glass, shoulders drooping.

Though he'd been reciting that litany to himself for years, he'd never quite managed to achieve those goals. He might only have fragments of memory from those early days, but he couldn't shake them—and they were still influencing his life.

However, given his history, given what his birth mother had done, there wasn't much chance she'd reformed, seen the light, gotten her act together—or decided to look for him.

Was there?

With that unsettling question hanging in the air, he yanked his cell phone off his belt and scrolled through his messages. Good. There were one or two requests he could work on tonight that were sufficiently complex to distract him.

He booted up his laptop, put a pot of coffee on to brew, and settled in at the kitchen table to dive into the first request.

Yet, fingers poised over the keyboard, he hesitated.

Would it hurt to check out this registry his mom had mentioned, see how it worked? Just in case, someday in the distant future, his curiosity was piqued enough to pursue her suggestion?

No.

His birth mother had made her choice years ago.

He might be stuck helping Maureen Chandler search for her own son, but as far as he was concerned, the woman who'd given him up didn't deserve a second chance.

6

David spotted her the instant she stepped into the restaurant. Maureen Chandler might have lost her wavy, russet hair, but she was still a stunning woman.

He rose from the corner table he'd requested at the chic café and lifted his hand.

Smiling in acknowledgment, she wove through the tables with an inherent grace and settled into the chair he held out.

"Sorry I'm a few minutes late. A student stopped by, and . . ."

"Your schedule fell apart. No problem. I'm just glad you had time for lunch, if your Mondays are as busy as mine. Based on our quick phone conversation, I had a feeling this might be a discussion better held in person."

"I agree—and thank you for suggesting it. This is quite an upgrade from my usual brown bag repast."

The waiter appeared and extended a menu to Maureen. "I can recommend the salmon. It's very fresh today."

"Sold." She waved the menu aside.

"A decisive woman. I like that." David handed the waiter his menu too. "Make that two." Once the man departed, David picked up the conversation. "From what you said earlier, I have a feeling your meeting with Keith didn't go well."

"It was cordial." She unfolded her napkin and draped it across her lap, brow puckering. "He's very polite, and he struck me as an intelligent, focused man."

"But . . ."

"But I picked up a sense of . . . *resistance* might be the best word for it. I have no doubt he'll do the job; his commitment to his work came across loud and clear. But I got the distinct feeling he doesn't want to take this on."

"So did I. I think he considers the time he'll devote to it a waste of resources."

"I expect that's true—yet by the end of our meeting, I was certain it went deeper than that." She tipped her head, her expression pensive. "Could there be something in his background that makes this assignment distasteful?"

"It's possible. As I said in your office, he's always been tight-lipped about his personal life. I do know he and his parents had a strong relationship, and he's still close to his mother."

"Hmm." She tapped a finger against the linen tablecloth. "I suppose he might have some moral objection to helping an unwed mother, if he's the judgmental type."

"I've never found him to be the least judgmental, except when I've asked him to evaluate the competence of an employee." The waiter delivered a basket of rolls, giving him a chance to ponder Maureen's feedback . . . and come to a troubling conclusion. "He offended you, didn't he?"

She lifted one shoulder and focused on selecting a roll. "Not by anything he said or did. It was just intuition—and I could be reading more into this than I should."

"Why do I think you're a sound judge of people?"

"I'm flattered . . . but we hardly know each other."

"That can be remedied."

She set her butter knife down, folded her hands, and focused those green eyes on him. "What are you suggesting?"

What *was* he suggesting? Those glib words had rolled off his tongue almost faster than his brain could form them. It was the kind of flirty thing he might have said forty years ago.

"Honestly? I'm not certain. I'm sixty-four, Maureen. Too old to play games—even if you make me feel young enough to want to try. Here's the truth. I still love my wife. Carol was a wonderful person, and we had a solid marriage for thirty-one years. That should be enough for any man—and I thought it was for me. Then I walked into your office, and I felt like a teenager. I guess what I'm saying is I'd enjoy getting to know you better. Perhaps a lot better."

"That's very direct."

"Candor comes with age."

"In that case, I'm eligible to reciprocate, since I'll be sixty in a few weeks. Why in the world would you want to get involved with someone who has cancer?"

Has.

Present tense.

His heart stumbled.

"The treatment wasn't successful?"

"I'll find out in five years."

"May I ask what kind of cancer you had?"

"Breast, stage IIA. A four centimeter tumor. On the plus side, it didn't spread to the lymph nodes. I had surgery, followed by chemo every three weeks for almost six months, finishing off with radiation five days a week for six weeks. Since it was early stage, the prognosis is good."

"All of that sounds positive." His spirits took an uptick.

"I hope so. But getting involved with me would be a gamble."

"A lot of things in life are. Sometimes the risk is worth it."

The server arrived with their food, and Maureen waited until he left before responding. "I'm flattered by your interest. And in the spirit of honesty, I'll admit I felt a bit like a teenager when we met too."

"That's a relief." He flashed her a grin and dug into his salmon. "I was afraid it might be one-way."

She picked up her fork but didn't eat. "You strike me as a very principled man, with a compassionate heart and high moral standards. Doesn't the skeleton in my closet bother you?"

"It happened a long time ago."

"I was old enough to know better—and that's not an answer."

Somehow he wasn't surprised she'd seen through his evasive maneuver. "I could use your perceptiveness in my boardroom."

"I prefer the classroom—and you're still avoiding the question."

Might as well own up to the truth.

"It bothers me a little, but I've learned through the years not to take things at face value. There's often more to a story than first meets the eye . . . and I have a feeling that may be true in your case."

She scooped up a forkful of whipped potatoes. "I might tell you my tale someday, and you can decide for yourself."

"Does that mean you're open to the idea of getting to know each other better?"

"I need to think about it."

"Are you this measured and thoughtful about everything?"

"Yes. A lesson learned in the school of experience." Regret darkened her eyes, but it was gone in a blink. "In the meantime, we should talk about Keith."

"Right." He did his best to redirect his thoughts to the original reason for their lunch.

"I was on the verge of killing the whole project—until I stopped in at my neighbor's house yesterday with some cookies. I complimented Claire on the job she did sealing her driveway the day before, and Haley piped up to tell me Keith had seen her struggling with the tub of sealer and hauled it from her trunk to where she needed it."

"That sounds like Keith—and I did ask him to introduce himself to your neighbor if he got the chance. Why did that change your mind?"

"For one thing, that act of kindness was a mark in the plus column for your assistant. For another, Claire got flustered when I asked about him."

Maureen fell silent, and David paused, fork poised in midair. "Is that significant?"

"Only if you know Claire. Her experience with romance has been less than favorable. She doesn't date, and not once in the year I've known her has she been anything but cool, calm, and collected when the subject of men came up. Keith threw her."

"Why?"

"She claims he reminds her of her ex."

"Maybe he does."

"That's very possible. But based on what she's told me about her marriage, that would disgust her, not fluster or rattle her."

How in the world did women pick up all these subtle emotional nuances?

David did the math—a woman in a tizzy after a nice-looking man came to her aid—and made his best guess. "You think she was attracted to him?"

Maureen finished off her potatoes and forked a piece of sautéed carrot. "Not that she admitted to me—and probably not to herself—but I have my suspicions. And while I might not yet be certain about your assistant, it's nice to see Claire noticing a man. It's a nudge in the right direction, if nothing else. As I've learned from her many kindnesses during my illness, she has a loving, caring heart. It would be a shame if she spent the rest of her life alone."

"Maybe she's content with her daughter and her career."

"A career is a wonderful thing—but there are gaps it can't fill."

"Yet you never married."

She looked down at her plate, using the tines of her fork to line up her last three carrots in a straight row. "For a long time after I gave my son away, I didn't think I deserved a husband and family. Eventually, after much prayer, I got past that."

"But . . . ?"

"The right man never came along." She set down her fork and lifted her gaze.

David wasn't an impulsive man, nor a demonstrative one. Public displays of affection had always embarrassed him. Yet before he knew what was happening, he'd lifted his hand and covered Maureen's.

"Maybe—"

"Dad?"

It took a moment for the single, shocked word to register. When it finally did, he raised his gaze to find Debbie and her husband standing beside their table. His daughter's face was pale, her lips were mashed together, and the disapproval in her eyes scorched him.

One more complication in their already complicated relationship.

Stifling a sigh, he retracted his hand and rose. "Hello, Debbie. Shawn." He shook hands with his son-in-law but didn't even attempt to hug his daughter for fear she'd break, her posture was so brittle. "What a surprise to see you here."

"I'll bet." His daughter cast Maureen a disparaging look.

When the silence lengthened, Shawn stepped in. "I had a meeting in this area and stole Debbie away from motherhood duties for an hour. Bobby's with our next-door neighbor."

"Impromptu lunches are the best kind. And speaking of that . . ." David gestured to his companion and did the introductions. "Maureen is an art history professor at Manchester Christian University."

Shawn shook her hand. Debbie gave a curt nod and turned her attention back to him. "Is this a working lunch?"

How best to answer honestly without raising any more hackles?

"We're working on a project together."

His daughter's eyes narrowed. "Since when have you been interested in art?"

"Deb . . ." Shawn glanced from father to daughter and took her arm. "I need to get moving or I'll be late for my meeting. Nice to see you, David. A pleasure to meet you, Dr. Chandler."

Before Debbie had a chance to respond, he ushered her out of the restaurant.

David slowly retook his seat.

"I see what you mean about mending fences." Maureen rested her elbows on the table and linked her fingers.

"Tell me about it." He poked at the last bite of his salmon, then pushed it aside and set his knife and fork on the plate.

"Me being here with you at a cozy restaurant like this isn't going to help matters. The resentment was so thick I could cut it with this." She picked up her knife. "She thought we were on a date."

"Close enough."

"I don't want to be the cause of any further estrangement between the two of you, David. Family ties are important."

"So is friendship."

"Ours is very new."

"But I value it already." He signaled to the waiter for the check. "I'll have a talk with her."

"Do you think that will help?"

"I doubt it. But ignoring the issue won't make it go away."

The waiter set the check on the table, and David put his credit card on top.

"I agree. So returning to the reason for this lunch—let's let your assistant see what he can dig up about my son . . . but send him back to my house first. I have some additional material I can share with him that might be helpful. And perhaps he and Claire will run into each other again."

"Doing a little matchmaking, are we?"

"Not matchmaking as much as fanning a spark. I care very much for Claire, and if I can get her thinking about romance again, she might at least start opening her eyes to the possibilities around her. Not that Keith would necessarily be the one, but he did stir up an ember. So one positive thing has come out of this project already."

"More than one." David smiled, signed the check, and rose. "Shall we?"

He walked her to her car, wishing he was young and carefree and impulsive enough to suggest they skip out of work this afternoon and go for a drive in the country.

But he had responsibilities and commitments—and she did too.

"Thank you for lunch." Maureen stopped at her car, keys in hand.

He rested a hand on the roof of the serviceable, older model Taurus. "It was my pleasure—and I mean every word of that. You brightened my day."

A faint flush crept over her cheeks. With a rueful shake of her head, she gestured to her face. "The bane of redheads—even if the red is now from a bottle. I never got over my propensity to blush at a compliment from a handsome man."

"Now it's my turn to blush."

"Not that I can see."

"On the inside."

She gave a soft laugh. "I see you have a silver tongue to go with that silver hair—a trait sure to impress the ladies."

"One lady in particular, I hope." He opened her door, and she slid inside. "I'll be in touch. Drive safe."

After closing the door, he stepped back, then waited while she backed out and started toward the exit. Once she pulled into traffic and disappeared down the street, he strolled back to his car.

What an interesting, appealing, and insightful woman.

Getting together with her again couldn't happen soon enough.

In the meantime, however, he had a daughter to talk to and an assistant to deal with. Neither were going to be receptive to what he had to say.

Fortunately, one of them had to listen.

And while it might be the coward's way out, he'd start there.

"So are you ready to talk about the scene at the restaurant?"

At Shawn's question, Debbie tightened her grip on the hairbrush and attacked her tangles. She could see her husband in the vanity mirror, stretched out on the bed, hands clasped behind his head on the propped-up pillows. He looked relaxed. Sounded relaxed. But after three years of dating and seven years of marriage, she could hear the undercurrent of concern—and determination—in his voice.

She was going to have to talk about this whether she wanted to or not—*not* being the operative word.

"Debbie?"

"It wasn't a scene."

"You could have fooled me. The tension pinging off the walls reminded me of Bobby after he drinks a glass of Mountain Dew."

Giving up any pretense of brushing her hair, she swung around on the vanity seat. "Dad was on a date."

"He said they were discussing a project."

How could men be so clueless?

"He was holding her hand, Shawn!"

"I didn't see that." He squinted at her. "Are you sure?"

"Yes. Or close enough."

"Okay. I'll take your word for it. So what's wrong with your dad having lunch with a nice woman?"

"Mom's only been gone two years."

"Maybe he's lonely."

"He has his job to keep him occupied. That was always plenty for him before."

"Before what?"

"Before Mom died." She rose and stalked over to the bed. "He never had time to take *her* to lunch on a workday."

Understanding dawned in his eyes. "Or help you with your homework or teach you to ride a bike or go to the spelling bee finals. I get it. You resent the attention he's giving this woman because he wasn't there for you or your mom."

Her spine stiffened. "That would be juvenile."

He watched her in silence.

She turned away and paced over to the window, jerked the drapes closed.

How come her husband was always right?

She *was* being juvenile.

"Look . . . I can't help how I feel, okay?" She clamped her fingers around the edge of the fabric, fighting the dull throb of the headache she'd been struggling to keep at bay since lunch.

"But he's trying to make amends. In the past year, he's cut back on work, and he spends a lot of time with Bobby and Grace. He also comes over whenever we invite him."

"It's too little, too late."

"Sweetheart . . ." His gentle voice held just a hint of recrimination. "Holding those hard feelings inside isn't going to fix the past. It's only going to ruin any chance to build a future with your dad. Why don't you try to meet him halfway?"

"You mean forgive and forget." She folded her arms tight against her chest.

"Forgetting is hard, but you might manage the forgiving part if you worked at it."

She swung back to him. "Why should I? Besides, he's obviously found someone else to care about now."

"That doesn't mean he loves you any less." He pulled back the blankets on her side of the bed and patted the mattress. "Climb in. It's late. Besides, I have a hard time concentrating with you standing there in that skimpy sleep shirt. We'll continue our conversation under the covers."

She played with the hem of the shirt. "I don't think you have talking in mind."

"I might."

"Liar."

"Why don't you test that theory?" He patted the bed again.

How was she supposed to resist her husband's bone-melting wink and come-hither smile?

She crossed the room and scooted in beside him. After rearranging his pillows, he pulled her close.

"You think I'm wrong to be cold toward my dad, don't you?" Somehow it was easier to put the hard truths into words snuggled up next to his solid chest, the steady beat of his heart beneath her ear.

"I think you have your reasons." He trailed a kiss along her temple. "But I know you have a tremendous capacity to love. And your dad is a good man, despite any mistakes he made in his priorities in the past. I just hope you can find a way to work through your resentment so someday you don't look back with regrets."

"Seeing him with that woman didn't help matters." She snuggled closer. "But there's one thing I'll never regret."

"What's that?"

"Marrying you."

"Now that's exactly the kind of thing a man likes to hear." He shifted toward her, until they were almost nose-to-nose, his hand resting on her hip.

"We're done talking, aren't we?" She traced the curve of his jaw with one finger.

"Uh-huh."

She reached back, groping for the switch on the lamp beside the bed. Grateful for the man beside her. Grateful for their life together, the home they'd built, the family they'd created.

Grateful for the reprieve from this discussion.

But as Shawn pulled her close, she knew the issues with her father would resurface in the light of day. Now that he was making a concerted effort to be part of her life, of her children's lives, things were going to come to a head. And it wasn't going to be pretty.

Because despite Shawn's counsel, she wasn't anywhere close to forgiveness.

7

∙∙

This was getting old.

As Keith turned onto Maureen Chandler's street for the second time in four days, he once again eased back on the gas pedal. He had reports to write, meetings to set up, quarterly results to review. On any other busy day, he wouldn't leave the office until after seven.

Instead, David had told him to cut out early and meet with the art professor to discuss some material she hadn't shared with him on his first visit.

Hopefully, this would be his last trip.

He parked in front of her house, same spot as last visit, taking a moment to examine the newly sealed driveway next door. Claire Summers had done a decent job, as far as he could tell. No sign of her today, however.

A twinge of disappointment rippled through him, and he frowned. What on earth was that all about? He ought to be glad she wasn't around. She might be pretty and appealing in a girl-next-door sort of way, but the lady had a serious chip on her shoulder, a sharp tongue, and attitude with a capital *A*.

No wonder she wasn't married.

Her friendly daughter must have inherited the congenial gene from her father, whoever . . . and wherever . . . he was.

Putting thoughts of Maureen Chandler's neighbor aside, he grabbed his notebook and started up the professor's walk.

She answered immediately, as if she'd been watching for him.

"Hello, Keith. Welcome back." Her greeting was warm, her manner gracious.

"She's been through a lot this past year. Go out of your way to be extra nice."

As David's parting admonition echoed in his mind, he forced up the corners of his lips. "Thank you."

He crossed the threshold, and she gestured toward the back of the house. "Would you mind if we talked in the kitchen? I've got dinner underway, and I'd like to keep things moving."

"No problem."

He followed her down the hall—but came to an abrupt halt on the threshold of the kitchen.

This wasn't at all what he'd expected based on the traditional style of the small brick house and the conventional furnishings in the living room.

The original kitchen had been totally redesigned and expanded. White cabinets gleamed beneath the skylights in the vaulted ceiling, and a long sweep of multicolored granite formed a huge island that featured a cooktop at one end with a rack of copper pots and utensils hanging above. A modern glass table supported by a stainless steel cube sat at the far end, in front of a wall of windows. Colorful modern-art prints added splashes of color on the cream-colored walls.

"You didn't say wow."

He transferred his attention to the professor. She was watching him with an amused expression.

"Everyone says wow."

He took another survey of the airy, open space. "I may not have said it, but I thought it."

"Not the decor you'd expect for a professor of medieval religious art, is it?"

"No."

"Just goes to show there's usually a lot more facets to people than one might think." Before he could come up with a suitable response, she waved a hand toward the island. "I've put some paperwork there for you to look through. If you'd be more comfortable at the table, feel free to move over there."

"This works." He slid onto one of the stools and reached for the first file.

"Let me know if you have any questions. Would you like a glass of iced tea or some coffee?"

"I'm fine, thank you."

"If you change your mind, say the word."

She walked over to the refrigerator, and he got to work.

The first file contained medical records from the professor's pregnancy. He scanned the sheets, pausing when he noticed that five months in, a new physician was listed in Boston. The change of location was consistent with what she'd told him during his first visit, though she hadn't explained the reason for it.

In any case, a ten-minute perusal of the medical material didn't turn up any information that appeared useful.

He moved on to the file about the private adoption agency. This one was thicker, the paperwork she'd filled out more than twenty years ago slightly yellowed at the edges. He pored over it for fifteen minutes, but as far as he could see, there was nothing to indicate the names of the adoptive parents. The only biographical information on the couple was a scribbled note in Maureen's hand indicating both were teachers.

Given her profession, it made sense that academic types would appeal to her as adoptive parents.

An enticing smell distracted him as he closed that file and picked up the next one. The aroma was spicy and savory and Italian—and it set off a rumble in his stomach. Chinese had been on the menu again tonight, but this smelled a whole lot better.

Too bad he'd have to wait until Sunday for another home-cooked meal.

Trying to ignore the appetizing scent swirling through the kitchen, he opened the third file. This one detailed her efforts to find her son, and corresponded to the information she'd given him on his first visit, albeit with a few more details. She'd listed herself on several of the kinds of registries his mom had mentioned, so either her son wasn't searching for her or he was looking in the wrong places. It didn't take long to read through the material.

"Can I interest you in some homemade salsa and chips?"

Without waiting for him to respond, she set a plate and small bowl in front of him. After helping herself to a serving, she returned to the other counter where she appeared to be assembling the ingredients for a salad.

His stomach rumbled again, prompting him to take a chip. The salsa was so tasty, he took another. And kept eating as he opened the file containing the PI's report.

The man had been thorough, no question about it. He'd even managed to track down a retired maternity nurse from the hospital where Dr. Chandler had delivered her baby and an employee from the long-gone adoption agency. However, neither had been able to offer any leads. Again, as far as he could tell from a first read, the file offered no further clues.

He'd give everything closer scrutiny later, when hunger wasn't—

A knock sounded on the back door, and the professor crossed the room to open it.

"Hi, Haley. Come on in. Where's your mom?"

"She's trying to fix a loose piece of gutter in the back. She said I should give you these and tell you she'll be here as soon as she can." She handed over a plate. "Mmm. It smells yummy in here . . . hey! You came back!"

The little girl scurried over to him as the older woman set a plate of dangerous-looking brownies on the island, next to the salsa.

"Is your mom up on a ladder, Haley?"

"Yeah."

The professor narrowed her eyes. "I'm not sure I like that."

"Mom does stuff like that all the time." Haley shrugged, then directed her next query to him. "The driveway turned out real good, didn't it?"

"Yes. Very nice."

She climbed on the stool beside him and snagged a chip, making herself at home—as if she spent a lot of time in the professor's kitchen. "What are you looking at?"

He closed the last file. "Some papers Dr. Chandler gave me."

"Keith . . . would you mind checking on Claire while Haley helps me set the table? I'm not a great fan of ladders."

He tapped the files into a neat stack. In general, he wouldn't hesitate to comply with such a request. Most women doing a gutter job would appreciate assistance.

Given her reaction in the driveway last Saturday, however, Claire was more likely to take a swing at him with her hammer than welcome his offer of aid.

"I asked if I could help, because the ladder's kind of rickety, but Mom said she could do it herself." Haley took another chip and scooped up a generous portion of salsa.

"Keith?" Maureen looked at him, concern scoring her voice.

He was sunk. He didn't much like the idea of her neighbor on a rickety ladder, either—even if the lady in question was bad tempered.

Sliding off the stool, he gestured to the rear door. "I assume I can get there from the back?"

"Yes." Maureen led the way to the door and pulled it open. "A row of arborvitae separates our property, but you can get through where one died." She pointed to a narrow opening in the hedge.

"That's the secret passage Mom and me use," Haley offered, still chowing down on the chips.

"I won't be long."

"No hurry. The lasagna I made won't be ready for another fifteen minutes."

Homemade lasagna.

Now *that* was a dinner.

At least he'd be out of here before they started eating.

He crossed Maureen's pristine lawn, slipped through the hedge, and stopped to take stock of the situation.

The rickety ladder was still at the back of the house, and the gutter was still sagging, but Claire Summers was nowhere in sight.

The temptation to retreat was strong. If she wasn't on the ladder, she wasn't in any danger, right?

But given the state of the gutter and the position of the ladder under the center of the sag, the job wasn't finished yet.

Sighing, he trudged across a patchy stretch of grass in need of a mow, passed a weed-filled plot of overgrown roses, and circled around an eighteen-inch-high wooden deck that featured more than a few rotted boards.

The gutter wasn't the only thing around this place that needed attention.

He stopped beside the ladder. A hammer rested on top, along with a gutter spike and its sleeve. The gutter was not only sagging, it was bent inward in the center of the sag.

Obviously, the woman had no clue what she was doing.

Expelling a breath, he fisted his hands on his hips. He ought to walk away, tell Maureen Chandler her neighbor wasn't on the ladder, and beat a hasty retreat.

He glanced toward the partly open sliding door at the back of the house. With dinner waiting for her next door, she couldn't spend a whole lot more time on . . .

A red splotch at the edge of the weathered deck caught his eye, and he moved closer.

Was that . . . blood?

He checked the rest of the deck.

A trail of red spots led to the sliding door.

Fresh, bright-red spots.

Pulse kicking into high gear, he picked his way across the dubious deck as fast as he dared, avoiding the most unreliable-looking boards.

At the door, he paused. "Ms. Summers?"

No response.

But the trail of red spots continued across the chipped tiles inside, disappearing through a doorway. When he strained his ears, he detected the sound of running water.

She must be in the bathroom, trying to deal with whatever injury she'd inflicted on herself.

When a second summons produced no result either, he followed his instincts and tugged at the door.

The stupid thing refused to budge.

He put both hands on the edge and gave it a yank.

This time it opened—under protest.

Was *everything* in this house falling apart?

Hoping she wouldn't prosecute him for trespassing, he followed the trail of red drops down the hall.

He found her bent over the bathroom sink, her right forearm stuck under the faucet, tears streaming down her face as the water gushed over a long, nasty gash.

Stomach clenching, he cleared his throat. "Ms. Summers."

With a gasp, she jerked toward him, eyes wide.

"I'm sorry. I didn't mean to startle you. When Dr. Chandler heard you were on a ladder, she asked me to come over and check on you. Looks as if she was right to be concerned. May I?" He nodded toward the oozing cut.

She gripped the counter with her other hand. "I can deal with this. Sorry you were bothered."

Her complexion was white, her whole body was trembling, and she seemed completely unaware of the tears coursing down her cheeks.

He gentled his tone. "Look . . . I know you're an independent and capable woman. You did an impressive job on your driveway. But it's going to be hard to deal with that cut one-handed—and left-handed, at that. Unless you're a leftie?"

"No." The word came out shaky.

"Then let me help."

If she told him to leave, he would—but for some reason he hoped she didn't. Maybe because he felt sorry for her, living in this house that Jack built. Maybe because he'd always been a sucker for a woman's tears. Maybe because she brought out his latent protective instincts, standing there trying to look strong when all she looked was fragile and vulnerable and . . . appealing.

Whatever the reason, he held his breath while she stared back at him with those big blue eyes fringed by damp, spiky lashes.

All at once the rigid line of her shoulders collapsed. "Okay. I have some first-aid stuff in the hall closet, middle shelf."

"Keep your arm under the water while I get it."

He found her medical supplies, picked out what he needed along with a clean washcloth, and returned as fast as he could.

As he deposited the items on the vanity, he gave the cut a closer inspection. "It's long and deep in the middle—but not deep enough for stitches, as best I can tell. Why don't you sit and put your arm on the counter while I clean it up?"

She took a step to the left and sat on the toilet seat in the small bathroom.

The cut was still oozing at the ends and bleeding in the center, but the flow was slowing.

She didn't make a sound while he worked on her arm, other than a few small intakes of breath as he carefully cleaned the wound with soap and water and applied antibiotic cream. By the time he'd bandaged it, adding an extra layer of gauze in the center, her respiration had evened out and her voice was steadier.

"You seem like you know what you're doing."

"I learned a lot on the way to becoming an Eagle Scout." He began gathering up the first-aid supplies. "So what happened out there? Did you fall off the ladder? Are you hurt anywhere else?"

"No to both. The hammer slipped, and as I grabbed for it, I ran my arm along the edge of the gutter. It was sharp."

"No kidding." He twisted the cap on the tube of antibiotic cream. "You know, you're supposed to drill a hole through the gutter first so it doesn't cave in when you hammer."

She stiffened. "Yes, I know. I read the instructions online. But you have to own a drill to use a drill. I did the best I could with what I had. Besides, what makes you an expert?"

"I repaired my mom's gutter last year."

He could feel her giving his Ralph Lauren dress shirt and Johnston and Murphy shoes a skeptical once-over. "Seriously?"

"Yeah. She's on a fixed income, and she won't take money from me. So I give her sweat. Let me wash the blood off your fingers."

She fell silent as he turned the faucet back on, positioned her hand under the stream of water, and gently scrubbed at the bloodstains with the washcloth.

Her hand felt small in his, and delicate, with long, slender fingers. But the palm had too many calluses, the nails were chipped and unpolished, and the cuticles still bore the faint, dark stain of driveway sealer.

His heart contracted with a sudden surge of tenderness.

Hands like these—a woman like this—shouldn't have to do the kind of hard, physical labor that seemed to be her lot.

"I think they're clean now."

At her soft comment, he released her hand at once, shut off the water, took a quick step back—and ran into the wall.

Smooth, Watson, real smooth.

"Dr. Chandler said dinner would be ready in fifteen minutes, and we've used up most of that." At least his voice hadn't come out in an adolescent squeak. "I'll walk you over."

He expected her to refuse—half hoped she would—but after a brief hesitation, she surprised him.

"Thanks. Give me a minute to change out of this and I'll meet you in the kitchen." She swept a hand over her bloodstained T-shirt, edged past him in the confined space, and disappeared down the hall . . . leaving a pleasing, floral fragrance in her wake.

And stirring in him a sudden longing to reach for her hand again.

A red alert began to beep in his mind, urging him to run fast—and far.

Because Claire Summers was dangerous. She wasn't the kind of woman he could date a couple of times, have a few laughs with, and walk away from. Claire was the white-picket-fence, ring-on-the-finger type—even if Haley's father was MIA. She also had a daughter who needed to be considered, and other issues—like a house held together with spit—that would only complicate his life.

Any woman he decided to get involved with had to come unencumbered. He had enough baggage of his own without taking on someone else's.

So he'd walk her back. Gather up Dr. Chandler's files. Say good night.

And hope he didn't cross paths again with the girl next door.

This was nuts.

She should have thanked him for his help, told him she was fine, and sent him on his way.

Instead, she was rooting through her closet like some frantic schoolgirl, trying to find the extravagant blue blouse she'd bought on a whim after that persuasive salesgirl had convinced her it was a once-in-a-lifetime perfect match for her eyes.

All because Keith Watson's touch had sent shock waves rippling through her.

How pathetic was that?

Claire heaved a sigh.

Was she really so desperate for male companionship that even a guy who reminded her of Brett could turn her on?

Except this guy had been an Eagle Scout—an achievement that required service to the community. And he helped his mother.

Brett had never cared about anyone but himself.

Claire snagged the blouse and pulled it on with fumbling fingers, frowning at her trembling hands. That had to be a delayed reaction to her injury and unrelated to the man waiting in her kitchen. Right?

Wrong.

Expelling a breath, she yanked the elastic band out of her ponytail and picked up her brush. Might as well admit the truth. She was attracted to Keith Watson. Had been from the moment he'd wrangled the tub of sealer out of her grasp last Saturday and hauled it up the driveway for her.

So she was human. So what? Any lonely woman's heart would

pitter-patter if a handsome guy appeared out of nowhere and came to her rescue.

But if he turned out to be as much like Brett as she'd initially thought, despite that Eagle Scout and good-son stuff, his appeal would evaporate.

In the meantime, why not enjoy it?

She found him waiting for her in the kitchen, examining the recalcitrant sliding door.

"It's on the list."

He swiveled around at her comment, and a spark ignited in his eyes as he focused on the silky blouse. Then he jerked his gaze back to her face and cleared his throat. "It could be a worn roller."

Maybe splurging on this blouse two years ago hadn't been a mistake after all.

"I wouldn't be surprised. I'll get to it one of these days. Ready?"

He stepped out, and she followed behind him. Before she could maneuver the door shut, he grabbed it and tugged until it slid into place.

"Thanks." She locked it and gestured toward the opening in the arborvitae. "I take it you found the secret passageway. Oh . . . watch your step." She grabbed his arm as he headed toward a board she didn't trust.

"Let me guess. Another project on the to-do list."

"Near the bottom. I'm starting with the small stuff."

"You don't use the deck, do you?" He gave it a wary inspection.

"Not much. Haley and I mostly just cut across it when we go over to Maureen's, but we know the safe boards."

He followed in silence as they crossed her neighbor's lawn and knocked on her door.

When Maureen opened it, her features flattened in shock. "Oh my goodness! What happened?"

Haley turned from the bowl of chips on the island, eyes wide with alarm.

"It's just a small cut. Mr. Watson bandaged it for me." Claire gave her daughter a reassuring smile as she entered. "How many of those have you wolfed down, young lady?"

The diversion worked. Her daughter's expression went from worried to guilty in a heartbeat. "I can't remember, but I'll eat my dinner. Cross my heart."

"Of course she will. It's my world-famous lasagna. Keith, will you stay? I have plenty. Even with four of us eating, I'll be freezing lots of leftovers. We set you a place."

"I appreciate that, but I wouldn't want to impose."

"It's not an imposition. Do you have other dinner plans?"

He cast a covetous eye at the pan of lasagna, the tossed green salad, the basket of Italian bread already on the table. He was tempted, but he was going to refuse. Claire could feel it.

"I wish you would. You deserve a nice meal after coming to my rescue, even if Maureen is providing the meal. But I contributed the brownies." Impulsiveness was one of the traits she thought she'd beaten into submission years ago, but apparently she hadn't tamed it after all.

Yet she didn't regret her spontaneous invitation.

"You should stay." Haley slid off the stool and joined them. "My mom makes the best brownies in the whole world, and Dr. Chandler's lasagna is awesome."

Keith checked his watch. "I do have some work to do tonight . . ."

"But you also have to have dinner." Maureen added a bowl of grated parmesan cheese to the table. "We won't be offended if you eat and run."

He did one more sweep of the table and let out a slow breath. "All right, I'll stay."

As they all took their places, Claire's heart suddenly felt lighter—even if his capitulation was due more to a homemade meal than her charms . . . whatever those might be. But it would be nice to share a meal with an attractive man here in the safety of Maureen's kitchen. And an hour in his company should help her determine if his resemblance to Brett was merely superficial . . . or significant.

Good food, adult conversation, perhaps some laughter.

For tonight, that was enough.

He shouldn't have caved.

The pace of the red alert beeping in his mind had gone from brisk to breakneck.

Keith helped himself to a second serving of lasagna, stealing a look at Claire. Her face was animated as she shared a story about one of her second grade students, her features relaxed, eyes bright, lips soft and smiling. Gone was the prickly, squeegee-wielding feminist from last Saturday.

That woman had been easier to dismiss.

This woman was engaging, interesting, smart, witty . . . and far too appealing.

But she came with a lot of baggage—including a house in desperate need of TLC. Money must be very tight, or she'd be hiring people to do the more urgent home repairs. And where was Haley's father? Why wasn't he contributing to the household income, helping make life more comfortable for his daughter, no matter his feelings for Claire?

"That story's a treasure. Don't you think so, Keith?" Maureen turned toward him.

Yanking his attention back to the conversation, he deposited the lasagna on his plate. Unfortunately, he'd been more interested in the storyteller than the story. Claire might as well have been speaking Greek for all he'd absorbed.

Irene Hannon

He was busted.

"Yes." His response might be lame and too brief, but it was safe—as long as they didn't ask him any other questions.

The quiver in Maureen's lips suggested she'd detected his problem. He braced, waiting for her to tease him, but instead she came to his rescue. "I don't imagine you have to deal with anyone in your job who insists he has a magic cape that gives him the ability to fly."

"No." He relaxed and dug into the lasagna. "But I've dealt with a few people who try to work creative magic with numbers."

"I bet. I can see where being a CPA would have its own set of challenges. Did you know Keith is both an MBA and CPA, Claire?"

"No. That's impressive."

Keith shoveled in another large bite of lasagna, willing the heat in his neck to stay below his collar as he shifted the conversation away from his professional accomplishments. "I can sympathize with the kid and the cape, though. When I was six, I had a cardboard box in my room that I believed had magic powers. For reasons I can't begin to fathom at this stage of my life, I became convinced all I had to do was crawl inside and I'd be safe. That the box was like a magic force field and would protect me. It took my mom and dad two years to convince me to let them trash it."

As his confession hovered in the air, he bunched the napkin on his lap into a ball. He'd never told anyone about his magic box. Why on earth had he done so tonight, with three people who were virtual strangers?

He did a quick survey of his dinner companions. Claire's expression was speculative. Maureen's, thoughtful. Haley's, matter-of-fact.

"I had a blanket for a long time, when I was little." Haley propped her elbow on the table and balanced her chin in her palm. "I used to take it to bed with me and carry it around. It made me feel safe, just like your box. But when I got older, I didn't need it anymore, because I figured out that the thing that really made me feel safe was being with Mom. Is that what happened with you?"

"More or less."

"Do you have a good mother?"

"The best."

"Yeah. Me too." Haley smiled at Claire, and the loving look that passed between mother and daughter tightened his throat.

He took a drink of water before he spoke. "I need to be on my way."

"Before dessert?" Haley gawked at him as if he'd just turned down a million bucks.

"I'm afraid so. I have some work to do tonight." And he didn't want to risk revealing any more personal tidbits. "Thank you for the great dinner, Dr. Chandler."

"It was my pleasure. And let's make it Maureen. No reason for formalities at this point."

"Is it all right if I take your files?" He released his grip on the napkin and stood. "I'd like to go over them more carefully at home. I can make copies and bring back the originals, if you prefer."

"No need. I trust you to keep them safe." She rose too. "I'll show you out."

As he gathered up the files, Claire circled around to the other side of the counter.

"Let me give you a couple of brownies to take home." She slid the plate toward her and retrieved a box of plastic wrap from a drawer. "Unless you don't like chocolate?" She hesitated and looked across the granite.

"I like chocolate."

Their gazes met.

Held.

An electrical charge jolted through him.

"Hey, Mom, how come your face is red?" Haley bounded over to snag a brownie.

Claire dipped her chin and fumbled with the plastic wrap.

"Sometimes people get flushed from the heat in a kitchen." Maureen glanced at Claire, then him. "Why don't you help yourself to another glass of milk to go with your dessert?"

"Okay." Haley returned to the table and grabbed her glass.

His lungs finally kicked in again.

Claire kept her head bent as she selected and wrapped two generous brownies. Only when she handed them over did she raise her chin.

Man, she had drop-dead gorgeous deep blue eyes—the color of the sky on a fresh, crisp autumn day.

He took the packet of brownies, his blood pressure edging up as their fingers brushed.

"How's the arm?" His question came out hoarse.

She moistened her lips. "Fine. Thanks for coming to my rescue."

"Listen . . . leave the gutter for now. I'll borrow my dad's drill on Sunday when I visit my mom and drop by your place afterward to reattach it—if that's all right with you."

"I don't want to put you out."

"It won't take long, and you're on my route home." Sort of. If he went the long way.

"What time?"

He did some fast calculating. Dinner at his mom's was always at five, and he usually stayed around until dusk. But he needed light for the gutter job—and he intended to fix the sliding door while he was at it. He'd just have to cut out early on his mom.

"Around seven?"

"That's fine. There's a youth program at church in the afternoon, but we'll be home long before that."

"See you then." He gathered up the files, cradled the brownies in his hand, and followed Maureen to the front of the house.

"Call me if you have any questions." She opened the door. "I'll be interested to hear your thoughts on next steps—if you can think of any. My PI wasn't hopeful he could uncover much more, and he didn't think the odds of success were high enough to justify the cost of additional digging. I have to give him high marks for being honest if nothing else."

"I'll do a thorough review of everything. Thanks again for dinner."

"It was my pleasure—and thank *you* for your help with my project. Enjoy the rest of your evening."

Brownies in hand, files under his arm, he headed toward the curb, trying to figure out why he felt a whole lot better walking down this path than he had walking up it two hours ago.

He could attribute his upbeat mood to his meeting with Maureen, which had gone better than expected. In fact, he was beginning to like the woman.

He could also attribute it to the great dinner.

But neither of those were the real reason.

The credit belonged to Claire.

He surveyed her driveway as he slid behind the wheel of his car.

Who'd have guessed the professor's prickly neighbor would turn out to be so appealing?

Or that he'd be looking forward to seeing her again?

Or that he'd end up hoping to find something in Maureen's file worth following up on that would give him an excuse to drop by again?

He set the files and brownies on the seat beside him, started the car, and pulled away from the curb.

None of that was good, of course. Claire might have been nicer to him tonight, but her attitude the day they'd met spoke volumes about her opinion of men. An opinion likely formed by her experience with Haley's missing father.

On top of that, she was struggling to make ends meet on her teacher's salary. Struggling to raise a daughter alone. Struggling to prop up a disintegrating house.

She didn't need a guy in her life who had a bunch of unresolved issues of his own, who . . .

Wait a minute.

He was the one who didn't want to be saddled with more problems, not the other way around. Right?

He pulled into the cross traffic, aimed the car toward his condo, and admitted the truth.

His view of this situation had done a one-eighty tonight, starting the moment he'd found her trembling in the bathroom, tears streaming down her face, her blood tinting the water pink.

Now he cared more about protecting her from his baggage than vice versa.

But how was he supposed to do that?

Get your act together if you want to spare her more grief.

He tightened his grip on the wheel, turned a corner. Excellent advice, but far easier said than done. He'd spent thirty years trying to banish the ghosts from his early years. What more could he do?

"If you connected with your birth mother, learned the reasons she did what she did, you might be able to move past that."

His mother's words echoed in his mind as he skirted around a stalled car.

Was she right?

Might such a meeting have a positive outcome?

But what if his birth mother was dead . . . or had disappeared . . . or worst of all, turned out to be as uncaring as she'd been nearly three decades ago?

He picked up speed again, fighting back a suffocating feeling of panic.

Chill, Watson. You don't have to take any immediate action. Let the idea simmer for a while. See how the next visit with Claire goes.

Maybe he could even pray about it—not that he'd given God a whole lot of attention in recent years. His job had taken precedence over everything, become his refuge. The world of numbers was comfortable, predictable, safe.

Kind of like that box in his bedroom.

But eventually that childhood box had become confining. So he'd ventured into the bigger world, trusting his parents to take care of him.

Maybe it was time to venture out again from the secure adult world he'd created—this time putting his trust in God.

Except stepping into the unknown was risky. There was no guarantee of reward.

Darkness began to fall, and he switched on the headlights to illuminate his route.

Too bad he couldn't do the same for the personal road before him.

But unfortunately, that one still lay in shadows.

8

....

"I thought I might find you out here on such a beautiful day."

As the sound of her father's voice carried over the spring breeze, Debbie shifted around on her knees at the edge of her weed-infested garden. He stood at the corner of the house, dressed in his field outfit of jeans, blue work shirt, and heavy boots, and he was holding a plant in a nursery container.

It *had* been a beautiful day—until now.

He hesitated for a moment when she didn't greet him, then walked toward her.

She settled back and watched him approach. He was in great shape for a guy his age, trim and fit and limber. Much better shape than he'd been in two years ago, when all of her mom's pleas that he watch his cholesterol, take up some regular exercise, and lose his paunch had gone unheeded.

Now he ate healthy food and visited the gym three times a week.

In memory of Mom—or to appeal to that woman in the restaurant?

She scowled at him as he approached, but he didn't seem in the least put off by her less-than-cordial welcome.

"I thought this might be a nice addition to your rose garden." He set the nursery container beside her, and she glanced at the tag. Double Delight.

The tea rose she'd been trying to find for two years.

"Where did you get this?" She fingered one of the velvety petals, leaned close to inhale the spicy scent of the two-toned blossom.

"A nursery in Wentzville. They ordered it for me, and I picked it up while I was out there at a job site this morning."

Was it a coincidence he'd chosen this particular rose—or did he know it was Mom's favorite?

He spoke as if he'd read her mind. "Your mom was partial to that one, you know."

"Yeah, I know—but I'm surprised you do."

"I was never into gardening like she was, but I admired her handiwork. And every now and then on a summer evening, we'd walk through her gardens." A wistful smile tugged at his lips. "She always had me smell this one when we got to the roses."

"Those little strolls can't have happened very often. You never got home before dark." The bitterness of her tone hung heavy in the air between them, lingering after the words faded away.

Sighing, he lowered himself to the ground beside her until they were eye to eye, regret etched on his face. "If I had it to do again, I'd make some changes."

To her horror, pressure built in her throat. She was *not* going to cry. Not. Going. To. Cry. Tears didn't solve a thing—and they wouldn't change the past.

"It's a little late for that." Somehow she managed to choke out the words.

"I know. And I'm sorry."

The pressure increased, and she turned away. Maybe if she went back to yanking out weeds, he'd get the hint and leave.

Instead, he dropped onto his knees and joined her. "There are some things we should talk about."

"Talk doesn't change anything."

"It can—if opinions have been formed without full information."

What was that supposed to mean?

She tugged on a tenacious dandelion, but the leaves pulled off, leaving the root firmly embedded in the earth, ready to send up another noxious sprout.

"You might have to use the trowel on that one."

"I know how to weed a garden." She picked up the trowel and attacked the root. "I also know what I saw on Monday. You were on a date with that woman—and I formed that opinion with full information. You were holding her hand."

"It didn't start out as a date, but it did end that way—and I plan to see her again."

At least he wasn't trying to pretend things between them hadn't been cozy.

Debbie stabbed at the earth with the trowel. "Mom would have enjoyed meeting you for lunch like that once in a while. But you never had time for her. For either of us. Even on important occasions."

"That was a mistake. I see that now. At the time, though, I thought I was doing the right thing."

"Neglecting your wife and daughter was the right thing?" She glared at him, her voice vibrating with hurt and anger. "It didn't seem very right the night I found Mom crying in your bedroom when I was twelve, on your anniversary. You'd called and said there was some crisis at the office, as usual, and you couldn't get away in time to take her to dinner. She'd bought a new dress, gotten her hair done, had a manicure. She was all ready to go. The tears were running down her face when I peeked in the bedroom door."

He rested a hand against the ground, and a muscle twitched in his cheek. "I didn't know that. She never said a word."

"Mom didn't complain about anything." Debbie tackled the stubborn dandelion root again. "She got herself under control and told me it didn't matter, that she understood why you couldn't get away, that she was just being silly and selfish. But I didn't think she was the one being selfish. I still don't."

"You're right. I should have realized how much a night like that would mean to your mom. But I was always more worried about keeping the business afloat."

"Get real, Dad." Sarcasm dripped from her words. "You run a very successful company. The issue isn't whether you can keep it afloat but how much more money you can make this year than last."

"The business hasn't always been as solid as it is now, Debbie. It was lean in the early years. Building a company from scratch can eat up your life. However, things were going well by the time you were twelve." His fingers tightened around the stem of a weed, lines of distress scoring the corners of his mouth. "I should have let someone else handle that crisis on our anniversary."

He yanked out the weed, tossed it onto the growing pile between them. When he continued, his voice was more subdued, his expression pained. "The truth is, I was always afraid things would collapse around me and I wouldn't be able to provide for you and your mom. I never got over that fear, no matter how successful the business became. That's what drove me to put in those long hours."

She slanted a look at him. He was staring at the dark earth, fingers clutched in the dirt. Not once in her entire life had she seen her self-confident father exhibit one iota of fear. Was this just some lame attempt to rationalize his skewed priorities?

As if sensing her perusal, he turned toward her, a profound sadness in the depths of his eyes. "There are a lot of things about my past you don't know. Things I shared only with your mother. She thought I should tell you about them after you got older, but I didn't want to dredge up all that garbage again. Maybe you need to hear them, though."

If this was a ploy intended to gain sympathy, her dad was giving an Oscar-winning performance.

"So tell me." The challenge came out stiff, bordering on confrontational, and she had a feeling he'd back off. Why offer explanations to someone who obviously wasn't receptive or willing to listen with an open mind?

But he surprised her.

After dusting off his hands, he sat on the grass at the edge of the garden, resting his forearms on his knees. "I told you my father was a businessman and that he died when I was very young. I lied about both."

She sat back on her heels with a frown. Her dad might have a lot of faults, but he'd always been scrupulously honest. "Why?"

"Because I was ashamed of him." He focused on the new spring grass at his feet, fingered the tender green stalks reaching for the sun. "He was the classic ne'er-do-well. A man with grandiose, get-rich-quick schemes that always went belly-up. We lived hand to mouth, sometimes with just enough heat to keep the pipes from freezing, sometimes with nothing more to eat than peanut butter and jelly sandwiches for a week at a stretch, never sure when we'd next be evicted. I remember spending one Christmas Eve in a homeless shelter with my mom while Dad was off chasing some new pot of gold in Oklahoma."

"Why did your mother stay with him?"

"She loved him. And he said he loved us. But I never understood how a man who professed to love his family could let his wife and son live the way we did. Oh, there were always great promises about the mansion he'd buy us and the servants we'd have once he hit it big, but in the meantime Mom worked two part-time jobs at minimum wage trying to keep a roof over our heads and food on the table. We bought our clothes at the thrift store and wore coats to bed in the winter. I remember wondering through more nights than I care to remember if I'd ever be warm again."

He paused, the mellow tones of the wind chimes on the patio filling the silence with a soothing resonance as she studied his profile.

"Why didn't you ever tell me any of that?"

"I never wanted you to worry about ending up that way. I didn't even want you to know people lived like I did growing up. I wanted you and your mom to have a secure life, to know you could count on me to provide for you, no matter what. I thought that was the best way I could demonstrate my love—and if that meant missing out on family events, that was a sacrifice I had to make."

He wiped a hand down his face, leaving a dirt stain on one cheek. "Carol knew my background, understood what drove me, and she tried to convince me that being a workaholic was an overreaction. That you needed my time more than you needed an expensive summer camp or ballet lessons or designer clothes. But I just couldn't downshift. I was so afraid if I slowed my pace, things would fall apart." He exhaled. "Your mom also urged me to share my history with you once you got older. But before I knew it, you went off to college . . . and life moved on."

Debbie jabbed her trowel into the ground. "I wish you'd told me."

"Would hearing about it as a teenager have made a difference?"

"I don't know." She was still trying to assimilate his revelation, to reconcile her image of a workaholic father who only cared about his job with one who cared so much about his family he was willing to sacrifice his personal life to provide for them. "What happened to your father?"

He picked up a clump of dirt, sifted it through his fingers. "When I was twenty, he got involved in some sort of easy money pyramid scheme. I'm not certain he realized it was crooked in the beginning. Mom never thought he did, but she had blinders on when it came to him. In any case, once he realized the mess he was in, once he knew he was going to be implicated in an illegal business that had swindled hundreds of disabled people out of their savings, he went down to the Eads Bridge one night and jumped off. Mom died of a heart attack two years later. She was only fifty-seven."

Shock rippled through Debbie. How could she have lived in the same house with this man for eighteen years and never picked up a clue about his traumatic youth, even if he *was* gone a lot?

"I'm not saying my background excuses the bad choices I made with my own family." Her father angled toward her, the grooves around his mouth deepening, his eyes sad. "But maybe it will help you understand that my intentions were good. I wanted to shelter you from the sordid side of life, to give you a childhood where you never had to worry about subsisting on peanut butter or shivering through a winter night. In hindsight, I know you needed more of me and less of the material things I provided, and I'd follow a more moderate course if I had it to do over. But since I can't alter the past, I'm hoping you'll give me a chance to make amends in the future."

The noonday sun highlighted the creases in his face that marked the passage of years . . . and reminded her time was running out to repair their strained relationship.

What he'd told her today did give her a new perspective. She could understand why he'd been so driven, so work-focused.

But long-standing resentment didn't evaporate overnight.

The best she could do was offer him the chance he'd asked for. To let him play a bigger role in her life . . . and see where things went from there. Shawn was right. She didn't want to look back someday with regret.

She picked up her trowel and began hacking again at the stubborn, imbedded root. "We're having a birthday dinner for Bobby a week from Sunday. You're welcome to join us if you're free."

He exhaled, as if he'd been holding his breath. "I'd like that. Thank you."

Then he settled in beside her again and went back to pulling weeds.

She snuck a peek at him. "Don't you have to get back to work?"

"I told the crew I had some important business to take care of. They can get along without me for another hour. Would you like me to help you plant that?" He gestured toward the rosebush.

"Are you sure you have time?"

"Yes."

She shoved her trowel as deep as possible, wiggled it around, and finally managed to pull out the dandelion root. "I have a dead bush I was going to replace over there." She gestured toward her rose garden. "The Double Delight will be perfect."

"Let's do it."

After tossing the deep-rooted weed on the heap, she stood. "I'll get the shovel from the garage."

"I'll meet you at the garden." He picked up the bush and started to move away.

Her heart began to hammer as she wrestled with the sudden urge to make an offer she wasn't at all certain was wise. Yes or no?

Just do it, Debbie.

"If you . . . if you want to bring your lady friend to Bobby's party, it's okay."

At her breathless overture, he stopped. Slowly turned. "Are you sure?"

No. At this point, she wasn't sure about anything. But somehow this felt right.

"If she's important to you, I'd like to get to know her. And please tell her I won't be so rude this time."

"She understood your reaction. And I think she'd like the birthday party. She doesn't have any family of her own."

Debbie picked a piece of dirt off her jeans. "She has cancer, doesn't she?"

His smile faded. "Had. I hope. The prognosis is good." He transferred the rose from one hand to the other. "Look . . . I want you to know that Maureen is a new friend. There's been no one since your mom died. I loved her with all my heart—like I love you."

He'd often said those words to her, told her he was proud of her, but somewhere along the way, his expressions of affection had become just words. They'd stopped registering. She'd measured love in terms of time and attention, and by her measure, he'd failed. Yet he'd demonstrated his love in the way he thought most appropriate—in concrete terms, by providing security and a comfortable life.

Had they both had tunnel vision all these years? Was there fault on both sides for the cracks in their relationship? Instead of keeping all her hurt inside, letting it build a wall of resentment between them, should she have told him what she needed years ago? Reinforced what her mother had apparently tried to communicate? Would that have made a difference?

When she didn't respond, he continued toward the garden—disappointed, no doubt, that she hadn't returned his sentiment.

But she had a lot of thinking to do first. A lot of emotions to sort through. She'd have to dig deep to dredge up the words he wanted to hear.

Her gaze fell on the pile of weeds, already wilting in the spring sun. She'd accomplished a lot in the garden today. Prepared the ground for the seeds she would soon plant and nurture until they took root and sent fragile shoots reaching toward the warmth.

Perhaps she'd done the same with her dad.

Time would tell.

"Thanks a lot for your help, Dr. Chandler." Jarrod rose and slung his backpack over one shoulder. "I'm sorry to keep you so late, but I was beginning to feel like a hamster on a wheel—running fast and getting nowhere."

"No problem. I don't have any special plans for Thursday nights as a rule. And you were right to stop by. I wouldn't want you to lose momentum on your thesis when you're making such great progress."

"I'm glad you think so. Some days . . ." He grinned and shook his head. "But I'm back on track now. Thanks again." Hefting the backpack into a more comfortable position, he lifted a hand in farewell and disappeared out the door.

After gathering up the papers on her desk and sliding them into her briefcase, Maureen glanced at her watch. How could it already be six? The day had flown—and she owed David a report on Keith's visit from last night. The lengthy faculty meeting, plus crises with two of her graduate students, had given her a legitimate reason to bump the call down on her priority list, but now she'd run out of excuses.

Yet her stomach churned at the thought of talking to him.

Because David McMillan made her feel the same way she'd felt that long-ago summer for those few magical days under the Italian sun.

Breathless. Alive. Happy.

And look how that had turned out.

She shifted her gaze to the redbud tree outside her window, the magenta flowers brilliant against the deep blue of the early-evening sky. The feeling this time was different in some ways, though. *She* was different. Older. Wiser. Cautious. More jaded, less gullible. And much less susceptible to brain fog just because she'd piqued the interest of an engaging, mature man. David seemed to be who he said he was, but Hal had too—and she wasn't going to make the same mistake twice.

The key was to move slowly, not get carried away. To approach this open-eyed rather than starry-eyed. If she stuck to those guidelines, she wouldn't get hurt again.

Doing her best to suppress the flutter of nerves in the pit of her stomach, she picked up his business card and tapped in his cell number.

He answered on the second ring, his tone clipped and distracted. "David McMillan."

"David, it's Maureen. Is this a bad time?"

"Never." Warmth chased the preoccupation from his voice. "It's nice to hear from you."

"I apologize for the delay in getting back to you after my meeting with Keith. My day was crazy."

"Mine too. I spent most of it on a job site trying to deal with a hawk's nest one of my crews discovered in a wooded area they were clearing. It seems the hawks objected to their presence and began a dive-bombing attack. Then we discovered the nest has eggs in it, putting it under the protection of federal law. Now we have to get a permit from Uncle Sam to relocate the nest. Since this is a multimillion-dollar project, and every delay dings the bottom line, we're hustling to get through the government red tape."

"A Herculean task, I bet."

"You've got that right."

"In light of your crisis, my day doesn't sound half bad. The worst part was a long, boring staff meeting—but even that had a few moments of levity when the professor emeritus nodded off and fell out of his chair. Fortunately, he only hurt his dignity."

David's deep chuckle came over the line. "I'll trade your professor's faux pas for my hawks any day. Now tell me how it went last night with Keith."

"Better than I expected. I invited Claire and Haley to dinner, and the three of us convinced him to join us."

"How in the world did you manage that?"

"It wasn't a hard sell." She gave him a quick recap of the evening's events.

"The lasagna was an inspired idea. Offer any bachelor a home-cooked meal and he's likely to cave."

"To be honest, I think he was hungry for more than lasagna. He and Claire might not have gotten off to the best start, but as of last night, I'd say your plan to convince your assistant there's more to life than numbers is off and running. There was some serious electricity pinging off the walls in my kitchen."

"Interesting. So with all that went on, did you and he have much opportunity to talk about your project?"

"No, but he did read through my files, and he took them home for further review. To be honest, though, I don't think there's much chance he'll uncover anything the PI overlooked."

"Maybe not, but it can't hurt to put some fresh eyes on it. And as far as I'm concerned, there've already been positive outcomes from this whole thing."

"I was thinking the same thing last night as I watched Keith and Claire. Wouldn't it be something if they actually hit it off?"

"Yes. But my comment had a more selfish motivation. If we hadn't started this whole thing, I'd never have met you."

Her heart stumbled.

Oh my.

Talk like that could turn a girl's head, no matter her age.

But Hal had been a smooth talker too. And while her instincts told her David was more sincere, those same instincts had let her down big time two decades ago.

"Thank you for saying that." The temptation to return the sentiment was strong, but she resisted.

"Moving on to another topic—I stopped by my daughter's this afternoon, and we had a long talk while we pulled weeds in one of her many gardens."

"Wow. Between that visit and the hawk situation, you had quite a day. Was she still upset about finding the two of us together at lunch?"

"At first. But by the time I left, I think we'd mended a few fences. She not only invited me to Bobby's birthday party a week from Sunday, she said you'd be welcome to attend as well. I'm hoping you'll accept."

He was asking her to a family event.

As the implications registered, warmth flooded her heart. He wanted their relationship to be open and aboveboard. He wasn't afraid to let her meet his family, nor vice versa. He was willing to share a very private, personal part of his life with her.

What a difference from Hal.

Her gaze fell on the small, framed verse from Jeremiah that she'd placed on her desk twenty-two years ago, when she'd been in desperate need of comfort and courage. Through all the ups and downs during the intervening years, those words of reassurance had sustained her.

"'For I know the plans I have for you,' declares the Lord, 'plans to prosper you and not to harm you, plans to give you hope and a future.'"

Funny. She'd written off romance long ago. She'd found her fulfillment instead in nurturing young minds, had assumed that was her destiny. But could it be that love was part of God's plan for her after all, even at this late date?

"I haven't told her anything about your background, in case you're wondering. But if you'd like to think about it, I understand."

David's voice drew her back to the present. "No. I'd love to join you, as long as my presence won't make things awkward."

"I can't guarantee there won't be a few uncomfortable moments, but those will have more to do with me and Debbie than with you. And you'll love Bobby and Grace. They're great kids—speaking with the objectivity of a doting grandfather, of course."

"Of course." Her lips curved up. "Just tell me when and where."

They finalized the arrangements and ended the call, but her smile lingered as a feeling of lightness . . . of hope . . . enveloped her.

And maybe that was okay. Maybe, after all the years she'd spent trying to fill up the lonely place in her heart with fulfilling work, God had saved the best for last.

9

· ·

"Do you mind if I borrow Dad's drill?"

Keith's mother refilled their coffee cups. "Of course not. It's on his workbench, where it's always been. Problem at the condo?"

He shifted in his seat. He'd been dreading this moment, trying to think of some excuse for needing the drill that didn't involve a certain blonde schoolteacher who was making it hard for him to concentrate at work for the first time in his career.

But short of lying—which he didn't do—there was no way around it except try to play down the charms of said school-teacher. Otherwise, his mom would start asking questions. A lot of questions.

And he didn't have any answers at this point—for her or himself.

All he knew was his assessment of Claire Summers had gone from hostile to hot so fast it had left him reeling.

"Keith?" His mother gave him a quizzical look.

"Maureen Chandler's neighbor has a sagging gutter, and she doesn't have the right tools to fix it." He took a sip of his coffee, keeping his tone nonchalant. "I offered to stop by on my way home tonight and take care of it."

She rejoined him at the table. "Is this neighbor the mother of the little girl who wrote that letter to your boss?"

"Yes."

"Didn't you say she was unfriendly on the phone the day you called her?"

"She was. But we, uh, got to know each other a little better the other night at Maureen's when she and her daughter, uh, came over while I was there."

"Her husband couldn't take care of the gutter problem?" His mother watched him over the rim of her cup.

"There's no husband in the picture."

"Divorced?"

He lifted one shoulder. "I don't know. Maybe she's never been married."

Silence.

He could guess what she was thinking, but he waited her out.

At last she carefully set down her cup. "I know I mentioned grandchildren to you the other day, but I wasn't thinking of the ready-made variety."

"Don't jump to any conclusions. Besides, Haley's a very nice little girl."

"I'm sure she is. But a single mother . . . she could have a lot of issues."

"Who doesn't? From what I've observed, she's strong and independent and very capable. She even sealed her own driveway. And she seems to be an excellent mother. Haley comes across as well adjusted and happy. I have a feeling she's also very good with the second graders she teaches." Hard as he tried to suppress it, a thread of defensiveness crept into his voice.

"My. You certainly managed to learn a lot about her and her daughter from a quick, casual conversation."

His mother would have made an excellent police detective.

"Maureen invited me to stay for dinner. I couldn't pass up homemade lasagna. Claire and Haley were there too."

"Sharing a meal with someone is a good way to get to know them, no question about it." She picked up her coffee and took another sip. "And it was nice of you to offer to help with the gutter—but I thought you bought a condo so you wouldn't have to deal with home repair issues."

"I did—and I don't plan to make this a habit. But she cut her arm trying to do it herself. I figured I could spare a half hour on my way home tonight to help her out."

"Where does she live?"

He was hosed. Claire's house wasn't remotely on his way home.

"Ballwin."

His mother arched an eyebrow, and he braced for her comment.

Much to his surprise, however, she finished off her coffee and stood. "I expect you'll need to leave soon, then. Why don't I cut you some carrot cake to take along? Your new friend and her daughter might enjoy some home baking."

"They're not exactly friends. We just met."

"It doesn't take long to know if you click with a person. I pegged your father as special ten minutes after we were introduced. The zing was there from the very beginning."

He coughed on his swig of coffee.

How had she known he'd felt a zing with Claire?

"Don't get any ideas about this, Mom." He wiped his lips on his napkin and stood. "She might be nicer than I thought at first. And pretty. But it takes more to build a relationship than zing."

"So there is zing." She gave him a pleased look as she set a generous wedge of cake on a plate and covered it with plastic wrap.

Busted again.

He was out of here.

"I'm going to take the fifth—but warn you again not to jump to conclusions."

"I only reach conclusions when evidence supports them." She handed over the cake. "Your Claire sounds very nice."

"She's not my Claire."

"She still sounds nice. I'm glad you finally met a woman who made you sit up and take notice. Since you're not the impulsive type, I doubt I have to warn you to take your time and be careful."

"No, you don't."

"Glad to hear it. Now you go on and fix that nice lady's gutter. I put enough cake on the plate for you too, in case you decide to stay for a chat afterward."

"I'm not staying. I have work to do at home."

"Then they'll have an extra piece to share tomorrow. But it's there if you change your mind."

"Good night, Mom." He leaned over and kissed her forehead.

"Good night. And have fun."

After a quick detour to his father's work bench, he strode down the front walk, cake plate in one hand, drill in the other.

Tonight's dinner had not gone the way he'd hoped. His mom had ferreted out far too much information—and despite her denial, she was jumping to conclusions about him and Claire.

Sheesh.

Three weeks ago, he hadn't known the woman existed. The two of them had never even been on a date.

Not that he was planning to ask her on one.

Not yet, anyway.

Down the road, however . . .

He stowed the cake on the passenger seat, put the drill in the trunk next to his toolbox, and backed down the driveway.

126

It would be interesting to see if this zing, as his mom called it, led to anything more than a surge of hormones.

Interesting . . . and unsettling.

Because his mother was right about something else too.

He and Claire both had issues. And if hers were half as entrenched as his, things could get very complicated.

"How come you're wearing lipstick on a weekend, Mom?"

Claire recapped the tube and dropped it in her makeup bag on the bathroom vanity. "I'm in a lipstick mood."

"Is it because Mr. Watson is coming over?"

Her daughter was growing up way too fast.

As she tried to think of a truthful but evasive response, the door chimes pealed.

Saved by the bell!

"Can I answer that?" Haley was already halfway down the hall.

"Sure." Taking a long, slow breath, she tried to put the brakes on her racing heart. This was ridiculous. She was thirty-two, not sixteen. The man had stopped by to do a home repair, period. This wasn't a date. He'd be in and out in less than fifteen minutes. She was letting herself get all worked up over nothing.

Except the man she found waiting in her foyer sixty seconds later was far from nothing.

Gone was the high-end corporate business casual look. Today, he wore sport shoes, worn jeans that sat just right on his lean hips, and a black T-shirt that hugged his broad chest and revealed impressive biceps.

Add in tall, dark, and handsome . . .

Whew.

Thankfully, he was angled away from her as he chatted with

Haley. That gave her a moment to regain her composure—and quash the urge to fan herself.

Haley spotted her first. "Hey, Mom, look! Mr. Watson brought us some homemade cake from his mom's house." She lifted a plastic-wrapped, dinner-sized plate.

He turned then, smiling as he gave her a quick but thorough sweep. She resisted the impulse to tug at the hem of her soft cotton top and rub her damp palms down the denim of her jeans. He looked a thousand percent better than she did, even in dressed-down mode. The man probably spent more on the shoes in his closet than she'd spent on her entire wardrobe.

Nevertheless, those brown irises warmed as he completed his perusal. "She insisted. I hope you like carrot cake."

"Yes."

"Can I have a piece now, Mom?"

"Yes."

"Awesome. Thank you, Mr. Watson."

"You can call me Keith . . . if it's okay with your mom."

"Yes."

Good grief. She sounded like a parrot.

Say something else. Anything. Just keep it innocuous.

"You, uh, look nice tonight."

The blush started at the base of her neck and crept up to the roots of her hair.

So much for innocuous.

Keith gave her a lazy smile. "So do you."

She bit her lip. Did he think she'd been angling for a compliment? Since her social skills were as rusty as the wobbly wrought-iron table on the deck left by the former owner, that was a very real possibility. She couldn't even remember the last time she'd bantered with a good-looking single guy.

When the silence lengthened, she swallowed and gestured to his hand. "I see you brought the drill."

"Yes. I have a few other tools in the car too. I wasn't sure how well-equipped you were—um, with tools, I mean. Not that you aren't . . ." He gave her another fast scan as his voice trailed off, his complexion turning slightly ruddy.

Maybe she wasn't the only one with rusty social skills.

"How come you guys both have red faces?" Haley looked from one to the other as she rejoined them, fork in hand.

Claire recovered first; Keith's awkwardness helped level the playing field a bit. "It's a little warm in the house. Did you cut yourself some cake?"

"Yes. Do you want any?"

"Maybe later. Keith came to fix the gutter, so I need to help him do that first, before it gets dark." Claire led him toward the kitchen, speaking over her shoulder. "I left the ladder out there."

At the sliding door, she gripped the edge to pull it open. Immediately another hand with a sprinkling of dark hair on the back grabbed it above hers, from behind.

He was so close she could smell the spicy scent of his after-shave. Sense the heat radiating off his chest. Feel the whisper of his breath on her temple.

The temptation to lean back was almost overpowering.

"Ready?"

She blinked at his question. For what?

Oh.

The door.

"Yes."

They tugged together, and it slid open—with a noisy protest.

"I might have to move this up on my to-do list." She snagged the hammer and gutter spike from the edge of the counter, willing her lungs to kick back in.

His touch on her arm sabotaged that effort. "How's the cut?"

"Better." *Keep breathing, Claire.* "You did a first-rate patch job."

129

"Nice to know my scouting skills can still come in handy." He gestured for her to precede him through the door. "Is there somewhere out back I can plug in the drill? I have an extension cord in the car if I need it."

"There's an outlet over there." She gestured to the wall of the house at the end of the deck, near the gutter. "Let me do it—I know which boards are safe to stand on."

After inserting the prongs, she rejoined him as he started up the ladder, gripping the legs to hold it steady.

"Where'd you get this ladder?" He popped a bit into the drill.

"The previous owner left it in the garage. I figured it was either a housewarming gift or trash no one bothered to haul away. I can't imagine which, can you?"

She hoped her teasing tone would elicit a smile. Instead, he frowned down at her. "Do you use it a lot?"

"When I need to. I had to clean the gutters last fall after the leaves fell. Mostly I use it inside."

"You might want to get a new one."

"It's on my wish list."

"What else is on there?" The furrows were still embedded in his brow.

Time to lighten the mood.

"Well, let's see. My most recent house-related wish was that a genie would magically appear to repair my gutter." She cocked her head and gave him a once-over. "You're not wearing the right clothes, and you didn't pop out of a bottle, but you'll do."

His lips quirked, and the frown eased. "In that case, I guess I'd better get to work."

He drilled through the center of the sagging gutter, bent the metal back into shape, and positioned the sleeve inside. Then he pushed the nail through the gutter and the sleeve and hammered it in.

The whole job took less than five minutes.

"I guess you do know your way around home repairs." She stepped back as he descended.

"A lot of this stuff is simple, if you have the right tools. Let me put the ladder away for you." He started to fold it up.

"You don't have to do that."

He froze. "Are you going to get mad if I do?"

She shoved her hands in her pockets and exhaled. "You mean like I did with the driveway sealer?"

"Yeah."

"I owe you an apology for that."

The taut line of his shoulders relaxed. "I was afraid you were going to whack me with the squeegee."

"That thought did occur to me. I don't have a lot of tolerance for domineering, autocratic men."

He winced. "Ouch."

"However, I think I was wrong in your case. I'm sorry I misjudged you."

"Apology accepted. And nice job on the driveway."

"Thanks. If I never do it again, though, it will be too soon."

"A professional sealing job isn't that expensive." He studied her, gaze probing. "Is money really that tight, Claire?"

Not what she'd expected him to say.

Straightening to her full height, she lifted her chin, prepared to tell him that was none of his business.

But he beat her to it. "Sorry. None of my business. Is it all right if I put the ladder away for you?"

She thought about feigning insult and insisting she and Haley were doing fine. But Keith was a smart, perceptive man. No one who had money to spare would let so many maintenance chores go unattended—or take on heavy-duty jobs most people left to more experienced professionals.

Why deny the obvious?

So she gave a curt nod. "I'll open the garage door for you from inside."

"Hang onto this, okay?" He handed her the drill.

As he disappeared around the side of the house with the ladder and hammer, she crossed to the recalcitrant sliding door. It took her several tugs to open it, several more to close the thing.

Once inside, she stepped into the attached garage through the kitchen door and activated the opener. The door squeaked, but at least it was working now, though she had no clue why. All she'd done was force it up the day it had gotten stuck, and it had been cooperating ever since.

Praise the Lord for small blessings.

Keith ducked under the door as it rose. "Where do you want this stuff?"

"I keep the ladder against the far wall"—she pointed to the spot—"and the hammer goes on the workbench in the corner."

After putting them back in their places, he returned to the front of the garage and picked up a toolbox. "I brought a few other tools from home. I can check out the sliding door, if you want me to."

Her first inclination was to refuse. Why further tarnish her image as a capable, competent, independent woman?

But the door did need fixing—and so far it hadn't responded to a liberal application of WD-40, a swift kick of the frame, nor evil incantations.

Swallowing her pride, she summoned up a smile. "Wow. Wish number two. You really are a genie."

"Is that a yes?"

"I'm not stubborn enough to turn down the offer of help with a door that's going to dislocate my shoulder one of these days. Come on in."

As he entered, Haley was licking the last bit of icing off her fork. "Your mom makes great cake, Keith."

"I'll tell her you said that."

"You gonna fix our door?" She rose from the table, deposited her plate and glass on the counter, and wandered over to watch him.

"I'm going to try."

"Don't get in his way, honey."

"She's not in my way." Keith winked at Haley. "Want to help?"

"Can I?"

"If it's okay with your mom."

Haley turned to her. Keith was just being nice . . . but it was sweet of him to consider her daughter. And it wouldn't hurt for Haley to be exposed to a man who seemed to have a lot more kindness and empathy than her own father had possessed.

"Sure." She hefted the drill. "Do you need this?"

"Yes." He took it from her and set it on the floor beside him.

"I've tried spraying the track with lubricant, but that didn't work." She wandered closer too.

"The rollers may be gummed up or damaged. Do you have a drop cloth or blanket? And I could use a rag or two."

"Those I can supply."

By the time she retrieved the items from the hall closet, Keith was down on his hands and knees with a screwdriver.

"What're you doing now?" Haley leaned in close to watch him.

"Adjusting the rollers. We'll try that first. It's the easiest fix."

Claire deposited the blanket and rags on the kitchen table.

He worked on the rollers on each end of the door, stood, and tried sliding it. It still stuck, but the improvement was significant.

"That's much better." Claire tried it herself. "My shoulder thanks you."

He planted his fists on his hips and shook his head. "It's not good enough. I'm going to take the door off and check the rollers. I don't suppose you have any sawhorses."

"No—but I do have two card tables. Would those work?"

"Are they sturdy?"

"As sturdy as a card table can be."

He eyeballed the width of the slider. "Let's try it. If you can set them up on a safe area of the deck, I'll take the door off. Haley, could you help your mom?"

"Sure."

The two of them retrieved the tables from the basement. Things might be tight, but at least they were past the days when one had functioned as a kitchen table, the other as a place to stack clothes that should have been stored in a chest of drawers in her bedroom.

As they set them up on the deck, Claire kept an eye on Keith. He finished unscrewing something overhead with the electric drill, then grasped the edges of the door and lifted it. Once the bottom was clear of the track, he swung it toward him and pulled the door free, balancing it in his hands.

Based on the bulge in his biceps, it was very heavy.

"I'm going to lay it across the card tables and take a closer look at the rollers." He maneuvered it through the opening and started across the deck, watching where he stepped.

"Mom."

"What?"

"You're standing in his way."

Jerking her gaze away from his muscles, Claire moved back. Carefully. If she put a foot through the deck on the heels of her close encounter with the gutter, Keith would think she was a real klutz.

He jockeyed the door onto the tables, checking their stability before he released it.

"What now?" Haley edged in.

"Now I look at the rollers and give them a thorough cleaning. I have a job for you back inside." He led the way to his toolbox, fished out two small brushes, and handed one to Haley. "While I work on the rollers, would you clean the tracks, especially the corners?"

"Okay."

As she dropped to her knees, he returned with the other brush, along with a cleaning solvent and a can of silicone spray. While he examined the wheels, Claire leaned closer. "What do you think?"

"They're very dirty. I'll clean them and we'll assess the condition."

"Can I help?"

"Thanks, but it won't take long."

He was right. In a matter of a couple of minutes, he had the rollers cleaned and lubricated. Then he examined them.

"What's the verdict?"

"They've seen some long, hard use." He fingered a worn area. "What I did will improve the operation, but your best bet would be to replace them."

"How much would that cost?"

"My guess is twenty to twenty-five dollars."

A gallon of high-quality paint for Haley's bedroom. And it had to be high quality. This was going to be their home for a long time, and she wanted paint that would last.

"As long as it doesn't stick anymore, I think I'll wait awhile to replace the rollers."

To her relief, he simply nodded and stood. "Let me check on my helper."

She watched as he knelt beside Haley to examine her work. Listened, throat tightening, as he praised her efforts. Swallowed as her daughter's face glowed.

The guy was good with kids, despite the preppy first impression he'd made.

Who'd have guessed?

"I think we make a great team. I'm just going to put some mineral spirits on this rag and run it over the track. That will clean up any grease still stuck there."

"What's mineral spirits?"

"It's stinky stuff. You might want to move away."

She scooted back.

Keith finished up quickly, then came back outside, adjusted the wheels, and hefted the door.

Once again, his muscles bulged.

The man must pay regular visits to the gym.

He had the door back up and readjusted in less than five minutes. This time, when he tested it, a firm one-handed push produced a smooth glide.

"It's not perfect, but it should buy you a few more months." He bent down and stowed his tools.

"Wow. You sure do know how to do a bunch of stuff." Haley opened and closed the door herself.

He grinned. "My dad was a great handyman. I learned everything I know from him."

"I don't remember my dad. He and Mom got divorced when I was five, and then he died."

Keith shot her a quick look, then went back to gathering up his tools. "I'm sorry to hear that."

"It's okay. He lived in California, and I never—"

"Haley." The word came out sharper than she intended, and at her daughter's surprised expression, Claire softened her tone. "Let's take down the card tables and gather up the rags."

"Are you going to stay awhile, Keith?" Haley began collecting the rags.

"I'm sure you both have things to do tonight."

That was true. But suddenly Claire didn't want him to leave. "Can I offer you a cup of coffee before you go?"

He hesitated, and she could read the indecision in his eyes.

In the end, though, he shook his head. "I've got a stack of reports waiting at my condo that I need to review before a meeting in the morning."

"I understand." She pasted on a smile despite the sudden deflation of her ego. "Haley has homework and I have papers to grade, so we'll all be busy. Thank you again for all your help tonight."

"No problem."

"I'll walk you to the door."

Haley trailed behind as they crossed the living room and emerged into the tiny foyer. Claire pulled the door open, expecting Keith to make a fast exit.

Instead, he paused. "Remember . . . you have one wish left."

She squinted at him. "What?"

"Genies always grant three wishes."

"What are you guys talking about?" Haley looked from Keith to her, clearly puzzled.

Claire brushed a wisp of hair back from her daughter's forehead. "It's just a joke." Wasn't it?

"Not really." Keith transferred the toolbox from one hand to the other. "If you have another priority item on your wish list, I'd be happy to oblige."

"Mom's always saying she wishes there were more hours in the day and more money in the bank."

"Haley!"

"Well, you do."

"Keith is talking about home repairs."

"Oh. Hey . . . maybe you could help paint my bedroom!"

"Is that next on the to-do list?"

"It's getting close, but you've done enough already." Claire sent her daughter "the look." Haley sighed but got the message and fell silent, "Have a nice evening, Keith—what's left of it."

"Thanks. You too. Hope the homework goes quick." With a thumbs-up at Haley, he turned and strode down the walk.

Haley crossed to the window and peeked through the curtains. "I hope he comes back."

Claire did too—but that wasn't smart. Romance would only complicate her life. It was better he hadn't stayed around tonight. She needed some space to get her bearings and figure out how to deal with an attraction she hadn't sought and didn't want.

"We have a lot of other stuff that needs fixing." Haley let the curtain drop back into place.

"He's not a handyman, honey. He has a very busy job. We're lucky he offered to help at all."

"I guess. But I think he liked being here."

"Why do you think that?" Claire bolted the door for the night.

"Because he smiled a lot. And when you left to get the card tables, he watched you with this funny look on his face. Kind of like Cap looks at me and you when he comes for a visit. Like he's glad to see us and he wishes he could stay forever."

Had Keith looked at her like that?

Hard to say, since she'd been focused on that chest-hugging black T-shirt and those impressive biceps.

"You smile more too." Head tipped, Haley inspected her. "Like now."

She flattened her lips. "Enough talk. You need to get to that homework, young lady, and I need to grade papers."

"Homework's no fun."

"Neither is grading papers. But life isn't all fun and games."

While her daughter trudged down the hall toward her room, Claire returned to the kitchen and pulled a bag of coffee out of the refrigerator. Drinking it alone wouldn't be much fun, but a jolt of caffeine might help clear her thinking.

She passed the cake on the counter. Stopped. She hadn't had any dessert for a few days. Why not indulge?

Without second-guessing the calorie splurge, she cut herself a generous wedge. After running her finger along the side of the knife to capture the excess frosting, she sucked off the gooey confection.

Mmm. Cream cheese . . . sweet, smooth, and yummy.

Kind of like the man who'd brought it.

Rolling her eyes, she headed for the coffeepot. Better brew it extra strong tonight to help banish such whimsical notions. She was too old for daydreams and fairy tales and romantic fancies.

But if she did still believe in all that . . . if life hadn't taught her that happy endings were only for storybooks . . . if the fear of making another mistake hadn't chased every romantic notion from her heart . . . she just might indulge in that genie fantasy she'd conjured up earlier.

And if she did, she knew exactly what her third wish would be.

10

Giving in to a yawn, Keith pulled Maureen's files out of his briefcase. He could take them home and work there, but the office was cozier. Weird to apply that word to his work space, but it was true—more so recently. These days, his condo felt sterile and forlorn. Every time he glanced out at his pristine deck or sat down to eat a solitary nuked dinner, he found himself wishing he was picking his way across the rotting boards on Claire's deck toward her back door, or joining her and Haley for a home-cooked meal around Maureen's table.

He was also losing sleep—not to mention job focus—thanks to a certain blonde schoolteacher.

Even worse, David was beginning to notice his preoccupation. After he'd drifted away and had to be reeled back in during the bid session for that new strip mall today, he'd caught his boss watching him more than once.

He was getting behind at the office too—the very reason he hadn't yet had a chance to review Maureen's files in detail.

But tonight was the night . . . even if he was here until midnight.

"Staying late?"

He looked up to find David on the threshold of his office, one shoulder propped against the door frame, arms folded in a casual, relaxed stance that didn't fool Keith for one second. After working closely with the man for three years, he'd learned to read every mannerism.

His boss was concerned—about him, instead of some over-budget, behind-schedule project.

Not good.

The last thing he wanted to do was disappoint his mentor . . . or put his upward trajectory here at risk.

"Not too much longer." He hoped.

"Did you have a chance to evaluate the cost report for the Donaldson project? I'm concerned our people might have underestimated labor, given the revised architectural renderings."

"Yes." He reached behind him and pulled a file from a stack on his credenza. At least he'd completed *one* thing today. "I finished it late this afternoon. I was going to give it a final look tomorrow before I passed it on. I think we're still on target, but the margins will be tight. Do you want to take it with you?"

"Tomorrow's fine. What are you working on now?" David inclined his head toward the files in the center of the desk.

"Maureen Chandler's project. I haven't had a chance to give much attention to the new information I picked up Wednesday night. But I did a quick read-through at her house, and she already seems to have taken most of the appropriate steps. I'm not confident I'll be able to find anything her PI missed."

"Just give it your best shot. I don't think Maureen's expecting miracles."

The professor and his boss were on a first-name basis?

Since when?

"You've talked to her?"

"Yes. We chatted last week, after your visit. She said you stayed for dinner, along with Haley and her mother."

That wasn't necessarily information he wanted his boss—or anyone else—to know. "She bribed me with homemade lasagna." He tried for a how-could-a-bachelor-like-me-resist tone.

"So she told me. I'm a sucker for homemade lasagna myself."

Was that a slight twinkle in his boss's eyes?

And if so, what did it mean?

He gave the man a cautious look. "It was very good."

"I'm sure it was. Now I'll let you get on with that." David gestured toward the files. "Don't stay too late. There's more to life than work, you know."

Again . . . since when?

Squinting after his departing boss, Keith tapped his pen against the stack of files in front of him. Robin was right. David had changed—a lot. In the past, his office light had usually still been burning when Keith shut down for the night. These days, the president of McMillan Construction beat him out the door four nights out of five . . . and he almost never showed up on weekends anymore.

Strange. You'd think losing a wife would drive a man to spend more hours at the office, not less. If you let work consume you, you didn't have to deal with messy issues like grief or regrets or traumatic pasts or complicated family relationships.

Not to mention romance.

Or was he confusing his own issues with David's?

Jaw clamped together, he forced the question from his mind. Dissecting that heavy subject did not belong on tonight's agenda. He'd stayed late to go through Maureen's files, and that's what he was going to do.

He opened the first file and peered at a smudge on the corner of the manila folder. Was that . . . salsa? Very possible. He'd helped himself to enough of it last Wednesday. Man, that had been great stuff. Haley had enjoyed it too, based on the way she was chowing it down until Claire intercepted her.

What a cute kid.

He brushed his finger over the stain. That impromptu dinner had been fun. A lot more fun than spending the evening at his desk. And he wouldn't mind doing it again. Even a pizza shared with Claire and Haley on her ramshackle deck would be better than sitting at the office.

But better still? A candlelight dinner at some romantic restaurant with Claire alone. And he knew just the place he'd . . .

Frowning, he cut off that wayward line of thought.

This was nuts.

How could a woman he'd met less than two weeks ago be dominating his thoughts like this? Where was his willpower? If he didn't start focusing on Maureen's files pronto, he really would be here until midnight.

Mustering every ounce of his self-discipline, he managed to keep his mind on the job at hand for the next hour.

Unfortunately, a second pass of the professor's medical file didn't yield any obvious clues, unless her physician in Boston had perhaps recommended her adoption agency and might have a connection to someone who'd worked there—assuming the man was even still alive. Had the private investigator pursued that?

Something to check out when he got to the PI file.

The adoption agency paperwork contained a lot of information about Maureen but nothing about the adoptive parents. No doubt the PI had tried to locate the caseworker who'd signed the forms, but he'd verify that too.

The third file, detailing Maureen's own search, offered nothing new.

That left him with the PI's report.

As far as he could tell, the man hadn't spoken with Maureen's doctor in Boston. He had verified, however, that the agency caseworker who'd handled the adoption had died. The PI had followed up on the few leads he'd uncovered, but all had been dead ends.

After closing the file, Keith drew a lined legal pad toward him. He had no idea what questions the investigator had asked Maureen, but he had a few more of his own, now that he knew her a little better. Maybe none of them would lead anywhere, but they were worth exploring.

As he jotted down his thoughts, he glanced at the phone on his desk. The most efficient way to handle his follow-up questions would be to give her a call. He didn't need an in-person meeting.

But if he did pay her another visit, there was a chance he might cross paths with Claire again.

The temptation to play those odds was strong—even though his life would be a lot simpler if he walked a wide circle around the lovely single mom. Why mess with a routine that had suited him fine until now? Work long hours, visit the gym, eat when and where he chose, visit his mom every Sunday. It was comfortable, predictable, and painless.

Yet all at once, it also felt boring, dull—and lonely.

Muttering under his breath, he threw his pen in the drawer. Slammed it shut.

How could a man go from satisfied and content to restless and unsettled in such a short time? And what was he supposed to do about it?

He didn't have a clue.

But hanging around the office wasn't going to give him any answers—nor quiet the rumbling of his stomach. The latter he could fix with a quick stop at one of the many fast-food drive-throughs on his route home. The former . . . not so easy to find.

With a sigh, he shut down his computer, stuffed a few reports into his briefcase, and turned off the lights in his office. Then he headed toward the exit through the quiet, deserted building.

Maybe he should go visit the professor in a day or two and put the outcome in God's hands. If he ran into Claire, fine. If he didn't, he'd consign their previous encounters to the two-ships-that-pass-in-the-night category.

Even if he had a sinking feeling that would be easier said than done.

Two days later, as Keith pulled up in front of Maureen's house, he scanned Claire's property. No sign of her or Haley. Given the weather, however, that wasn't a surprise.

He cringed as a streak of lightning slashed through the angry, dark-gray sky, followed seconds later by a loud crack of thunder. Could he have picked a worse night for this meeting?

But he'd made the appointment yesterday morning, when the meteorologists were predicting partly cloudy skies with a slight chance of showers. Ha. Considering their dismal record this spring, he should have figured that forecast wouldn't hold.

Too late to back out now, though.

Drops of rain began to spatter his windshield, and he grabbed his briefcase, slid out of the car, and took off at a jog for the door. As he stepped onto the porch, the heavens opened, disgorging sheets of rain.

That had been close.

He pressed Maureen's bell and inspected the whipping branches of the maple tree above his car. Not the smartest place to park. But if he ventured out in this gale, he'd be drenched before he got halfway down the walk.

Resigned, he turned his back. All he could do was hope for the best.

As usual, Maureen answered quickly and ushered him inside. "I can't believe the turn in the weather. We could have rescheduled, you know."

"It wasn't that bad when I left the office. And it might let up before we're through." Another boom of thunder shook the house.

"I like your optimism." She gestured to the living room. "Why don't we talk here? I love the kitchen and sunroom in nice weather, but with all those windows and skylights, it feels a bit too open to the elements in a storm like this."

Apparently there'd be no home-cooked treats tonight.

He ignored the pang of disappointment. "Sure. That's fine."

"What can I offer you to drink?"

"A Sprite, if you have it."

"I'm well supplied with a variety of soda. My younger neighbor likes it, and Claire lets me spoil her now and then. Make yourself comfortable. I'll be back in a minute."

She disappeared through the door that led to the kitchen while he claimed the same seat he'd occupied on his first visit. As he pulled her files and his notebook from his briefcase, another flash of lightning strobed through the room, followed almost at once by a bone-jarring boom of thunder. The lights flickered, then steadied.

Good thing he'd repaired Claire's gutter or she'd have a waterfall outside her kitchen window and a river next to her foundation. Given the condition of her house, that was the last thing she needed. He'd lay odds either the basement or the roof leaked.

Maybe both.

"I don't want to ruin your dinner, but since you seemed to enjoy the salsa the other night, I made a new batch."

He turned as Maureen entered with chips and salsa, plus their drinks.

146

Rising, he reached for the tray. "Let me take that—and I won't turn down the salsa. It was great."

Once they settled in and he'd taken the edge off his hunger with a couple of chips, he set her files on the coffee table. "I'm finished with these. Thanks again for letting me borrow them."

"Any new insights?"

"Nothing dramatic. But they did raise a few questions. Your PI may have covered them, but I didn't see any notes to that effect in his report." He wiped his fingers on a paper napkin and opened his notebook. "It doesn't appear he tried to contact the doctor you saw in Boston. Is that correct?"

"Yes. My obstetrician had no connection to the adoption agency or the adoptive parents."

"What about the pediatrician who took care of your baby once he was born?"

"He was chosen by the adoptive parents. I never met him." She looked down at the ice melting in her glass. When she continued, a thread of regret wove through her words. "I never saw my son after he was born, except for a few minutes in the delivery room."

"Was that your choice?" As the words spilled out, Keith tightened his grip on the pen. That question wasn't on his list.

He was about to retract it for fear he'd overstepped when Maureen surprised him by responding.

"Yes. I was afraid if I held him in my arms, I'd never be able to let him go."

"So why did you?"

Again, the question was out before he could stop it.

Again, she responded.

"I taught at a conservative Christian school, Keith." Her voice was quiet, her eyes sad. "A college in those days, not a university. We were a small community, bound by a strict moral code—which I violated. I was afraid I'd lose the position I'd worked so hard to attain if the administration found out about my mistake. Our faith might preach forgiveness, but the faculty was also expected to set a high moral standard for students. What I did was hardly role-model material."

"So the school never knew?"

"No. When I discovered I was pregnant in September, I asked for a six-month sabbatical beginning in the spring semester, ostensibly to work on a research paper about Italian manuscript illumination in the fifteenth century. It was rather short notice for such a request, but I was well liked, and they accommodated me. By the time I returned to campus, I'd completed my paper and given away my baby." Her voice choked, and she took a sip of her soda.

A gust of wind shook the shutters on the house, and the lights flickered again.

Maureen rose and crossed to the front window. "I don't like storms." She drew the drapes closed, still facing the window as she continued. "But sometimes it's better not to run away from them. Sometimes it's better to hunker down and endure the lightning and thunder and rain. The storm might change the landscape—but who's to say it wouldn't be a better landscape?"

"Does that mean you'd keep the baby if you had a second chance?"

She returned to her chair, looking older and more weary than she had minutes ago. "I don't know. Beyond the selfish and fear-driven reasons for my decision, I've always believed a child does best with two parents. I was already thirty-eight, and there wasn't a husband anywhere on the horizon. So perhaps I made the right decision." She grasped her glass with both hands. Swirled the clear liquid. "In any case, I'm sorry I didn't find some way to follow his life—though adoption wasn't as open back then."

Silence fell between them, broken only by the low rumble of thunder and the relentless beat of the rain against the windows.

Keith shifted in his seat. Strange how a person's perceptions could change. When he'd read Haley's letter, he'd had no sympathy for the mother who'd walked away from her child. In some ways, he still didn't. At thirty-eight, as a highly educated woman, Maureen could have provided for herself and a child. If she'd lost her job, there were other colleges and universities that would have welcomed someone with her experience and qualifications. And while a single-parent household might not be optimal, lots of children in that situation did fine. Like Haley.

Bottom line, the primary reason Maureen had opted for adoption was selfish—she hadn't wanted to face the humiliation of an unwed pregnancy.

Yet her regret and remorse, her uncertainty over whether she'd made the right decision, were real. He still might not agree with what she'd done, but her choice to give up her child wasn't nearly as black and white as he'd assumed in the beginning—and even after all these years, it was a source of anguish.

Might the same be true with his own birth mother?

"I don't mind answering your questions about my past, Keith, but I'm not sure how any of this will help you find my son."

At her gentle comment, he picked up his notebook again and forced himself to refocus. "Those last few won't. I was just trying to understand what happened from your point of view. But let me get back on track. Is there anyone you became friends with during your time in Boston who might, in any way, have had a connection to the adoption agency?"

"No. I kept to myself for the most part. I was ashamed about what I'd done and didn't want to have to explain my situation. I avoided the neighbors in my apartment building, and while I was acquainted with a few people at the Boston Public Library who helped me with data searches for my research, I didn't confide in any of them. My doctor and the agency knew I was an unwed mother, but I didn't offer details. There was only one person who knew my whole story. In fact, he referred me to the agency I used. He died several years ago, however."

"I didn't see anything about that in the PI's report."

"I doubt I mentioned it to him. As I said, my friend died, and everything we discussed was held in strictest confidence."

"Still . . . his connection to the adoption agency could be important. Do you mind sharing his name?"

"Father Kevin Ryan."

Keith darted her a surprised look. "A priest?"

"Peculiar how that worked out, isn't it? Me, a professor at an evangelical college, confiding in a Roman Catholic priest."

"How did you even meet him?"

"I didn't want to attend services of my own denomination while I was in Boston, since I was trying to stay under the radar, but I missed being in church. So I began stopping in at this lovely old church in my neighborhood for quiet reflection. The doors were always open, and it was one of the few places where I felt at peace.

"One day Father Ryan came in while I was there. He welcomed me and introduced himself. After several such encounters, we began to talk. He was a wonderful listener, with amazing empathy, and he never exhibited one iota of judgment. In the end, I told him my story and he referred me to the agency. We remained friends until he died."

Keith jotted down his name. "What was the name of his church?"

"St. Columba, but he was transferred several times after that. He spent his final years in a retirement center for priests."

He jotted down the name of the facility when she offered it.

"Would you mind if I . . ." His voice trailed off as the lights flickered again. This time they went out, leaving the room in shadows.

"Oh dear. I was afraid of that. We often have outages in bad storms. Would you like me to light a few candles? I keep some on hand for emergencies." Maureen started to rise.

"I can see well enough for now, and I think we're almost finished."

"All right." She sat down again. "Where were we?"

"I was about to ask whether it would be okay if I checked into the connection between St. Columba and the agency you used."

"I don't believe there was a connection. I got the impression from Father Ryan that he was acquainted with the woman who was the director at the agency. And everything was handled very discreetly. He wouldn't have shared more than the basics with her; everything we discussed was kept in confidence. Besides, he's been gone for five years."

"Still . . . it might be worth some legwork. And I'll see if I can find out anything about the pediatrician. Try to make a connection that way."

"My PI mentioned that too. But as he warned me, HIPAA laws being what they are, it would be difficult to justify the additional expense of such an attempt given the small chance of success. Besides, the hospital probably had many pediatricians on staff, and I expect it would be hard to track them down."

Keith helped himself to a few more chips. "Since I work for salsa—and lasagna—the expense won't be an issue."

"Good to know. My PI's hourly rates had me second-guessing my choice of profession."

Another boom of thunder shuddered through the house, and he tucked the notebook back in his briefcase. "I'll get on this as soon as I can."

She followed him to the foyer. "There's no hurry. After waiting this long, another few days or weeks won't make that much difference." She pulled open the door and eyed the steady rain. "Would you like to borrow an umbrella?"

"No, thanks. I'll make a run for it."

"I suppose that's a viable option when you're young and strong." She touched his arm. "But be careful driving home."

"I will. And I'll be in touch soon."

As he exited onto the porch, he cast a quick glance at Claire's house. Of course no one would be out in a storm like this. There'd be no chance meeting tonight.

Quashing his disappointment, he aimed his automatic opener at the Infiniti, unlocked the car doors, and sprinted through the rain.

He was fast—but not fast enough. As he slid behind the wheel, the damp cotton of his shirt was clinging to his skin.

He needed to head home and change.

But instead of starting the engine, he sat there looking at Claire's dark house. How were they coping with the electrical outage? Was Haley afraid of storms? Was Claire? Would she even admit it if she was?

Probably not. The lady had grit and determination and an independent streak a mile wide. Was it possible those traits had caused the problems in her marriage that led to divorce?

Or were they the *result* of problems in her marriage?

So many questions . . . so few answers.

He ought to drive away. Forget about the duo inside the crumbling house.

And he would too.

Soon.

But first, he'd jot down a few more notes from his meeting with Maureen—just in case God had a change of heart about arranging a chance meeting with the professor's neighbor.

11

. . . .

"Hey, Mom . . . Keith's out in front!"

At Haley's announcement, Claire's pulse shifted into high gear. Why in the world would David McMillan's executive assistant be paying her an unannounced visit?

After ascending the last few basement steps in double time, she dashed over to the kitchen table and deposited the oil lamp she'd dug out of a box of Christmas decorations. Then she joined her daughter at the front window. At least with the lights out, they could see the street without being seen.

"He ran out of Dr. Chandler's house and jumped in his car, but now he's just sitting there with the dome light on."

Meaning he hadn't come to visit her.

Even as Claire's spirits plummeted, logic kicked in. There was no reason for the man to stop by. He was probably afraid she'd hand him another chore if he stepped onto her property again.

"Can we invite him in, Mom?"

And put him on the spot, when he obviously hadn't intended to pay a call?

Not a smart move.

"No. We're . . . uh . . . not dressed for company."

Flimsy, but true. They were both splattered with paint from head to toe, and her jeans were so old and filled with holes, they'd do a punk rocker proud.

On second thought . . . she ought to be grateful he hadn't detoured to their house.

"I bet he wouldn't care what we're wearing."

Maybe not . . . but she did.

"We're not prepared for company. Maybe we'll see him again the next time he comes over to—"

All at once, every light in the house seemed to come on at once—spotlighting the two of them in the window just as Keith looked up.

Wonderful.

Short of being rude, she couldn't pretend she didn't see him—especially when he was looking right at her.

Edging behind Haley to hide as much of her scruffy attire as possible, she forced up the corners of her lips and lifted a hand in greeting.

Keith waved back.

Five seconds later, he opened his door.

"Hey, look! He's getting out! I think he's going to come over and say hi."

Her daughter's conclusion was verified a moment later when he made a dash through the rain toward their small front porch.

Yanking the rubber band out of her ponytail with one hand and fluffing her hair with the other, she bolted for the hall. A full makeup job was out of the question, but if she could add a touch of lipstick and—

The bell chimed, and she froze as Haley raced over and yanked the door open.

Was the man ever going to see her when she looked normal?

"Hi, Keith! Come in." Her daughter pulled the door wide.

"It looks like someone's been painting."

"Yeah. We started on my bedroom, but after the lights went out, it got too dark. Are we gonna finish now, Mom?"

Keith swept a bead of rain off his forehead as she approached. Despite his clinging shirt, he looked good. Spectacular, even.

Damp was definitely a flattering look for him.

"Um . . . I don't know." She forced her gaze higher, resisting the urge to comb her fingers through her hair. "We have company now. Hi, Keith."

"Hi." He gave her an amused once-over. "I didn't mean to interrupt you in the middle of your redecorating project. And I do mean middle. Did you guys have a paint fight, or what?"

"No." Haley examined her T-shirt. "I guess painting is messy. We're changing my walls from gross brown to awesome pink."

"So I see. The new color complements your complexion." He grinned and tapped Haley's paint-splattered nose with his index finger. "Your mom's too."

Claire stifled a groan. Just how much paint was on her face? Too much, based on the hint of laughter in his brown irises. Time to divert his attention.

"Were you visiting Maureen?"

"Yes. I think I might have a couple of leads. A pediatrician and a priest, of all things."

"You mean you might be able to find her son after all?" Haley's eyes widened. "Mom said not to get my hopes up, but I've been praying really hard."

"I'm going to try—but keep praying, okay?" He looked back at Claire over her daughter's head. "Listen . . . I didn't mean to interrupt. I just wanted to make sure you survived the storm."

"The basement leaked again, but we're used to that. Want to help us paint?" Haley sent him a hopeful look. "We have extra brushes."

"He's not dressed for painting, honey."

"Maybe he could wear one of your old shirts. Do you think it would fit?"

As Haley sized up her chest, Keith's eyes flicked down. Zipped back up.

She crossed her arms as warmth spilled onto her cheeks. Why, oh why, couldn't she have picked a T-shirt a touch less threadbare?

He cleared his throat. "You know . . . my gym bag is in the trunk. If you could use another pair of hands, I could make a quick change. I still owe you one wish, remember?"

"I don't expect you to spend your evening painting after working all day."

"You are."

"True. But it's *my* house. You probably have stuff to do at your own place."

"Not that much. I live in a condo."

"We could have a painting party!" Haley clapped her hands. "I could put on some music and we could sing along while we work."

"If I sing, you'll throw me out. But I wouldn't mind listening to the two of you do some harmonizing. So . . ." He held out his hands, palms up. "Want to cash in your third wish?"

The dimple in his cheek was hard to resist.

"Are you sure?"

"I wouldn't offer if I wasn't."

"You'll get paint on your gym clothes."

"Doesn't matter. They're old."

She was out of excuses. And spending the evening in the company of a handsome man was far preferable to a ladies-only event, much as she enjoyed being with her daughter.

"Okay. Wish number three has now been officially redeemed."

"Give me five minutes to grab my stuff and change, and we'll get this painting party started."

"Yes!" Haley pumped her fist in the air.

Reining in his grin, Keith tipped his head toward her daughter. "Is she always this listless?"

"You should see her when we go ice-skating."

He raised an eyebrow. "You ice-skate?"

"Yeah! Mom's really good. She knows how to go backwards and do spins and everything."

"I'm impressed."

"Don't be. I learned when I was a little girl, and it's like riding a bicycle." Claire smoothed her palms down her jeans. "I'll reopen the paint cans and round up another roller and brush for you."

"Sounds like a plan."

While Keith retrieved his clothes and changed in the hall bathroom, she also set out a plate of cookies and a carton of lemonade.

Once he rejoined them, she handed him an extra painter's cap and tried not to stare at the well-developed hamstrings below his gym shorts. "You're going to end up with paint all over your legs."

"Nope. I'm a very careful painter." He pulled the cap over his hair. "So what do you want me to do?"

She held up a roller and a brush. "Your choice. Edge around the baseboards and molding, or roll."

"Door number two, no contest." He reached for the roller and inspected the walls. "You've made a lot of progress. When did you start?"

"Monday. I did the ceiling first, then we put a coat of primer on the walls. I've got parent-teacher meetings the next two nights, which will slow things down, but with you pitching in tonight, we should finish up Saturday morning."

"I see you're still using that." He gestured toward the wobbly ladder.

"I only had to go up two rungs."

He eyed the furniture clustered in the center of the room. "Who moved all that?"

"Mom." Haley grabbed a cookie from the plate on top of the plastic-covered dresser. "I helped, though."

"I'm sure you did." Keith took another inventory of the furniture, then dropped the subject. "Okay. Let's roll—pardon the pun." He aimed a grin at her and went to work.

Haley cranked up the music loud enough to drown out the rain, and for the next two hours they laughed and painted and chatted. Mostly they laughed.

It was one of the nicest evenings she'd spent in years.

By the time they called it a night at nine o'clock, the first coat of pink was finished.

"Wow." Haley did a three-sixty pivot. "It doesn't even seem like the same room."

"That was the whole idea." A sharp twinge of pain struck as Claire turned her head, and she tried to discreetly rotate her neck and flex her shoulders.

"Sore?"

The man didn't miss a thing.

"Teaching requires a whole different set of muscles than painting. On the plus side, this house gives me more of a workout than a gym. I'm in a lot better shape now than when we moved in a year ago." Out of the corner of her eye, she caught Haley pilfering another cookie. "Enough, young lady. That's number four."

Her daughter retracted her hand with a disgruntled sigh. "I think moms have eyes in the backs of their heads."

"I'm inclined to agree with you." Keith chuckled and pulled off his baseball cap. "I was never able to put one over on my mother, either. I still can't."

"Go wash up and do your teeth." Claire took Haley's paintbrush. "After you get into your pajamas, I'll come in and kiss you good night."

"Where are you bunking while your room's all torn up?" Keith dropped down onto the balls of his feet and fitted the lid back on the can of paint.

"I'm sleeping with Mom. There's plenty of room for both of us in her bed. You want to see?"

"Haley." Claire interrupted before Keith could respond, firing a stern look at her daughter. She didn't want any man taking a tour of her bedroom—especially a certain executive assistant. "Stop dillydallying."

"Okay, okay. Thanks a lot for helping, Keith."

"You're welcome."

"Are you leaving now?"

"After I help your mom clean up."

"I can take care of this." Claire bent to retrieve some of the rags. "You did enough already. Why don't you head home?"

"Trying to get rid of me, huh?" His tone was teasing, but his eyes were serious. Searching.

"No." She met his gaze steadily. "It was nice having you here tonight. But you don't need to hang around now that we're done."

"I don't mind. And I always clean up my messes." Several charged beats ticked by before he broke eye contact. "Where do you want this stuff?"

Based on the firm set of his jaw, his decision to help was not a negotiable subject.

Fine. She could live with that.

Because there was something to be said for men who refused to leave messes in their wake.

"There's a utility sink in the basement."

"I'll find it while you get Haley settled for the night."

"Do you want to come back Saturday morning and help us finish?" Her daughter sent him a hopeful look.

"Haley." Claire summoned up her don't-argue-with-me voice. "He's helped enough already."

159

"But . . ."

"No buts." She pointed to the door. "Bed. Now."

Shoulders drooping, Haley trudged toward the door. "'Night, Keith."

"Sweet dreams." He put the brushes in one of the pans and stood. "Basement door's in the kitchen, I presume?"

"Yes. Be careful going down."

"Let me guess. The steps are shaky."

"No. Solid as a rock. The railing, on the other hand . . ."

"I get the picture. Take your time with Haley. I need to clean myself up too."

She gave him a quick once-over. "Other than two tiny pink specks on one cheek, you don't need much cleanup. How come you didn't splatter paint all over your clothes, like I did?"

One side of his mouth hiked up. "Genies repel paint."

"Cute."

"True. Trust me. We genies have magical powers." With a wink, he disappeared out the door.

For a few moments after he left, while she inhaled the smell of fresh paint and listened to the muted sounds of her daughter's singing coming from behind the bathroom door, she surveyed the fruits of their labors. Together, they'd transformed a room that was drab and bleak and uninviting into a place that was warm and welcoming and happy. And they'd had fun doing it.

It was only a room . . . but could it symbolize more? If she let Keith into their lives, could he do for them what he'd done for this room? Add lightness and vibrancy and joy?

Of course, that assumed he *wanted* to be part of their lives.

But she was getting the distinct impression he did.

She picked up a damp rag and scrubbed at a spot of pink paint on the back of her hand. Slowly it disappeared—but the effort to eradicate it chafed her skin, leaving an angry red blemish.

Kind of like the lingering blemish left on her heart after Brett's betrayal and their breakup.

Sighing, she squeezed the nubby rag tight in her fist. A few minutes ago, Keith had said to trust him—and she wanted to. Wanted to believe that if she followed her father's advice and tossed a line into the sea, she wouldn't end up with a shark this time.

Given her track record, however, fishing was risky.

Yet despite her lurking fear, the temptation to let herself believe things might be different with Keith was strong. Very strong.

"Mom!" Haley called down the hall from the bathroom. "There's paint stuck in my hair."

"I'll be right there."

Claire tossed the rag into the pile on the floor and exited the bedroom. In the basement, she heard Keith turn on the water as her genie prepared to clean up.

Her lips lifted in a wistful smile. He'd been joking when he'd told her he had magical powers, but her life was, indeed, a lot brighter since he'd started coming around.

As for trusting him . . . that was no joke. In the end, the question about whether to let this thing between them progress came down to exactly that. To move forward, she had to trust him.

But could she?

Should she?

The answer eluded her as she walked down the hall.

At the bathroom door, she paused. She didn't spend enough time in prayer these days, but God had always been her go-to source when she needed direction—and he had impeccable credentials in the trust department.

So closing her eyes, she put the problem in his hands.

Lord, I could really use some guidance here. If Keith is meant to be more than a casual acquaintance, could you help me discern that? Because I can't afford to make another mistake. For Haley's sake . . . or mine.

12

Keith finished rinsing the last roller, set it aside, and surveyed Claire's basement.

It was a pit.

Literally.

No, the cement wasn't crumbling and bats weren't swooping over his head. But based on the style of houses in the neighborhood, this bungalow was at least five decades old—and the basement looked every day of its fifty years.

He glanced again at the pile of wet rags near one of the walls, marking the leak Haley had referenced.

What on earth had Claire been thinking when she bought this problem-plagued place? Had she realized the scope of the work that needed to be done before she signed on the dotted line? Did she ever feel overwhelmed—and discouraged—as she watched her to-do list mushroom?

All of those questions bothered him.

But one question bothered him more.

Why did he care so much about the troubles of a woman he'd just met? An acquaintance too new to even qualify as a friend?

Frowning, he grabbed the bar of soap on the edge of the sink and sudsed up, checking out his hands. Claire was right. Somehow he'd managed to avoid most of the paint thrown off by the roller.

But during their painting party, something more intangible and elusive had seeped into his heart, leaving him upbeat, energized, and filled with a sense of contentment—as well as hope.

It was kind of how he'd always expected love to feel when he met the right woman.

He scrubbed at the few flecks of paint on his fingers. This wasn't love, though. It couldn't be. Love happened gradually, over time.

Still, the happy mood Claire engendered in him could explain why he was beginning to care too much, too fast. And every time he saw her, every time they interacted, her appeal grew. She never complained about her lot in life—and it was a challenging one. She just did what had to be done, day in and day out, working hard to provide a home for herself and her daughter with grace and courage and even humor.

As far as he was concerned, that was the definition of a hero.

And he'd like to get to know her better.

A lot better.

But therein lay a problem.

He rinsed off his hands, snagged the towel hanging over the edge of the sink, and faced the truth.

Building a relationship was a two-way street. If he expected her to share the details of her past with him, to trust him with her hopes and dreams and fears, she'd expect the same in return.

And that was tricky. It would require a leap of faith he wasn't sure he was ready to make—and an acknowledgment that he'd lied earlier when he'd told her he always cleaned up his messes. Instead of dealing with the untidy jumble of baggage from his past, he'd tried to marginalize it, to convince himself it was old news that didn't matter anymore.

But his mom was right. It did matter. Hard as she and his dad had tried, they hadn't been able to compensate for the bad stuff that had happened in his early years. Not that he even remembered the particulars—thank God. But Mom had filled in some of the blanks, and he'd never forgotten the main trauma . . . nor how it had made him feel.

He wadded the towel in his fist, the familiar hurt echoing in the recesses of his soul—a reminder that he had unfinished business. That if he wanted to pursue Claire, he needed to get his act together.

And his mom's advice on that score could be right too. Connecting with the woman who'd borne him might help.

On the other hand, what if it opened a whole new can of worms?

A dull throb began to pulse in his forehead, and he massaged his temples. He'd like to attribute the ache to the paint fumes, but why kid himself? While the headaches that had once plagued him on a regular basis had subsided, stress could still bring one on. And thinking about wading back into his past was a huge stressor.

But he didn't have to deal with all that junk this very minute. Why not take tonight at face value—as a pleasant couple of hours with a lovely woman and her charming daughter?

Decision made, he slung the towel back over the edge of the sink and ascended the stairs, testing the railing as he went.

More than wobbly.

When he emerged into the kitchen, he found Claire filling a glass with water.

"Let me guess—the standard put-off-going-to-bed trick." He closed the basement door behind him.

"Bingo." She tossed the reply over her shoulder, wincing as she twisted her neck. "How did you know?"

"I used that line as a kid too."

"Oh. I thought you might have nieces or nephews or . . . maybe even children of your own, from a previous relationship or something." She threw him a quick look, her circumspect query reminding him how little he'd shared with her about his past.

Perhaps it was time to crack the door, test the waters.

"No siblings, so no nieces or nephews. I was adopted when I was three by an older couple, and I guess one like me was enough." He tried without much success for a smile.

Her eyes widened. "I had no idea you were adopted. Does Maureen know?"

"No. I don't usually announce it to the world."

She studied him, head cocked. "She's not quite the world. And it's kind of an area of mutual interest."

"The circumstances were completely different." He needed off this subject. Fast. Before he lost control of the headache that was primed to morph from dull ache to sharp throb. "As for your other question, there's no divorce or children in my past, either."

He could read the next question in her eyes, and though she didn't ask it, he answered. This was a far easier topic than adoption.

"It's the classic story. I never met the right woman. Plus, work consumes a lot of my life."

"Yeah. I know all about demanding careers." She caught her lower lip between her teeth, her expression conflicted, as if she was waging some sort of internal debate. A few seconds ticked by before she spoke again. "Give me a minute while I take this in to Haley. Or do you need to leave?"

Did she want him to?

Hard to tell.

That had been his plan, though. Their evening together had been an unexpected and enjoyable bonus, but he had several reports in his briefcase to review for tomorrow.

Yet suddenly he was in no hurry to go.

"No. I can stay a little longer."

"I'll be back in three minutes."

While she was gone, he wandered over to the sliding door and gave it a test glide. Still working, but those worn rollers were nearing the end of their life. As for the deck . . . He propped his hands on his hips and peered at the rotting boards illuminated by a dim security light. It was a lost cause. She'd be better off tearing it down and starting over.

Except decks were expensive, and she could fix a whole lot of other problems for the cost of replacing it.

"Would you like a drink, or another cookie?"

He turned as she set the barely touched water glass on the counter and faced him. He wasn't in the least hungry. Yet when he opened his mouth to refuse, different words came out. "I wouldn't mind another cookie."

"I could put some coffee on too, if you like."

"Will you join me?"

"As long as you can handle decaf. Otherwise, I'll be awake until three in the morning."

"Decaf is fine." He gestured to some mugs hanging on hooks over the counter. "Are those okay to use?"

"Yes."

While he retrieved them, she got the coffee going.

"This won't take long. Have a seat and . . ." She winced again as she gestured to the table.

"You really did a number on those muscles." He set the mugs beside the coffeemaker. "Is it your shoulders or neck?"

"I'd call it a draw . . . and the ceiling is the culprit, not what I did tonight. I spent hours with my head tipped back while I used the roller."

"I might be able to work out some of the kinks." He moved to the table and pulled out a kitchen chair. "Want me to try?"

She gave the chair a guarded look. "More Boy Scout training?"

"No. I had a neck issue a few years back after I overdid it at the gym with weights. I ended up needing physical therapy for a few weeks, which included some neck massages. I don't claim to be an expert, but I remember what my therapist did and I might be able to give you some relief."

She stuck her hands in her pockets. "I can just use the heating pad again after you leave."

"Has that been helping?"

"Some."

"This might be more effective."

Still she hesitated, keeping her distance. Almost as if she was afraid.

Too afraid, given the circumstances.

He was a respected businessman, not some stranger she'd picked up at a bar. He'd been sent to help with Maureen's project by a high-profile executive known for his integrity, and had done nothing during the time he'd spent with Claire to give her any reason to mistrust him. Her daughter was sleeping in the next room.

So what had happened to make her wary? Was her fear—and caution—about being touched fallout from her failed marriage? Was her experience with her ex-husband the reason for her jitters?

Had the man hurt her physically?

Given her skittish reaction to his offer, the latter possibility seemed more than plausible.

And it didn't sit well with him.

At all.

As his blood pressure spiked and a muscle contracted in his cheek, Claire folded her arms across her chest and retreated a step.

Uh-oh.

She was picking up his tension.

Time to regroup. Lighten the mood.

Coaxing his taut lips into a smile, he propped a hip on her table, feigning a nonchalance he didn't feel. "How about this—I'll give you a money-back guarantee. If your neck and shoulders don't feel better after I work on them, the genie will grant you an extra wish. What do you say?"

Silence fell, broken only by the hiss and spit of the brewing coffee.

She moistened her lips. Gripped her fingers around her upper arms. Swallowed.

Just when he thought she was going to ignore his question, she spoke.

"Touching scares me."

Whoa.

His heart stuttered as his theory about her ex-husband morphed from possible to probable.

Putting a lid on the anger simmering in his gut, he managed to speak in a conversational tone. "May I ask why?"

She didn't respond at first—and he couldn't blame her. He understood how hard it was to share painful secrets. In fact, he wouldn't be surprised if she shut down, told him to mind his own business. In her position, he might do the same.

In the end, however, she parroted his words from a few minutes ago back to him. "I don't usually announce it to the world."

He waited, wondering if she'd add an excepting "but," then proceed to offer an explanation.

She didn't.

Quelling his disappointment, he pushed the chair back in. "Sorry. I didn't mean to pry. But just so we're clear, you don't have to be scared of me. And in case you were concerned about my intentions, I had no ulterior motives. I was planning to touch your neck and shoulders, nothing else."

The facsimile of a smile twisted her lips. "To be honest, you're not the one I was worried about." Without giving him a chance to process that, she gestured to the coffee. "Would you like cream?"

"No. I take it straight."

"Help yourself." She put the plate of cookies on the table and moved to the pot to pour their coffee.

He took a cookie he didn't want and bit into it to give his mouth something to do, since any limited gift of gab he possessed had deserted him.

"The rain stopped and it's a warm evening. Would you like to sit on the front porch while we have our coffee?" She handed him a mug without making eye contact.

Near as he could recall, there weren't any chairs on the small front porch . . . but some instinct told him to accept her overture.

"Sure."

She led the way out. The storm had, indeed, blown over, leaving behind air that smelled fresh and a brilliant full moon that cast a silver glow on the landscape.

His quick scan confirmed there was no seating on the porch, but she set her mug on the railing and pulled two woven-mesh folding chairs from under a tarp in one corner. Like the house, they looked as if they'd seen better days.

"Another gift from the last owner?" He gave the flimsy aluminum frame a dubious inspection as he opened the one she handed him.

"No. I found them at a garage sale. They're okay for now, but someday I'm going to hang a swing over there." She gestured to the other side of the porch. "And I want to put a rose arbor behind it to create privacy. I like to think about sitting there in the evening when all my tasks for the day are done, watching the sun set and smelling the roses."

Given the multitude of chores and responsibilities on her

plate, she might have a shot at achieving that dream sometime in the next century.

She settled into her chair, and he did the same—gingerly. But it held. Must be stronger than it looked.

Kind of like the owner of this house.

In the silence that followed, he sifted through the questions running through his mind. Could he find a way to ask about that touching comment without shutting her down? Or should he stick to some careful probing about her reasons for buying this house? He could also venture into . . .

"Are you a praying man, Keith?"

At her out-of-the-blue question, his strategy deliberations stalled. "What?"

"Sorry." She gave a self-deprecating laugh that sounded stiff. Nervous. "That came out of left field, didn't it? I was attempting to set the stage for a conversation I want to have with you, but that wasn't the smoothest opening."

"A conversation about what?"

"Me. My background. Us. A bunch of stuff. I brought up praying because it's what I do when I need guidance—and I needed some tonight. So I had a quick word with God while you were in the basement. Two minutes later, after I kissed Haley good night, her comment seemed like an answer to my prayer." Claire paused, wrapped her hands around her mug, and took a sip of her coffee.

Intrigued, he leaned forward. "What did she say?"

"She mentioned how much fun she'd had tonight, how our house was happier whenever you were here, and she said we should invite you to come over more often. To use her words, 'Keith makes our house brighter. Even tonight, when it was rainy and stormy outside, the sun was shining inside.'" Claire looked over at him. "I feel the same way."

As her soft words infiltrated his heart, Keith took a slow, deep breath. The porch was dim, only a few far-flung streetlights and the luminescent moon providing illumination, and he couldn't read her face.

On the plus side, that meant she couldn't read his, either.

Because based on the pressure behind his eyes, she might catch him tearing up.

"I embarrassed you, didn't I?"

"No." He steadied his own mug with a two-handed grip. "I'm just . . . surprised. And very flattered. No one except my parents has ever said anything that complimentary to me."

"Seriously?" Her tone spelled skepticism in capital letters. "You're single, successful, attractive. Translation: chick magnet. It's hard to believe your female friends haven't had some very nice things to say."

Okay. She had a point. A few of the women he'd dated a time or two after his infrequent happy hour sojourns had been on the gushy side.

"I've had an admiring comment now and then. Most of them weren't very sincere. It was just flirting stuff."

"This isn't."

"I know that." Otherwise, it wouldn't have packed such an emotional punch.

She took a sip of coffee, then stared into the dark depths. "Here's the thing. I vowed a long time ago that I wouldn't waste one more day or night fretting over how someone feels about me. It's too gut-wrenching and stressful and exhausting. I also decided that when—or if—I ever again met a man who interested me, I was going to be up-front with him."

Lifting her chin, she looked over at him. "I don't have any time for or interest in playing games. I believe in honesty and trust and candid communication. If those kinds of parameters scare a guy off, so be it. Better that than let myself get carried away about a man who could end up disappointing me."

At the quiver in her final words, his stomach tightened. "I appreciate your honesty. And you haven't scared me off."

He was tempted to reach for her hand, twine his fingers with hers, and assure her she could count on him to be the kind of man she deserved.

But he didn't.

Because while she hadn't disclosed the specifics of her background, one thing was clear. This was a woman who had suffered more than her share of hurt and betrayal. He wasn't about to make any promises until he was certain he could commit to moving forward without putting her heart at risk again.

"That's good to know." Her words were positive; her tone wasn't. There was a distance, a coolness in it that hadn't been there before.

And he knew why.

She'd just given him one of the greatest compliments of his life, and he hadn't said one word to indicate the feeling was reciprocated—even though it was.

Yet how could he acknowledge the mutual attraction without creating expectations?

On the other hand, if he didn't offer some affirmation, she was going to withdraw.

That wasn't an acceptable option, either.

Perhaps the solution was to dig deep and match her candor with some honesty of his own.

He set his mug on the concrete floor beside him and took a steadying breath. "To be frank, I'm not used to having conversations like this. None of the women I've dated have been so forthright—and to tell you the truth, if they had been, I would have run in the opposite direction."

"That's what I was afraid of."

"But I don't feel that way about you."

The shadows made expressions difficult to read, but he could feel her searching gaze. "So how *do* you feel?"

He shifted, the chair squeaking in protest as he formulated his response.

"I like being with you. I think there's potential—and I know there's some serious electricity." He paused, cherry-picking his words. "However, even before this conversation, I'd concluded there are things in your background that might make you . . . vulnerable. So I'd decided to move slowly, see how this develops. The last thing I want to do is cause you any more grief."

"I'm fine with slow. More than fine." She ran a fingertip around the rim of her mug, making a full circle. "And you're right. I've had plenty of grief, and I'm not in the market for any more. On the flip side, I don't want to saddle an unsuspecting guy with my baggage, either. That's why I think it's only fair to give you some history before you get too involved with Haley and me—if you'd like to hear it."

He hesitated. Not because he was unsure of his answer, but because an affirmative response carried an obligation to share in return. Maybe not tonight, but at some point in the future.

That scared him.

But having this woman shut him out scared him more.

Decision made.

"Yes. I would."

She leaned back in her chair, putting a bit more distance between them. Perhaps to create a bigger comfort zone of personal space?

As she lifted her mug to her lips, the plaintive wail of a distant train whistle echoed in the silence. A gentle breeze drifted past, the sweet scent it carried familiar but elusive. Overhead, a stray cloud drifted across the moon, leaving the world in shadows.

Just when he began to think she'd had second thoughts, she spoke.

"I haven't shared the details of my past with many people. And the odd thing is, you were the last person I ever expected to connect with."

"Why?"

"In a lot of ways, you remind me of my ex-husband."

That wasn't the best news he'd ever heard, especially if some of his speculations about her ex turned out to be accurate. "What ways?"

"He was a numbers guy too. Public accounting. The job consumed his life. All he ever thought about was work and getting ahead."

"That's not all I think about." Not anymore. Not since he'd met her.

"Still, on a superficial level, the parallels are striking. You wear the same kind of upscale clothes and drive a similar sporty, expensive car."

"Is that why you weren't too friendly the day we met over a tub of sealer in your driveway?"

"Yeah. That, plus your take-charge manner."

"I was only trying to help."

"I know, but at the time, it rubbed me wrong."

"So your ex was a take-charge kind of guy?"

"More a my-way-or-no-way kind of guy, I guess." She rose and walked over to the railing, angling away from him as she gazed into the darkness. "I'm going to back the story up a bit, okay?"

"Sure."

"I grew up in Charleston, and my childhood was idyllic in many ways. My dad operated a charter fishing boat. Still does. My mom worked part time at the local bank. We were a close-knit, loving family. Everything was perfect until I was twelve. That's when my older brother, Steve, was killed in a car accident while he was out with a friend who'd just gotten his license. He was only fifteen. Things were never the same after that."

He listened as she told him how she and her parents had struggled to make peace with the tragic loss, about her mother's demise from early-onset Alzheimer's, about her father's financial struggles after medical bills depleted his savings.

A car passed by, the headlights piercing the gloom and illuminating a young couple walking hand-in-hand down the dark sidewalk. Claire watched them for a moment, then turned the opposite direction. "So that brings me to Brett."

"Your ex?"

"Yeah. A world-class jerk." Her words curdled with an almost palpable bitterness. "We met in college. He was two years ahead of me, a big-man-on-campus type. Handsome, popular, star of the debate team. A real smooth talker—and I fell for his charm and flattery hook, line, and sinker. No surprise, I guess. I'd lived a sheltered life as the coddled surviving offspring, working summers on the *Molly Sue* with my dad, singing in the church choir. I never even went on a date until I was seventeen. I guess you could say I was a late bloomer."

"It's hard to believe the guys weren't knocking your door down."

"Not if you'd seen me as a teen. I was gawky, with braces and acne and a skinny, boyish figure. Besides, after working on the boat with Dad all day, it was kind of hard to lose the fish smell. Trust me, eau de mackerel can't compete with Chanel No. 5 for attracting male attention."

Amazing how she'd managed to keep her sense of humor through experiences that would have permanently soured a lot of people.

"By the time Brett entered the picture, I wasn't too hard on the eyes. I caught his attention in the cafeteria the first week of school. I was lonely and vulnerable—a fish out of water, to continue the nautical analogies. I guess he sensed I was easy pickings, and before long we were a couple. We ended up getting married a month after he graduated. I dropped out of school and got a job as an administrative assistant to support us while he went on to get his MBA and CPA."

"How did your parents feel about that?"

"Not happy." Claire leaned back and braced herself against the railing, fingers curled around the pitted wooden beam. She was facing him now, but with the moon still shrouded in clouds, her features were indistinct. "They begged me to wait, to finish school, to date a few more people before I committed to someone for life. But I was caught up in the euphoria of young love. I thought they were being old-fashioned and that everything would be rosy."

"Except it wasn't." Keith picked up his coffee, but the night air and cool concrete had chilled it. After one sip of the unappetizing brew, he set it back down.

"No. I got pregnant right away, which wasn't part of our plan. Brett was less than thrilled, but I promised him it wouldn't be a problem. That I'd arrange everything so he could finish school without disruption."

"What about the disruptions in your life? You gave up college so he could go on for an advanced degree."

"Somehow that got lost in translation. Anyway, once he got a job, I was able to stay home with Haley, and that was a joy. But Brett, being an entry-level public accountant, was either working long hours or on the road. As a result, our marriage suffered. Plus, he started drinking—more than I thought was prudent. I raised the issue, but he didn't agree."

Was this where it was going to get nasty? Alcohol abuse could turn some people very ugly.

"How exactly did he express his disagreement?"

Despite his measured, neutral tone, she got the gist of his

question. "He never abused me—or Haley. We had a lot of fights, but there was no physical violence. He expressed his displeasure in a different way. Since life at home wasn't fun and games, he found those elsewhere. In particular, with another CPA in the firm who was assigned to many of the same accounts and often traveled with him. Her name was Tiffany."

After psyching himself up for a battered wife story, it took Keith a moment to process this unexpected twist.

Claire's husband had cheated on her.

That was a whole different kind of abuse. A battering of the heart rather than the body, but just as damaging.

Jerk was too mild a word for the guy.

Claire was obviously waiting for a response, but words failed him. "I don't know what to say. I'm stunned."

"Yeah. I had the same reaction the day I came across an incriminating email from her on his cell. I didn't want to believe it. I hoped Brett might have some logical explanation. But he didn't even try to deny the affair. I think he was glad I'd found that message. For all I know, he set it up so I would."

The man hadn't even had the guts—or basic humanity—to break things off in an honest way.

Keith flexed his fingers. Too bad her ex wasn't standing here now. Knuckles on jaw would feel eminently satisfying—a rather unnerving reaction, considering he'd never picked a fight in his entire life.

Then again, he'd never felt this protective of a woman before.

"To wrap up this unhappy tale, I thought my world was ending." Claire's voice wavered. Steadied. "Brett had no interest in trying to work things out, so we divorced. He took a position in a West Coast office of his firm, and I continued to work while I went back to school part time and finished my teaching degree. I graduated at twenty-nine, got my current job, and bought this house. Life is finally on the upswing."

Given the condition of her house, he wasn't sure about that final comment. But he'd come back to that. "Haley said her father died."

"Yes. Last year, in a one-car drunk-driving accident. Haley was the beneficiary of his life-insurance policy, which went straight into her college fund. He didn't leave much else. Brett wasn't one to stockpile for a rainy day."

Too bad. Even a small infusion of cash would have gone a long way toward alleviating some of Claire's rainy days.

"Tell me about the house. How did you end up here?"

"I hated paying rent on an apartment. It felt like throwing money into a black hole. So I saved every penny I could until I had enough for a decent down payment. Then I found this. An elderly man owned it, and he couldn't keep up with the maintenance. After he died, his heirs just wanted the cash and they sold it as is."

No kidding.

"Did you have it inspected before you bought it?"

"Of course. I know the house has cosmetic issues, but it's structurally sound and has lots of potential. Plus, the neighborhood is great, the school district is excellent, and the location is perfect. It was a real find."

Keith wasn't certain about that. "It's also a lot of work."

"That can be done over time." She flipped a hand, dismissing that subject. "So have I scared you off yet?"

Her inflection was teasing, but the subtle thread of tension woven through her words betrayed her anxiety.

"Not even close. And I appreciate your willingness to share all that with me."

"It only seems fair. I wouldn't want you to get too . . . interested . . . and then have all this garbage dumped in your lap. You need to know I come with serious baggage."

"Don't we all."

"Some is worse than others. I have a feeling any baggage you carry is going to look like a Disney movie compared to mine."

This was his chance to give her a hint about his early history. Tell her she wasn't the only one toting around a less-than-ideal past.

But he was already on overload. He needed to think through everything she'd told him, figure out next steps before he started spilling his guts—because the two of them were in different places. Claire's past might have had a huge impact on her life, but she'd faced it, dealt with it, and moved on.

He hadn't.

And until he did, it was better to leave his skeletons in the closet.

Bending down, he snagged his mug, then stood. "To be honest, your Disney comparison isn't accurate. My pre-adoption years weren't all that great. But why don't we defer that discussion to another day? We both have to work tomorrow."

She twisted her wrist toward the streetlight and peered at the face of her watch. "I guess it is getting late."

"So what time does the painting party start on Saturday morning?"

She blinked at him. "You're coming back to help us finish?"

"Genies always see a wish through to the end."

"Haley will be thrilled."

"How does her mother feel about it?" He joined her at the railing.

"Also thrilled. But what happens after I've used up all my wishes?"

"We can cross that bridge when we come to it."

The cloud over the moon drifted away, and the shimmering orb once again bathed the rain-washed landscape in a silver light that gave the world—and the woman inches away from him—a magical, dreamlike quality.

He could see her face clearly at this close range. In the ethereal light, she was beautiful . . . appealing . . . tempting.

Too much of all of the above for him to resist.

He lifted his hand, his fingers tingling as they anticipated making contact with her smooth, silky-looking skin.

But all at once she backed off, folding her arms over her chest and breaking the spell.

He let his hand drop to his side. Waited a moment for his pulse to decelerate. "Should I apologize?"

"No." She swallowed. "It's just . . . I'm not ready for that. Not because I don't trust you, but because I don't trust me. That's what I meant earlier when I talked about touching. I want you to touch me, and that's scary. I don't even know you very well yet."

That was true—and it wasn't a problem he could remedy tonight.

Summoning up a smile, he held out his mug to her. "I admire your self-control."

She took it, careful to avoid his fingers. "Does the offer still stand for Saturday?"

"Of course."

Some of the tautness in her features eased. "Come whenever you get up. We'll start early and finish about noon—I hope."

"Expect me about eight."

"If you want to sleep in, you can come later."

Trade an extra hour of sleep for an extra hour with Claire? Not a chance.

"I like to get up early."

"Okay."

"Let me grab my stuff."

He detoured into the house, snagged his gym bag, and rejoined her. She'd picked up her own mug, and she lifted it in salute. "See you Saturday. And thank you."

"My pleasure." He backed toward the steps. "Good night."

Not until he slid behind the wheel did he look back. She was still standing near the door, juggling the two mugs in her hands.

He hated to leave.

But it was time.

As he shoved the key in the ignition, put the car in gear, and pulled away, a question she'd asked him earlier in the evening echoed in his mind.

"Are you a praying man?"

He'd never responded.

Yet after his roller-coaster emotional ride tonight, he had a clear answer.

More so now than ever.

Because he needed all the guidance he could get.

13

· ·

"Come in, ladies. Welcome to the I'm-glad-it's-Friday party."
Maureen pulled the door wide and ushered in Claire and Haley.

"I've never been to a Friday party before." Haley crossed the
threshold, toting a plate of gooey butter cookies.

"Me, neither. But I felt like celebrating. It's spring and the
sun is shining and we have the whole weekend ahead to enjoy."

"Mom and me made these." She held out the plate.

Maureen took it and gave Claire a hug. "These look wonderful, but you didn't have to provide dessert."

"It was the least I could do after you went to the trouble of
making the whole dinner."

"It was no trouble. I'm glad I have the energy—and appetite—to enjoy cooking again. Now let's get this party started."

"This is so much fun. Two parties in one week!" Haley fell
in beside her as she guided them back to the kitchen.

"Two parties?"

"Yeah. Keith came over on Wednesday night after he visited
you, and we had a painting party."

The very subject she'd wanted to introduce—and one of the reasons she'd arranged this impromptu get-together.

"I did notice his car parked in front after he left here. Did you have fun?"

She directed the question to Claire, and while Haley provided the verbal answer, the subtle blush on Claire's cheeks was just as telling.

"It was awesome! We laughed a lot and sang songs. Well, I sang. I didn't want to go to bed when we were done, but Mom made me, even though Keith stayed for a while." Haley grabbed a carrot stick off the veggie tray on the island and turned to her mother. "What did you guys do, anyway?"

"We sat on the porch and had a cup of coffee."

Haley rolled her eyes. "B-o-r-i-n-g."

Maureen set the cookies on the counter and pulled two oven mitts out of a drawer. Based on Claire's lingering blush, her little tête-à-tête on the porch with Keith had been anything but boring.

"Haley, if you want to fix a plate with some veggies and dip and go out on the patio, you might see the fawn and doe I told you about. They often show up about now to munch in my garden. At this rate, I doubt any of my hostas are going to manage to poke their heads more than three inches out of the ground this season."

"Cool."

While Haley loaded up her plate, Maureen checked on the chicken and rice casserole. It was doing fine all by itself, just as she'd planned, leaving her free to chat—and ask a few exploratory questions.

"So how was your week?" She took off the mitts and gestured to the stools at the counter, then helped herself to a stalk of celery.

"Busy." Claire slid onto the adjacent stool. "Sorry the parent-teacher meetings ran long and you had to delay dinner."

"Not a problem. We'll be very cosmopolitan and eat on European time." She twirled her celery in the dip. "How's Haley's room coming?"

"We made a lot of progress this week. I think we'll finish it tomorrow."

"It was nice of Keith to pitch in."

"Yes." Claire made a project out of selecting a grape tomato.

"He seems to be a very conscientious and responsible man."

"Seems to be."

"Of course, after all the time he spent at your house on Wednesday, I'm sure you've gotten to know him far better than I have."

Claire picked up a tomato. Examined it. Put it back. "Actually, I did most of the talking."

That was news, considering she'd known Keith less than a month. Despite the rapport she and Claire had developed over the past year and her neighbor's many kindnesses during her treatment, it had taken months before Claire had offered more than a peek into her background. Nor had she been all that talkative in the early days of their friendship.

Very interesting.

"What did you talk about?" She did her best to keep her tone casual as she munched on her celery stick.

Claire continued to scan the tray for the perfect tomato. "I told him about Brett."

Maureen masked her surprise—and delight—as best she could. It was about time Claire gave the opposite sex another chance, and from everything she'd seen so far, Keith was a worthy candidate for her trust. "He must be a very good listener."

"Too good. I told him more than I intended."

"Maybe that's not a bad thing." She swirled another stalk of celery in the dip. "He strikes me as the honorable sort, and David speaks very highly of him."

Claire tipped her head. "David? As in David McMillan?"

"The very same." She bit into her celery.

"When did you two transition to first names?"

Maureen chewed the veggie stick. Better to be up-front about their developing relationship. Perhaps it would encourage Claire to take the leap too. "A while ago. We've been chatting on and off since this whole thing began. We had lunch too."

"And you didn't tell me?" Claire gave up all pretense of selecting a tomato.

"You didn't tell me about your painting party with Keith."

"That just happened two days ago. I haven't seen you until now."

"True. So in the interest of full disclosure, I'm also attending a birthday party for his grandson on Sunday."

Claire's mouth dropped open. "You mean you two are dating?"

"It's only been one lunch that was partly business and a child's birthday party."

"But it could lead to real one-on-one dating, right? You do like him?"

Like was too mild a word . . . but she wasn't ready to admit to anything more—even to herself.

"He's very nice, and I enjoy his company."

Claire touched her hand. "I'm happy for you, Maureen." Then she tipped her head, her expression pensive. "Who would have guessed Haley's letter would lead to all this?"

"It's strange how God works, isn't it? Sometimes he offers us opportunities and second chances when we least expect them. Keith may be another example of that, you know. If a man gives up his free time to paint a little girl's room, I think it's safe to assume he's got more on his mind than redecorating."

Her neighbor's jaw firmed. "I know. But I'm not going to let myself get carried away. He hinted he'd tell me about his background at some point—especially the adoption—but we'll see."

Maureen stared at her. "Keith is adopted?"

Claire's hand froze as she reached for a tomato, dismay flattening her features. "I shouldn't have said anything. He told me that in confidence."

"But . . . why on earth wouldn't he share that with me, given my own background?"

"I asked him that. He said the circumstances were completely different. I got the impression his adoption story isn't a happy one. Listen . . ." She leaned closer, features taut. "You won't say anything, will you? I don't want him to think I was gossiping behind his back."

"No worries. This will stay between us." She patted Claire's hand and rose. "Now why don't you call your daughter in and we'll divvy up my casserole."

Still mulling over Claire's surprising piece of news, Maureen went to retrieve the main dish. What an odd coincidence.

Yet in some ways, it explained a lot. If Keith's history was as unhappy as Claire had suggested, his initial aloofness—and her impression that he didn't want to work on her project—made sense. He would probably prefer to have nothing to do with an adoption-related assignment.

She slid her hands back into the oven mitts and took a firm hold of the glass baking dish. Warmth seeped into her thumb through a worn area, and she transferred the dish to the table as fast as she could, touching it as briefly as possible.

Kind of like the way she'd handled the events that had gotten her into a mess twenty-two years ago.

She paused beside the table, pulling the protective mitts from her fingers. Like the hot casserole, her story had the power to burn. That's why she'd avoided telling it. Only a few people were privy to her secret. Father Ryan. Her dearest friend, now gone. Claire. Each time she'd shared it, she'd worried about being judged. Instead, each friend had validated her trust in them by treating her with love and compassion.

David had earned her trust too, despite their short acquaintance. The man radiated kindness and integrity. And if they did end up becoming a couple, she wanted no secrets between them. It was time he knew the full story, not just the outcome. And no matter what happened between them as a result, he'd respect her confidence.

Until now, Keith hadn't been on her confidante list. But perhaps, if he had a troubling adoption history, her story would help him understand how mistakes could be made even by people who otherwise led exemplary lives.

"I'm starving!" Haley burst through the door, empty plate in hand.

"Did you see the deer?" Maureen tucked the insulated mitts back into their drawer.

"No. I think maybe they saw me and got scared."

Very possible. Fear was a powerful motivator. It was often easier to hide in the shadows than face danger.

For deer . . . and for people.

So as Haley and Claire joined hands with her at the table for the blessing, she added a silent prayer of her own—for the courage to tell her story to the two new men in her life . . . and to do it sooner rather than later.

"Hey! Watch the drips!"

At Keith's warning, Claire glanced down from her perch on the ladder. He'd stopped rolling the wall below her to wipe a large drop of paint off his arm.

"I thought genies repelled . . ." She stopped. Cocked her head. "Was that the doorbell?"

"Don't ask me." Keith finished wiping off the pink spot. "I can't hear a thing with the music cranked up so loud."

"Haley."

No response.

She increased her volume. "Haley!"

A blonde head popped up from behind the plastic-draped furniture. "Yeah?"

"Turn off the CD."

Her daughter moved over to the portable player, and the room went silent.

A moment later the doorbell rang.

"I'll get it." Haley jogged toward the hall.

"Check to see who's there before you open the door."

"I will." Her muffled voice drifted back.

"Beat you." Keith finished rolling the last wall, a full hour ahead of schedule.

She made a face at him. "Edging is harder."

"Ha. Rolling takes a lot more effort and—"

"Cap!" Haley's squeal bounced off the walls.

Claire's eyes widened. "What in the world . . ." She descended the shaky ladder as fast as she dared.

"Who's Cap?"

"My dad."

She took off for the front door at a jog.

Sure enough, her father was standing in her foyer, an overnight bag on the floor beside him, hugging Haley. He grinned at her when she appeared.

"Surprise!"

She gaped at him. "What are you doing here?"

"I told you to keep your eye out for a surprise, didn't I?"

"Yes, but . . . I was expecting a package in the mail."

He chuckled. "A surprise is supposed to be something unexpected. So I guess I succeeded. Now are you going to stand there all day with your mouth open like a flounder, or are you going to give your old man a hug?"

She didn't need a second invitation. Throat constricting, she flew into his arms.

"That's more like it." He held her tight, just the way he had since she'd been a little girl, his arms as strong and comforting as she remembered. "This is why a man travels halfway across the country." His words came out hoarse beside her ear.

When he finally released her, she stepped back and looked him over. Not much had changed since their last visit. Same unruly gray hair that was always a tad too long, same twinkling blue eyes, same ready smile, same lean, wiry build. The crevices on his face were deeper than they'd been a year ago, the tanned skin more weathered, but overall he appeared fit and vigorous.

Thank you, God.

"It's so good to see you." Her own voice choked.

He patted her shoulder, his other hand still holding Haley close. "It's good to see you too. Since you wouldn't commit to making a trip out my way, I took the first opportunity I had to come visit my two favorite ladies."

"You didn't drive, did you?"

"No. I didn't have that much time. Business is picking up for the season. I took off for the weekend, but I've got charters every day next week."

"Did you fly, Cap?" Haley looked up at him.

Claire frowned. He couldn't afford that. If he'd shelled out big bucks for a ticket, he'd be eating macaroni and cheese for weeks. She should have told him they'd come out to visit this summer, found some way to scrape up the gas money and . . .

"Hey." He smoothed out her brow with a gentle touch, just as he had when she'd gotten her britches tied up in knots over some inconsequential thing as a youngster. "I didn't break the bank to do this."

"What does that mean?" Haley sent him a confused look.

"It means I got a free ride—literally. I had a local charter customer last month who happens to be a pilot, and he has clients in the Midwest. When I mentioned I had family in St. Louis, he said if I ever wanted to hitch a ride with him, just pick up the phone. So I did. He's in town for some kind of charity thing tonight and lunch with clients tomorrow, then we head home. I guess you could say I've officially become a jet-setter."

Claire sent him a dismayed look. "Does that mean we only get the pleasure of your company for twenty-four hours?"

"More like twenty-seven—and I intend to make the most of them. Except . . ." He gave them both an inspection. "You two look like you're in the middle of a painting project."

"We're making my bedroom pink. Wanna see?" Haley took his hand and tugged him toward the hall.

He started to follow . . . but came to an abrupt halt as Keith stepped into the foyer.

Good heavens! Claire clapped a hand to her mouth. She'd totally forgotten about him!

"Dad." She moved beside her father. "Let me introduce Keith Watson. He's the . . . he's my . . . he's, uh, helping us paint Haley's room." Heat flamed in her cheeks. "Keith, this is my father, Frank Flynn."

After the two men shook hands and exchanged greetings, Keith looked at her. "I'll clean up the pans and rollers and get out of your hair so you can enjoy your visit."

"Don't leave on my account. I'm the one who dropped in uninvited." Her father turned to her. "Why don't you round up a brush for me and I'll pitch in?"

"We're almost done. Besides, I want to visit with you, not paint." Out of the corner of her eye she saw Keith disappear down the hall.

Her father leaned closer and lowered his voice. "Am I interrupting anything?"

She tucked her arm in his. "No. Keith was only planning to stay until noon, and we really were wrapping things up."

"In that case, I won't feel guilty. But I am curious."

No surprise there. Before her dad's visit ended, there'd be lots of questions . . . unless she stuck close to Haley. He wouldn't probe too much in front of his granddaughter.

That plan worked fine all afternoon and evening. They gave him a tour of the house, introduced him to Maureen, ate grilled burgers on the deck after she delineated the safe areas, and capped off the day by going out for ice cream.

But after they both kissed Haley good night and returned to the kitchen, he pounced on the topic she'd been dreading.

"So tell me about your painting buddy." He helped himself to a soft drink. "Haley is certainly taken with him."

Might as well face the inquisition.

She grabbed a Coke, opened the kitchen window, and joined him at the table. "Warm night."

"Very pleasant." He sipped his drink, watching her. Waiting.

She gave him the condensed version of how they'd met, downplaying any suggestion of a relationship.

Except he didn't buy it.

"Come on, sweetie. This is your father here. I've known you for thirty-two years. Seems to me you've finally decided to throw your line in and do a little fishing—and I approve. That young man made a very nice first impression."

She swiped up a stray drop of mustard left from their dinner, the cheerful hue reminding her of Haley's comment about Keith brightening up their house.

"I wouldn't go that far. Fishing is proactive, and Keith just showed up. I'm going with the flow but not making any special effort."

"Is that right?" His eyes twinkled as he took a swig of soda.

"You always wear such nice clothes and fix up your hair and put on eye shadow when you paint?"

She was busted.

"Okay, so I like him. But we met less than a month ago, and I'm not going to let myself get carried away. Fool me once and all that."

"Caution is fine—as long as you don't let it paralyze you." He surveyed the kitchen. "Though I must say, a bit more caution in house-hunting might have been prudent. This place needs a lot of sprucing up."

"The price was right, though."

"I like bargains myself. Still . . . you think you might have taken on a little too much?"

"No. I can make this work, Dad."

He covered her hand with his. "I know that. You can do anything you set your mind to, and don't you ever doubt that. I just wish things had been easier for you. And I wish I could help you out with a few bucks now and then. That deck out there is downright dangerous."

"We don't use it much."

"I'm glad to hear that."

"As for finances, we're doing okay. I have a to-do list, and I'm working my way through it item by item." Of course, every time she crossed one repair job off, two others appeared—but there was no reason to mention that. "And the house has wonderful potential."

"I can see that. The basic construction appears to be sound, and the neighborhood is very nice. That lilac bush on the side is a beauty too." He angled his head toward the open window and sniffed. "I can smell it all the way in here. Reminds me of your mom."

"Yeah?" She took a sip of soda. "How come?"

"She was always partial to them."

"Really? She never told me that. Why didn't we plant one in our yard?"

"They won't flower in Charleston. We tried transplanting some cuttings from her parents' house after we got married, but turns out they need a long period of winter chill in order to bloom." He leaned back in his chair, his expression thoughtful as he looked at her. "Sometimes that's true for people too."

She traced a trail of condensation down the side of her can. "And sometimes it isn't. Sometimes winter kills instead."

"That's the pessimist's view. I like to believe winter makes us more appreciative of—and ready for—spring. Seeing Keith here today gives me hope that spring might be just around the corner in your part of the world . . . in more ways than one." A breeze wafted through the room from the open window, and he sniffed again. "Smells like a piece of heaven, doesn't it?"

Claire inhaled. "Yeah, it does. Life's been so busy I've never paid much attention to that bush."

"You should go over there at least once a day and take a whiff while it's at the peak of bloom. I can't say I've ever seen a lilac that laden with blossoms. Mother Nature orchestrated the seasons perfectly to produce what your mom would have called a lilac spring."

"Lilac spring. That has a nice sound to it."

"Yes, it does." He finished off his soda and stood. "Now this old jet-setter is going to put his weary bones to bed. What time are services at your church tomorrow?"

"Nine and eleven." No need to tell him she wasn't always diligent about attending. That was between her and God. Besides, maybe her father's visit would be the impetus she needed to prod her back into the habit of weekly attendance.

"Let's make it nine. That will give us a few more hours together afterward."

"Works for me. Are you sure you'll be okay on the sleeper sofa? Haley and I don't mind giving you the bedroom."

"I wouldn't think of putting you out of your bed. I'll be fine." He leaned down and kissed her forehead. "Good night, sweetie."

"'Night, Dad."

While he got ready for bed, she made up the sofa bed for him. Then she tidied up the kitchen.

The last thing she did was close the window. But before she lowered it, she took another whiff of the sweet fragrance.

Lilac spring.

A soft smile played at the corners of her mouth. Wouldn't it be nice if her dad was right? If a long, cold winter could lead to abundance in the spring—for both lilacs and people?

It was something to hope for, anyway.

14

As the doorbell chimed, Maureen took a steadying breath. Prayer had led her to this moment, and she would *not* let second thoughts undermine her resolve. God would see her through— whatever the outcome.

She rose and summoned up a smile for Keith. "Excuse me while I get that."

"If you're expecting company, I could finish my update by phone later. I was about done, anyway."

"No—that's okay. Besides, I had one other thing I wanted to talk to you about, if you can spare a few more minutes."

He shrugged. "Sure."

Smoothing a hand down her skirt, she walked to the door and pulled it open.

David turned from perusing his assistant's car. "Is Keith here?"

"Yes. He was giving me an update, but we were just finishing." She managed to hold onto her tremulous smile. "I appreciate you coming a little early."

"It was my pleasure." He gave her a discreet but appreciative scan and dropped his voice. "You look very lovely today."

"Thank you." The linen skirt and crisp blouse had been a smart choice. The attire for his grandson's birthday party might be casual, but David could have stepped out of the pages of *GQ*. No jeans for this guy. Razor-creased slacks, open-necked shirt, summer blazer that set well on his broad shoulders.

Talk about distinguished looking.

Plus, the man had the physique of someone half his age.

Their gazes met, and she got lost in the blue of his eyes.

Only when the sound of a throat being cleared finally penetrated her consciousness did she remember her other guest.

She turned. Surprise lurked in the depths of Keith's eyes as his gaze darted from her to David.

"I, uh, should probably be going. David." He acknowledged the other man with a cautious nod from across the foyer.

"Actually . . . I hope you'll stay a few more minutes." She tightened her grip on the knob. "There's something I'd like to share with the two of you."

They gave her an inquisitive look, but David spoke first as he moved into the house. "I'm sure we'd both like to hear whatever you have to say."

Since that didn't leave Keith much choice, he followed his boss back to the living room and retook his seat.

After both declined her offer of a beverage, she perched on the edge of the upholstered chair by the fireplace. It would have been so much more comforting to sit beside David on the couch—but leaving some space between them would allow her to better observe the reactions of the two men.

She cleared her throat. "Given all you've both done for me, I felt I owed you a few more details of my story . . . including how I got myself into the predicament that precipitated the adoption."

David gave a firm shake of his head. "That's not necessary, Maureen. We intend to see this through no matter what."

"I know that. And I'm grateful. But I'd like to share this with you—and I feel confident, after getting to know you both over these past few weeks, that you'll respect my privacy and keep it to yourselves."

"Of course." There was no hesitation in David's response.

Keith shifted in his seat. "You really don't have to share those kinds of private details with me if you'd rather not."

"I want to." Maureen locked gazes with him. "It would be a favor to me if you'd stay and listen. It's time this story was told—at least to trusted friends."

A flicker of surprise—and pleasure?—softened his eyes, and he dipped his head in assent. "All right."

Her pulse picked up.

The time had come.

Folding her hands in her lap, she took a steadying breath. "I'm sure you've both wondered how a professor at a Christian college managed to find herself pregnant at the mature age of thirty-eight. And it's a valid question. Why did I violate the moral laws I believed in and encouraged my students to follow?"

"Can I say something before you continue?" David locked gazes with her.

Her heart tripped, and she braced herself. "Yes."

"Nothing you tell us will change my opinion about you. What happened twenty-two years ago is ancient history. I don't think one mistake, or even sin if you will, should condemn a person for life. We'd all be in sad shape if that was the case. Lives should be judged as a whole, not by isolated incidents."

She exhaled. "Thank you for that."

Knitting her fingers into a tight knot, she plunged in. "It happened in Italy. I'd always wanted to see in person the art I knew only through books or reproductions. I spent a week on my own in each of three cities. Venice was my last stop. I'd just arrived, and was eating dinner at a sidewalk café. There was another

American there, a handsome, sophisticated-looking man. I guess he heard me speaking English to the waiter, and as I finished my meal, he came over and asked if he could join me for dessert."

She paused, reaching deep for the words she'd spoken to so few people. "He said he was there on business and gave me a card from a major company, one you'd both recognize. Then he asked if he could meet me for dinner the next night. For a woman who'd spent her life with her head in books, whose experience with romance was confined to old Cary Grant movies, it all felt magical. Story-bookish. Since he said he was a widower and he wasn't wearing a ring, I agreed."

"Let me guess. He lied about his marital status." David's lips were set in a grim line.

"I honestly don't know, though I suspect he did. I'll explain that in a minute."

With a nod, he leaned forward and clasped his hands between his knees.

"To make a long story short, we shared dinner every night for the week I was there. We went on gondola rides. Met to watch the sun rise over St. Mark's square. Visited the Rialto Bridge. He wooed me with words—and then with wine. That was my downfall."

Her fingers began to tingle, and she loosened her clasp to let the blood flow back into her white knuckles. "On my last night in Venice, he insisted I try some of the local wine. I wasn't a drinker, but I finally gave in, planning to have only a small glass. He kept refilling it, though, and I lost track of how much I drank. The moonlight was shimmering on the canals, the gondoliers were singing love songs, couples were strolling by arm in arm. It was magical. The next thing I knew, we were in my hotel room. The rest, as they say, is history."

"So the next morning he just said good-bye and walked out?" David's expression was fierce.

She gave a mirthless laugh. "He wasn't even that polite. When I woke up, he was gone . . . along with all the empty promises he'd made about the future. I called the hotel he'd told me he was staying at, but there was no one registered under his name. That's when I realized I'd been had. That he was just some traveling businessman who picked up gullible women to amuse him in his free time." Hard as she tried to prevent it, a bitter note crept into her voice.

Now it was Keith's turn to lean forward. "Did you contact the guy later?"

"I hadn't intended to. After I left Italy, I was determined to forget about him. But once I discovered I was pregnant, I panicked and called his company, hoping he might take some responsibility. Turns out the business card he'd shown me had also been a fake. There was no one working there with that name. Hal Wright didn't exist in real life."

Anger flashed in David's eyes. "There are words for people like him—but they're not suitable for polite company."

She managed a sad smile. "I must confess, I've thought a few of them, even if I've never said them. But there are words for women who do what I did too—and they're not pretty, either."

"Alcohol can take away inhibitions and loosen morals."

She shook her head. "No. I'm not going to blame the alcohol. I hate those drunk-driving campaigns that say alcohol kills. Alcohol doesn't kill. People who use alcohol irresponsibly kill. That's what happened in my case. I could have stood firm, refused to drink. I could have listened to the voice of my conscience after things started to accelerate, but I ignored it. The blame is mine."

"The man who seduced you shares some of it." David's tone was adamant, his jaw hard.

Maureen shrugged, suddenly weary. "It doesn't matter anymore."

"So you faced this all alone."

"Yes."

"What about your parents? Other family?"

"I was an only child and had nothing but distant relations. Dad was a chaplain at the U.S. Naval Hospital in Okinawa. I visited my parents once a year, during my summer break, so the timing of the pregnancy was providential in that regard. They never knew about it. I never *wanted* them to know. I was too ashamed. My one solace was my faith, but in the beginning I felt distanced even from God. Eventually, though, I found the courage to ask him for forgiveness, and I made peace with my mistake—or so I thought. But after cancer struck, I realized I had unfinished business."

"So you'd never considered trying to find your son before your diagnosis?" Keith fixed her with an intent look.

"Yes, I did. My best friend, Linda Barrett, urged me to. I met her when I was in my early forties and she was in her fifties. She was a childless widow and didn't have any family, either. We clicked like sisters. After we'd known each other several years, I told her my story, and she encouraged me to try and connect with my son. She thought it could have a positive impact on both our lives. I wrestled with the idea but never followed her advice. Before she died three years ago, she brought it up again. In hindsight, I think she was right. That's why I'm grateful to both of you for agreeing to help me."

"Speaking of that. . . ." David shifted toward Keith. "Any progress?"

"I have two leads. My plan is to follow up on both of them early this week."

"There's no urgency." Maureen directed her comment to Keith. "And I appreciate you stopping by today with an update. I also appreciate your understanding. The circumstances of my situation don't condone what I did, but they do give it context.

200

I suspect many women who give up their children make that decision under similar duress—and perhaps live to regret it."

He narrowed his eyes slightly, as if he was wondering what had prompted her last remark. But he didn't comment. Instead, he checked his watch. "If we're finished, my mother is expecting me to come by early today and help her clean out her garden."

"I won't keep you any longer, then." She stood. "Let me walk you to the door."

He rose and looked at David. "Are you leaving too?"

"No. Maureen and I have plans for the afternoon."

"Oh." He shifted toward her. "Well, uh, I'll be in touch as soon as I have any information on the . . . two sources we discussed. And thank you for sharing all that background with me. It was very . . . enlightening."

"Thank *you* for all you've done to help me in my quest." She preceded him to the foyer and opened the door. "Enjoy your afternoon."

"You too." With one more glance back toward the living room, he exited.

When she rejoined David, he was standing. She positioned herself behind one of the wing chairs and rested her hands on the back. "Keith seemed a little confused by . . . us. I take it he doesn't know you and I have become friends."

"He does now." He strolled over, stopping in front of the chair, close but not close enough to invade her personal space. "Why do I have a feeling you had an ulterior motive for including him in your story today?"

"Because you're a very perceptive man?"

He raised an eyebrow. "I appreciate the compliment—but is that all I get?"

"Sorry. I can't divulge a confidence."

"Enough said. I admire people who can keep a secret. And I'll keep yours."

She moistened her lips. "To be honest, I wasn't certain how you'd react. I sense you're a man of high moral values, and I'm not proud of violating mine."

"Maureen . . . I doubt there's a person alive who hasn't on occasion violated their values or made mistakes they regret—like the ones I made with my wife and daughter. You had a moment of weakness; my mistakes went on for years. I live with guilt and remorse too."

She sighed. "Why does life have to be tainted by regret?"

"That's a question only God can answer. But I'll tell you one thing I don't regret—meeting you."

Pressure built behind her eyes. "Thank you. That's one of the loveliest things anyone has ever said to me. And for the record, I feel the same way."

"Dr. Chandler, you just made my day." He held out his hand. "Now what do you say we two imperfect people go to a birthday party and play pin the tail on the donkey with a four-year-old?"

She looked at his extended hand . . . firm . . . steady . . . waiting—and knew it was an invitation for more than a birthday party.

He was asking her to take a leap into the unknown.

Just as Hal had.

But this time, her conscience wasn't blasting out a red alert. This time, her heart was singing, not quaking. This time, her decision was being made with full control of her faculties.

Stepping out from behind the chair, she placed her fingers in his. "Let's join the party."

"Isn't that Keith's car?"

As Haley leaned forward, straining against the seat belt to

peer through the front windshield, Claire inspected the sporty vehicle rolling down their street toward them.

Unless another late-model red Infiniti happened to be visiting her neighborhood, it was Keith.

But why would he be here two days in a row?

"I think so." She eased back on the gas pedal.

The other car slowed too.

As they drew alongside one another, the tinted window on the driver's side of the Infiniti rolled down.

She lowered her window too. "What are you doing here?"

"A command performance with Maureen that included my boss." He leaned sideways to see past her. "Hi, Haley."

"Hi, Keith."

"Is everything okay?" Claire rested her elbow on the window.

"Fine. She had some more background information she wanted to pass on. Is your dad gone?"

"Yes. We just dropped him off at the Spirit Airport terminal—how the other half travels, I guess. Talk about plush."

"I wouldn't know. McMillan employees fly commercial, not corporate—and I have the leg cramps to prove it. Speaking of sore muscles . . . how are your shoulders and neck?"

"Better." Sort of. But she didn't want to invite another offer for a massage.

"So did your dad have a good time?"

"We all did."

"Yeah." Haley had unlocked the seat belt and was now hanging over the wheel, almost in her lap. "Cap is lots of fun. You should have stayed around. I think he would have liked that, 'cause he asked a bunch of questions about you."

Trying not to cringe, Claire changed the subject. "So where are you off to?"

"My mom's. I told her I'd help her clean out her annual gardens."

203

"Perfect day for it."

"Yeah."

A car backed out of a driveway down the street, and she gestured toward it. "I think we're about to hold up traffic."

Despite a quick check in the rearview mirror, he didn't move. "Listen . . . I know the bedroom is finished, but if there's anything else you could use a hand with, I'm available."

He was looking for another reason to see her.

Meaning her data dump about Brett hadn't scared him off.

Thank you, God . . . I think.

"You don't have to be a genie or a handyman to come visit. Maybe next time, we could do something fun."

"Hey . . . we're going skating next Saturday." Haley leaned her elbow on the steering wheel. "You want to come?"

"Ice-skating in May?"

"It's an indoor rink."

The car pulled up behind Keith with a toot of the horn.

"You're welcome to join us. Think about it and let me know. No pressure, though. Ice-skating isn't everyone's thing. Have fun at your mom's." With a quick wave, Claire rolled up her window and accelerated.

Haley bounced back to her seat.

"Buckle up."

"We're almost home."

"Most accidents happen close to home."

Grumbling, she complied. "Do you think Keith will go skating with us?"

"Hard to say. Not everyone likes to ice-skate."

"If he doesn't, could we invite him to do some other fun thing?"

"Maybe."

"Like what?"

"We'll have to think about it."

Haley went silent for a few moments. "My school picnic is in a couple of weeks. He might like that."

No way was she showing up at a family event with Keith in tow. That would look too . . . cozy.

"That's a thought. But I bet we can come up with a bunch of other ideas too."

"Yeah."

As they passed in front of Maureen's house, her neighbor came out the front door with a trim, silver-haired man. Haley gawked as they pulled into their driveway.

"That looks like the man from the newspaper picture. The one I wrote the letter to. Keith's boss."

Claire tried to observe the duo a bit more discreetly. "I expect it is."

"Is he helping find her son too?"

"I guess so." At the very least.

While she pulled into the garage, Haley settled back in her seat. "With two people looking, I bet we'll find him. I'm really glad I wrote that letter. This might be the best birthday Dr. Chandler ever had."

Claire slid out of the car, catching one more glance of the couple before the garage door trundled down and blocked them from view.

It very well might.

Whether they located her son or not.

15

. . . .

"Nervous?" David paused outside Debbie's front door to check on his date.

Maureen smoothed a hand down her skirt. "Is it that obvious?"

"Not at all. But I'd be nervous if I thought I might be walking into the kind of tense family situation I described to you."

"What's the worst that can happen? Debbie gives me the cool treatment." She shrugged. "I'll have fun with the children no matter what."

"I like how you look on the bright side of things." And there was plenty more to like too.

"It makes life more pleasant than the alternative."

"I agree. Ready?"

"Or not."

Flashing her a grin, he pressed the bell, then motioned to the brightly wrapped package she was holding. "You didn't have to do that, you know. I had the gift covered." He hefted the box in his arms.

"With children, two presents are always better than one."

Footsteps sounded on the other side of the door, and a moment later Shawn pulled it open. "Welcome to the nuthouse . . . or should I say, birthday house. Nice to see you again, Dr. Chandler. Please, come in."

"Only if you call me Maureen."

"An easy request to accommodate. We're not the formal type."

As they stepped inside, Bobby barreled down the hall, skidding to a stop in front of them. Although he stayed a safe distance away as he eyed Maureen, it was obvious he was intrigued by the presents in their arms. Grace sidled in too, but she wedged herself behind Shawn.

"Hey . . . don't I get a hug from the birthday boy?" David got down on one knee, set his gift on the floor, and held out his arms.

His grandson threw himself into the embrace. "Did that lady bring me a present too?"

At his grandson's theatrically loud whisper, David felt Maureen drop down beside him.

"Yes, she did. I heard you were four today, but you look so grown up—are you sure you aren't six or seven?"

Backing off from the hug, Bobby gave Maureen a once-over, his chest puffing slightly. "No. I'm only four." He squinted at her head. "You have funny hair."

"Bobby!"

Bobby sent his aghast mother a confused look as she came to an abrupt halt on the threshold of the foyer.

David rose, ready to step in—but Maureen handled the situation with aplomb.

Why was he not surprised?

"It's okay." His date directed the reassurance to Debbie, then refocused on Bobby, staying down on his level. "It is kind of funny, isn't it? But it makes me feel like Rope Girl."

He scrunched up his face. "Who's that?"

"You don't know about Rope Girl?" Maureen widened her eyes.

"No."

"I bet your sister does." She shifted to get a better view of the little girl. "Have you heard of Rope Girl, Grace?"

"No." Grace eased out from behind her father and moved closer to her brother, obviously intrigued.

"Rope Girl is one of the Disney heroes. She's a member of Teamo Supremo and uses a magic jump rope to capture her enemies. Do you like to jump rope, Grace?"

His granddaughter nodded.

"I thought so. I bet you're good at it too. Anyway, Rope Girl has hair just like mine—short and spiky—except hers is purple."

"I like red better." Bobby inspected her.

"I do too." Maureen patted her hair.

Bobby cocked his head. "Is it sharp?"

"Not at all. Would you like to touch it?"

After shooting his mother an uncertain glance, he gave it a tentative pat. "Hey! It's soft!"

"That's right." Maureen smiled at Grace. "Would you like to touch it too?"

"Yes." As she edged closer, Maureen bent her head so the little girl could check it out.

"Are you a superhero?" Grace's question came out in an awed whisper.

"No. I don't have a magic jump rope. But I do have something else you might like." She dug into the tote bag slung over her shoulder and withdrew a small, wrapped package. "I know it's not your birthday, but since it's my first visit, I brought you a little treat too."

"Say thank you, honey." Shawn stepped closer and laid a hand on his daughter's shoulder.

"Thank you." Grace sent Maureen a shy smile.

"You're very welcome."

"Wow. My mom said you probably wouldn't bring a present

208

even for me, but you brought one for both of us." Bobby beamed at her. "I'm glad you came."

"I'm glad too. Besides, what would a birthday be without a lot of presents?"

"Yeah! So can I open it now?"

"After dinner, Bobby. With all the other presents." Debbie wiped her palms down her apron and took a step toward Maureen. "That was very nice of you." The words were polite, but her tone was stiff.

David frowned. Debbie was trying to be cordial—but it was clearly an effort. Had he made a mistake bringing Maureen, after all? Should he have waited until he and Debbie had smoothed things out a bit more?

Too late for second thoughts, though. They'd just have to make the best of it.

As Maureen started to rise, he cupped a hand under her elbow, sending her a silent apology. But her eyes seemed to say, "I'm fine. Everything will be okay."

He hoped she was right.

"Thank you for including me in the party, Debbie." She smiled at his daughter, still the epitome of graciousness. "Your father mentioned that you have several gardens. I hope you can find a place for these." Again she reached into the tote bag, this time withdrawing a small gift bag tied with a frilly ribbon. "Asiatic lily bulbs. The man at the nursery assured me they could not only be planted in the spring, but would survive the winter. I included the receipt in case you'd prefer to exchange them for some other kind of flower, though."

"Thank you." Debbie hesitated, then took the bag. "You didn't have to do this."

"It was my pleasure. I love flowers, but I'm afraid I was born with a brown thumb. If we have time later, I'd enjoy seeing your gardens."

"There isn't much to see yet."

"Not true." Shawn put his arm around her shoulders. "Your azaleas are spectacular." He turned to Maureen. "She won't tell you herself, but she's a master gardener and the president of our neighborhood garden club."

"Shawn!" Soft color suffused Debbie's cheeks.

"That's wonderful!" Genuine delight lit Maureen's face. "I've always admired people who can make things grow."

"I learned most of what I know about gardening from my mother."

A beat of awkward silence ticked by.

Just as David prepared to step in, a raucous alarm sounded in the back of the house.

Debbie's eyes widened. "Oh no! I forgot about the gravy!"

As she dashed for the kitchen, Shawn shook his head. "I told her not to go overboard. Bobby would have been happy with hot dogs."

"Or pizza." His grandson was still examining Maureen's present. "But I like turkey and mashed potatoes too." He cast a worried eye toward the kitchen. "Do you think Mom burned the gravy again, like on Thanksgiving?"

"Could be, champ."

David leaned close to Maureen's ear and lowered his voice. "My wife was a wonderful gardener, but cooking wasn't her forte. Debbie takes after her in both respects."

Maureen looked past him, toward the kitchen. "Do you think she'd be offended if I offered to help?"

"I don't know, but I, for one, would be grateful. I've heard stories about your homemade lasagna, so I expect you know your way around a kitchen."

"You make lasagna? From scratch?" Shawn was practically drooling.

"On occasion."

"I'll tell you what . . . why don't we all offer to help? The adults, that is." He put his hands on the children's shoulders. "Guys, it might be better if you go watch that video for a little while."

"Yeah." Grace was still clutching her present. "Mom gets crabby every time the smoke alarm goes off. Come on, Bobby." She took her brother's hand and tugged him toward the family room.

"Shall we?" Shawn gestured toward the back of the house.

"I'm game if you are." David deferred to Maureen. So far, she was batting a thousand in the prepared-for-any-contingency department.

"Lead the way."

Instead, he linked arms with her as they followed Shawn to the kitchen.

The alarm was silent now, and Debbie had opened a window, but the smell of smoke hung in the air. David muffled the cough tickling his throat. No sense adding fuel to the fire.

His daughter gave them a frenzied look. "I've got it under control. Shawn, why don't you give Dad and . . . his guest a drink in the living room?"

"Actually, we all were going to offer to pitch in. Right, David?"

"Right. Maureen likes to cook."

"I'd be grateful if you'd let me help, Debbie." Maureen disengaged from his arm and moved a few steps closer to his daughter. "I hear a turkey dinner is in the offing, and since I have no family I've never had a reason to prepare a Thanksgiving-type meal. But I do love to cook, as David said, and I'd enjoy contributing in some way."

Debbie hesitated, then gestured to the stove. "I had a little trouble with the gravy. Do you do gravy?"

"My mom taught me to make great gravy, just like your mom taught you about flowers." She dumped her tote bag on a convenient chair and moved to the stove. "Let's see what we have here."

As the two women conferred, Shawn inclined his head toward the breakfast nook. "Why don't I fix us some drinks and we can observe from the sidelines?"

"Good suggestion."

While Shawn got their beverages, David took a seat and tuned in to the conversation between the two women.

"Yes, that strainer will work fine." Maureen took the utensil his daughter offered. "Lumps are such a nuisance with gravy, aren't they?"

"Yes." Debbie leaned closer to examine the roasting pan. "What about the burned part?"

"I think we can work around that." Maureen gestured to another pot on the stove, which looked about ready to boil over. "Why don't you test the potatoes while I take care of this? They might be about ready."

Debbie turned her attention to the pot of spuds and grabbed it just in time to prevent a reenactment of the Mt. Vesuvius eruption.

"Thank the Lord your friend showed up when she did or we'd be sending out for pizza." Voice pitched low, Shawn settled into the chair beside him. "She's been a nervous wreck about this whole party, wanting to impress you and your friend. I told her she was overextending."

David caught Maureen giving her watch a discreet glance as Debbie slid a pan of rolls into the oven. At least he didn't have to worry about choking down burned bread.

"She doesn't have to pull out the stops for me, and I don't think Maureen is all that difficult to please."

"I get that impression." Shawn inspected the twosome at the stove. "I have to admit, Debbie wasn't the only one concerned about this get-together. But I think my worry was misplaced. Your friend is very gracious and charming. I doubt it'll take her long to win Debbie over."

"Let's drink to that."

They clinked glasses—and much to David's relief, Shawn's words proved prophetic. By the time they all sat down to a superbly salvaged meal, Debbie was far less tense and chilly. Her reserve melted even more as Bobby and Grace opened Maureen's thoughtful gifts—a LEGO set for the birthday boy and a sparkly necklace for his sister. Later, when she offered without any prompting to show Maureen her garden, David knew the evening was a success.

He told Maureen that as he drove her home in the twilight.

"I thought it went well too, but I'm glad to hear you say so. I enjoyed myself very much."

"Did you really?" He sent her a quick look in the fading light.

"Yes. Bobby and Grace are darling, Shawn's a fine man, and Debbie's . . . I think she did great, given the background you shared with me."

"What did you two talk about in the garden?"

"Flowers."

"Is that all?"

She gave a soft laugh. "You want to know if she gave me the third degree about us."

"Guilty as charged."

"In a very subtle way. I was discreet. Just so you know, when she asked how we met, I simply said I'd had some dealings with McMillan Construction."

"True enough."

"As far as it went. I'm not ready to tell my story to any more people yet."

"I'm fine with that. I'm also fine with whatever you decide to share—or not share—in the future. Now I have a couple of questions for you. Where on earth did you come up with Rope Girl, and when do I get to try this great lasagna I've heard about?"

She laughed again. "Knowing how inquisitive and outspoken

children can be, I thought my hair might attract some attention. So I did my research. We professors are very good at research, you know. As for my lasagna—I'll check my calendar and get back to you."

Not the definitive answer he'd hoped to hear.

Flexing his fingers on the wheel, he swallowed. "That's not an easy letdown, is it?"

"No."

The queasiness in his stomach dissipated. "Good. I've been out of the dating game a long time, and I've forgotten a lot of the rules—but I'm beginning to remember that unsettling feeling I used to get when I was trying to read the signals from a girl I liked. Except back then, I'd have spent days in agony, wondering if she was getting ready to dump me. Having the guts to ask is one of the pluses of growing older, I guess."

"In that case, I have a question for you too. Are we dating?"

"I hope so." He pulled into her driveway, shut off the engine, and angled toward her. There was only a touch of light in the sky now, but he could see the smile on her face and the warmth in her green eyes. "Assuming the lady's willing."

"Very." She let out a soft sigh. "This has such an air of unreality about it."

"How so?"

"I thought all this had passed me by. That the only romance I'd ever enjoy would be the vicarious kind, through my old Cary Grant movies."

He gave a rueful shake of his head. "I'm afraid I'm no Cary Grant."

"Don't sell yourself short."

As he returned her steady gaze, pressure built in his throat. "No one's ever compared me to Cary Grant."

"I guess it's all in the eye of the beholder, but it seems obvious to me. Cary had an image of being smart, urbane, charming, considerate, sincere, and honorable. A true gentleman in every sense of the word. From everything I've seen so far, that image fits you."

Warmth filled his heart. Overflowed. "Thank you for that." He reached over and gently stroked her face, the red spikes at her hairline tickling his fingers. "The kids were right. Your hair is soft."

"It's also funny looking . . . and not very sexy or glamorous."

She dipped her head, but he slid his hand down to her chin and tipped it up again. "I think you're beautiful—inside and out. And I'll prove it."

Without waiting for a response, he leaned closer and claimed her lips in a tender, lingering kiss.

When he at last drew back, her hands were resting on his arms and there was a shimmer in her green irises. "No one's ever kissed me that way. Like I was precious and rare and special."

Even Hal.

She didn't say that—but she didn't have to. The man had been a user, pure and simple. A smooth talker whose words were intended to manipulate. But this woman who'd come so unexpectedly into his life, putting new spring in his step and adding light to his days, deserved better.

And as he said good night at her door a few minutes later with a final kiss, then drove home in the dark, he resolved to do his best to make up for all the years she'd spent date nights with Cary Grant.

"Done." Shawn flopped into his favorite easy chair in the family room and closed his eyes. "Sugar-high birthday boy is finally asleep. How much cake did he eat?"

"Too much. So did Grace. Tag-teaming bedtime was an in-

215

spired idea." Debbie yawned and scanned the floor from her prone position on the couch. Several scraps of wrapping paper and what looked like dried-up cake crumbs stared back at her. "I should run the vacuum."

"It can wait until tomorrow. Let's not risk waking the kids."

"Good point."

"That was an easy sell."

"I was just looking for an excuse to put it off." She maneuvered herself into a half-sitting position. "So how do you think it went?"

Shawn opened one eye. "You first."

"The dinner was okay . . . thanks to Maureen."

"She seems adept in the kitchen."

"Yeah." Debbie snagged a throw pillow and hugged it against her chest. "The kids had fun, and Bobby loved his presents."

"It was nice of Maureen to bring gifts for everyone."

"She liked my gardens too."

"Who wouldn't?" Shawn opened his other eye. "So are you glad you told your dad he could invite her?"

"I guess. I think he appreciated it, and I can't fault her manners."

"I agree. She seems like a very nice person."

Suddenly restless, she rose and wandered over to the window. Night had fallen now. It was dark and silent and empty outside.

A chill rippled through her.

Nice as the day had turned out, something had been missing.

Some*one* had been missing.

All at once Shawn's arms came around her, and he rested his chin on her head. "You're thinking about your mom, aren't you."

Her throat clogged. How had she ever managed to find a man who could tune into her feelings with such precision?

"Yes." She swallowed, blinking away the tears clinging to her lashes. "I know she's been gone awhile now, and we've been through other holidays and family events without her, but today the loss felt fresh again."

"Because Maureen was here instead of her."

"I guess. You know, I wanted to resent her—especially after I caught Dad looking at her like some moonstruck kid, as if she were some kind of gift from heaven. But I couldn't. She was too nice. And Dad seemed happier than he's been since Mom died. Except now I feel guilty, like I'm being disloyal to Mom."

With gentle pressure, he turned her around until she was facing him, then looped his arms around her waist. "You want my opinion?"

"Am I going to like it?"

"Some of it."

She sighed and rested her hands on his shoulders. "Lay it on me."

"I think wanting to resent Maureen is normal. She's getting attention from your dad you never got growing up. He's making time for her that he didn't make for you or your mom. She's also filling a gap for him left by your mom's death—a gap that's still huge for you. Sound plausible?"

"Yes. But there's more, isn't there?" Of course there was. Shawn was a lawyer. He knew how to structure an argument, and one of his techniques was to begin with the sympathetic stuff.

"Not much." He gentled his voice and stroked her hair. "Maureen is nice. Your dad does seem happier. Those are positives. He's also trying very hard to reconnect with you, to make up for being an absentee father. Based on what you told me after his visit the other day, I think it's clear he realizes his mistakes and understands his approach to providing for his family, while well intentioned, was misguided."

"His new insights don't change the past."

"No . . . but yours can change the future, now that you know what motivated him—if you let them soften your heart. As for

Maureen being a gift from heaven for your dad . . . that may be true. And if we welcome her into our family, she might be a gift to all of us. This could be a new beginning for everyone."

Debbie laid her cheek against Shawn's chest. "Do you know how annoying it is being married to a guy who's always so smart and insightful?"

A chuckle rumbled against her ear. "I'll remind you of that remark the next time I get us lost on a road trip."

"That wouldn't happen if you'd stop and ask directions."

"And destroy the male stereotype? No way. I'll leave that to a braver man than me." He kissed the top of her head. "Feel any better?"

"Some."

"Ready to call it a night?"

"Yeah. I'll check the doors and meet you in the bedroom."

With one final squeeze, he released her and started toward the hall, stooping to pick up a stray, sparkly bow en route. Turning, he tossed it to her with a grin. "Bling for my lady."

She made a face and threw it back. "I prefer the real thing."

He caught it one-handed, stuck it in an . . . interesting . . . place, and waggled his eyebrows. "That'll be waiting for you in the bedroom."

As he disappeared down the hall, Debbie smiled. If she'd searched the world over, she couldn't have found a better man. What a blessing it had been the day she'd slipped in an icy parking lot and found herself saved from a nasty spill by a pair of strong arms that were destined to hold her for always.

Did Dad feel that way about Maureen? Did he count his meeting with her as a blessing too?

And was Shawn right? Could Maureen be a gift to all of them?

Questions bouncing through her brain, she verified all the doors were locked, flipped off the lights, and padded down the hall.

Funny. She hadn't expected to end the evening feeling receptive to her father's new friend, no matter how nice she was. But maybe it was time to stop looking at everything through the lens of the past.

Maybe it was time to follow Shawn's advice and open her heart to a new beginning.

16

"Robin?" Keith stuck his head out of his office.

She swiveled around in her desk chair. "What's up?"

"I need an uninterrupted hour. If any drop-ins wander by, can you head them off at the pass?"

"You got it—though I doubt you need to worry this early on a Monday morning. No one's caffeine has kicked in yet. Hot project?"

"I need to make some headway on the little girl's letter David sent my way after that article about the donation to the children's hospital."

"Is that still on your desk?"

"Not for much longer, I hope. So buy me some time if you see anyone lurking."

She gave him a mock salute.

Once he closed the door and returned to his desk, Keith pulled out the contact information he'd dug up on the Net last night for his two leads.

He started with the hospital. Finding a list of pediatricians with admitting privileges twenty-one years ago hadn't seemed like an impossible task when he'd broached the idea to Maureen, but there were only twelve years' worth of annual reports on the hospital's website—and none of them contained a full list of physicians affiliated with the hospital.

This was going to require some phone time.

Unfortunately, after being routed through several departments—none of which were able to offer any help with historical data—he was forced to conclude the hospital was a dead end. As one harried-sounding woman in human resources told him, hundreds of doctors were associated with the hospital, and the list was in constant flux.

Meaning identifying doctors who were on staff twenty-one years ago on a particular day would be hugely time-consuming—and the list would be overwhelming even if he did.

No wonder the PI hadn't bothered to pursue this angle. HIPPA laws aside, trying to find the right pediatrician would be like looking for a needle in a haystack.

On to the priest.

An older-sounding woman answered the phone at St. Columba rectory, but after he introduced himself and explained that he was trying to find some information about Father Kevin Ryan for a friend, she tut-tutted.

"You have the right church, Mr. Watson. I've been the housekeeper here for thirty years, and I remember Father Ryan well. He was a fine man and an outstanding priest. But he died five years ago."

She'd been at St. Columba for three decades?

Maybe his luck was turning.

But how best to play this? Clandestine stuff wasn't his forte—yet telling the woman about Maureen wasn't an option. He couldn't betray the professor's confidence.

"Yes, we knew he had passed away." He'd be as truthful as possible, but discreet. "According to my friend, he was living at . . ." Keith consulted his notes and gave the woman the name of the retirement center.

"That's right. I used to visit him every few months. He only had one sister, and with her arthritis she couldn't get out to see him too often after her husband died."

Keith's pulse took an uptick. "Is his sister still living?"

"Last I heard. In fact, up until a few years ago, she volunteered at a children's agency not far from here."

"Would that have been . . ." Again, he checked his notes and read off the name of the adoption firm Maureen had used.

"Oh no. That burned down long ago, more's the pity. They did fine work. She used to be active there too, though."

He did his best to sound cool and composed despite the sudden spike in his adrenaline. "Was St. Columba involved with that agency?"

"Not officially. But Father Kevin knew the director through his sister, and on occasion he sent people there who were in need of such services. Several of the priests after him did the same, until the place burned down. Not that any of them ever shared details with me, you understand. Being priests, they kept that kind of information in the strictest confidence."

"Of course."

Still . . . if Father Ryan's sister had volunteered at the agency and was close to her brother, might there be a chance she'd have a piece of information that would help him in his search?

He needed to get her name—or convince this woman to pass his name on to her with a request that she give him a call.

"Young man . . . you aren't a reporter, are you?" The woman suddenly sounded nervous.

"No. I work for McMillan Construction in St. Louis. I'm happy to give you the name and phone number of the company president if you'd like to confirm that. As I said, I'm just making inquiries on behalf of an older friend who admired Father Ryan very much."

"Hmm. Well, if you're willing to give a reference, I suppose you're legit. But a person can't be too careful these days, with all the scandals. And I wouldn't want anyone to be trying to dig up dirt on a fine priest like Father Kevin."

"I assure you, that's not my intent. But I have a feeling my friend would enjoy talking with his sister." He dismissed the notion of asking for her name, given the woman's sudden wariness. "If I left my phone number, would you be willing to pass it on and ask her to call me?"

"We haven't been in touch since Father Kevin died . . . but I might be able to track her down. I'd be happy to give it a try."

"That would be great." Keith gave her his name again, as well as his office and cell numbers. "Thank you again for helping me with this."

"I won't make any promises, but I'll see what I can do. Have a blessed day."

After they said their good-byes, Keith tapped his notes into a neat stack and slid them back into his briefcase. The odds weren't great the priest's sister would have pertinent information, but it was worth pursuing. Because if this lead didn't pan out, they'd be back to square one.

And he didn't like leaving things unfinished.

Then why are you dragging your feet about sorting out your own background?

At the prod from his conscience, he swiveled slowly toward his computer and stared at the screen saver of symmetrical geometric shapes. But instead of soothing him, as usual, the predictable pattern simply reinforced the disparity between his work life and his personal life.

His conscience was right. After Maureen's story yesterday, and after more or less promising Claire he'd share information about his adoption at some future date, he ought to check out the Missouri Adoption Registry site.

223

Even if he did decide to follow up, though, the odds his birth mother would be on it were minuscule. From the little he knew about her, the last thing she'd wanted in her life was a kid. Yet might the mere act of trying to make a connection be enough to close out that chapter in his life once and for all?

Perhaps it was worth a try.

Without second-guessing, he entered the name of the registry in his browser. In a couple of clicks, he was on the site.

There was only one page, and he gave it a quick scan. The process was simple—but not fast. Mail in a hard copy of the form and wait up to three months to find out whether there was a match?

Archaic.

Then again, what was another few months after waiting decades?

At least the form was simple. Two pages, asking for basic data. It would take all of five minutes to complete.

He printed it out. Glanced through it again. Started to slide it into his briefcase.

Just do it, Watson. Putting it off isn't going to make it any easier.

As he slowly reached for a pen, his palms began to sweat.

He frowned at them.

This was crazy.

Completing the form wasn't a commitment. He could fill it out and hold onto it until he was ready to drop it in a mailbox. It was nothing to get nervous about.

Gripping the pen tighter, he went to work.

In less than the five minutes he'd estimated, the thing was done. He signed it, addressed an envelope, and slipped it inside. He even put a stamp on it. Then he slid it into his briefcase.

One of these days soon, he'd mail it.

But not today.

At the sudden jingle of the phone on the kitchen counter, Claire's pulse took a leap. Her hand jerked, sending a long red squiggle across Susie Ward's spelling test.

Oh, for goodness sake.

Huffing out a breath, she rose to answer it. All week, she'd been jumpy as the skittish deer who nibbled on Maureen's hostas, hoping Keith would call to say he'd decided to join them on Saturday for skating.

How pathetic was that?

She was way too old for that kind of teenage stuff—especially four days' worth of it.

Still, she couldn't control the sudden hitch in her respiration as she checked caller ID.

But it wasn't Keith.

Curbing her disappointment, she pressed the talk button. "Hi, Dad."

"Hi, sweetie. Did I catch you at a bad time? You sound out of breath."

"I'm fine. I was correcting papers."

"Hmm. I was hoping that nice young man might have dropped by for a visit."

"No. I haven't spoken to him since last weekend."

"Too bad. How was your week otherwise?"

"Good."

Liar, liar. All you did was mope around wishing Keith would call.

This had to stop.

"How about you? Did those charters you told us about last weekend work out well?"

"Perfect. Sunny weather, pleasant people, and the fish were

225

biting. Not to mention the extra cash I have in my pocket. What's not to like? So, about Keith . . ."

She rolled her eyes. Her father had a one-track mind when something piqued his interest.

"There's no reason you can't initiate an invitation, you know. I understand that's done all the time these days by women."

No way was she going to tell him she'd already tried that and been rebuffed.

"I'll give it some thought. Would you like to talk to your granddaughter?"

"You're evading the subject. I'll take that as a positive sign."

"Don't get your hopes up, Dad. Keith appeared in my life out of the blue. He could disappear just as fast."

"He might too, if you don't take some initiative."

"So do you want to talk to Haley?"

"Fine. I get the hint. Yes, of course I want to talk to Haley—especially if you don't have anything else to say."

"Not on that subject, anyway. Hold on while I get her."

Phone in hand, she stuck her head into the hall. The music booming from her daughter's refurbished bedroom was as loud as when they'd all been painting. Shaking her head, she walked toward the room and pushed open the half-shut door.

Haley was gyrating to the tune, reading a science book as she moved to the beat.

From the doorway, Claire flagged her down. Once she had her attention, she pointed to the phone and mouthed the word "Cap."

Instantly Haley shut off the music and bounded for the door.

"Here she is, Dad. Talk to you soon." Without waiting for a response, she handed the phone over and marched back to the kitchen. She wasn't going to waste one more minute tonight thinking about a certain handsome young executive. She would focus on correcting papers. Period.

Through sheer force of will, she succeeded—more or less. By the time Haley returned to the kitchen with the phone ten minutes later, she'd finished the papers and was preparing to review her lesson plan for tomorrow.

"Did you have a nice talk with Cap?" Claire lifted her glass of iced tea to her lips and pushed the spelling papers aside.

"Uh-huh." Instead of returning the portable to its cradle, however, Haley walked over to the table and held it out. "The phone rang as soon as I hung up. Keith wants to talk to you."

The iced tea went down the wrong way.

Gasping for breath, she began to cough.

"Are you okay, Mom?" Alarm flashing across her face, Haley touched her shoulder. "Should I hit you on the back?"

"No." Somehow she managed to choke out the word between hacks. Holding up a finger to communicate she needed a minute, she gestured to the phone, then pantomimed that her daughter should talk to Keith.

Keeping an anxious eye on her, Haley spoke into the receiver. "Hey, Keith, Mom's coughing, so she can't talk to you for a minute . . . Yeah, I think so . . . Uh-huh, but her face is red and her eyes are dripping."

Claire tuned out the conversation and rose to retrieve a paper towel. As she swiped at the tears running down her cheeks and blew her nose, the coughing subsided in increments until at last she could breathe again.

"Haley." The word came out ragged. She cleared her throat and tried again. "Tell him I'll be with him in a minute." Still raspy.

While her daughter complied, she shoved a glass under the faucet, filled it a quarter of the way, and took several small, careful sips.

With a last swipe of her nose, she reached for the phone.

"Are you okay?" Haley relinquished her grip.

"Yes. Go finish your homework."

Haley leaned close and whispered in her ear. "He's going to come skating with us on Saturday! I already asked."

Her heart began to bang against her rib cage, and she suddenly felt breathless again.

At least Keith would assume she was winded because of her coughing spell.

Moistening her lips, she tried for a casual tone. "Sorry about that. The iced tea went down the wrong way."

"Are you sure you're all right?" The concern in his taut voice was unmistakable.

"Yes. Fine." She sank back into her chair. "Haley said you're going to join us for skating."

"True—although I may live to regret it. I haven't been on a rink in almost twenty years. You're going to show me up big time, aren't you?"

"I'm not that good."

"That's not what Haley just told me. According to her, you're another Dorothy Hamill."

"Trust me, that's a huge exaggeration." She leaned back. "We could do something else if you'd rather, though."

"Or we could do two things. Like skate and eat. The eating will compensate for any negatives from the skating. Food has a way of putting a better light on almost anything. So what time should I pick you up and which rink have you designated for my public humiliation?"

She gave him the details while she used her paper towel to wipe up some splatters of iced tea on the table.

"Okay. I'll be at your door at one-fifteen on Saturday. How's everything else been going?"

"No complaints." Not anymore. Not since he'd called. "How about you? Are you making any progress with Maureen's project?"

"I've chased down my best lead and made the contact. Now

it's a waiting game. If this doesn't pan out . . . well, much as I hate to admit defeat, I'm not certain what else I can do."

"I think Maureen understood the long odds from the beginning, given that her PI couldn't turn up any information. I know she's grateful for the attempt, though. And she's benefited in . . . other ways."

"Yeah. It seems she and my boss have connected."

"So you know about that."

"I put two and two together. David's dropped a couple of hints, and he told me they had plans together last Sunday afternoon."

"They went to his grandson's birthday party."

"No kidding." A beat of silence ticked by. "Taking someone to a family event is significant."

"That's what I thought, though Maureen is downplaying it."

"I'm sure she's cautious, given her bad experience in the romance department."

"Aren't we all." No harm reminding him she was a slow mover—even if her heart seemed to be gearing up for a sprint rather than a marathon.

"Yeah. I get the caution thing. I've got some old stuff—not romance-related—I need to work through too."

Stuff he'd suggested he might share with her . . . but hadn't.

And until he did, until he trusted her enough to be as open about his past as she'd been about hers, she would keep her emotions in check.

"Slow and easy isn't a bad plan, given the circumstances." She kept her tone neutral. "In the meantime, I'm looking forward to Saturday."

"Me too. See you then."

When the line went dead, Claire lowered the phone to the table, grateful Keith had called after she'd spoken with her father. Otherwise it would have been tougher to sidestep his suggestion about issuing the man an invitation. This way, she could see how things went before she mentioned their date.

Date.

She frowned.

Was it a date, with Haley in tow?

Yeah, it was. Not a candlelight and music and flowers kind of date, but a date nonetheless.

And if it went well . . .

Her lips tipped up as she rose to rinse out her glass and straighten up the table.

Maybe down the road she just might find herself on that other kind of date.

17

. . . .

Keith slid his laptop into its case, reached for his briefcase, and stood.

"Are you leaving already?" Robin strolled in and dumped a stack of papers in his in-box.

"It's five o'clock."

"I know. I'm out of here too. It's Friday—date night for me and my hubby, remember? What's your excuse?"

"Do I need one?" He picked up the laptop.

"Normal people wouldn't. Workaholics like you . . . yes." She narrowed her eyes, then smirked. "So who is she?"

"I don't have a date."

Not tonight.

Tomorrow . . . that was a different story.

And Robin didn't need to know about that.

"Seriously?" Her face fell.

"Seriously. I've got to pick up some stuff at the hardware store to fix a leaky faucet."

"Since when did you become Mr. Handyman?" She propped

her hands on her hips. "I thought you paid people to do that kind of stuff at your condo."

"I do, but my mom's on a fixed income." That was true. But it was also a non sequitur—even if Robin would assume there was a connection.

In fact, the leaky faucet was in Claire's kitchen sink.

"Oh. Well, at least for once you won't be the last person out of here on a Friday. That's a—"

His phone began to ring, and he glanced at caller ID.

It was a Boston area code.

Pulse picking up, he set his computer case back on the desk. "I need to take this."

"The best laid plans, huh?" She rolled her eyes. "Don't stay too long."

"I won't. Would you shut the door on your way out?" He picked up the phone.

"Sure. Have a good weekend."

He waited until the door clicked before speaking. "Keith Watson."

"Mr. Watson, this is Father Ryan's sister, Delores Kohler. I understand you'd like to speak with me."

Yes!

"That's right. I have an acquaintance who was a close friend of your brother." He sat back down. "Let me tell you her story."

He gave her an abbreviated version of the background—including the efforts Maureen had made to locate her son—though he never mentioned the professor's name. If the woman asked for it, he'd have to call her back after clearing the breach of confidence with his unofficial client. There'd been no sense doing that in advance and raising Maureen's hopes. The woman might never have called.

"So your friend is hoping to connect with the son who was placed through the agency my brother recommended."

"Yes. The lady I spoke with at St. Columba said you used to volunteer at that agency. May I ask when that was?"

She recited the dates of her tenure, and he did the math.

Delores Kohler had been there when Maureen's baby was adopted.

Trying to tamp down the sudden surge in his pulse, he told her the boy's birth date. "Since your brother recommended the agency, I wondered if you and he might ever have discussed cases?"

"On occasion—but never names, or even very many details. Both of us respected the confidentiality of the information shared with us."

Not promising.

He tapped his pen against the desk. "May I ask what you did at the agency?"

"I helped adopting parents deal with logistics and paperwork. It was quite rewarding to see couples who yearned for a child finally have their wish fulfilled. I got to know many of them well, because the adoption process is long and involved. I exchanged Christmas cards with some of them for a few years afterward. There were a handful I kept in touch with far longer."

"Any from the year in question?"

"I'd have to check through the cards to refresh my memory. Twenty-one years is a long time, and those days are a bit fuzzy now. Do you have any other details about the birth that might help me determine whether any of the parents I've had contact with is a possible match?"

"Yes." He flipped open his briefcase, pulled out Maureen's medical file, and read her the name of the hospital, time of birth, and the baby's weight. "I also believe that both of the adopting parents were teachers."

"All right. I've jotted that down. Give me a day or two to look through my files. I'm not certain I can pinpoint dates, but I'm willing to make the effort. It sounds as if your friend has gone to a great deal of trouble."

"Yes, she has. I can't thank you enough for calling me back and for offering to help."

"Well, it's best not to get your hopes up. Many couples came through our doors, and I stayed in touch with only a small percentage. On the other hand, stranger things have happened. God works in mysterious ways, you know."

"Yes." All the unexpected happenings in his own life these past few weeks were proof of that.

"I'll be in touch, then. Good-bye."

As the woman severed the connection, Keith dropped the phone into its cradle and rocked back in his chair.

Despite the dubious odds, he had the strangest feeling he was on the verge of a big discovery. That Delores Kohler might be the key to solving Maureen's puzzle.

And if such a long shot ended up paying off in the professor's case, might something equally surprising come from the application for the Missouri Adoption Registry he'd pried out of his fingers and dropped in the mailbox on Tuesday?

If it did, though, would the surprise be good—or bad?

"You were holding out on me." Haley on her heels, Claire glided over to Keith, who'd just executed a perfect hockey stop near the edge of the rink.

"Yeah! You're almost as good as Mom!"

Keith grinned at them. "I guess skating is like riding a bicycle. Although I expect I'm going to have a very sizeable bruise on an unmentionable part of my anatomy after that eye-popping fall I took three minutes out. And I do mean eye-popping." He bent down to Haley's level. "Are my eyeballs still in their sockets?"

When she leaned in for a closer look, he crossed his eyes.

She giggled. "Yeah. They are."

"Whew. I wouldn't want to lose one out here on the rink. Otherwise we'd have to have a game of chase the eyeball."

Haley giggled again.

"I take it you played hockey." Claire moved out of the path of a twosome skating hand in hand.

"For a couple of years. But I can't do any of the fancy stuff figure skaters do."

"I bet you could."

"Nope. I rented a pair of figure skates once on a high school date after the girl convinced me it was easy. Ha! I kept getting the toe pick caught and falling flat on my face. I was the laughingstock of the rink. She never went out with me again."

"We'll go out with you again even if you fall a whole lot," Haley promised.

"That's a relief. Are you speaking for your mom too?" He glanced her direction.

"Yes, she is."

"Excellent. Then what do you say we give that a try?" He gestured to the cozy couple circling the rink.

Claire adjusted one of her gloves, giving the duo a quick perusal. "I was never into pairs skating."

"Me either, but I'm willing to give it a try. It might take a few circuits to get our rhythm in sync, but I have a feeling we can make it work."

She looked over at him. His mouth was smiling, but his eyes were serious.

He was talking about more than skating.

Her heart skipped a beat.

"Go ahead, Mom. I bet neither of you will fall."

"If one of us does, though, we'll both go down." She continued to watch Keith.

"Or we'll hold each other up." As the music switched to a waltz beat, Keith pulled off one glove and held out his bare hand.

He wanted to skate skin to skin.

When had this simple ice-skating excursion turned into *that* kind of date?

"Chicken." Keith said the word so softly only she could hear it. Under his teasing tone, however, was a subtle dare.

It was the sort of challenge designed to rankle . . . and goad her into accepting the gauntlet.

And it was working.

She could do this without letting herself get carried away. She'd just pretend she was holding hands with her dad. Imagining she was a little girl again letting him teach her how to skate would take any hint of romance out of the equation.

Lifting her chin, she put her hand in Keith's.

Instantly her plan disintegrated.

Because Keith's warm, firm, strong grip didn't feel anything like her dad's.

Nor did she feel like a little girl.

"I'll follow you guys, okay?" Haley moved away from the edge of the rink and waited.

"Ready?" Keith glided out a few inches, until their linked arms were stretched.

No.

But she wasn't backing down now.

Pushing off, she fell in beside him.

The first time around the rink was a struggle as they tried to match their pacing. Once, she stumbled. He grabbed her, and they both remained upright. Then he lost his balance, and despite her efforts to help, they both ended up in a heap on the ice.

Haley glided up beside them as they untangled themselves. "Are you guys okay?"

"I am." Keith reached over and brushed some frost off the sleeve of her jacket. "How about you?"

"I've had worse falls." Claire rubbed her elbow.

He rose and held out a hand, which she regarded warily. "Maybe I better get up on my own."

"Uh-uh. We're in this together."

Capitulating, she put her hand in his again. He braced and pulled her to her feet. "We're going to get this right. You'll see."

She wasn't as certain—but to her surprise, after a few more circuits, they managed to establish a gliding pattern that was comfortable for both of them.

Keith's eyes twinkled down at her. "You know what? I wasn't real keen on this skating idea, but I'm glad Haley suggested it."

She searched his face as she concentrated on matching him pace for pace. "Why?"

"What's not to like about holding a beautiful woman's hand?"

She tottered again, and his grip tightened.

He'd called her beautiful.

She refocused on the frozen expanse in front of her—but the slippery ice wasn't the only thing throwing her off balance today.

"Hey."

At his soft summons, she sent him a hesitant look.

"That wasn't an empty compliment. You *are* a beautiful woman, and I like spending time with you. I'm being honest, not manipulative."

Like Brett was.

He didn't say those words, but the message hung in the air between them.

"I believe you." And she did. "It's just that we don't know each other very well yet. I don't want this to get too . . . personal . . . until we do."

In silence, he guided her over to the railing. When he faced her, faint creases marred his forehead. "I'd buy that . . . except you told me some very personal stuff the other day."

Yes, she had. Because it had felt right—and she'd hoped he'd reciprocate.

But she didn't intend to share her rationale. If he ever decided to tell her his story, she wanted it to be by choice, not under duress.

"You caught me at a weak moment."

"Hey, Keith." Haley zipped over to them, her own hockey stop spraying them both with ice crystals.

"Haley!" Claire put up her hands to shield her face.

"Sorry." But Haley's unrepentant grin said otherwise. "Want to have a race?"

"I'm game." With one more look at her, Keith slipped his glove back on.

Claire did the same, stifling a pang of disappointment. No more hand-holding today, apparently. "Not me. I'll be the starter. Two laps. Get ready. Set. Go!"

The two of them took off, Haley's shorter legs working twice as hard as Keith's but giving him a run for his money. Despite his height advantage, her daughter had practice on her side. It was neck and neck, making the outcome hard to predict.

Kind of like the outcome of her relationship with Keith.

It was clear he liked her and that he had romance on his mind. So did she.

But she was older and wiser now. Less susceptible to charm and pretty words and a handsome face. Yes, Keith appeared to be a fine person. The more she learned about him, the less he reminded her of Brett. But she wasn't going to settle for a man who kept parts of his heart—and his past—off limits, no matter how nice he was.

This time around, she was going to hold out for the whole package.

And if Keith couldn't offer that, she wasn't going to let this go any further.

No matter how much she wanted to.

"That was great pizza, Keith." Haley buckled herself into the backseat of his car as he held the door for Claire.

"I'm glad you liked it. It's one of my favorite places. Are you in?" He pulled Claire's seat belt out for her.

She took it and clicked the buckle. "All set."

He closed her door, then circled the car. As he slid behind the wheel, his phone began to vibrate, and he pulled it off his belt to check caller ID—just in case. Not that there was much chance it was his boss. David's weekend calls had tapered off to almost nothing over the past few months.

When his mother's cell number showed up on the screen, he frowned.

"If you need to take that, it's not a problem." Claire tugged off the knit headband she'd worn for skating.

"I think I better. This is the second call from my mom in the past few minutes, and that's not like her." He pressed the talk button and put the phone to his ear. "Hi, Mom. What's up?"

"Oh, thank goodness." She expelled a loud breath. "I was afraid I might have to call 911."

His heart stuttered. "What's wrong?"

"It's the silliest thing, really. You know that flip lock I have on my basement door for extra security?"

"Yes." Of course he did. He'd installed it at her request, for whatever good it did. The thing was meant more for childproof-ing than deterring burglars who might break into a basement window and come up the stairs to the kitchen. But hey, if it made her feel safer . . .

"Well, I guess it must have been positioned just right—or I should say wrong—because the door banged shut behind me when I came down to do some laundry, and the lock flipped over. Now I'm stuck in the basement."

He unclenched his fingers from around the wheel. "How long have you been down there?"

"An hour or so. I've been jiggling the door, hoping I could shake it loose, but it hasn't budged."

"It wouldn't be much of a lock if you could."

"True. Thank the Lord I had my phone. That was a smart idea of yours, to carry my phone around with me at home. Listen . . . I hate to bother you, but can you run over and let me out? Or are you in the middle of something?"

Keith slid a glance toward Claire. "I'm, uh, a little tied up, but I'll be there as soon as I can. An hour, tops. Can you hold out that long?"

"I can—but I'm not so sure about my bladder. Just do the best you can. See you soon."

The line went dead.

Keith tapped a finger against the wheel, then removed the phone from his ear.

"Is everything okay?" Claire angled toward him.

"It's not a catastrophe." He slid the cell back onto his belt, not certain his mom would agree, given her lack of bathroom access. Too bad she'd shared that tidbit. Otherwise, he'd have had no qualms about taking Claire and Haley home first. Now he'd feel guilty if he made his mom wait unnecessarily. On the other hand, if he took the two of them with him, she'd get all kinds of ideas he didn't want to encourage.

"What's not a catastrophe?" Haley unbuckled her seat belt and bounced forward to rest her elbows on their seats.

Might as well come clean.

"My mom locked herself in the basement."

Claire leaned toward him, concern etching her features. "Is she okay?"

"Yeah. Embarrassed more than anything, I think."

"Where does she live?"

"South County. Not far from the mall."

"If you want to stop by and let her out before you take us home, that's fine. I don't have any plans for the rest of the evening."

"I don't, either," Haley chimed in.

"Yes, you do, young lady. Homework. We're not going to leave it until Sunday this week. But we have time for a quick side trip."

It would definitely be closer to swing by his mom's rather than backtrack. Besides, he wanted to see if he could fix that faucet at Claire's tonight.

Could he ask her and Haley to wait in the car while he ran in—or would that look suspicious . . . like he didn't want them to meet his mother?

Possibly the latter—and Claire was cautious enough already.

But prolonging his mother's ordeal wasn't an option, either.

"If you're sure you don't mind, I think it would be best if I stop by." He fitted his key in the ignition. "It won't take more than a minute."

"That's fine. Haley—buckle up again." Claire settled back in her seat too. "I take it your mom is alone?"

He put the car in gear and pulled into traffic. "Yeah. Dad died suddenly two years ago of a stroke. He was seventy-three, but he'd never had any health issues. It was a shock to both of us."

"I'm sorry. That kind of abrupt loss is especially hard. How's your mom doing?"

"She's hanging in. Some days are better than others."

"Do you have any brothers or sisters?"

At the query from the backseat, he flashed Haley a quick glance in the rearview mirror. Claire must not have shared any of the minimal background he'd offered. "No, it was just me. But I always thought it would be cool to have brothers or sisters."

"Me too," Haley said.

Claire shifted around. "You never told me that."

Her daughter shrugged. "I didn't figure it would do any good, since you're not married. How come your mom and dad didn't have more kids, Keith?"

"Haley . . . it's not polite to ask personal questions." Claire sent the little girl a warning look.

"It's okay." He switched lanes and picked up speed. "I was adopted, and my parents were older when they got me. So they didn't want to take on any more children." He checked out her reaction in the rearview mirror. No shock. Not even surprise.

"I have a friend at school who was adopted. Her name is Jennifer. She's really nice. I like her mom and dad too. Is your mom nice?"

"Very."

"Do we get to meet her?"

"It will be faster if we wait in the car, Haley."

Keith looked over at Claire. Was she offering him an out—or didn't she want to meet his mother?

Whatever her motivation, he should be grateful. That would keep things simpler.

For some weird reason, however, different words came out.

"You might as well come in and let me introduce you. Mom would enjoy meeting you."

Too much.

That was the problem.

But he'd deal with it later.

"Are you sure?" Claire scrutinized his face, as if she was aware of his conundrum.

"Yes." His response came out sounding more confident than he felt.

"For a minute, then—but we'll wait in the car until you have a chance to talk with her. After being locked in the basement, she might not be in the mood for company."

"Oh, I think she'll be very receptive to meeting you."

Chomping at the bit was more like it.

"Goody!" Haley grinned at him in the rearview mirror. "I like meeting new people."

"Miss Gregarious." Claire shook her head. "Not from my genes."

"I wouldn't say that. Your dad seems like the outgoing type."

"Oh, he is. He meets new people all the time, on his boat. And he's a lot of fun!" With that, Haley launched into a chorus of praises for her grandfather that lasted the rest of the drive.

Only when they pulled into the driveway of a small ranch-style house did she wrap things up and focus her attention outside the window.

"Is this where you grew up, Keith?"

"Yep." He set the brake. "Home sweet home. Sit tight while I release the prisoner and see what she has to say about visitors."

"Take your time." Claire rolled down her window. "It's a beautiful day."

Yeah, it had been.

So far.

And as he slid out of the car, he hoped it stayed that way.

18

. . . .

"Here he comes!" Haley leaned over the front seat again as Keith exited his mother's front door and started toward them. "That didn't take long. Do you think we're going to get to go in?"

Claire studied Keith. He looked . . . nervous. Considering how reluctant he'd been about sharing his background, that must mean his mother wanted to meet them—and he was worried about what she'd reveal.

"I think so."

Confirming her conclusion, he detoured around the driver's side and opened her door. "Command performance."

He gave her a smile . . . but she knew him well enough by now to pick up the strain around the edges.

Haley bounded out of the car, but Claire hesitated. Might as well offer him one final chance to bail. "If you'd rather not be delayed, we could skip."

"Too late. Mom's touching up her lipstick and combing her hair. You're stuck."

She didn't feel stuck . . . but it was pretty clear he did.

"Taking someone to a family event is significant."

His comment about David inviting Maureen to his grandson's birthday party replayed in her mind. This wasn't a family event, and it hadn't been planned, but Keith was a private person. Perhaps he'd never even mentioned her and Haley to his mother until today.

On the other hand, he could have taken them home first. Coming here had been his choice.

Stop analyzing every move, Claire. Go with the flow for once.

Taking that advice to heart, she got out of the car.

Keith shoved his hands in his pockets as they walked toward the house. "I, uh, haven't said anything to Mom about us." So her guess had been correct. "I don't typically talk about women I, uh, go out with. And I've never brought any of them here."

It wasn't difficult to follow his line of thought from there.

He was afraid his mother was going to jump to conclusions—and he didn't want her to.

Not the best omen for their future.

Claire's spirits took a dive.

"Don't worry. I won't say anything to suggest we're more than friends." Her words came out stiffer than she intended.

He noticed.

Touching her arm, he stopped and faced her. "That's not what I meant. It's just that my mom's been after me lately to think about settling down, and given your . . . caution . . . I don't want her to make assumptions that might not be true from your end."

Her wariness was the reason he was less-than-enthusiastic about this meeting? He wasn't confident in how interested *she* was?

Could that be on the level?

Maybe.

After all, she had been dragging her feet. It made sense that he wouldn't want his mom to get too enthusiastic about a woman who might not be in his life in a month or two—or even next week.

"Hey! Are you guys coming?" Haley sent them an impatient look from the front porch.

"We'll be right there." Claire waved at her, then turned back to Keith. "I understand your reasoning." She read the disappointment in his eyes—almost as if he'd hoped she'd reassure him about her interest. But she wasn't going to make promises she might not be able to keep, depending on how things went between them. "We'll play this low-key, okay?"

"Sure." He gestured toward the door. "Shall we?"

His mother was waiting in the foyer when they stepped inside, and before Keith could introduce them, Claire found her hand taken in a warm clasp.

"Welcome, my dear. It's so nice to meet you." She sent her son a reproving glance. "You didn't tell me she was such a beauty. Of course, my son doesn't tell me much of anything about his personal life."

"We've only known each other for a few weeks. It's nice to meet you too, Mrs. Watson."

"Please, call me Alice. And you must be Haley." Keith's mother turned to her daughter. "And you're just as pretty as your mother. What did the three of you do today?"

"We went ice-skating."

At Haley's response, Alice's eyebrows shot up. "Is that right? I can't recall the last time Keith was on the ice." She sent her son a speculative look.

"He did real good, except for one bad fall in the beginning and another when he was skating with my mom. But we had a lot of fun."

"Well." Alice gave them all a sunny smile. "I'm sure you did. Now I imagine you must be hungry after all that energy you expended skating. I have some sandwich fixings in the—"

"We already went out for pizza, Mom."

"But thank you," Claire tacked on.

"Oh." His mother's face fell for a moment, then brightened. "In that case, can I tempt you with dessert? I made some cheese-cake brownies for tomorrow's dinner, and there's way more than Keith and I can eat."

"That sounds great!"

At Haley's enthusiastic response, Claire stepped in. "Except I know a little girl who has a whole pile of homework waiting in her room."

Her daughter wrinkled her nose.

Based on Alice's crestfallen expression, Keith's mother was clearly as disappointed as Haley.

Claire bit her lip. Alice seemed so nice . . . warm and welcoming and radiating kindness. The kind of woman Claire would enjoy getting to know. Would it really hurt if they stayed long enough to eat one brownie?

As if reading her mind, Keith spoke for the first time—to her. "I wouldn't mind having a preview of my mom's efforts, if you can spare another ten minutes."

She searched his eyes. Odd. They didn't appear conflicted anymore. Either he'd resigned himself to the situation, or he didn't figure another ten minutes was going to make things any worse.

"The majority rules. Besides, I'd love to sample one of those brownies too."

"Yay!" That from her daughter.

"Wonderful!" Alice gestured toward the back of the house. "Let's go into the kitchen."

Claire followed the older woman. She looked to be around seventy, yet her step was spry and her face reflected a youthful enthusiasm. Kind of how she'd expected her own mother to be at this age, had Alzheimer's not dimmed the spark in her eyes and stripped her of everything except her physical body. Though that, too, had withered away in the end.

"Claire?" Keith placed a hand on her arm.

Swallowing past the lump in her throat, she refocused. The three of them were watching her, and warmth stole over her cheeks. "I'm sorry. I zoned out for a minute. I was thinking about my mother. You remind me of her in some ways, Alice."

"I take it she's gone home to God?"

"Yes. Alzheimer's."

"I'm so sorry, my dear." Keith's mother placed a hand on her other arm. "That's a terrible disease. But I hope you have good memories to sustain you, from happier times."

"Yes."

Odd. With Keith's hand on one arm and his mother's on the other, she suddenly felt far less alone than she had in a very long while.

"That's a blessing, then. Happy memories are a great comfort." Alice patted her hand.

"Mom asked if you'd like some coffee, Claire."

At Keith's gentle prompt, she nodded. No wonder they'd all been looking at her. "If it's not too much trouble."

"None at all. I always keep a pot going. One of my few vices." She winked. "Have a seat while I serve up the brownies."

Claire kept an eye on Keith as they ate their dessert and chatted, doing her best to direct the conversation to innocuous topics. Although he demolished his brownie in a few bites, his tension appeared to have dissipated. Even when his mother offered them a quick tour of the house—including his old room, which had been converted to a guest room albeit with plenty of Keith's life still on display—he didn't seem perturbed.

So it wasn't his history in this house that was off-limits, apparently.

Just the pre-adoption stuff.

"What's that for?" Haley pointed to an impressive trophy on a shelf in the corner of the guest room.

"Keith won that when he was on the debate team in high

school." Alice moved into the room and began to give them an inventory of the various trophies, awards, certificates, and ribbons displayed on the walls and shelves. It seemed he'd excelled in both sports and scholastics, and he even had a commendation for coaching a league-champion youth baseball team.

On top of all that, he was an Eagle Scout.

Impressive.

Only after Alice crossed to another bookcase did Keith grow uncomfortable. "Mom . . . they don't need to hear about all that stuff. It's old news. You ought to put some of it away."

"Why? I'm proud of it—and proud of you."

"Your son is quite accomplished." Claire aimed her comment at the woman, bending to examine a math commendation.

"Modest too."

Haley was still staring wide-eyed around the room. "Wow. This stuff is awesome. All I have is a science project award and a spelling certificate."

"You have plenty of time to earn more, kiddo. Life is just getting started for you." Keith drained his coffee mug. "Are you ladies ready to go home?"

"Yes. Because winning awards like these takes a lot of effort— an excellent incentive to focus on that homework waiting in your room." Claire sent her daughter a pointed look. "The reprieve is over."

Haley's shoulders drooped.

"I think that's our cue." With a wink at Haley, Keith led them back to the foyer.

Claire extended her hand to his mother at the front door. "Thank you so much for the wonderful dessert and tour."

Instead of taking her hand, Alice pulled her into a hug. "It was my pleasure. You come back any time." Then she turned to Haley and gave her a hug as well. "The same goes for you, young lady. This visit was too short."

"Yeah. But I loved your brownies. That cheesecake stuff on top was yummy."

"I'm partial to that myself—even if my waistline isn't."

"You're trim as ever, Mom." Keith leaned down and gave her a kiss on the forehead. "I'll see you tomorrow."

"The highlight of my week." She patted his cheek. "Reverend Patterson is preaching, though, and I'm staying for the social afterward, so don't come too early. In the meantime, I hope you enjoy the rest of your day—and I'm sure you will." She aimed a knowing look toward Claire.

Taking Haley's arm, Claire guided her daughter out the door, Keith on her heels.

Haley jabbered almost nonstop on the way home, asking questions Claire wouldn't have considered broaching—but she was just as interested in the answers as the little girl. And Keith didn't appear to mind the cross-examination.

"Do you go visit your Mom every Sunday?"

"Yes."

A dutiful son. Nice.

"Do you go to church first?"

He hesitated. "Sometimes."

Meaning he wasn't the most diligent Christian—but who was she to point fingers? At least he believed.

"Did you have a bunch of friends on your street when you were growing up?"

"Not a bunch—but I was close with a couple of them. I spent a lot of time studying, so I wasn't the most social kid."

He was selective in his companions and a bit of an introvert, preferring books to socializing. Not bad qualities, either.

By the time they pulled into her driveway, she'd also learned he missed his father a lot, didn't remember either set of grandparents, rarely took vacations but when he did enjoyed solo camping trips in the mountains, and jogged three miles every other morning.

Her daughter would make a fine police interrogator.

But the easy give-and-take evaporated as he pulled into her driveway and shut off the engine.

"Your mom is nice." Haley unhooked her seat belt.

"Yeah, she is. I had two great parents."

"Did you ever meet your real mom and dad?"

At the innocent question, he froze. Despite the distance separating them, Claire could feel his sudden tension.

"No."

Time to run some interference.

"Haley, would you grab our coats?"

"Okay."

As her daughter gathered up the outerwear piled on the backseat, she picked up the conversation before Haley had a chance to continue her previous line of questioning. "Would you like to come in for a few minutes?"

Brow furrowed, Keith flexed his fingers on the steering wheel. "Actually, I brought along a few tools. I thought I'd take a stab at fixing that leak in your kitchen faucet—if you'd like me to."

"Yeah, we would. That plop, plop, plop is driving us crazy, isn't it, Mom?" Coats bundled in her arms, Haley pushed her door open and clambered out.

Claire angled toward him and lowered her voice. "You don't need an excuse to stay. You're welcome to come in, no strings—or handyman jobs—attached. And I'll head off any other uncomfortable questions."

He gave her a smile that held no mirth. "I forgot how inquisitive kids can be."

"This particular kid is about to be relegated to her room with her schoolbooks." She checked her watch. "Well past the agreed-upon start time, thanks to your mother's kind offer of dessert."

"Mom enjoyed it."

"So did I. She's a very nice woman."

"Who's also very inquisitive." He sighed. "I'll get the third degree tomorrow . . . but I'll deal with it." He gestured toward the trunk. "Shall I get the tools? You're wasting a lot of water in there—an environmental no-no. Plus, leaks increase your water bill."

"When you put it that way . . . how can I refuse?"

"Give me a minute to gather up my equipment and I'll join you inside. Sit tight while I get your door."

"I've already got it." She lifted the handle and scooted out, then bent down to look back at him. "I'll settle Haley in with her homework while you get your stuff."

With that, she closed the door and joined her daughter on the porch.

"Is Keith staying?"

"Yes." She dug out her key and fitted it in the lock. "But you, young lady, are done partying for today. That grade on your last geography test wasn't acceptable. Go work on those maps."

"Oh, Mom."

"Don't 'oh, Mom,' me." She shouldered the door open and guided Haley inside. "As it is, you're only going to get in half an hour of studying before it's time for bed. It's already eight-thirty. You'll have to finish up tomorrow."

Her daughter didn't seem in the least upset about deferring the bulk of her homework to another day.

Haley dumped their jackets and gloves on the nearest chair. "What are you guys going to do after he fixes the faucet?"

"I expect he'll leave then."

"Maybe he'll stay and talk for a while again."

"Maybe. But you'll be in bed." She gave her a gentle push in the direction of her room.

With a theatrical sigh, Haley trudged down the hall.

As for whether Keith would linger . . . she wasn't hopeful. A discreet glance out the sidelight revealed he was still sitting behind the wheel. Perhaps second-guessing his decision to stay, despite her promise to divert unwanted questions?

She half expected him to put the car back in gear and drive away.

Because even if the adoption issue had been dodged tonight, the more they saw of each other, the higher the probability it would come up again. Keith had to know that as well as she did—and it was clear he found it disturbing.

The question was, why?

What was he so afraid to share?

He couldn't keep sitting in the car. Claire was waiting for him inside.

But after everything that had happened today, he needed a couple of minutes to develop a game plan.

Lifting his right hand, he examined it. It looked the same as it had this morning—but it sure didn't feel the same. It was still tingling from the warmth of her fingers clasped in his at the rink . . . a completely unplanned, spur-of-the-moment intimacy.

What had come over him, anyway? Hadn't he labored over the pros and cons of her invitation before accepting? Hadn't he decided to go, but play the whole thing cool—fun, friendly, laid-back? Hadn't he resolved not to push her past her boundaries, give her a chance to get comfortable with the notion of romance before initiating any touching?

Yes, yes, and yes.

But one look at her standing next to him on the ice, those blue eyes fixed on him as if no one else in the world existed, her lips soft and appealing, and he'd caved.

Yet he didn't regret his impetuousness—because from the instant their fingers intertwined, he'd felt complete. Like he'd been waiting all his life for this woman to appear and claim his hand . . . and perhaps his heart.

Keith raked his fingers through his hair. This was crazy. He was a methodical, balance-sheet kind of guy. He'd never been rash, never made decisions without thorough analysis. But this thing with Claire defied logic. He'd known her . . . what? A month? Yet he was thinking seriously about a future with her.

Very seriously.

Not that he'd rush into anything, of course, or make any kind of commitment. It was too soon for that. Still . . . he could begin laying the groundwork. *Should* begin laying the groundwork if he had intentions that might involve a ring down the road.

And therein lay the problem, as he'd recognized early on.

He had to tell her about his past, as she'd told him about hers. She needed to understand why he always worked so hard to prove himself. Why he found it difficult to trust. Why, even now—and despite his success in the business world—he was often afraid everything he'd worked for would disappear tomorrow.

And this day was probably as good as any to share his story.

A flutter of nerves took flight in his stomach. Too bad he'd eaten that brownie. But maybe by the time he fixed her faucet, his food—and his nerves—would settle down.

Yet forty-five minutes later, after wrestling the lime-encrusted faucet off the sink, replacing the washer, and getting everything back in working order, his stomach didn't feel any better.

Nor did his nerves.

"Mom says I have to go to bed, so I came in to say good night."

As Haley spoke over his shoulder, he dropped the flathead screwdriver back into his toolbox and turned. Despite his apprehension, her psychedelic-patterned hot pink and neon purple sleep shirt tickled him. No shortage of color in this little girl's life. "Did you get a lot done on your homework?"

She grimaced. "Some, but there's a ton more for tomorrow."

"The skating and brownies were worth it, though, right?"

Her face brightened. "Yeah. Well . . . I guess I'll see you around."

"I hope so." It all depended on how Claire felt after she heard his story.

"Mom said to tell you she'll be out in a minute."

"Okay." He closed his toolbox but fumbled the catch.

He checked out his fingers.

They were shaking.

"Can I tell you a secret?" At Haley's whispered question, he looked over at her.

"I guess so."

She crept closer. "I think Mom likes you a lot."

He tightened his fingers around the handle of the box. "Why do you think that?"

The little girl grinned. "'Cause she's in the bathroom putting on lipstick and combing her hair—again."

A confidence boost just when he needed one.

Thank you, God.

"That's nice to know. So how do you feel about your mom liking me?"

"It's awesome! She's a lot happier now. Sometimes she even sings while she's cooking dinner. And she smiles a lot more than she used to. I like you a lot too—so it's okay if you want to hang out with us even more."

"I'll keep that in mind. Now you better get to bed or your mom will come looking for you."

"Yeah. Good night."

As she disappeared around the corner and down the hall, he took a slow, steadying breath. He could only hope Haley was right, that her mother liked him as much as she thought.

Because Claire was a lovely, accomplished woman who could have her pick of men if she ever decided to get back into the dating game. Men who came from normal backgrounds and weren't carrying around a lot of ancient excess baggage. She didn't need to settle for a guy who was still lugging around a bunch of unresolved feelings.

But he prayed she would—for one very simple reason.

He was finding it harder and harder to think about a future that didn't include a certain blonde-haired schoolteacher and her charming daughter.

19

. . . .

Keith was stowing his tools when Claire returned to the kitchen, and he sent her a weary smile.

Of course the man was tired.

He'd taken a couple of hard falls while slipping and sliding around a skating rink for two hours, spent another forty-five minutes with his upper body wedged under her sink in a space designed for someone the size of a two-year-old, and given those impressive biceps a workout yanking at her stubborn faucet.

The man was either a really good sport or a glutton for punishment.

"Sorry about that." She gestured to the sink. "It was a much bigger job than I expected."

"Yeah. A common problem with home repairs. That's why I prefer to leave them to the experts. Unfortunately, despite my best efforts, you might have to replace that faucet sooner than you'd like."

She sighed. "The story of my life. Thanks for the temporary patch job."

"Not a problem." He propped a hip against the counter—and winced.

She sent him a sympathetic look. "A souvenir of our ice skating outing, I take it."

"A very colorful one—but I'll live." He shifted his weight, transferring the pressure to a less-bruised part of his anatomy. "Is Haley settled for the night?"

"Depends on how you define settled. She's in bed—but I suspect she's already got her latest Nancy Drew book propped under the covers and is reading by penlight. It's hard to fault a child for liking books, though."

"True."

Silence fell between them—caused by something less benign than mere fatigue, if her instincts were accurate.

Tension began to ping in her nerve endings.

Shoving her hands into her pockets, she swallowed. "Is everything okay?"

"Yes."

That was a lie.

Keith looked more stressed than tired now, the faint web of lines at the corners of his eyes signaling strain rather than weariness.

Panic nipped at her composure.

She was getting bad vibes.

Very bad vibes.

Balling her hands into fists, she tried for a nonchalant tone. "Would you like a drink?"

"Water would be great."

She busied herself with the task, retrieving a glass from the cabinet, filling it with ice, twisting the tap.

When she turned and handed it to him, he took a long swallow, then met her gaze. "Could we sit outside for a few minutes? I'd like to talk to you about something."

Her breath jammed in her lungs, and her stomach bottomed out.

He was going to tell her he didn't want to see her again.

God, why would you bring this man into my life, then snatch him away right when I was beginning to believe he might be destined to be part of my future?

The Almighty didn't answer her silent, torn-from-the-heart question—and why should he? This was her fault. She'd dumped too much on Keith about her past too soon. She'd been too prickly, too demanding, too—

"Claire?"

She blinked, willing the pressure behind her eyes to dissipate. "Sure. We can talk. Let me grab a sweater."

If he was going to break things off, there was no sense delaying the inevitable.

As she started for the coatrack by the back door, he snagged her arm.

"Hey."

She paused, forcing herself to look back.

"I'm not walking out, okay? I just want to tell you some stuff about my background."

It took a few seconds for her to shift gears. To realize that not only was he not leaving, he was laying the groundwork to move forward.

He was thinking long-term.

All at once, her legs felt as unsteady as they did on the rink after an extended absence from skating.

She groped for the back of a kitchen chair. Hung on. "Sorry. The last time I had a c-conversation like this, the guy left. Forever."

"That's not in my plans. The leaving part, that is."

Meaning he had hopes for forever?

A tiny light began to shine in a long-dark corner of her heart.

One Perfect Spring

"The only problem is, after you hear my story and realize what a flawed guy I am, you may be the one who wants to leave." His tone and expression were grim.

The man was seriously worried she might turn tail and run based on what he was going to share with her.

Her first instinct was to deny that. To tell him the mere fact he was willing to trust her with his secrets guaranteed she'd stick around.

But she held back. Her days of blind faith were over—in terms of men, at least.

"I don't think that's going to happen, Keith." She tried to be honest, to encourage without making any guarantees. "I like you very much, and I've been hoping you'd get to the point where you'd trust me with your history. I didn't feel secure about moving forward until you did. So your willingness to take that step means a lot."

"Let's hope you feel the same way after I'm finished." He gestured toward the front porch. "Do you want to sit out there?"

"I moved the chairs to a safe spot on the deck. You can smell the lilacs better back there."

After following her to the door, he reached over her shoulder to roll it back. "At least this is still holding up. I guess if I ever find myself looking for work, I could always become a handyman."

He sounded half serious.

"I thought your job at McMillan was secure." Under the dim glow of the dusk-to-dawn light, she led him in a crisscross path to the two folding chairs on the side of the deck, dodging decaying boards.

"Is anything?" He tested his chair, then gingerly sat.

She studied him. "That comment doesn't quite fit the image I have of you as a very confident, take-charge, I'm-in-control kind of guy."

His mouth curved, but there was no humor in his demeanor.

"Just goes to show how appearances can be deceiving, doesn't it?" A breeze whispered past, and he cocked his head, sniffing. "Is that scent the lilacs you were talking about?"

"Yes. The bush is bowed down under the weight of the flowers. My dad says my mother would have called this a lilac spring—a profusion of blooms after a long, cold winter."

"Nice analogy." He took a sip of his water. "Bitter weather giving rise to lush growth."

"I thought the same thing."

"Except harsh conditions can also stunt growth."

Their backs were to the light and the night was dark, leaving his face in shadows. But based on his resigned tone, it was obvious that's what he felt his background had done to him, despite all the evidence of his success.

From Maureen's house next door, quiet classical music drifted through the night, the melodic harmonies soothing. Calming.

A welcome antidote to the tension on this side of the hedge.

Thirty seconds ticked by. Forty-five. Sixty.

Just when she began to wonder if he'd changed his mind, he spoke.

"It's hard to start. I've never told this story to anyone."

Anyone?

Her heart missed a beat, and she had to fight a sudden urge to reach over and twine her fingers with his.

"I feel honored."

"I hope you still do at the end." He took a drink of water, his throat working as he swallowed. "My pre-adoption years weren't pretty—and the truth is, I'd prefer not to talk about them. But in the past few weeks, it's become clear to me that all the garbage I thought I'd thrown out is still polluting my life."

Garbage. Polluting.

Strong words.

"Sometimes it helps to talk through bad stuff. I felt better after I shared my past with you."

"You took a risk, though. What if I hadn't hung around?"

He had a point.

"Keith." Quashing her caution, she followed her heart and covered his hand with hers, praying for the right words. "Whatever happened to you as a child may have been traumatic, but at that age, you were a victim. How could I hold that against you?"

"It's the longer-term effects that concern me. The first three years of a child's life are a critical development period, and I didn't spend them in the best environment. They had a lasting effect on me."

"Do you actually have memories of that time?"

"No. But I remember the cloud of fear and anxiety that always seemed to hang over my head. And I have a vague recollection of the incidents that occurred the day I was taken from my birth mother."

"Taken, as in her parental rights were terminated by the court?"

"Yeah." Without relinquishing her hand, he set the half-empty glass of water on the deck beside him.

"What about your birth father?"

"She never identified him—and I don't know a whole lot about her, either. Just what the agency passed on to my adoptive parents. She'd had brushes with the law since she was a teenager, and ended up serving time for a drug-possession felony conviction after I was removed from her custody."

A rustling at the edge of the wooded common ground behind her house drew his attention, and he looked toward the back of the yard.

"Probably deer." She peered into the darkness, but they were difficult to spot at night.

"Very high-strung animals. Easy to spook. Hard to approach."
He turned to her. "That might describe me too."

"I don't think you're hard to approach." She squeezed his
fingers. "And if the rest is true, it sounds like you have a good
excuse. Based on what I remember from my child psych classes,
a lot of children who come from abusive backgrounds, whose
emotional needs aren't met, also turn out to be violent and dis-
ruptive and defiant. They tend to be impulsive and act based on
instinct instead of reason. None of that describes you."

"I don't have any recollection of being abused by my mother.
The people she associated with—different story. The last druggie she hung around with in particular."

"Do you remember specifics?"

"Mostly impressions of terror. He only hurt me once that I
recall—the last night I was with my mom. From what my adoptive parents learned, he was getting his kicks heating the tines of
a fork until they were superhot and burning patterns of parallel
lines on my back. I have the scars as a souvenir."

A shudder rippled through her, and she fought back a wave
of nausea.

"Hey . . . it's okay. There are only three or four, and they've
faded to almost nothing."

No, it wasn't okay. While scars might fade, the memory—and
psychological damage—didn't.

"Considering all you went through, I can't believe you turned
out so normal."

He gave a brief, mirthless laugh. "I wouldn't go that far. I
struggled with anxiety and guilt and shame for years. I still have
trouble trusting people—including myself. I've always had this
sense that the floor's about to drop out from under me."

"Did you ever get counseling?"

"Yeah. My parents did all the right things. But even with the
therapist, it was hard to talk about my past. And I had lots of

problems with self-image, as many adopted kids do. We tend to feel unwanted and unworthy no matter how much love our adoptive parents give us."

"Because your birth mothers didn't want you." She didn't need to dredge up more data from her child psych classes to understand that. It was common sense.

"Yes. It's hard to ever feel good enough, or worth loving, after your mother rejects you. All my life I've felt driven to prove myself, to show the world I have something to offer, that I'm worthy." His voice rasped, and he picked up the glass of water. The melting ice clinked as he took a long swallow. "As you might have guessed, I've done a bunch of research on the topic. A lot of the emotions I've experienced are normal. In my case, though, the feeling of unworthiness has always been worse."

"Why?"

Bowing his head, he drew a long, unsteady breath. "My birth mother tried to commit suicide. I was the only one with her at the time. It was like she couldn't take being around me for one more minute."

As his revelation reverberated through the darkness, the ache in Claire's heart deepened.

"What happened?"

His Adam's apple bobbed. "She rented a room at some flea-bag motel, took an overdose, and almost died while I sat in the room watching a video until I fell asleep. The maid found me the next morning, trying to wake her up. That's when I was taken away. Or so goes the story my adoptive parents got from the agency."

And here she'd thought she was the one bringing the heavy baggage to this relationship.

But she'd been an adult when her trauma occurred, and she'd brought much of it on herself by ignoring the reservations she had about Brett and letting herself be swept away on a sea of romantic fantasies. At least her early years had been loving and happy, giving her a solid self-image that eventually reemerged from the ashes of her adult ordeal.

Keith, on the other hand, hadn't had that nurturing foundation of love and stability, nor the all-important sense of safety and security, during his critical formative years. Given that kind of legacy, it was no wonder he still struggled.

To make matters worse, the baggage that came with a normal adoption had been compounded by his mother's attempted suicide—an act Keith viewed as the ultimate rejection. That might not be true, but Claire couldn't argue with the fact that her need to escape whatever mess she was in appeared to have been stronger than her love for her son.

She tried to think of some way to express how bad she felt for all he'd gone through. Came up blank.

Instead, she scooted her chair closer and kept it simple, willing him to read what was in her heart. "I'm so sorry."

"Me too. And I'm also more unsettled than I've been in years. I thought I'd dealt with my issues. Then I met Maureen . . . and you . . . and everything changed. My birth mother was no college professor, but hearing Maureen's story made me wonder about her background. What was her own upbringing like that she ended up taking drugs and having an illegitimate child? Why did she keep me for three years if she didn't want me? And why did she abandon me in the end?"

He set the glass back on the deck, covered their linked fingers with his free hand, and leaned close, his breath a warm whisper on her cheek.

"As for you . . . from the moment we met, I knew you were special. I also knew I had to deal with the lingering questions about my background before things could get serious. You deserve a man who has the courage to dig into his past and try to resolve the issues that have been plaguing him for thirty years."

"But what can you do?"

"I already did it—or took the first step. I signed up with the Missouri State Adoption registry. If my mother is still alive and happens to be looking for me, we'll connect."

She frowned. "Given her history, the odds might not be in your favor."

"I know. I have no illusions about her. There's a good chance she got back into drugs after she was released from prison. She might even be dead. But if she's not . . . who knows? According to my parents, other than the burns on my back, I was in decent condition when the state took me. One of my only memories from those early years is sitting at a table drinking milk and eating oatmeal. I have a feeling I remember it because it was a daily ritual, which would suggest my mother did try to take care of me . . . for a while, anyway." He exhaled and shook his head. "I have no idea what I'll discover, but I can't ignore the questions anymore."

"How will you feel if there's no response?"

He shrugged. "No worse than before, and possibly better. I'm hoping taking that proactive step will let me put the past to rest so it won't continue to be a shadow over my future. A future I'd like to think includes you—assuming you can handle all the skeletons in my closet."

"They can keep mine company."

Despite the dim light, she caught a sheen in his eyes. When he spoke, his voice was hoarse. "I'm no bargain, Claire."

"Neither am I."

"I may always work too hard to prove myself."

"Maybe not . . . once you realize you don't have to prove yourself to me. That I already recognize and admire your many fine qualities."

The breeze picked up, the cool air bringing with it another swirl of lilac-scented air. A chill rippled through her.

"Cold?" He rubbed her hand, cocooned between his.

"A little. We're barely past April, after all."

"I think we can fix that."

He rose, tugging her up with him as the romantic strains of Mozart's "Concerto for Flute and Harp" played softly on Maureen's side of the hedge.

He fingered a strand of her hair. "It's almost as if someone scored this scene, isn't it?"

"Sort of."

He touched her cheek, the contact of his fingers feather light against her skin. Her eyelids drifted closed, and she waited. Expecting more.

It didn't come.

When she looked up, she found him watching her, an unmistakable yearning in his eyes.

But he wasn't acting on it.

"What's wrong?" Her question came out in a whisper.

"Nothing. I'm just . . . I don't want to make a mistake. Rush you. Scare you off, like one of those deer." He gestured toward the common ground.

"I'm not scared."

To prove it, she put her arms around his neck, tipped her head back, and stepped close. Closer still, until his arms came around her.

The blatant invitation surprised her as much as it seemed to surprise him.

But he made a fast recovery. The next thing she knew, his lips were on hers in a kiss as gentle and sweet and stirring as the music drifting over the arborvitae and the scent of lilacs suspended in the air around them.

The rest of the world melted away.

Claire had no idea how long the kiss lasted—but it wasn't long enough.

When at last he broke contact, dipping back down for another brief touch of lips before straightening up, she was glad he kept his arms around her.

Because for the second time tonight, her legs felt as shaky as they did at the rink after a long absence.

"I think we just took a quantum leap forward." His voice didn't sound any steadier than she felt.

"Yeah." The single word was all she could manage.

"It's a little scary."

"Yeah."

"But I have no regrets."

"Me, neither." She finally managed to open her eyes. He was looking down at her, and the tenderness and warmth in his gaze turned her insides to mush.

He lifted his hands and framed her face with his palms, gently brushing his thumbs over her cheeks. "Just so you know, I don't make a habit of kissing women on the first date."

First date?

Yes, she supposed it was.

"It doesn't seem like a first date."

"To me, either. It's kind of odd, really. I feel as if I've known you for a long time."

"Same here."

But in truth, it had only been a few weeks—and moving too fast could lead to mistakes, despite the powerful bond growing between them.

She had to remember that.

"We need to be careful, though. I don't think either of us wants to risk making a mistake."

"I can't imagine this being a mistake." He traced the line of her jaw with one finger. "But I agree. Caution isn't a bad thing."

"Right." Even if it felt wrong. Even if she had to use every ounce of her willpower to keep from melting against him again.

The music from next door ended with a final flourish of harp and flute, and quiet descended.

"I think that's my cue to leave."

Yet for a long moment he didn't move.

At last, with a sigh and a final brush of his thumbs, he removed his hands and stepped back.

She missed his warmth at once.

He picked up his glass, and she followed as he crossed the deck. Once inside, she kept her distance, watching him from across the room. Otherwise, she might succumb to the tide of longing sweeping over her.

"Everything all right?" He scrutinized her as he hoisted his toolbox.

"Yes." *Liar, liar. Just tell the man the truth.* "No. You're very . . . tempting."

A spark ignited in his brown irises, sending a bolt of electricity surging toward her. "That goes both ways."

"Will I . . ." Her voice squeaked, and she cleared her throat. "Will I see you soon?"

"The sooner the better. I'll call you tomorrow after I get home from my mom's." He started toward the front door.

Twenty-four hours before she heard from him?

A lifetime.

Rolling her eyes, she followed him to the door. She needed to get a grip.

On the threshold, he turned and reached for her hand, tugging her close. "One more for the road?"

"Sold."

"That was easy."

"You're a good salesman who has an excellent product and obviously understands the value of sampling."

With a soft laugh, he cupped her neck with his free hand, leaned down, and gave her one more quick but satisfying kiss.

"My product has many line extensions." He opened the door and winked. "Tonight was the mild variety. Wait until you try the hot and spicy version."

Her pulse tripped into double time, and she had a sudden urge to fan herself.

"I see I've piqued your interest." He propped a shoulder against the door frame and grinned.

She gave him a small shove out the door. "Go home, Keith."

"I'm going. But I'll be back." With a jaunty salute, he strolled down the walk. At his car, he turned and gave one final wave.

She waved back—and stayed at the door as he backed down her driveway and drove away.

Only after his taillights disappeared did she close the door and wander back to the kitchen. She picked up his glass, swirling the ice that was quickly melting in the heat of the house.

Warmth could melt so many things.

Including hearts.

Who'd have guessed a simple skating outing would end up with a toe-tingling kiss—and the promise of more to come?

She emptied the glass. Ran her index finger around the rim. Brushed it over her lips.

A quiver rippled through her.

Keith might have a lot of issues, but the man sure knew how to kiss.

As for the insecurities and peccadillos that were the legacy of his traumatic past—he'd persevered and succeeded despite them. And now he was trying to put that past to rest and pave the way for a future with her, searching for answers to a lot of tough questions.

That kind of risky quest took guts. Based on the story he'd told her, the odds for any positive contact with his mother weren't great. Best case, he'd know more about the circumstances of those first three years. Worst case, his ego and self-esteem would take another beating.

So as she put the glass in the dishwasher, flipped off the lights, and climbed into bed, she prayed that any answers he might find would lead to closure rather than more angst.

But it would take a lot of prayer and God's mercy to make that happen.

And as she bunched the pillow from the empty side of her bed in her arms and stared at the dark ceiling, she hoped that in the event of a worst-case scenario, the love of his adoptive parents—and the new love growing between the two of them—would compensate for any more hurt that might be lurking in his future.

20

As Keith juggled the two cheesecake brownies from his mother in one hand and fitted the key in the door of his condo with the other, his cell began to vibrate.

Might it be Claire, so anxious to talk to him she couldn't wait for his promised call?

Grinning, he shook his head. Man, he had it bad.

And why not? After her sympathetic response to his story last night, he was feeling optimistic about the future—which his mom hadn't failed to notice. Despite his dodging and weaving as she peppered him with questions, she'd jumped to all kinds of conclusions.

He hadn't tried too hard to temper them, either.

Because they were accurate.

Carefully nudging the door open with his bruised hip, he stepped inside, put the brownies on the small table in his foyer, and pulled the phone off his belt.

It wasn't Claire's number—but the Boston area code was familiar.

Might more good news be in store?

He pushed the talk button and put the phone to his ear. "Keith Watson."

"Mr. Watson, this is Delores Kohler, Father Ryan's sister. Is this a convenient time to talk?"

"Yes."

"Well, despite the long odds, I think we have a match."

His pulse took an uptick, and he strode to the kitchen. "One of the couples you kept in touch with adopted a baby about the time my friend gave birth?"

"Yes. And he was born at the same hospital where your friend had her son, on the same day. Plus, both of the adoptive parents were teachers. I was able to find their telephone number from the address on their last card, and I spoke with the mother this afternoon. She also recalled the agency telling her the baby's birth mother was a highly educated woman, which wasn't the norm for our expecting clients."

It all fit.

Still, it was best not to get carried away, just in case this turned out to be a dead end.

"That sounds very promising—but I have no experience with things like this. Could two clients at the agency have adopted children born the same day at the same hospital?"

"I volunteered there for more than six years, and I never heard of that happening."

Yes!

They had a match.

He was sure of it.

"Does their son know he's adopted? And are they willing to talk with my friend to verify the link?" He stopped beside the counter and pulled a notepad and pen out of a drawer.

A few beats of silence ticked by.

"They told their son at a very young age that he was adopted. Apparently, he never expressed any interest in meeting his birth mother, though his parents offered to try and make the connection for him if he ever changed his mind."

Not so good.

Maureen wouldn't want to disrupt her son's life if he preferred not to meet her—but perhaps learning about him would be enough.

"I can assure you of my friend's discretion. She wouldn't impose herself on the family unless they were receptive. But I think it would give her great comfort to at least have a few details about his life, if the parents would be willing to talk with her."

"They are—but there's another piece to this story that I need to tell you before we take this any further."

As Delores began to speak, Keith groped for the stool at the small island in his kitchen. The painful pressure against his bruise hardly registered as the woman's words began to sink in.

This wasn't at all the outcome he'd expected. Nor did he have a clue how to deal with it.

But David might. And since his boss had started this whole thing—and become friends with Maureen along the way—who better to decide on next steps?

Maybe that was passing the buck . . . but the minute he hung up, he was handing off the latest development to David.

Because it was way out of his league.

"That was the finest lasagna I ever had." David set his napkin beside his plate and smiled at Maureen across her kitchen table.

"Then you've led a sheltered life culinarily speaking . . . if there is such a word."

"On the contrary. I've eaten in some of the finest Italian restaurants on The Hill. This ranks right up there with the best of them—and that's not an empty compliment."

A soft flush suffused her cheeks, adding to her beauty. Funny how the first thing he'd noticed the day they'd met was her stubby hair. Now he saw stunning eyes and model-like cheekbones and a smile as warm as a toasty fire on a cold winter night.

"In that case, thank you. I'm flattered to have my efforts favorably compared to the best Italian-food enclave this side of Italy. Would you like some coffee with dessert?"

"Dessert?" He groaned and patted his stomach. "I can see that spending time with you is going to cost me—in calories."

"You're in great shape. I don't think indulging your sweet tooth once in a while will hurt your boyish figure."

As she rose to clear the table, he captured her hand and winked. "I can think of far less fattening ways to indulge my craving for sweets."

She gave a soft laugh, her eyes twinkling. "I haven't been flirted with in years."

"And I'm pretty rusty at it."

She squeezed his fingers. "You don't sound rusty to me."

"I'm more than half serious, you know."

"I know. But let's not rush things, okay? I'm out of practice with this dating thing."

"I am too. As for being patient—one of the virtues of age is learning that good things are worth waiting for. On the flip side, however, another virtue is learning to know your mind and to go after what you want. But I'll be happy to bide my time . . . as long as my intentions are understood."

"Understood—and accepted."

"Excellent." He released her hand and rose. "I'll help clear the table."

"There isn't much to clear."

"Still, many hands and all that. This way, we can get to dessert—"

His cell began to vibrate, and he checked caller ID. Frowned.

"Something important?" Maureen picked up the empty bread basket.

"Could be. It's Keith, and he generally doesn't bother me on weekends for trivial things."

"Go ahead and take it. I'll get the coffee started."

Moving to the side of the room, he put the phone to his ear. "Hi, Keith."

"Hi. Sorry to bother you on a Sunday night, but I had some news I wanted to share. Do you have a few minutes?"

"Yes. I just finished having dinner at Maureen's house, and we haven't yet moved on to dessert. What's up?"

A few beats of silence ticked by.

"Keith? Are you there?"

"Yes. Look . . . it might be better if we talk later. I have some news about her son that I'd rather share in private."

"Positive or negative?"

"Some of both."

"Hold on a minute."

He glanced over at his hostess and muted the phone. "I'm going to step onto your patio for a minute, if that's okay."

"Sure. Chase away the deer if you see them eating my hostas."

"Will do."

But deer were the last thing on his mind.

Once on the patio, he closed the door behind him and faced the woods at the back of her property. "I'm outside. What do you have?"

As he listened to Keith recount his conversation with Delores Kohler from a few minutes ago, David suddenly lost his appetite for dessert.

"So based on everything she said, I think it's very likely we have a match. I'm sure if Maureen talks to these people, they'll be able to verify that." Keith paused. "I thought it might be better if this news came from you."

Yeah, it would.

But he didn't relish sharing it.

David pulled a pen out of his pocket and dug around for the small notebook he always carried. "Give me the names and phone number again."

As Keith complied, David sat at the patio table and jotted down the information. "Does Maureen know you made contact with the woman at the Catholic church?"

"No. I didn't see any reason to raise her hopes until I had some concrete information."

"All right. Thanks for your diligence with this. I'll share the news with her tonight."

"Is there anything else I can do?"

David gazed into the shadows at the rear of the property. "Pray."

And as he severed the connection and tried to psyche himself up for the conversation to come, he took a moment to follow his own advice.

Maureen set a cannoli on each place and poured their coffee, keeping one eye on David through the sliding glass patio door. His back was to her, but his call was over. The phone was resting beside him on the glass-topped table.

So why hadn't he come back in?

She waited another sixty seconds, then opened the door. "Dessert's on, if you're ready."

He stood slowly—with an almost palpable reluctance—and turned toward her.

At his grave expression, her heart faltered. "What is it? What's wrong?"

"Why don't we sit out here for a few minutes?"

Trying to tamp down her growing trepidation, she stepped through the door and closed it behind her, all thoughts of dessert fleeing.

She perched on the edge of the chair he pulled out for her, gripping the arms. Once he retook his seat, he pried one of her hands free and folded it in his.

But even his firm, steady grip didn't reassure her.

Something was very wrong.

For several long beats, David didn't speak. Nor did she ask any more questions.

Instead, she braced.

When at last he began, his tone was gentle. "Keith is fairly certain he's located the couple that adopted your son."

Again, her heart stumbled.

Her prayers had been answered!

Except . . . why didn't David look pleased?

"That's good news, isn't it?"

He took a long, slow breath. "There's no easy way to lead up to this, Maureen. I'll give you all the particulars—or as much as Keith was able to learn—in a moment, but I'm very sorry to tell you that the boy we think was your son was killed in the Middle East two months ago while serving with the Marines."

As the words hovered in the air between them, the rest of the world went silent.

The evening song of the birds stilled.

The faint hum of car engines from the main road a block away faded.

The tinkle of the wind chimes on the patio ceased.

The only sound she heard was a rushing in her head—and the keening wail of a silent "No!" echoing and reechoing in her brain.

She'd been in this terrible place once before, on that fateful day she'd called Hal's hotel in Venice and listened to the clerk tell her no one by that name had been registered. As she'd struggled to accept that the man she'd given her heart to had vanished without a trace, the bottom had fallen out of her world.

Now it was falling out again.

The son she'd never known was dead.

No! No! No! No! No!

"I'm so sorry, sweetheart."

The faint words came from a distance. From another realm.

She blocked them out, struggling to process the news.

It wouldn't compute.

Her son was dead?

Killed in a foreign land, at the peak of his youth?

God, how can this be?!

She sucked in a breath as pressure built behind her eyes, and a choked sob ripped past her throat.

Someone touched her face, pulled her close. Beneath her ear, a heart beat steady and sure.

But her son's heart had been stilled forever.

A tear trickled down her cheek even as numbness began to creep over her. She didn't try to stop it. The dulling effect of shock would allow her to gather information and sort through the facts without emotion clogging her brain. Later, when she was alone, she could fall apart. David didn't need to be dragged into the muddled mire of her anguish.

With a self-discipline she didn't know she possessed, she eased out of his arms. He refused to relinquish her hand, but that was okay. She needed something solid to cling to.

"Tell me what you learned." Her voice sounded hollow, disembodied.

She listened as he told her how Keith had tracked down Father Ryan's sister through the woman at St. Columba rectory. How the priest's sister had kept the cards and notes from couples she'd worked with during her volunteer days at the agency. How the timing of the adoption fit. How both adoptive parents had been teachers.

It was a match.

She knew that as surely as she knew God had led her to this moment for reasons known only to him.

"Tell me about my son." She looked down, focusing on their entwined fingers. Drawing as much strength as she could from this man, so new in her life but already so much a part of it.

"I don't have a lot of details, except that he was killed while on routine patrol with his unit."

"What was his name?" She choked out the question as her composure began to slip again.

"Paul Phillips."

"Paul." She whispered the name, savoring it on her tongue.

"The adoptive parents are more than happy to talk with you if you want to contact them." David slid a small piece of notepaper toward her across the table.

She read the names. Beth and Joseph Phillips. Under the names, David had written a phone number.

With her free hand, she picked up the sheet of paper—her only link to the son she'd never known. Would never know.

The pressure in her throat built again as she stared at the names. "David . . . I think I need some time alone to . . . absorb all this."

He stroked her face again, and she made herself look at him. Compassion had softened his features, and his eyes were filled with kindness and empathy.

"I don't mind staying if you want company."

She swallowed. "I appreciate that. But I'll have company. God and I have a lot to talk about it."

"Are you certain?"

"Yes, but thank you for offering to stay. That means a lot."

After studying her for a few seconds, he rose and brushed his lips over her forehead. "I'll let myself out. Will you call me later?"

"Yes. In an hour or two. Thank you for understanding."

"Always." After one more tender touch, he moved toward the house.

She didn't watch him leave, but she heard the sliding door open, then close, behind her.

For a long while she sat there, the paper cradled in her hands, letting the news—and its implications—sink in.

She'd missed her chance to meet her son . . . to explain . . . to apologize . . . by two months.

Why, God?

Why did you bring me this far, let me get this close, only to snatch away any hope of a reunion?

As she wrestled with that question, the sun set.

Darkness fell.

And still no answer came.

The breeze picked up, and she shivered in the evening chill. At last she rose and made her way back inside.

David had cleared the table of their uneaten dessert but left the coffeepot plugged in. She wandered over and poured herself a cup . . . but the brew was bitter on her tongue.

Or was that the taste of regret?

She dumped it down the sink.

A glance at the clock on the far wall told her she'd been outside for two hours. Hard to believe. Time had just . . . stopped. But she owed David a call.

He answered on the first ring, as if he'd had his phone in hand, waiting for her. "How are you doing?"

"I'm still in shock."

"That's understandable. I'm so sorry it ended like this."

"I have to believe God had his reasons." Though what they were, she couldn't fathom.

"Are you going to contact the Phillipses?"

She examined the paper clutched in her hand, soggy around

the edges now from the moisture in her fingers. "I think I'll sleep on it before I make that decision."

"I could spend the night on your couch if you don't want to be alone."

Her heart contracted with tenderness.

"My couch is meant for sitting, not sleeping. You'd have a crick in your neck for a week."

"I wouldn't mind."

No, he wouldn't.

The man was a gem.

"Thank you for offering, but I'll be fine. I'll call you tomorrow, okay?"

"Or tonight if you can't sleep."

"No sense both of us being awake."

"I'm not certain I'll sleep very well, anyway. I want you to promise you'll call if you need to hear a friendly voice—or just feel like talking."

"If it comes to that, I will. Otherwise, I'll call you tomorrow."

"I'll be thinking of you—and praying."

"I appreciate that. Good night."

Once the line went dead, she locked up and wandered back to her bedroom. It was too early to turn in, but maybe a long, hot soak in the tub would help her relax.

If only.

Still, a bath would use up a small portion of the dark, lonely hours she'd have to face until dawn signaled the start of a new day.

But even when the sun rose tomorrow, she had a feeling it would be a long while before light would manage to penetrate the darkness in her grieving soul.

21

Claire sank into a chair in the teachers' lounge, pulled her cell out of her tote bag, and started to tap in Keith's number.

Stopped.

Scowling, she set the phone in her lap and unwrapped the turkey sandwich she'd retrieved from the refrigerator.

There was no reason to bother Keith at work.

So what if he'd seemed distracted when he'd called last night? That didn't mean he was having second thoughts about sharing his past with her. Maybe his mother had asked a lot of questions about them yesterday during their weekly dinner and he was annoyed. Or some issue might have come up at work that had him worried, like those job-site problems in Springfield he'd referenced while they were skating. His preoccupation probably had nothing to do with their relationship.

Still, it would be nice to talk to him. Just to make sure.

She reached for the phone again.

Stopped.

"You might as well call whoever's got you twisted into a pretzel." Plastic container of salad in hand, the fourth-grade teacher dropped into the chair beside her. "You went through the same drill a couple of hours ago, on break."

Great.

Now other people were tuning in to her anxiety.

"It can wait." She took a bite of her sandwich.

"Yeah?" Ruth tore open a packet of dressing and drizzled it over her chicken Caesar. "Doesn't look like it. Must be a guy."

Warmth crept over her cheeks. "Don't jump to conclusions." She forced herself to take another bite of her sandwich, praying it didn't get stuck in her throat.

"What else could it be?" Ruth speared some lettuce, jabbed at a piece of chicken. "I've been there—too many times to count. That's why I've sworn off men. They're more trouble than they're worth."

In other words, she'd broken up with her latest beau. But her resolve wouldn't last long. The thirtysomething double-divorcee never went more than a month without a man in her life.

"I'm sure there are a few good ones out there."

Ruth sent her a skeptical glance. "You couldn't prove it by me. All of the guys I've been involved with started out looking like Porsches but ended up being clunkers with a capital *C*." She crunched a crouton. "I didn't think your opinion of men was all that high, either."

Not for the first time Claire wished she'd kept her opinions to herself when Ruth had probed about her past during her early days on the job. She hadn't said much . . . but the other woman had gotten the gist.

"I'm trying to keep an open mind."

"Since when?" Ruth tipped her head. Narrowed her eyes. "You *have* met a guy, haven't you?"

Claire choked down another bite of her sandwich and checked her watch. "I need to run a quick errand before lunch break ends." She stuffed the remainder of her sandwich in her tote bag, along with her phone, and stood. "See you later."

"I'll be around." Ruth sent her a smug smirk.

Once in the hall, Claire paused to take a deep breath.

This wasn't good.

She was letting Keith get under her skin. Fretting over how he felt about her, where she stood with him—the very things she'd vowed never to do again after the Brett fiasco—and it was stressing her out. Enough that other people were noticing.

But she'd also vowed that if she ever again met a man who interested her, she was going to be up-front with him rather than stew about her concerns.

So she *would* make that phone call. Ask him straight out what was going on, and settle this thing.

Striding down the hall, she exited the building and tucked herself into a quiet nook on the side. Her fingers weren't quite steady as she tapped in his number, but at least she was being proactive instead of passive.

He answered on the first ring.

"Claire? Is everything okay? Are you at school?"

He didn't sound distracted today. He sounded the way he usually did—warm, welcoming, glad to be talking with her. But she also heard a thread of concern, thanks to her out-of-the-blue, middle-of-the-day call.

She'd overreacted—big time.

"Yeah, I'm fine. Sorry to bother you at work."

"It's no bother. Hearing your voice is the bright spot in my day. I was going to call you after school, but you beat me to it. What's up?"

The muted shouts of children at play drifted her way from the back of the building.

Just be honest, Claire. You're too far in to back out now.

She held on tight to the handle of her shoulder tote. "I have a confession to make."

"Okay." His tone grew more serious.

"I've been kind of worried since you called last night. You seemed very distracted, and I wondered if you might be having regrets about confiding in me on Saturday."

She heard him expel a breath. "Trust me, my distraction had nothing to do with you."

Her pounding pulse slowed a hair. "That trust thing is . . . it's still hard for me."

"I know. Listen, I'm sorry about last night. I wish I was there right now to give you a hug."

The tension in her shoulders eased, and she leaned back against the side of the building. "Can I get a rain check?"

"Absolutely. In fact, this is two-for-one day. But I'm sorry to say you'll have to wait to redeem them. Those problems in Springfield I mentioned to you got worse. I'm heading there this afternoon to sort things out. I could be gone until Friday."

She wouldn't see him the whole week?

Bummer.

"Is that why you were distracted last night?"

"No. I didn't find out about the trip until this morning. Last night's preoccupation involved Haley's birthday project. I had some news. Have you spoken with Maureen today?"

"No. Did you find her son?"

He hesitated. "I think it might be better if you talk to her directly. I know you and she are friends, but David and I promised her total confidentiality."

"I understand. And I respect your commitment to that promise. I'll touch base with her later."

"I think that might be a good idea."

Why?

She bit back that question—and the others clamoring for answers. Keith was right. It was up to Maureen to decide what she wanted to share.

"I'll stop in at her place tonight. In the meantime, have a safe trip. Are you driving?" She watched a robin land in a nearby tree and poke a few twigs into a half-completed nest.

"Yes—but I plan to be back in time for dinner Friday. Are you free?"

"As a bird." The robin took off on another scavenging mission. "My usual Friday night consists of eating tuna casserole with Haley and watching an old movie."

"If you can part from your daughter for one night, I had more upscale fare in mind."

Her heart skipped a beat. "Are you asking me out on a real date?"

"Yeah. Interested?"

"Very. I'll just need to line someone up to watch Haley."

"My mom might volunteer, unless you have another preference."

He was willing to ask his mother to babysit . . . and let her grill his date's daughter?

That had to be a super positive sign.

The bell rang, signaling the end of recess, and Claire pushed off from the building. "Maureen's watched Haley on the few occasions I've needed a sitter for a school-related function—but my instincts tell me it might be better to have someone else do it this time."

"Trust your instincts. I'll run the idea by my mom and call you with details. Now I better let you go. I remember that bell from my youth—and the consequences for ignoring it."

"For students, not teachers. But I do need to get back to my classroom." She walked around the side of the building, ran up the steps, and pushed through the door. "I'm looking forward to Friday."

"Me too. Talk to you soon."

As she ended the call and tucked the phone back in her purse, she spotted Ruth approaching down the hall. "Friday, huh? That open-mind thing must be working for you." With a wink, the other teacher continued on her way.

This time, though, the woman's comment didn't fluster her in the least.

Because it was true—and to sweeten the deal, she had a double-hug rain check waiting to be cashed.

Maureen slipped her rarely used Do Not Disturb sign on the knob, closed her office door, and returned to her desk.

The hour she'd chosen had arrived.

At six o'clock in Boston, most people would be at home, eating or preparing dinner.

Including Beth and Joseph Phillips.

After a restless night, much prayer, and two encouraging phone conversations with David, she was ready to talk to the only parents her son had ever known.

And having that conversation in the familiar, predictable, orderly professional setting where she felt most in control would help her get through it in one piece.

She hoped.

Heart pounding, she picked up the slip of paper David had left with her and tapped in the number.

Three rings in, just when she began to think the phone would roll to voice mail, a woman answered.

"Mrs. Phillips?"

"Yes."

Her mouth went dry, and her fingers tightened on the receiver. "This is Maureen Chandler. I believe Delores Kohler spoke with you about me last weekend, though not by name. I've been trying to locate the son I gave up for adoption twenty-one years ago, and from all indications it appears you and your husband were the adoptive parents. She said you were receptive to a call from me."

"Oh my. Yes. Yes, of course. Let me just . . . I'm going to sit down here at the table." The scraping of a chair sounded in the background before the woman spoke again. "I was so surprised to get that call from Delores after all these years. But . . ." The woman's voice broke. "Did she pass on our sad news?"

"Yes." Maureen swallowed past the lump in her throat. "I'm so sorry for your loss."

"Thank you. Paul was our only child. It was . . . there are no words. He had such a promising future. We tried to convince him to finish college and save the military for after graduation, but he said college would be there when he came home and he wanted to serve his country now, when the need was great." Her words choked, and a sniffle came over the line. "Joe and I tried to instill patriotism in him, but I think we did too good a job."

Maureen agreed. If he hadn't joined the Marines, she might have had a chance to meet him. But she kept that selfish thought to herself.

"It sounds like he was a remarkable young man."

"Yes, he was." The woman sniffled again. Cleared her throat. "From what Delores said, I don't think there's much doubt you're Paul's birth mother, but I do have one other piece of information that might help verify that. When we were at the agency shortly before Paul's birth, I caught a glimpse of the name of a doctor in our case file. I don't think I was supposed to see it, so I didn't say a word. But I looked him up later and discovered he was an obstetrician. Was Walt Ziegler, by chance, your doctor?"

Maureen closed her eyes as the name conjured up the image of a face that had receded into the recesses of her memory. "Yes."

"Then I think we have a match. May I ask where you live?"

"St. Louis."

"Oh. Not close." Disappointment scored the woman's words.

"I thought if you were nearby, you might like to visit. Even though we don't know each other, we share a very dear connection. Meeting you would be like another link to Paul."

Maureen pulled her calendar toward her and gave it a quick scan. If she couldn't meet her son, at least she could meet his adoptive parents, see where he'd lived, hear stories about him. It was better than nothing—and a gracious gesture on the part of Beth Phillips.

"If you're sincere about that invitation, Mrs. Phillips, I'd be willing to make a trip to Boston."

"Of course I'm sincere. And it's Beth. When would you like to come?"

"Would this weekend be too soon? I could fly up Saturday morning and visit with you in the afternoon."

"We don't have a thing planned for this weekend. Our life has been very quiet since . . . since we lost Paul." Once more, her voice broke.

"Let me see if I can make some arrangements on such short notice and I'll call you back."

"You're welcome to stay here that night, if you like. We have a guest room."

Pressure built behind her eyes at the unexpected kindness. "Thank you. But this could be a very emotional meeting. We both may need some space afterward."

"I suppose that's true. But you'll stay for dinner, won't you?"

"Yes. Thank you."

"In the meantime, would you like me to email you a picture of Paul?"

A photo of her son.

Her lungs stalled.

"That would be wonderful." Her reply came out shaky.

"I'll do it the moment we hang up, if you'll give me your email address."

Maureen recited it, then rang off with a promise to call as soon as her travel arrangements were set.

For a full ten minutes she remained motionless behind her desk, waiting for the familiar ping from her computer that would signal the arrival of an email.

When it finally came, her heart stuttered.

In a few seconds, with just a few clicks, she'd be face-to-face with her son.

Slowly she swiveled in her chair. Opened her email.

A note from Beth was there, along with the jpeg attachment. She read the woman's words first.

This is a shot of Paul taken in full-dress uniform six months ago. He was a corporal with the 1st Battalion. I have many other photos I'll share with you when we meet. Albums full. I hope taking a pictorial tour of his life, and knowing he lived it fully and well, will give you some comfort and closure. We will be forever grateful you shared your son with us. His presence in our lives for twenty-one wonderful years was a gift beyond measure. And though he is gone, his memory will live in our hearts until we meet him again in God's presence.

Fighting back tears, Maureen moved the mouse to the attached jpeg and downloaded it.

A photo filled her screen—and she stopped breathing.

Because now no doubt remained.

The young man staring back at her had Hal's slightly crooked mouth and her big green eyes.

This was her son.

No DNA test could prove it more conclusively.

A tremor coursed through her as she leaned close to examine the handsome young man in his black-brimmed white cap, dark blue jacket with red trim and brass buttons, and white belt with gold buckle. Ribbons and insignias were lined up in military precision above the left pocket.

But it was the face she scrutinized. Strong and confident and proud, with a firm jaw and eyes that held a hint of daring and mischief, this was a man who seemed happy and content and comfortable with his place in the world. A man who'd been raised well and loved much.

Beth and Joseph Phillips had done a good job with her son.

She lifted her finger and traced his features on the screen. This young man could have been part of her world if fear of condemnation—and worries about job security—hadn't colored her decision.

Yet from all indications, he'd led a happy, full life with two parents who'd given him a loving and stable home. Perhaps a better one than she could have provided. And along the way, he'd enriched their lives too. Good had come from her decision in spite of the heartache.

But what might have been if she'd made a different choice?

Straightening her shoulders, she ruthlessly cut off that line of thought. It was useless to second-guess lost opportunities.

Yet a new opportunity had been dropped into her lap, thanks to Beth Phillips's gracious offer.

And she didn't intend to pass this one up.

So with her son's photo on one side of her screen, she opened her browser, typed in the name of her favorite airline, and made reservations for a weekend trip to Boston.

"Done." Claire swiped off the suds clinging to the sides of the stainless steel sink, hung the dishcloth on the rack under the counter, and faced her daughter. "Now I'm going to run over to Dr. Chandler's and return that plate from the cookies she brought us last week."

"Can I go? Maybe she baked some more." Haley stowed the last pot from dinner.

"Not tonight. You have an English paper to write. If you get behind this early in the week, you'll be buried by Friday—and I don't think you want to spend your whole weekend doing homework, do you?"

"No." She sighed. "But could you bring me back some cookies if she has any new ones?"

"If she offers. Remember . . . don't open the door for anyone while I'm gone."

"Yeah, yeah. I know."

After grabbing a sweater, Claire tucked her keys in her pocket and headed for the front door. Maureen hadn't called, so it was possible she didn't want to share the news Keith had alluded to this afternoon. But he seemed to think she might welcome some company, and he had better instincts than most men about such things. If Maureen wasn't in the mood for a visitor . . . well, it was a short trip home.

She double-checked her neighbor's driveway as she crossed the lawn to her front door, but there was no sign of David's car tonight.

No need to worry about interrupting anything.

Juggling the empty plate in one hand, Claire pressed the bell.

Fifteen seconds ticked by. Twenty. Thirty.

Claire's pulse picked up. She'd seen Maureen walk down to get her mail from the box on the street earlier. Why wasn't she answering? Had she gone out again? Had David picked her up? Was she ill or . . . ?

All at once, the lock was turned and Maureen opened the door.

Claire stopped breathing.

Her neighbor was as pale as she'd been during her cancer treatments.

What in the world . . . ?

Maureen gave her a tired smile. "I look that bad, huh?"

"No. I mean, you seem . . . It's just that . . . Is everything all right?"

"It's been an eventful day. I was about to call you." She looked past her. "Is Haley with you?"

"No. I, uh, ran over to return your plate." She held out her flimsy excuse for a visit.

"Tell Haley I'll fill it again next week." Maureen took it from her. "After I get back from Boston."

The town where she'd given birth.

Maureen answered before Claire could formulate the question.

"Keith found the people who adopted my son." Her neighbor stepped aside and motioned her in. "If you have a minute, I'll fill you in."

She entered the house, trying to make the pieces fit. There was no elation on Maureen's face. None of the joy she'd expected to see if Keith's search was successful.

"I'm getting the feeling that isn't necessarily good news." She sat on the edge of the couch while Maureen took a seat beside her. "Doesn't he . . . doesn't your son want to meet you?" What else could dampen her enthusiasm?

But as she listened to her neighbor explain what Keith had discovered and her conversation with Paul's adoptive mother, her stomach kinked.

"Oh, Maureen." She reached for the older woman's hand. "I'm so sorry."

"I am too. Though your first guess may have been correct, if he'd been living. I understand he never expressed any interest in meeting me. That he was perfectly content with his adoptive parents. And I'm glad of that, glad he had a happy life. So we might never have become acquainted in any case. I'm just grateful for the opportunity to visit the Phillipses and learn more about him."

Claire studied her. "You seem . . . at peace with this."

"I am, now that I've recovered from the initial shock."

"But aren't you even a little angry or . . . or resentful about the timing? After all these years, that two months could make such a difference . . ." Her voice trailed off.

"I was upset at first—and I'm still sad. But I've spent a lot of hours in prayer since David told me the news last night, and I've given this to God. I may not understand why the situation unfolded the way it did, but he does. I have to trust he has plans for my welfare, not my woe."

"Jeremiah."

Maureen raised an eyebrow. "For someone who claims her faith isn't as strong as it once was, I'm impressed you know that reference."

"I read the Bible. And I'm making an effort to bolster my relationship with God—including regular church attendance."

"You won't regret it. Time spent with the Lord's Word and in worship is never wasted. It gives you a wellspring of faith and hope to draw from when bad things happen or situations arise that can't be explained in human terms. Maybe my quest didn't turn out the way I'd hoped . . . but it did turn out the way God intended. And I did accomplish my main goal. I found my son. It's just that our meeting will have to wait until the next life."

Claire blinked to clear the mist from her vision and looked down at their clasped hands. "I wish I had your strong faith— and your trust. I worry too much about things I should give to God."

"You're talking about Keith, aren't you?"

So Maureen had realized things were heating up between her and David's assistant.

"Yes—but also myself. I'm so afraid of making another mistake."

"Fear can be a terrible cross. One that keeps us from moving forward and taking advantage of the opportunities God sends our way. But caution and prudence are virtues too. Finding the right mix is the challenge."

"I know. I'm struggling with it."

Maureen squeezed her hand. "Aren't we all—especially with the men in our lives."

"So is it official now? David is the man in your life?"

"That would be fair to say, I think." The phone trilled in the kitchen, and Maureen gestured toward it. "We've talked three times already today, and I'd be willing to bet that's him again, offering to come over and keep me company."

Claire gently tugged her hand free. "Then by all means, answer it. I don't want to stand in the way of romance."

"I'll call him back in a few minutes. This conversation is important too—and he'll understand. That's how you know when you have a good guy, by the way. He puts you before himself."

Kind of like Keith had done with her. By giving her the space she needed. By doing odd jobs around her house when he preferred to leave maintenance chores to professionals. And most of all, by embarking on his own painful quest to clear the way for a future with her that was unencumbered by his past.

"I think you're right." She rose. "But I do have to go. I don't like leaving Haley alone for too long, and you have things to do if you're planning a trip to Boston."

"I always have time for you, Claire." Maureen stood too. "You've been such a blessing in my life this past year—fixing meals, running errands, picking up prescriptions, doing a hundred other things that needed doing despite your own busy schedule. I don't see how I would have made it through the surgery and treatments if you hadn't moved next door. I may never get to meet my son in this life, but you're the daughter I never had."

Tears pricked Claire's eyes. "The blessing goes both ways."

"Thank you, my dear." Maureen gave her a hug, then walked her to the door. "Don't forget to tell Haley to expect those cookies."

"I won't. And call if you need anything this week—or if you want to talk."

"I'll do that. God bless."

As the door closed behind her, Claire stepped off the porch and wandered back across the lawn.

Strange.

She'd come over to console her neighbor, and instead she'd been consoled.

God *had* blessed her—in ways she was just beginning to notice.

The scent of lilacs wafted past, and she inhaled the sweet fragrance that epitomized spring . . . and new beginnings.

Maybe her long, dark winter of mourning and weeping was over at last and this was her time to laugh and dance and love. To do as Maureen had counseled and believe God had a plan for her. That he'd led her to this place for a reason.

Maybe it was time to let new life burst forth and put her hope—and trust—in him.

22

....

"Robin, would you mind copying these two reports for me? I need to run in and see David." Keith checked his watch as he paused beside her desk and handed them to her. This quick side trip to the office on his way home from Springfield had been a lot less quick than he'd planned.

"No problem on the copies—but you missed David. He left about fifteen minutes ago."

"For the day?"

"Yeah. I think he had a hot date."

That made two of them—and he didn't intend to be late for his.

"Would you still mind running the copies? That way I can return the two calls that came in while I was on the phone with the foreman at the St. Charles site."

"Sure." She stood, weighing the reports in her hand. "But what's your hurry? It's only quarter to five. You usually stay late on Friday."

"Not tonight. I had a full week and a long drive."

"That never stopped you before."

"Just make the copies, okay?"

"You don't have to get huffy about it." She propped a hand on her hip and looked him up and down. "You wouldn't by any chance have a hot date too, would you?"

No sense evading the question. She'd find out soon enough if his relationship with Claire continued to escalate.

Make that *when*, if he had anything to say about it.

"Maybe."

"Hallelujah!" She grinned at him. "It's about time. Go ahead, finish your calls. I'll take care of this."

"Thanks." He strode back to his office. The sooner he was out of here, the sooner he could go home and prepare for the evening he'd been anticipating all week.

Him and Claire. Alone. At a romantic restaurant.

Now *that* was a Friday night.

He was still smiling when Robin deposited the reports on his desk several minutes later.

"All I can say is, she must be something. I don't recall ever seeing you this . . . I don't know. Animated? Eager? Happy?"

He clipped the note he'd written to the reports. "Could you put these in David's in-box. I'm out of here."

"You're leaving *early*? Wow. This must be serious."

Ignoring that comment too, he picked up his computer case and circled the desk. "Good night. Enjoy your weekend."

"Oh, I will. But not as much as you, I suspect."

Her chuckle followed him down the hall.

But he didn't care. In an hour and a half, after a shower and change of clothes, he'd be picking up Claire.

Nothing could dim his spirits at this point.

Yet twenty minutes later, after he pulled into his garage and retrieved his mail, the letter on top of the stack did just that.

It was from the Missouri Department of Social Services.

Home of the adoption registry.

He stared at the return address as his pulse began to beat a staccato rhythm.

How could this be? It was supposed to take three months for a response, and he'd sent in his form less than two weeks ago.

Did this mean there'd been no match, so it had been easy to respond quickly?

Or was the contact information for his birth mother inside?

He weighed the slim envelope in his hand as he entered the condo. It didn't feel as if it contained more than a single sheet of paper.

He had no idea what that meant—nor did he especially want to know tonight. Either way, it would ruin his evening.

Talk about crummy timing.

Letter in one hand, travel bag in the other, he continued toward his room. All week he'd been looking forward to a few pleasant, relaxed hours in Claire's company. They'd laugh, they'd talk, they'd sample some great food. It was supposed to be a real date, minus all the baggage that had plagued their relationship to date.

Unfortunately, it wasn't getting off to a great start—and opening the letter wouldn't improve things.

On the other hand, could he tuck it away and forget about it for the evening?

Doubtful . . . but worth a try.

An hour later, however—less than thirty seconds after he and Claire had been seated at an intimate corner table in the French bistro he'd chosen—she foiled his valiant attempt to banish thoughts of the letter.

"You might as well tell me."

"What?" Was it possible she'd sensed the presence of the unopened envelope burning a hole in his coat pocket?

"If you were any more on edge, you could do one of those fancy figure-skating moves you claim are beyond you." She leaned closer and touched his hand. "If you want me to butt out, say so. Otherwise, why don't you tell me what's bothering you?"

He squinted at her. "How come you know me so well already?"

She draped her napkin across her lap. "I think we're simpatico. That's not a bad thing in a relationship—unless the other person has secrets he or she wants to hide."

"I'm through hiding things . . . from you, anyway. It's just that there's been an unexpected development."

Slowly he withdrew the envelope and laid it on the table.

She leaned closer to read the return address, then sent him a confused look. "Is this from the adoption registry?"

"I assume so."

"I thought it was supposed to take three months to get a response?"

"That's what the website said. I guess they had a slow couple of weeks."

She caught her lower lip between her teeth. "You're not ready for this, are you?"

"No. But I'm not sure I ever will be."

"Do you want to open it now?"

Did he?

He picked up the slim envelope again. Weighed it in his hand.

The waiter delivered a basket of bread and the menus, then filled their water glasses. "Welcome to Café Provence. May I start you off with a beverage?"

They gave their orders, and as the man walked away, Keith laid the envelope beside his fork. "Let's decide on dinner first. Then I'll open it."

She picked up her menu and gave it a quick scan, her eyes widening. "Wow! One entrée is more than I spend on a full week of dinners for Haley and me." The instant the words left her mouth, she gave him a chagrined look. "Whoops. That wasn't very polite. Let me try again. I'm flattered you brought me to such a high-end place."

"Don't look at the prices, okay? I want to give you a memorable evening, and this meal won't break the bank. I've saved my pennies for the past nine years."

"Yeah?" She squinted at him. "You wear expensive clothes, and that car wasn't a bargain basement item."

"I'm expected to dress like an executive assistant on the job, but you know jeans are more my style off duty. As for the car— guilty as charged." He gave her an unapologetic grin. "I always wanted a sporty little number, and the salesman saw me coming a mile away. But my point is . . . enjoy your meal. I won't miss the money."

She shifted in her seat as she skimmed the menu again. "It's kind of hard to get out of the frugal mind-set after all this time, even when it's someone else's money."

He studied her knitted brow, hating that she always had to watch every penny. Someday, if things went the way he hoped, she wouldn't have to.

In the meantime, she was right about them being simpatico— because it didn't take him long to figure out what was going on in her mind. She was doing mental math, adding up the prices and thinking of all the stuff she could fix around her house for the cost of this meal.

Too bad he hadn't given her reaction more thought beforehand and chosen a less upscale place, one that didn't come across as in-your-face, as a way to brag about how successful he'd been and—

"Hey." She touched his hand, her eyes contrite. "I'm sorry. I didn't mean to throw a damper on the evening. Can we start over?"

"It's not too late to go somewhere else if you'd rather."

"No." She gave her head a firm shake. "I haven't been to a

restaurant like this in years, and I'm going to enjoy every minute of my meal. In fact, I was going to order the least expensive thing on the menu, but we have chicken so often I sometimes think I'm going to start cackling. So I plan to indulge and order my very favorite main dish. Lamb chops."

The tension in his shoulders eased, and his lips flexed. "That's the other extreme."

"Will we have to wash dishes if I order them?"

"Not quite."

"Then I'm splurging." She set her menu aside and gave him a teasing look. "Bet you'll think twice about bringing me to a place like this again."

"Not on your life. You have a standing invitation to any restaurant in town any night of the week."

Before she could respond, the waiter returned and they placed their orders.

Once he left, the lightheartedness evaporated as Keith picked up the envelope again. "I feel as if there should be a drumroll."

"Does my pounding heart count?" Claire folded her hands into a knot on the table.

"Added to mine, I think it does." He took a deep breath. "Here goes nothing."

Slipping an unsteady finger under the flap, he ripped the envelope open, extracted the single sheet of paper, and gave it a fast scan.

His pulse began to race.

"According to this, my . . ." His voice rasped, and he tried again. "My mother's name is Laura Matthews."

"She was in the registry." Claire's hushed comment was equal parts shock and wonder.

"Yeah."

"Does it say how long she's been in it?"

He did another read through. "No."

"Where does she live?"

"Kansas City."

"Not that far."

"No." He refolded the paper, slipped it back in the envelope, and returned it to his pocket.

"This must feel surreal to you after all these years."

"That's putting it mildly." He picked up his water and took a sip, gripping the glass with both hands to keep the liquid from sloshing out.

"What happens now?"

"Signing up for the registry is an acknowledgment you're open to contact from the other party. My birth mother would have received a similar letter."

"You know . . . depending on how long ago she sent in her form, this might be a huge shock to her too."

"That's possible." He set the glass back down.

The waiter delivered their salads, and once he left, Claire covered Keith's hand with hers, her slender fingers warm and comforting against his skin. "Would it make you uncomfortable if I said a short prayer before we eat?"

"No. I need to get back into that habit myself. It's how I was raised."

"Me too—and I've also been remiss." She bowed her head, and he did the same. "Lord, thank you for the gift of friendship and for the chance to share this meal. Thank you for guiding Keith on his journey so far, and please give him discernment and fortitude as he decides on next steps. And thank you for the grace and blessings you send us even when we fail to notice or acknowledge them. Amen."

After he added his own amen, she picked up her fork. "So what happens next?"

"I'm not planning any rash moves. I want to think about this for a few days. But it's possible my birth mother may call me."

"I have a feeling she won't. That she'll leave it up to you to initiate contact."

"I hope you're right. I'd rather do this on my timetable—and my terms." He speared some lettuce with his fork. "That's another of my quirks, you know. I feel more secure when I'm in control of stuff like that. Remember, I warned you I have a lot of idiosyncrasies."

"No more than I have. It should be interesting to see how we manage to sort them out as part of this relationship."

"Agreed. But why don't we put all that on the back burner for tonight and enjoy our meal?"

"Great idea." With that, she dug into her salad and proceeded to distract and entertain him with hilarious stories about her second grade students, her daughter's escapades, and her experiences on the *Molly Sue* with her father during her growing-up years.

By the time he drove her back to his mother's to pick up Haley, he was more relaxed than he would have believed possible.

Yes, the letter resting inside the pocket of his jacket would have to be dealt with. But not tonight.

Tonight was for Claire.

And it wasn't over yet.

"Thank you again for watching Haley, Alice." Claire rested her hand on her daughter's shoulder as they all stood in the foyer of the older woman's house. "I'm sorry we were a bit later than expected."

"I'm glad you and Keith had a nice, long dinner. And we had a marvelous evening, didn't we, Haley?"

"Awesome! We had hamburgers for dinner and made ice cream sundaes for dessert. Then we tried on a bunch of jewelry and painted our fingernails. See?" She held up her hands to display the pearl-finish pink polish.

"Girl stuff." Keith grinned at her.

"Yeah!"

"I hope the nail polish was all right with you, Claire?"

"Absolutely." She sent Alice a reassuring look. "Haley's been after me for ages to let her try it, but somehow it keeps dropping to the bottom of my priority list."

"Under propping up your house and cooking meals and grocery shopping and teaching and correcting homework papers and—"

Claire laughed and put a hand up to stop Keith. "Please. You're making me tired."

"The life of a working mother is busy and exhausting, I'm sure." Alice patted her arm. "But I must say, you don't look in the least weary tonight. You're positively glowing. And in case my son neglected to mention it, your outfit is stunning. I especially love that silk blouse. It's very stylish."

Also a great and inexpensive find at the resale shop where she bought most of her clothes.

Claire smoothed a hand down her black pencil skirt, also a resale purchase. Not that the source mattered. As she recalled the sweep Keith had given her when she'd answered the door, and the way his eyes had begun to smolder, she smiled. "He was very complimentary."

"I should hope so. A man would have to be blind not to appreciate a lovely young woman like you."

Her date for the night rejoined the conversation. "Are you ready to go? I know it's past Haley's bedtime."

In other words, the discussion was getting too personal for his taste.

"Yes. Thank you again, Alice."

"Anytime. Haley and I had a lot of fun. It was invigorating to have a youngster in the house again."

"We may take you up on that offer, Mom." Keith leaned over and kissed her forehead. "I'll see you Sunday."

"I'll look forward to it. And guests are welcome, you know." She sent a meaningful glance toward Claire and Haley.

No subtlety there.

Quashing her chuckle, Claire turned Haley toward the door. "Let's hit the road. Keith still has a lot of driving to do tonight."

He followed her out.

Once in the car, her daughter dominated the conversation at first, giving them a blow-by-blow description of her evening. But after a few minutes she yawned and fell silent.

Keith glanced in the rearview mirror. "I think she's out."

"That doesn't surprise me. She had an exciting evening—and so did I."

The dim light masked his features as he captured her hand and gave it a squeeze, but she could hear the smile in his voice. "In that case, I think we should plan a repeat performance very soon."

"No objections from me—nor from Haley, I'm sure. It's obvious she had a great time with your mom."

"I think the experience was mutual."

They lapsed into silence for most of the remainder of the drive, but the quiet was relaxed. Peaceful. The kind that spoke of hearts in harmony and spirits in sync.

She could get used to this.

With a contented sigh, she settled back in her seat and focused on enjoying the feel of Keith's warm, steady hand holding hers.

Once they arrived at her house, he parked in the driveway, circled the car, and opened her door and Haley's.

"Come on, kiddo. You're home."

Claire took Keith's arm as they started for the house, but when Haley lagged behind, she looked back at her. "Are you still waking up?"

"I guess."

The energy she'd exhibited earlier seemed to have evaporated, and Claire scrutinized her while she dug for her keys. "Are you okay?"

Haley shrugged.

Frowning, Claire fitted the key in the door and ushered her daughter inside. Once under the brighter lights, she examined her face. It was slightly pinched and flushed, and a quick hand laid on the youngster's forehead confirmed her fears.

Haley had a fever.

"Everything all right?" Keith moved beside her.

"She's running a temperature."

"I think it's my ear." Haley's shoulders drooped. "It's been kind of hurting since this morning . . . but it's worse now."

"For goodness sake—why didn't you tell me?"

Her daughter dipped her head. "I didn't want to miss going to Keith's mom's house tonight."

Claire opened her mouth to reprimand her. Closed it. As a kid, she might have done the same thing if she was afraid she'd miss out on some fun event.

Truth be told, even as an adult she'd be similarly tempted if admitting sickness meant giving up an enjoyable evening—like the one tonight with Keith.

"Okay. You know the drill. Get into bed while I round up the thermometer and ibuprofen."

Haley trudged toward the hall, stopping on the threshold to look back. "I'm still glad I went. Your mom is really nice, Keith. Good night."

"'Night." Keith waited until she disappeared, then lowered his voice as he turned to her. "This sounds like a routine occurrence."

"Not anymore. She had a lot of ear infections in her early years, but they've lessened in severity and duration as she's gotten older. She hasn't had one in more than a year."

"Is there anything I can do?"

"No. We'll watch it for a couple of days. In most cases, they clear up by themselves. Sorry to finish the evening on a down note."

"I have to admit, this isn't how I hoped our first real date would end. And it didn't start off too hot, either."

"The middle part was great, though." She linked her fingers with his and gave a gentle squeeze. "Besides, you don't have to leave yet. It won't take me long to get Haley settled."

She could read the temptation in his eyes, but after he scrutinized her for a moment, he shook his head. "I think we've both had enough excitement for one day—and I suspect you're not going to have the most restful night."

All of that was true—but she'd been looking forward to some time with him after Haley went to bed. Still, worry about her daughter would take some of the pleasure out of that, anyway.

"May I at least walk you to your car?"

"I'd like that."

He kept a firm grip on her hand as they strolled down her walkway, dodging one section of concrete that had buckled in the spring thaw. A recent addition to her to-do list.

Once they stood beside his Infiniti, he pulled her into his arms. "I'd hoped to do this in a more private setting, but I'm not leaving without a kiss."

She draped her arms around his neck. "I didn't intend to let you. I have a rain check for two hugs, remember."

"I'll trade you the two hugs for one kiss."

"Deal."

"Easy sell."

"Willing customer."

Letting out a slow breath, he fingered some strands of her hair. Touched her face. Traced the line of her jaw. "I've been wanting to hold you all evening."

"I've been wanting you to."

"But this has also been on my mind."

And with that, he bent and captured her lips.

The kiss started out oh-so-gentle . . . soared to passion-ate . . . and finally deposited her back on earth with a loving tenderness that bordered on reverent and left her yearning for more.

It was a kiss more about giving than taking.

It was what a kiss should be.

When he at last backed off, she clung to him until her world settled back on its axis.

"Wow." It was all she could manage.

"Ditto." He leaned down again and rested his forehead against hers. "I'll call you tomorrow."

"Okay."

Several seconds ticked by. At last, with obvious reluctance, he backed off. "You need to see to Haley."

Right.

She had a sick daughter inside.

"Drive safe going home—and thank you again for a wonder-ful dinner."

"We'll do it again soon."

"I'd like that. And next time I won't mention the menu prices."

She backed off as he slid behind the wheel, then watched as his taillights disappeared down the street.

When she returned to the house, she found Haley waiting for her in the foyer, already dressed in her sleep shirt, a huge grin plastered on her face.

"What?" She closed the door and faced her daughter.

"You guys kissed."

Warmth flooded her cheeks. "Were you spying on us?" Best to go on the offensive until she decided how to respond.

"No. You left the door open, and I looked out to see where

you went. It was just like a scene in one of those old romantic movies we watch sometimes." She let out a dreamy sigh. "So are you guys going to get married? Because it's okay with me. Keith is awesome."

Her daughter was already thinking marriage?

Better put the brakes on that, pronto.

"Haley, we only met each other a few weeks ago. Sensible people don't start thinking about marriage that fast. But if I ever do decide to get married again, I promise you'll be the first to know." She pointed toward the hall. "Under the covers, young lady, while I grab the thermometer and ibuprofen."

"But I want to talk about—"

"Now."

Turning on her heel, Haley marched back down the hall, muttering under her breath.

By the time she ducked into the bathroom to retrieve the items she needed and filled a glass with water, Haley was back in bed. Before her inquisitive daughter could ask anything else, she stuck the digital thermometer under her tongue.

Too bad it wasn't the old-fashioned mercury kind that took a whole lot longer to register, since the instant she removed it, the questions started again.

"If you married Keith, would his mom be my grandmother?"

Claire angled the thermometer to read the number in the window.

"Yes, but that would be a long way down the road—if it ever happens. Right now we're going to worry about that earache. Your temperature is 100.4. I can't believe you didn't tell me sooner." She handed her the pill and the glass of water.

Haley swallowed the medicine in one gulp.

"Drink some more."

After she complied, Haley handed the glass back. "Cap told me he fell in love with Grandma the first time he saw her and they got married real fast. Did you fall in love with Keith right away?"

Her hand tightened on the glass. "I didn't say I was in love with him."

"Then why did you kiss him?"

Oh, brother.

"We'll talk about it tomorrow. You need to go to sleep."

As Claire rose and tucked in the covers, Haley's expression grew solemn. "Is this one of those grown-up things you think I'm too little to understand?"

Claire smoothed out the edge of the blanket and straightened up. "As a matter of fact, you're growing up way too fast to suit me. But romantic stuff can be . . . complicated."

"Why?"

"Because a lot of times, things happen to people that make it hard for them to trust someone else."

"Like when you and Dad got divorced?"

"That's one example."

Haley bunched the pillow under her cheek. "I don't think it has to be complicated. If you love someone with all your heart, and they love you back the same way, it should be easy. You just have to make sure you find someone who loves you as much as you love him. And you know what? I think you did."

Deep inside, she did too—but no way did she intend to admit that yet.

"Despite what Cap told you, it's too soon to be talking about love."

Her daughter smiled and closed her eyes. "You don't always have to talk about love to know it's there. 'Night, Mom."

Out of the mouth of babes . . .

Claire flipped off the bedside light and wandered back down the hall, her fingers straying to her lips.

Haley was right.

While neither she nor Keith were ready to use the L word, the signs were all pointing that direction.

Perhaps her daughter was also right in saying it didn't have to be complicated. Maybe, if you found the right guy, it was easy.

And more and more, she was beginning to believe she had.

23

As the plane touched down at Logan International Airport on Saturday afternoon, Maureen's pulse quickened.

She was back in the city she'd never intended to visit again—arriving alone, just as she had the first time.

Except twenty-one years ago, she'd had no choice. Or none she'd considered viable.

This time, she could have accepted David's offer to accompany her, one he'd repeated again even in the moments before she'd left him at Lambert Airport security in St. Louis five hours ago.

But somehow it seemed fitting that this journey, like the first, be solitary.

Still, once it was over, David would be waiting to fold her in his arms and welcome her home—and that blessed certainty buoyed her strength and courage and determination to see this quest through to the end, difficult as it might be.

Overnight bag in hand, she deplaned and wove through the crowds, following the signs to ground transportation. By the time she filled out the rental car paperwork and was on the road, it was close to three o'clock.

The landscape around her was unfamiliar as she followed the route she'd mapped out before leaving St. Louis. Much had changed in the city during the past two decades.

The suburb the Phillipses called home was one she'd never visited, but their white frame Cape Cod style house was easy to find, thanks to the printout from MapQuest.

Braking to a stop in front, she braced her hands on the wheel and examined the well-maintained structure with the curving walk and trimmed lawn.

This was the yard where her son had played as a child. These were the sidewalks and streets where he'd ridden his bike. This was the driveway where he'd shot baskets, based on the hoop above the garage.

Her throat tightened.

Being here made him seem so much more tangible and real.

Yet the unkempt gardens and the empty stone planters on either side of the front door suggested that someone who had once taken great joy in flowers wasn't up to the task this year.

That life-disrupting trauma lay within these walls.

Blinking to clear her vision, she picked up her purse from the passenger seat and followed the curving path to the front door.

Seconds after she pressed the bell, a trim woman dressed in black slacks and a dark-green sweater answered, the gray roots of her ash-blonde hair long overdue for a touch-up. Behind her, a slender, gray-haired man with glasses and a pleasant face rested a hand on her shoulder.

"We've been watching for you." The woman gave her a tremulous smile and folded one of her hands in both of hers. "Welcome. This is my husband, Joe."

The man shook her hand, and they ushered her into the cozy living room. Couches and chairs were clustered around the fireplace, but her eye was drawn to the grouping of family photos on the mantel.

One shot showed a high-school-age Paul in a soccer uniform, holding a trophy. A later picture put him front and center again, standing between his parents on a beach, his arms over their shoulders, all of them grinning. The formal portrait of him in uniform that Beth had emailed to her also had a prominent place. And finally, on the far side, was a recent picture of the three of them in front of some fir trees, wearing Santa caps and holding snowballs.

A Christmas-card picture, perhaps?

"May I offer you a soft drink?"

At Joe's question, she redirected her gaze. "Yes, thank you. A white soda would be fine, if you have it."

"I pulled out the family albums." Beth gestured to a pile of books on the coffee table. "Joe said the stack would overwhelm you, but I thought you might like to at least glance through them."

"Yes, I would. Very much."

"Please . . . make yourself comfortable." She indicated the couch.

Maureen settled in, Beth beside her and Joe in an adjacent wing chair after he returned with her drink, and for the next two hours she asked questions and listened to stories about her son's growing-up years, soaking everything up as they paged through the albums. The Phillipses never inquired about the circumstances of Paul's birth, nor did she offer details. Clearly, that history was irrelevant to them. From their perspective, all that mattered was the blessing Paul had been in their lives.

Only when they reached the final pages of the last album, and shots of a uniformed Paul in the Middle East began to appear, did she broach the difficult subject of his death. "Would you mind very much telling me what happened? All I heard was that it happened during a routine patrol."

"Joe . . ." Distress deepened the lines in Beth's face, and she turned to her husband as she fumbled in her pocket for a tissue.

He cleared his throat and linked his fingers. "That's right. The patrol came under fire from insurgents. One of the guys in his unit was wounded and left exposed after everyone scrambled for cover. Paul was in a protected spot, but he crawled back out to get him. He managed to pull him to safety, and the young man did survive, but Paul suffered fatal wounds in the process." Joe's voice broke, and he stared at his clenched fingers for a moment before continuing. "A nomination for the Medal of Honor is working its way up the chain of command. We're told, given the circumstances, that's nothing more than a formality."

Her son had been a hero.

Swallowing past the lump in her throat, Maureen looked back at the photo of the handsome, confident young man in the formal Marine portrait on the mantel. "You must be very proud of him."

"Yes." Joe brushed his hand across his eyes. "But pride doesn't begin to make up for the empty place his passing left in our lives—and in our hearts."

Silence fell, broken at last by the sonorous chime of the grandfather clock in the foyer marking six o'clock.

Rubbing her palms down her slacks, Beth stood. "I'm sure you must be getting hungry. I knew we'd want to spend time with the albums, so I put a stew together and it's been slow cooking."

Maureen didn't feel in the least hungry, but her stomach was reacting to the savory aroma that filled the house, reminding her it had been almost twelve hours since her last meal.

She rose too. "If you'll point me to the bathroom, I'd like to freshen up."

"Of course." Beth led her down a hall, stopping at a closed door. "This was Paul's room. We didn't change anything after he went away to college because we wanted him to know this room would always be waiting to welcome him whenever he came home for visits." She opened the door and flipped on the light, though she kept her eyes downcast. "Feel free to look around if you like. No need to rush. It will take me a few minutes to heat up the bread and put out the food. The bath is the next door on your right."

As her hostess retreated down the hall, Maureen took her place in the doorway of her son's room.

The albums she'd viewed and the stories Beth and Joe had shared had given her many insights into the man her long-ago baby had become. But this room . . . this captured his personality best of all.

In the bright, geometric-patterned bedspread she saw his love of vibrant color and precision. In the shelves crammed with an array of fiction and nonfiction she saw his love of books and learning. In the framed certificates for academic achievement she saw his intelligence. In the high-quality prints of contemporary painting she saw his love of art. In the plaque on the wall containing a quote from Amos, she saw his motivation for enlisting in the Marines, his personal code of living, and his deep faith in God.

"Hate evil and love good, and let justice prevail at the gate."

Tears once more blurred her vision.

The world had lost a good man when her son died.

And the credit for his goodness belonged to the man and woman in the next room, who mourned him with a profoundness her own grief could but distantly echo. Their sorrow was for a boy they'd nurtured and taught and encouraged and lavished with love. For a son they'd laughed and cried with, nursed through various childhood illnesses, protected with every ounce of their ability—only to stand by and accept a flag as he was commended to God and committed to eternal rest while the haunting melody of "Taps" played.

318

Her grief, by contrast, was for a fine young man who was no more than a stranger. For a lost opportunity. For one night of loose virtue that had led to a lifetime of regret.

No matter the different sources, heartache hung in the air as she joined her hosts for dinner. They all made a valiant effort to chat, and they got through the dinner, but it was clear her decision to stay at a hotel had been wise.

All of them were drained.

She could see it in Beth's pallor as the woman pressed an album into her hands at the door—copies of some of their favorite photos of Paul for her to keep; in Joe's slightly unsteady hand as he shook hers and told her she was welcome to visit anytime; in her own numbing fatigue as she drove through the darkness to her hotel, needing sleep but suspecting it would be elusive as she tried to mentally prepare for her final stop tomorrow before flying home.

And that suspicion became reality while the long, bleak hours until dawn crept by and thunder rumbled overhead.

Yet her exhaustion vanished as she drove through the entrance to Massachusetts National Cemetery and followed the directions Joe Phillips had given her.

After winding through the well-kept grounds, serene and park-like on this overcast Sunday morning, she parked and reached for the single yellow rose and feathery fern tied with a golden ribbon on the seat beside her.

No one else was about at this hushed early hour as she crossed the manicured grass, passing between the uniform white headstones, each marking the grave of a soldier, many of whom had fought for freedom on distant shores.

At last she came to Paul's.

There was nothing to distinguish it from those on either side—except the engraved name.

Paul Joseph Phillips.

She lowered herself to her knees beside the fresh, tender new grass and traced the name with an unsteady finger.

Then she read the remaining information. Rank. Branch of service. Birth date. Day of death. Finally she traced the words that had been cut into the stone at the bottom.

Beloved Son.

Yes, he was.

By two mothers.

How ironic that she should finally meet up with him on Mother's Day.

Choking back a sob, she gently set the rose at the base of the stone, closed her eyes, and bowed her head.

I'm sorry I never got to meet you, Paul. But I'm grateful you had such fine parents and such a happy life. I only wish it could have been longer. That I could have told you face-to-face why I made the decision I did all those years ago, and that I've prayed for you every single day since. Thank you for the joy you brought to Beth and Joe, and know that you will always be remembered—and loved—by both of your mothers. Rest in peace, my son.

She stayed there, her fingers splayed on the cool marble, until a drop of rain splashed against the back of her hand.

Another followed.

It was time to go.

Rising, she pressed her fingers to her lips, then to the engraved name. She let them rest there for a few seconds, caressing the grooves in the smooth stone. At last, blinking to clear her vision, she removed her hand and forced herself to walk away.

The rain intensified as she wove through the grave markers, but despite the moisture seeping into her sweater, she stopped beside her car for one last look back.

Just as she turned, the sun broke through the gray clouds, bathing the world in glistening light—and her breath caught.

For in the distance, in the final moment before the clouds once more covered the sun, a rainbow appeared, come and gone so fast she wondered if she'd imagined it.

But no.

It had been real.

She gripped the edge of her door, staring at the spot where the translucent arc of colors had appeared for no more than a few heartbeats. The science was easily explainable, of course. The raindrops had acted as tiny prisms, breaking the light entering them into a spectrum. A phenomenon of nature, not some celestial sign or message.

Nevertheless, as she slid behind the wheel, she felt strangely comforted—and more at peace than she had since she'd started the quest to locate her son.

She also felt ready to put her past to rest and step into her future . . . a future that included the man waiting for her at home. A kind and loving and generous man who'd entered her life thanks to a son she'd never known. A son who, in turn, had blessed the lives of a childless couple.

Her quest might not have ended as she'd expected—or hoped—yet much good had come from it.

And as she exited the cemetery and aimed her car toward the airport, she gave thanks.

For unexpected blessings.

For a future filled with hope.

And for the transforming power of love.

"That was a delicious meal, Keith. Your idea to celebrate Mother's Day on my patio with a takeout dinner from that fancy gourmet shop was inspired. This is so much better than fighting the crowds at one of those impersonal brunches or squeezing into a packed restaurant. The service was excellent too." Alice lifted her coffee cup in a toast as he cleared away the empty plate that had held her double-chocolate torte.

"I'm glad you enjoyed it."

"I have only one complaint."

Pausing on his way to the kitchen to deposit their dessert plates, he half-turned. "What's that?"

"You seem very distracted. You didn't even respond to that comment I threw in about running off to join the circus."

She hadn't said that . . . had she?

Maybe.

Truth be told, he'd spent most of the dinner trying to figure out how to lead up to the subject he wanted to discuss.

Too bad it was Mother's Day. Any other Sunday, the topic would have been far less problematic to introduce.

He shifted his weight as she leaned back in her chair and gave him that appraising look he remembered from his teenage years. The one she'd gotten whenever she was trying to ferret out what was going on his brain.

Usually she'd succeeded.

Come to think of it, she'd have fit in well in a circus. No doubt she'd be an excellent mind reader.

"Let me get rid of these and we'll talk." He hefted the dishes, then escaped to the kitchen.

Taking his time, he stowed them in the dishwasher and set the machine humming. But delaying wasn't going to make this any easier. Might as well follow the advice of that sport shoe ad and just do it.

When he turned, he tried for a smile as he retook his seat. "I guess you still have that old ESP I used to dread."

"Mothers develop it, at least where their children are concerned. Even adoptive mothers."

The perfect opening.

"About that . . ." Slowly he withdrew the folded Missouri Department of Social Services envelope from his pocket and laid it on the table. "I got this in the mail on Friday. It's from the adoption registry."

If she was taken aback by his news, she gave no indication of it.

"That must mean you decided to follow through on my suggestion." She lifted her cup of coffee and took a sip, hand steady, voice calm.

"Yes. I got the answer a lot faster than I expected. My birth mother was in the registry."

"Is that right?" Slowly she set her cup back in the saucer. "Have you spoken with her?"

"Not yet. I wanted to talk with you first. I know you encouraged me to do this, but somehow it feels disloyal to you and dad. You were wonderful parents, and you're still the best mother in the world. I don't want to do anything that would hurt you or make you think I have any feelings for my birth mother beyond curiosity. The only reason I'm even considering contacting her is to get answers to some of the questions that have always bothered me."

"Keith." His mother leaned forward, grasped his hand, and locked gazes with him. "Everything I said to you a few weeks ago stands. Your father and I knew your traumatic early years continued to haunt you at some subliminal level. We often discussed it. And we agreed that connecting with your birth mother, finding out more about those years, might resolve some of your issues and give you a sense of closure. We always wanted what was best for you."

She gave his fingers a fierce squeeze. "As for hurting me—don't you worry about that. I know in my heart how much you love me, and I also know no one can ever take my place in your life. I support you in this 100 percent."

Blinking, he let out a slow breath. "You're the best, you know that?"

She gave a soft laugh. "Hardly. Your dad and I made plenty of errors along the way while we were learning to be parents—but you turned out fine despite our blunders."

"I can't think of a single mistake."

"Spoken like the loving and dutiful son you are." She picked up her cup again. "Let's have a toast, shall we? To closure, peace of mind, and a bright future."

"I'll drink to that." He lifted his own cup, clinked it with hers, and took a sip of coffee.

"So now that you've gotten that off your mind and I have your full attention, let's talk about Claire. I'm picking up some strong electricity between the two of you. Is my ESP still working?"

He grinned. "Close enough."

She gave a satisfied nod. "Excellent. Maybe I'll get those grand-children that have been on my mind sooner than I expected."

Keith didn't respond. It was way too premature to have *that* discussion.

In truth, though, his mother's prediction could very well come to pass . . . perhaps later rather than sooner, however, given Claire's caution. Once burned, twice shy, and all that.

But even if she tested his patience to the limits, he wasn't going anywhere.

Because as far as he could tell, Claire Summers was a woman worth waiting for.

24

. . . .

"Am I interrupting anything?"

Keith swiveled away from his computer. David stood on the threshold of his office, a file folder in hand. "Nothing that can't wait. What's up?"

As his boss strolled in and sank into a chair across from his desk, Keith studied him.

The man's hair was as silver as ever. The age- and sun-induced creases on his face hadn't diminished one iota. The slight wince as he sat suggested the arthritis that occasionally plagued him had flared up.

But he looked ten years younger than he had a few weeks ago, and there was a new spring in his step.

The metamorphosis had to be due to Maureen.

His boss must be falling for her. Fast. And it was having a positive impact on his whole demeanor.

He could relate.

"We've had a call about taking over a project from a builder that's about to file bankruptcy. The details are in here." He slid the folder across the desk. "Would you go over the numbers, evaluate whether we might be able to salvage this at a profit?"

"Sure. You want me to do a site visit too?"

"If the financials merit it. I'll take a trip out there too, if your research suggests it's warranted."

"Where's the project?" He started to open the file.

"Kansas City."

His hand froze.

Kansas City?

Where his birth mother lived?

Talk about a coincidence.

Or was it?

"Everything okay?"

"Yes." He flipped open the file and pretended to examine the documents inside, though the numbers were a blur. "I'll get on this right away. Would next week be soon enough for my visit, if it comes to that?"

"Sure. Just keep me updated." David rose. "Will you be able to make Maureen's birthday party on Saturday?"

"I wouldn't miss it. I've already given Claire my RSVP. By the way, I got a very nice thank-you note from Maureen yesterday."

"That sounds like her." A smitten smile played at his lips.

Yeah. His boss was going down for the third time.

"She gave me far too much credit, though. Finding the woman at St. Columba was a fluke."

"Fluke or not, you got better results than her PI did."

"I worked cheaper too."

"True." Grinning, David walked to the door. "I've got a busy Friday, but if you're ready to talk about this bankruptcy project by tomorrow, don't hesitate to grab me between meetings."

"I won't."

Once his boss disappeared, he refocused on the file. He had plenty of work to keep him busy well into the evening already

. . . but this was now top priority. Because if his due diligence warranted a trip west, that might give him the push he needed to make the call he'd been putting off all week.

And if it didn't . . .

He'd still make the call—but he wouldn't rush things.

Decision made, he shut his door, saved the document he'd been working on when David came in, and settled in to do some serious number crunching.

"Parties are so much fun, Mom!" Haley examined the pack of balloons and the rolls of crepe paper they'd purchased on the way home from school. "Do you think Dr. Chandler is excited?"

Claire dumped the contents of the ice maker into a plastic bag, secured it with a twister, and stowed it in the freezer. Making extra ice rather than buying it the day of the party would save a couple of bucks she could put toward the pork steaks she was planning to grill—not to mention the ingredients for the side dishes.

"Absolutely." She smiled at her daughter, back in fighting form now that the ear infection had cleared up, and tested the potatoes she was boiling for potato salad. Almost done.

"I wish she could have had a chance to meet her son, though. That would have been a better present than a party." Haley rested her elbow on the table and propped her chin in her palm. "When I asked Mr. McMillan to try and find him, I wanted it to be a happy surprise, not a sad one."

Claire slid into the chair beside her daughter and smoothed the fine wisps of hair back from her forehead. "I know it didn't turn out the way any of us expected, but she did find out all about her son. That made her happy. She even has pictures of him now. If it hadn't been for your letter, she'd always have wondered about him."

"I guess." Haley played with the package of balloons, her expression pensive. "It's kind of strange how sometimes when we pray for one thing, God gives us something different. It might not be what we wanted, but it can be just as good."

"What do you mean?"

"Well, I prayed that Mr. McMillan would find Dr. Chandler's son. And he did—or Keith did. It's really sad he got killed in the war . . . but other good stuff happened because we tried to find him. You and me got to meet Keith, and Dr. Chandler got to meet Mr. McMillan. Now everybody's happier. Dr. Chandler smiles all the time, and you laugh and sing more. Those lines between your eyes are even going away. I think maybe that's what God had planned all along."

Claire pulled her daughter into a hug. "You are one smart little girl, you know that?"

"You're just saying that because you're my mom."

"Nope. Because it's true." She ruffled her hair and stood. "Now why don't you finish that birthday card you're making for Dr. Chandler while I set the barbecue grill up on the deck so it's all ready for Saturday?"

"Okay." Haley picked up one of the colored pencils on the table and went back to her artwork.

As Claire turned down the potatoes and retrieved the grill from the garage, she mulled over Haley's insights. Not bad for an eleven-year-old.

And the little girl's wisdom had implications beyond the present situation. God's ways might often be difficult to understand, but it seemed—usually in hindsight—that even negative experiences could have positive results.

Like her marriage to Brett.

Had she not made a mistake in judgment with him, the little

girl who graced her life with love and light and laughter wouldn't be sitting at her kitchen table right now.

Perhaps good came from most things, but the benefits were only visible from a distance.

After stepping through the door Keith had fixed, Claire slid it closed behind her and set the small barbecue grill on the deck. The fragrance from the lilac bush was growing faint now that the blooms had peaked.

But it lingered in her heart—along with a new, more positive perspective . . . and a bright and shining hope.

Keith tapped the stack of papers for the bankruptcy project into a neat pile, slid them back into his file folder, and checked his watch.

Eight o'clock.

This was the latest he'd stayed at the office in weeks.

The time had been well spent, however. Based on his review of the spreadsheets and reports David had passed on to him, a trip to Kansas City was more than justified.

Meaning there were no more excuses to delay a call to his birth mother.

His pulse picked up as he stowed the file in his credenza. After locking it, he pulled the adoption registry letter from his briefcase. The envelope was getting dog-eared from being carried around for the past week, but the sheet of paper he pulled out was still pristine.

After spreading it flat on the desk in front of him, he reached for his phone.

Stopped.

Closed his eyes.

Though he'd been remiss in his relationship with God, and

daily prayer was a habit he needed to cultivate, the entreaty he sent heavenward flowed straight from the heart.

Lord, you've led me to this place for a reason. I believe you want me to do this. Give me the strength to carry through and to put my trust in you that all will turn out well.

Then, clamping his fingers around the handset, he took a steadying breath and punched in the number the registry had provided.

After two rings, a man answered.

"Is this the correct number for Laura Matthews?" The question came out clipped and taut.

"Yes. May I ask who's calling?"

"Keith Watson."

A beat of silence passed.

"Please hold a moment."

Much more than a moment passed as he waited.

After thirty seconds, he wiped his damp palm on his slacks.

Maybe his birth mother didn't want to talk with him after all.

Maybe she'd filled that form out years ago and had had a change of heart.

Maybe she—

"Keith?" The female voice was breathless. Tear-laced. "This is Laura Matthews. I'm so glad you called. I'd given up ever . . ." Her voice broke, and in the background he could hear a soothing baritone, though the words were indistinguishable.

He waited her out, jaw clamped. He would *not* let her emotional response to his call affect him. He did *not* intend to feel anything for this woman. He just wanted answers.

"I'm sorry." She was back, sounding shakier than before. "It's just that it's been so long. When I got the notice from the adoption registry, I could hardly believe it. I wanted to call right away, but Dennis—my husband—convinced me to wait. He said you might just want to know my name and didn't intend to get in touch. I'm so glad you did."

The ball was in his court.

He cleared his throat. "I almost didn't. But there are questions that have bothered me for a long time, and I'd like some answers. I'm going to be in your area next week on business, and I hoped we might be able to get together."

"Of course. Anytime. Would you like to come to my house?"

"No." His answer was swift and sure. No way was he venturing onto her turf. He wanted a neutral place where they could meet on equal terms. "I'd prefer a coffee shop or café. Even a park."

"All right. Where in town will you be staying?"

He found the address of the job site and read it off. "That's where I'll be working, and I'll stay nearby. I'm not familiar with Kansas City, and I haven't booked a hotel yet."

"Why don't I meet you in the lobby of your hotel, assuming it has a coffee shop? You can let me know where after you make your reservations. If that doesn't work, I'll find a spot nearby. Starbucks is everywhere."

Fine with him if she wanted to travel to where he was. That would make things easier.

"That works for me. I'll be in touch tomorrow once my travel arrangements are set." His tone was businesslike, impersonal. Probably not what she'd hoped to hear.

Too bad.

"That sounds fine. I'll wait for your call. And Keith . . . thank you for following up. It means a lot to me."

He didn't return the sentiment. "I'll be in touch. Good-bye."

With a trembling finger, he pressed the switch hook, severing the connection.

For a full minute, he sat unmoving, giving his pounding heart a chance to slow down. When it finally did, he picked up the phone again and tapped in Claire's number.

Haley answered.

"Hi, Keith. Guess what we're doing?"

The youngster's innocent exuberance helped restore his equilibrium. "I haven't a clue, kiddo. What?"

"Getting ready for Dr. Chandler's birthday party. Mom's cooking and I'm making a card. We have a bunch of balloons to blow up too."

"Sounds like you two ladies are busy. Do you think your mom might have a minute to talk to me?"

"Oh, sure. She always likes to talk to you. She says a phone call from you is better than chocolate. Hang on a sec."

He was still smiling when she picked up. "So I'm better than chocolate, huh?"

She huffed out a breath. "I need to begin teaching that girl the rules of the dating game—starting with the one about looking too eager. A lot of men take women who are too accessible for granted."

"Not this man."

"Nice to know. What's up?"

The corners of his mouth flattened. "I made the call."

"Oh, Keith. Hang on." He heard the sliding door open. Close. "I moved outside. I wish I was there to give you a hug."

"I think you stole my line from the day you called me on your lunch break at school. But yeah . . . I wish you were too."

"How did it go?"

He filled her in on the KC job and his promise to his birth mother that he'd call back and set up a meeting. "We haven't picked a date yet, but by this time next week, it will be history."

"Did she sound . . . receptive?"

"More than."

"That's good, then. You're more likely to get the answers you're looking for if she's cooperative. Did you find out anything else on the phone?"

He swiveled around in his chair and gazed at the screen saver on his computer, but the predictable, balanced design didn't soothe him as much as usual. "She's married. Her husband answered."

"Did he sound . . . normal?"

"Very. So did she."

The bitter thread that wove through his words surprised him—and didn't get past Claire.

"That seems to bother you." Her tone was cautious.

He rose, suddenly restless, and began to pace. "It's just not what I expected, I guess. I mean, she was into drugs. She served time in a federal prison. She tried to commit suicide. None of that suggests stability or a normal life."

"But that was thirty years ago. Some people do learn from their mistakes and make big changes in their lives. It's possible she's one of them."

He stopped beside the window and stared into the night, dredging up a painful truth from the darkest corner of his heart. "You know . . . I'm ashamed to admit this, but I think part of me didn't want her to change. That way, I could get my answers and write her off. I wouldn't have to think a whole lot about forgiveness, or feel too guilty about carrying a grudge. But it's harder when people have remorse—and I got the feeling she's carrying around a boatload of it."

"I understand your dilemma. Forgiveness can be a very tough struggle. Maybe once you meet her, though, you'll see things differently."

"Maybe." But he wasn't holding his breath.

"Will you call me again tomorrow?"

"Yeah. I might be bending your ear a lot until I get past this."

"I'm available any time. You're still coming to Maureen's party, aren't you?"

"I wouldn't miss it."

The sound of a sliding door came over the line, followed by

Haley's muffled voice. "Mom, can you help with the rabbit I'm trying to draw? It looks like a dopey dog."

"I'll be right in."

"Go ahead and help your daughter. Thanks for listening."

"Always. In fact, I'll do more than that. I'll pray about this every day."

"I'd appreciate that."

And as he rang off, gathered up his briefcase and computer, and turned off the lights for the night, he hoped she would follow through on that pledge.

Because in the days to come, he would need all the prayers he could get.

25

. . . .

"I think the youngest member of our group has called it a night." David gestured to four-year-old Bobby, out cold in the corner of Claire's living room where he'd sprawled on the floor to play with his LEGOs.

Debbie glanced at her watch and stood. "That's the one downside to having young children. Late night parties won't be on our social calendar for a few years yet."

"But these two munchkins are well worth the sacrifice." Shawn rose too, and scooped up his son. "Could you gather up the LEGOs, Grace?"

The little girl trotted over and started collecting them.

"I'll help." Haley followed her, the two girls chattering away, just as they had all evening.

From her seat beside David on the couch, Maureen surveyed the group that had gathered to celebrate her sixtieth birthday—a milestone she'd expected to mark much more quietly . . . and alone.

Until Claire and Haley and Keith and David and a whole cast of multigenerational characters had become part of her world.

This was the kind of family gathering she'd yearned to be part of all her adult life—and it was a treasure beyond price.

The presents she'd received tonight were treasures too. The painstakingly hand-drawn cards from the children. The homemade book of coupons from Claire for odd jobs, from weeding gardens to grass cutting to home-cooked meals, offering the precious gift of time that was already in such short supply in her young neighbor's busy life. The soft-as-a-cloud cashmere sweater from Keith that matched her eyes. A full day of pampering at a spa from Debbie and her husband. A gold Tiffany heart necklace from David.

Still, the chance to be part of a family celebration like this—that was the best gift of all.

"Shall we take our leave too?" David spoke close to her ear.

"Yes. I'm as ready as your grandson to call it a night."

"May I walk you home?"

She smiled into the warm blue eyes that had become so dear to her. "I was counting on it."

His fingers found hers and gave them a squeeze.

In the flurry of good-byes, she managed to draw Claire aside for a moment. "I can't thank you enough for this lovely evening. I'll cherish the memory always."

A flush of pleasure tinted her friend's cheeks. "I wish it could have been fancier. Filet mignon instead of pork steaks."

"The meal was perfect—and all homemade. I know how many hours it took you to prepare for this party, and that labor of love means more to me than filet mignon any day."

"Nothing is work when it's done with love."

"Thank you for that." Eyes misting, Maureen pulled her into a hug. "Why don't you let me stay and help with the cleanup? Many hands, you know."

"Absolutely not! It's your birthday."

Keith moved beside her and winked. "I volunteered for KP, so you're off the hook."

"In that case . . . I'll say good night. And thank you again—both of you—for everything you did to give me the best birthday I've had in forty years."

She joined David at the door, and after another round of good nights, he tucked her arm in his and led her across the lawn toward her house.

"That was a lot of fun." He squeezed her fingers. "Much more relaxed than the last family gathering for Bobby's birthday."

"I thought that one turned out fine too, once we got over the initial awkwardness."

"You mean resentment."

She shrugged and dug her key out of her purse. "Whatever it was, it's evaporating. I never expected such a personal and caring gift from Debbie and Shawn. Did you know about it?"

"Yes." He turned the knob after she twisted her key. "She called to run the idea by me. She said after all you'd been through with the cancer treatments, you might find it relaxing. I approved—and commended her on her thoughtfulness."

"She's a lovely young woman. I hope, over time, we can become friends."

"Trust me, you're well on your way toward that goal. I think you won her over when you salvaged Bobby's birthday dinner without making her feel like a complete failure in the kitchen." He propped a shoulder against the door. "Are you going to invite me in?"

In answer, she took his hand, tugging him along as she crossed the threshold.

His deep chuckle followed her.

"Would you like any more coffee?"

"If I drink another cup, I'll float home. Why don't we just sit for a few minutes?"

"That sounds perfect. And I'm ditching these heels too. Vanity and my protesting toes have been slugging it out all night, and my toes finally won."

She stepped out of them, then sat on the couch.

He joined her—close, but not too close.

Hmm.

Some interesting vibes were wafting her way.

"That necklace looks very nice on you." He perused the heart on the gold chain clasped around her neck.

She fingered it. "I've never had anything from Tiffany's before. You're going to spoil me."

"I hope so. In fact, I have something else for you—also from Tiffany's." He reached into the pocket of his jacket and withdrew another robin's-egg-blue box tied with a white bow.

It was smaller than the first one.

Ring sized.

Her breath stalled in her lungs.

Dragging her gaze away from the box, she searched his face.

The smile he gave her seemed a little shaky. "It's exactly what you think it is."

"But . . ." She looked down at the box again. Back at him. "We only met a few weeks ago."

"I know. And I'm not an impulsive man. But I am a decisive one, and at this stage of my life I know my mind." He shifted toward her and took her hand. "I also recognize a gift from God when I see it. From the day I walked into your office, I knew you were special. Every minute I've spent with you since has confirmed that impression."

He paused and examined their entwined fingers. "The truth is, I never expected to love again. To *find* someone to love again. Nor did I have any intention of looking. One happy marriage in a lifetime seemed blessing enough, and I was resigned to spending my remaining years alone. Yet the good Lord apparently had other ideas." His Adam's apple bobbed, and his gaze met hers. "I love you, Professor Chandler, and I would be honored if you would be my wife."

As the words she'd given up hope of ever hearing resonated in the room—and in her heart—every nerve in her body began to vibrate.

At sixty years of age, she'd received her first marriage proposal.

It was surreal.

Incredible.

Exhilarating.

She struggled to breathe. To speak. "This is . . . it's the most amazing moment of my life."

"Is that a yes?"

She tried to sort through her jumbled thoughts. To think as well as feel.

It wasn't easy.

"I do want to marry you." That much she knew—without a doubt.

Faint grooves dented his forehead, and he tipped his head. "I sense a 'but' in there."

"There is one—but it doesn't have anything to do with you or with my feelings." She spoke slowly, still trying to organize her thinking. "I've just had a bout with cancer, David."

"And the treatment appears to have been successful."

"I won't know that for sure for five years."

"I'm not waiting five years." His jaw tightened, as did his grip on her fingers. "Look, I recognize there's risk. I get that. But here's the thing—it doesn't matter to me. I want you in my life, as my wife, for as long as God blesses me with your presence, whether that's months or years or decades."

A tear leaked out of her eye, and she swiped it away. "I love you for saying that."

"I mean every word."

"I know you do." She touched the unopened box in his hand. "I just don't want you to end up losing two wives within a few years."

"Is there something you haven't told me?" The creases on his brow deepened, and a note of alarm sharpened his tone.

She lifted her hand and touched his cheek. "No. The last scan was fine. I'm hoping and praying the next one will be too. But for my own peace of mind, I'd rather wait until then to make plans."

"When is it?"

"Four months. September."

He gave an impatient shake of his head. "That's too long. Besides, no matter what the scan shows, do you really think I'd walk away at this point? I'm in for the duration . . . whether we're married or not."

A rush of tenderness tightened her throat. What had she done to deserve such a man?

As the warmth of his fingers seeped into hers, she fought down the selfish impulse to capitulate. "In fairness to you, though, I'd like to have a little more assurance the duration will be longer rather than shorter."

A shadow swept across his face. "Life doesn't offer those kinds of guarantees—with or without cancer."

She couldn't argue with that. That painful lesson was one they'd both learned.

"David." She touched his arm, trying another tack. "It's only been a year since my diagnosis. Give me these four months. If I marry you now, I'll just worry until the next test—and I don't want worry to be part of our honeymoon if it doesn't have to be."

He studied her in silence for a long moment. "You feel strongly about this, don't you?"

"Yes."

He weighed the box in his hand. Exhaled. "Okay. Here's my counter offer. The engagement is official as of today. We wait for the scan to get married. But no matter the outcome, the ceremony takes place two weeks later. Deal?" He held out the box.

Her eyes misted. It was one thing to take a vow about sickness and health when illness was some vague possibility on a distant horizon. It was another thing entirely when that possibility was a mere whisper away—and would be for several years to come. Yet this man, who'd already lost one wife in the recent past, was willing to take that risk. *Insisted* on taking it, despite the very real concerns she'd voiced.

His persistence spoke volumes about the depth of his love—and chased away the last of her doubts.

She took the box. "Deal."

The tension in his face evaporated. "Man. That was more stressful than any boardroom deal I ever brokered." He released an unsteady breath and gestured to the box. "Go ahead . . . open it."

Fingers trembling, she tugged off the ribbon and flipped up the lid of the velvet-covered case inside the classic Tiffany box. A huge, square diamond with a triangular stone on either side winked back at her.

"Oh my." Her awed words were more breath than sound. "This is . . . it's too much."

He took her hand, forcing her to look over at him. "It's not too much. You've waited a long time for this ring, and you deserve a knockout."

"This certainly qualifies."

He pulled it from its velvet nest and slipped it on her finger, his touch gentle yet sure. "I love you, Maureen . . . and I'll be counting the days—no, make that the hours—until we say I do. But I intend to start laying the groundwork right now for that honeymoon you mentioned. Any objections?"

Joy bubbled up inside her, sending a delicious tingle to every nerve ending. "Not a one."

His smile was slow and warm as he pulled her close, this man who'd come so unexpectedly into her life, brightening her world with laughter and joy and love. And as he claimed her lips in a loving kiss that told her just how much he cherished her, her heart rejoiced.

For God had, indeed, saved the best for last.

"She's finally settled down." Claire reentered the kitchen to find Keith emptying the dishwasher. "You don't have to do that."

"I don't mind. You put the whole party together and did all the cooking. So Haley didn't want to go to bed, huh?"

"No way, no how. Between all the new people she met and giggling with Grace all evening and ingesting too much sugar, I was afraid she'd be bouncing off the walls until midnight." She clapped a hand over her sudden yawn and sent him an apologetic look. "Sorry. It's not the company."

"Lucky thing I'm not the sensitive type." He stowed the last plate and turned to her. "I should go home so you can get some sleep. Didn't you say you were going to an early service tomorrow?"

"Yes. They're having a children's program afterward, and I'd like Haley to get more involved with the youth group. You're welcome to join us."

"I would . . . except I told my mom I'd take her to the late service."

He was following through on his pledge to get back on track with God, just as she was.

One more check in his pro column.

"Looks like two lost sheep are heading back to the fold."

"Not lost as much as distracted." He draped the dish towel over the sink and took her hand. "Walk me out?"

"Sure."

When they reached the front door, he moved aside to let her precede him. As he joined her on the porch, she motioned toward Maureen's driveway. "The birthday girl still has company."

"Strange how her whole adoption quest turned out, isn't it?"

"Strange but good."

He grew quiet as they ambled down the driveway to his car. All evening he'd been more subdued than usual . . . and she knew why. But she hadn't had a minute alone with him until now to ask about the latest with his birth mother.

"Did you finalize all the arrangements for Kansas City?" She stopped beside the Infiniti, mere inches separating them. Storm clouds had gathered, darkening the night and throwing his features into shadow, but she could feel his tension.

"Yes. My birth mother returned my call right before I came over tonight. Our meeting is set for three o'clock on Wednesday at the hotel coffee shop. I'll drive home after we're finished."

"When do you leave?"

"First thing Monday morning."

"I'll be thinking about you—and praying."

"I appreciate both."

"If you want to talk after you see her, I'll keep my cell phone handy."

"I may take you up on that. On the other hand, I might need every minute of the four-hour drive to sort things out."

She stepped closer, until his arms came around her. "I have a feeling it's going to go well."

"I hope so. To be honest, though, I'm not certain how to define 'well.'"

"God does. That's all that matters. Now . . . could you use a hug?"

Instead of replying, he pulled her tight against him and buried his face in her hair. The embrace was about comfort, not romance. So was the kiss they shared before he drove off. Both were filled with need, as if he was trying to draw strength and courage from her.

And that was okay.

Because as she watched his taillights disappear, as a low, ominous rumble of thunder reverberated in the distance, she had a feeling he would need mega doses of both as he prepared to confront the woman who'd given birth to him—and to face the past that had haunted him for thirty long years.

26

Keith saw her across the hotel lobby before she saw him. Even if Laura Matthews hadn't told him she'd be wearing a blue shirt, he'd have known it was her.

They shared the same profile.

It was . . . bizarre.

For an instant, his courage wavered. Walking away would be so much easier.

But he hadn't come this far to back down.

He had to see this through.

Straightening his shoulders, he stepped out from behind the pillar near the elevators and crossed the lobby toward her.

She spotted him at once. Her eyes widened, and she groped for the hand of the man beside her.

Keith's step faltered as they both rose.

He didn't want an audience for this reunion—and she'd said nothing about bringing her husband along.

As if sensing his urge to bolt, the woman hurried toward him, tugging the man along with her.

No escape now.

She stopped a few feet away, and for a long moment they assessed each other in silence.

Given her sordid background, Laura Matthews wasn't at all what he'd expected. She looked the way she'd sounded on the phone.

Normal.

Like any suburban mother who drove carpools and took kids to soccer matches.

She was dressed modestly, in a khaki skirt and knit top, her dark hair falling in soft waves around her face until it brushed her shoulders. She didn't appear to have applied much makeup beyond lipstick and perhaps a touch of mascara. Slender and on the short side, she wore flats instead of the spikes he'd half expected, and her manner was discreet and quiet rather than loud and flashy.

The man beside her came across as normal too. About five-nine, wearing dress slacks and a golf shirt, he had short hair that was more pepper than salt. His kindly face was creased with concern as he draped his arm around his wife's shoulders and gave her a gentle hug.

They seemed to be an average, middle-aged couple.

But how could a guy who was normal marry a woman like his birth mother, after all the seedy stuff she'd done?

And what had happened to bring about such a dramatic transformation in her life?

"I can see you have a lot of questions. And I'll do my best to answer them." As the woman across from him uttered the shaky words, she attempted a smile. Failed. "I'm Laura—and I'm so grateful to meet you at last." She held out her hand.

He looked down at her slender fingers. They were trembling.

The temptation to ignore her gesture of greeting was strong, but in the end good manners trumped his personal feelings . . . though he didn't return the sentiment.

Her fingers were like ice as his closed over them.

At least he wasn't the only one stressing out over this meeting.

"This is my husband, Dennis." She indicated the man beside her.

Keith shook his hand too. It was rock solid.

"Laura's been praying for this moment for years. We both have."

His drug-addicted, promiscuous, felony-committing birth mother prayed?

Nothing was adding up.

"I'll leave you two to talk." The man leaned down and kissed his wife's cheek. "Call me when you're finished. I won't be far away."

"Okay."

He held onto her hand for another few seconds, gave Keith a nod, then walked toward the exit.

Once they were alone, Laura motioned toward the coffee shop off the lobby. "I checked that out before you arrived. It's not very crowded at this hour. We should be able to find a quiet corner." A quiver ran through her words, and she sounded out of breath.

"That's fine."

He followed her over the polished floor, to a table for two in the far back corner of the almost-deserted coffee shop. She slid onto a chair and set her purse beside her, but he remained standing.

"What would you like?"

She fumbled for her purse and started to rise again. "Let me get the drinks."

"I'm already up. Just hold our table."

After slanting him an uncertain look, she sank back down. "Black coffee is fine."

He chose an Americano with an extra shot of espresso.

When he returned with the drinks and some napkins, her hands were crimped together on the small round table.

He acknowledged her subdued thank-you with a dip of his head and took his seat.

"I have to tell you . . . after all these years, receiving that letter from the adoption registry was a shock. A happy one, though."

"How many years ago did you sign up?" He loosened his grip on the cardboard cup when dark liquid spurted through the sip hole.

"Fifteen. Not long after Dennis and I got married. Much as I'd always wondered what happened to you, I didn't think you'd want to have anything to do with me. But he encouraged me to register, and after I prayed about it, I decided it was the right thing to do."

Another mention of prayer.

Had she had some kind of born-again experience in prison?

She leaned closer. "I'll be happy to tell you anything you want to know, but may I ask why you decided to contact me now, after so many years?"

To buy himself a moment to frame his response, he took a sip of his drink.

The hot liquid burned his tongue.

"I've been wrestling with a lot of questions for a long time, and they've been keeping me from moving forward with some things I want to do. To be honest, signing up for the registry was a shot in the dark. My mother suggested it, but I never expected to actually connect, based on what I'd heard about you."

Sadness filled her eyes. "What did you hear?"

"Enough. Drugs, illegitimate pregnancy, attempted suicide, prison."

"All true, I'm sorry to say. But the Laura who gave birth to you died long ago." She wrapped her fingers around her cup. "Do you remember anything about your first three years?"

"I remember being scared and cold and hungry. I remember

being burned. I remember the hotel room where you tried to take your life."

She flinched, but he steeled himself. She'd asked the question. Why cut her any slack?

Yet he found himself adding one more memory to that list.

"I also recall sitting at a table, drinking milk and eating oatmeal. I have a feeling I did that often."

"Every single morning."

He locked gazes with her. "I need to know if you ever hurt me."

"No!" Her reply was fervent. "I loved you as much as any sixteen-year-old mother could love her child."

He stared at her.

Sixteen?

Mom had told him his birth mother was a teenager—but she'd been barely old enough to drive?

He frowned. "I didn't know you were that young."

"Yes." She lifted the cup with both hands and took a cautious sip. Set it back on the table. "Why don't I tell you about my life—and our life together? That might answer a lot of questions without you having to ask them."

"All right." He picked up his drink and leaned back in his seat, giving her—and himself—some space.

"I was raised in an abusive home. My stepfather was a drunk who beat my mother on a regular basis. Much as I wanted to run away, I felt I'd be deserting her if I did. But when he started making advances to me, I knew I had to get out."

She spoke in a dispassionate, clinical tone that suggested she'd long ago dealt with—or buried—the emotional trauma of her childhood.

"I left when I was fifteen and became a street kid. Essentially I traded one hell for another. One out of three teens who stays away from home more than forty-eight hours is lured into prostitution, and within two weeks seventy-five percent are involved in theft, drugs, or pornography. The only part of that I avoided was the pornography."

Keith furrowed his brow. "Why didn't you go to the authorities?"

"I heard horror stories from the other street kids. They said I'd be sent back or put in a foster home that might be worse. I knew my way around the streets by then, and I figured, better the devil you know. Or so I thought, until I got pregnant."

"Do you even know who the father was?"

"No. The truth is, it could have been any one of several different customers." She confessed that without flinching, but the raw pain—and shame—in her eyes tugged at his heart.

He looked down and fiddled with his lid, trying to remain aloof. "Since you obviously didn't want me, why didn't you have an abortion?"

After a few beats of silence ticked by with no response, he glanced over at her.

A single tear was streaking down her face.

Great.

Crying females could erode male resolve faster than an August scorcher in St. Louis melted ice.

"I know I did a lot of bad things." Her voice was subdued now. Shaky. "But I couldn't kill my own baby. I thought . . . I hoped . . . that once I had you, things might get better. I even managed to lay off the drugs while I was pregnant. After you were born, though, one of the succession of losers I shacked up with got me hooked on heroin. It was all downhill from there. The last guy I was with was a dealer, and I got sucked into that too. Plus, he did very bad things when he was high—which was most of the time."

A muscle in Keith's jaw spasmed. "I know. I have the scars to prove it."

Her throat worked as she swallowed. "Do you remember what happened that day?"

"Not in any detail, thank God. But I do have lingering memories of terror—and pain."

Another tear slipped out of her eye. She picked up one of the paper napkins and wiped it away.

"That's the day I knew I had to take desperate action."

"So you tried to kill yourself." Anger erupted in his gut, so sudden and violent that the hand holding his coffee jerked, sending dark liquid spurting onto the tabletop. He grabbed a napkin and scrubbed the stain away. "You were saddled with a kid and a life you didn't want, so you decided to take the easy way out and leave me with that scumbag."

"No!" Her eyes flashed. She fisted her hands on the table and leaned forward, her body taut. "I loved you! But I knew I couldn't take care of you. I thought about dropping you off at a church, and maybe that's what I should have done. But I was afraid Les might follow me, and I couldn't take that risk. He got some kind of perverse pleasure out of frightening you, and I wanted you away from him, from me, from the life I was living. I wanted you to have a chance for something better."

She reached up and massaged her forehead, as if she had a headache.

That made two of them.

"To be honest, I wasn't thinking straight the night I took off after he started hurting you. When he went to the bathroom, I grabbed you and some money and some drugs and ran. Once we were safe at the motel, I hit bottom. I couldn't see anything but darkness ahead, and I decided you'd be better off without a druggie mother lurking somewhere in the background who was likely to go to prison. So I tried to overdose. I knew the cleaning people would find you the next morning, that as far as you were concerned, I'd just be asleep. You'd be safe and I'd be free. Except . . . I didn't die."

"No. You went to prison." A muscle clenched in his jaw. "How long were you in?"

"Two years."

"Is that where you found God?"

"No. That came much later. But I did connect with a vocational counselor who convinced me I could make something of my life and inspired me to get my act together. I owe her a debt I can never repay. By the time I got out, I had my GED and I'd been accepted at college. She helped arrange low-cost housing for me, and I worked nights while I went to school. It took me eight years, but I finally got my degree. Then I got a job—and I've worked ever since."

"Doing what?"

"I'm a caseworker with the Children's Division of Social Services. My degree's in social work."

In other words, she was helping kids who were in the same situation she'd been in growing up.

Much as he didn't want to, and grudging as it was, he had to admit that deserved some respect.

He cleared his throat and softened his tone. "Where did you meet your husband?"

For the first time, the corners of her mouth lifted. "Through my job. Dennis does a lot of work with young people in his ministry."

Ministry?

"Is he a . . . cleric?"

"Yes. He's the reason I found my way to God. My life was going well, and I knew I was doing worthwhile work, but something was missing. He showed me what it was—the redeeming love of God and his infinite capacity for forgiveness. We became friends as well as business associates. He'd lost his wife a few years before we met and was raising his two boys alone, and things between us clicked. I give thanks every single day for his presence in my life."

Keith took a long, slow sip of his drink while he processed all she'd told him—and the picture that emerged was 180 degrees from what he'd expected.

His birth mother, too, had known trauma as a child. She'd run from one kind of trouble to another. She'd made serious mistakes—and paid a steep price for them. Yet she'd worked herself out of the mess she'd created and now lived a happy, productive life.

There was much to admire in her story.

Yet bottom line, she hadn't loved him enough to get her act together and fight for the chance to be a real mother.

"Keith." She laid her fingers on his hand, her touch tentative, and spoke as if she'd read his mind. "I want you to know that the night I tried to take my life, my biggest regret was that I wouldn't be there to see you grow up. But I had no hope at that point things would ever get any better, and I knew it was just a matter of time until I ended up dead or in prison. I wanted you in a better place sooner rather than later, and I knew, if I had one breath left in my body, I would selfishly want to hold onto you. Ending my life was the only way I could guarantee you a better one."

As her impassioned words hung in the air between them, his heart stuttered.

She hadn't tried to commit suicide because she didn't want him.

She'd done it because she wanted him too much—and knew her presence in his life would hurt him.

That night in the motel room hadn't been about escaping from him.

It had been about escaping *for* him.

It had been about unselfish love, however misguided.

"That's not what you expected to hear, is it?"

Her soft question burned through the fog swirling in his mind.

"No."

"I hope knowing the truth will bring some closure for you."

He hoped so too—but at the moment his brain was on overload.

When the silence lengthened, she spoke again. "Do you have any other questions?"

"I can't think of any."

"Then may I ask a few?"

He forced himself to switch gears. Of course she'd have questions too. Might as well answer some of them. "Yes."

"Were your adoptive parents good to you?"

"More than good."

"Are they still living?"

"My mom is."

"And you . . . have you had a happy life? Are you married? Any children?"

"My life's been very happy. No wife or children." He almost added *yet*, but bit that back. He needed time to think through all he'd learned before he decided how much more of his life—if any—to share with this woman.

Perhaps sensing his reticence, she didn't press.

"I want you to know you're welcome to call or visit anytime if questions arise or if you'd like to get better acquainted. Our boys are grown now, and we have plenty of room for guests."

"I appreciate that." But he wasn't making any commitments. Swigging down the last of his coffee, he glanced at his watch. "I have a long drive back. I better get on the road."

She picked up her cup and stood. "I understand. If you're lucky, you may still miss the going-home traffic."

He rose too. "Do you want to call your husband? I can wait around until he comes back if you like."

"Your mother raised you well." She gave him a melancholy smile. "But no, thank you. I'll be fine in the lobby. Besides, I could use a few minutes alone."

They walked to the door of the coffee shop. Pitched their cups. Faced each other.

Now what? Would she expect him to give her a hug? Offer an assurance that he'd stay in touch? Would she kiss his cheek?

She took the awkwardness out of their parting by simply laying a hand on his arm. "Have a safe trip back."

Then she walked away.

He watched as she crossed to the center of the lobby, dug her phone out of her purse, and settled into a chair.

Once she placed the phone to her ear, he headed for his room to retrieve his bag, start the long drive back—and do some serious soul-searching.

Claire peeked through the drapes and checked her watch. Again. Factoring in both the snarl of rush-hour traffic as he left KC and the brief stop at his mother's house before swinging by here, Keith should have arrived by now. He'd said to expect him around eight-thirty when he'd called two hours ago, and it was approaching nine. She'd even made Haley go to bed early to give them some privacy, much to her daughter's disgust—though the promise of a trip to Ted Drewes for frozen custard tomorrow had helped mollify her.

Her phone trilled in the kitchen, and she let the drapes at the front window fall back into place as she dashed to answer it.

The name in the digital display wasn't Keith's, however.

Propping a hip against the counter, she snagged the portable out of the charger. "Hi, Dad."

"Hi, sweetie. You sound a little out of breath. Everything okay?"

"Fine. I was in the other room."

"I was kind of hoping you were out having another fancy meal with Keith."

She rolled her eyes. Why, oh why, had she told him about that dinner date? Now he brought it up every time they talked.

"No. Home for the evening. What's up with you?"

"Well, I happened to notice in the paper today that Delta's running a rock-bottom special on flights to select cities—and St. Louis happens to be one of them. Since I have a daughter who's going to be celebrating a birthday next month, I figured two tickets would be a great present. What do you say?"

She'd love to say yes. What a birthday treat that would be! A chance for her and Haley to spend some quality time with Dad. Trips on the *Molly Sue*, the familiar roll of the waves underfoot and a salt breeze whipping past. A low country boil. Mmm. She could almost taste the shrimp and spicy sausage and corn on the cob.

But practicality intruded—as it always did.

"Depends on how much this will set you back."

"You're not supposed to ask the price of a gift."

"Come on, Dad. I know money is tight on your end, just like it is on mine."

A sigh came over the line. "First off, I'm fully booked next week, and I'm at capacity with most of the groups. So I'm not going to be eating macaroni and cheese for weeks if I do this. Second, this is as much a gift to me as it is to you. That visit with you and Haley last month was wonderful but way too short. I need to see my two favorite ladies more often. Third, the tickets are a steal."

When he told her the price, her eyebrows rose. "Wow. That *is* a great deal."

"Told you so. You accepting?"

"Yes."

"Hot dog! You tell Haley we're going to take us some fine trips on the *Molly Sue*. By the time your visit is over, she'll be my honorary—" He stopped as a chime pealed in the background. "Is that your doorbell?"

Keith *would* show up now.

"Yes." She started toward the door.

"Kind of late for callers, isn't it?"

"It might be Keith. He's, uh, been in Kansas City on business all week and he might be, uh, stopping by on his way back into town." She peeked through the peephole.

The man under discussion stood on the other side.

"I'll wait until you make sure. You can't be too careful these days."

She flipped the lock. "It's him, Dad. I just checked." Opening the door, she motioned Keith in and angled away.

"Then I expect you'll have a far more enjoyable evening than I will. I only have a book to cuddle up with."

Warmth flooded her cheeks. "I'm hanging up now."

His chuckle came over the line. "You do that. It wouldn't be nice to keep that young man waiting after such a long drive. We'll work out the arrangements for your trip tomorrow. Give Keith my regards."

Ending the call, Claire turned back to her visitor. "Dad says hi."

One side of his mouth hitched up. "Based on your blush, I suspect he said more than that."

The warmth in her cheeks heated up a few degrees. "Maybe. He approves of you."

"Nice to know, since I expect he and I will be seeing a lot of each other down the road."

As she let that comment sink in, she looked him over. There were fine lines at the corners of his eyes, suggesting he'd put in some long hours on the job while he was away—and probably spent some restless nights in anticipation of today's meeting.

However, despite his fatigue, there was a new calm about

him. Gone was the subtle tension she only recognized now, in its absence.

The knot that had been in her stomach all day eased. "It went well, didn't it?"

"Yeah."

"I set up the chairs on the deck if you'd like to talk out there."

"Sure."

"Can I get you something to drink?" She tossed the question over her shoulder as he followed her through the house.

"I had coffee on the road and soda at my mom's. I'm full up. Where's Haley?"

"In bed."

"Kind of early, isn't it?" He reached around her to open the sliding door.

"That's what she said. I bribed her with Ted Drewes."

He chuckled as he took the chair beside her. "I bet that worked like a charm. It would on me."

"I'll tuck that piece of information away for possible future use." She shifted her chair toward him. "I could hardly concentrate at school today for thinking about you—not that anyone noticed. The kids are always hyper the last week of classes. So tell me how it went. You didn't say much when you called from the road."

"I was still processing everything I learned." He took her hand, lacing his fingers with hers as he filled her in.

Claire listened to his account of the meeting all the way through without interrupting.

When he finished, she expelled a long breath. "Wow. That's an amazing story—and not what I expected. Your birth mother really turned her life around after she hit bottom." She studied his face, trying to read his enigmatic expression. "Are you going to keep in touch with her?"

"To some degree. Maybe a card at Christmas, a call on occasion. But as I told Mom when I stopped in at her place, Laura Matthews is a stranger, linked to me only by blood. I didn't go to today's meeting intending—or wanting—to like her. My goal was simply to find answers. I got those . . . and while I did end up feeling sorry for all she went through and admiring the person she's become, my most important takeaway was a sense of peace and closure. For the first time in my life, I don't feel weighed down by the past. I'm ready to move into the future . . . a future I hope includes you."

A bird trilled in the warm spring air, its sweet song filled with joy.

The same joy that was in her heart.

For while Keith may have been the one on a journey to the past, seeking answers and closure and direction, she'd found all those same things since he'd come into her life.

She gave a contented sigh. "I like the sound of that."

"I hoped you might." He leaned close and gave her a quick kiss.

Too quick.

And way too distracting.

She had to force herself to focus on his words when he continued.

"So here's my suggestion. Let's have a real courtship this summer. We'll go on dates. I'll put up a porch swing for you and we'll spend some quality time there after Haley goes to bed—if you get my drift." He waggled his eyebrows, and she smiled. "We'll plan outings for the three of us too. Family stuff. And we'll pray about this. I think I already know where it's going to lead, but let's take our time and do this right. What do you say?"

In response, Claire stood, tugged him to his feet, and put her arms around his neck. "As my father used to say on the *Molly Sue* once we got past the obstacles in the harbor: 'Open up the throttle and let 'er rip.'"

Keith grinned. "I'm looking forward to getting to know him better."

"The feeling is mutual. But at the moment . . ." She snuggled closer against his solid, broad chest. "Why don't we get to know each *other* a little better?"

"I like how you think, Ms. Summers. Let's act on that suggestion."

And as he dipped his head to claim her lips in a gentle kiss that quickly escalated to a preview of the passion to come, she knew that here, in the circle of his arms, was where she belonged.

For always.

Epilogue

—— 4½ Months Later ——

"I think the excitement finally got to her." Keith grinned into the rearview mirror at Haley, who was passed out in her wedding finery on the backseat.

"I'm not surprised." Claire glanced over her shoulder. "I don't think she slept a wink last night."

"The professor was quite the diplomat, choosing Haley as maiden of honor. But it made sense, since she was the catalyst for this whole thing. Besides, it saved Maureen from having to pick between you and Debbie. No sense ruffling the feathers of the new in-laws."

"True. But she did ask me to sign as witness, which was very sweet." Claire sighed and leaned back against the headrest. "Wasn't it a lovely wedding? So intimate in the small chapel, with harp music in the background. And those elegant place settings at the dinner, plus the chair covers and tropical flowers and string quartet . . . perfect."

"The food was good too."

She gave him a playful jab. "Spoken like a stereotypical man."

"Guilty." He sent her an unrepentant grin, then grew more serious. "But I do appreciate the finer things in life. In fact, I'm sitting next to one of them."

"Hmm." He could hear her smile, even though he kept his gaze on the road. "You just redeemed yourself." She picked up the nosegay resting in her lap, and the scent of roses wafted his way.

"Interesting that you caught the bouquet."

Claire gave a soft laugh. "How could I not? She aimed it straight at me." She took a whiff and set the flowers back in her lap. "I'm glad everything turned out well. Maureen kept up a good front, but I know she was sweating it out until she got the results of the scan. I'm so glad the news was good." She sighed and fingered one of the rose petals. "Wasn't she a beautiful bride? That lace sheath was perfect for her, and the headpiece was stunning now that her hair has grown out long enough to have some soft waves."

"She looked very nice." But as far as he was concerned, the most stunning woman at tonight's event had been his date. In that sleek black cocktail dress with the flirty little slit in the back and a subtle clinginess that showed off her curves to perfection, Claire was a knockout. Once she stepped into the room, every other woman had paled in comparison—including the bride.

Best of all, she was his girl.

And she'd soon be more . . . if all went well.

"I hope they have a wonderful time in Hawaii."

It took him a few seconds to refocus. "I don't think there's any doubt of that. Knowing David, their honeymoon will be first class all the way." He swung into Claire's driveway. "Home sweet home. Sit tight and I'll get your door."

Usually she was out of the car before he could circle it, but tonight she waited for him.

"This fancy dress deserves the full treatment." She smiled up at him in the moonlight as she slid out.

"No. The lady in it does." He captured her hand and pressed her fingers to his lips. "Have I told you how beautiful you look tonight?"

"Several times—but a woman never gets tired of hearing compliments."

"Then expect to hear them often." He released her hand and opened Haley's door. She stirred and blinked up at him groggily. "We're home, kiddo."

Yawning, she retrieved her own miniature nosegay and climbed out of the car. "That was the most awesome wedding I ever went to."

"Also the only one." Claire put her arm around her daughter's shoulders and guided her toward the house. "Straight to bed for you, young lady. It's after eleven."

For once, Haley didn't protest.

Keith followed them up the narrow path. "Need any help inside?"

Claire fitted the key in the door and twisted the knob. "I can manage. Are you leaving?"

"No. I thought I'd wait for you out here." He gestured to the porch swing.

"Are you sure you don't want to sit on that great deck you built for my birthday?"

"The deck *we* built, you mean."

"You did all the heavy stuff."

"Nope. You more than pulled your weight—like you always do. But we'll have plenty of time to sit out there. I'm in a swinging mood tonight."

"Is that right?" She batted her eyes and sent him a saucy grin. "Hold that thought and give me ten minutes. Say good night, Haley."

"'Night." The little girl's farewell was more yawn than word.

Once mother and daughter disappeared inside, he strolled

over to the swing where he and Claire had spent many a summer evening after Haley was tucked in for the night. Where attraction and friendship had grown into deep, abiding love—just as he'd expected them to back in May. In light of Claire's bad experience in the marriage department, however, he'd resolved to give her time to get comfortable with their relationship, to be certain her future did, indeed, include him.

But her time was up.

Setting the swing in motion with a push of the toe, he double-checked the inside pocket of his jacket.

The small box was right where he'd tucked it.

Now he just had to wait—and try not to hyperventilate.

By the time Claire returned in less than the ten minutes she'd estimated, he was reasonably calm.

Yet the minute she appeared in the doorway, his pulse took a leap.

So much for cool and composed.

She sat beside him, scooting close as she always did, settling into the crook of the arm he'd draped over the back.

"That was fast." He bent his head to breathe in the scent of her hair. She felt so good resting against him. So right. So . . . perfect.

"Haley went out like a light the instant her head touched the pillow. But I have a feeling we'll be discussing Maureen's wedding for weeks to come. It did have a fairy-tale quality about it, don't you think?"

"Their meeting and courtship even more so. Who would have guessed all of this would come about because of a simple letter?"

"I know. It changed multiple lives—including mine. I never thought I could be this happy again."

That was his opening.

His heart skipped a beat, and he cleared his throat. "I think you could be even happier."

She shifted around to look at him, her expression quizzical, but before she could speak, he reached up and withdrew the black velvet case from his pocket.

Her eyes widened.

"You remember back in May how I said we should take the summer to get to know each other better?" His voice hoarsened, and he swallowed.

"Yes."

"The summer's over." He flipped up the lid to display the marquis-cut diamond in the gold setting.

Her sharp, indrawn breath was the only sound in the night, other than the gentle rustle of summer-weary leaves in the breeze.

He removed the ring from the box and held it with fingers that were suddenly shaky. "I've known almost from the beginning of our relationship that if I could get my past straightened out, my future would belong to you. And I hope you feel the same way, because at this point I can't imagine my life without you. You're the first thing I think of every morning and the last thing I think of every night. I spend half my time at the office daydreaming about you instead of working. Just ask Robin—she's always giving me a hard time about it. If David hadn't been going through the same thing with Maureen, my career would be toast."

He took her hand and folded it in his. Her eyes were shimmering when she looked up at him—a positive sign, he hoped.

"I know I'm no great bargain. I have a lot of quirks, and I expect I'll always try too hard to prove myself. But that also means I'll spend the rest of my life striving to be worthy of you. And I promise you this: no matter what our future together holds, I'll give you my fidelity, loyalty, devotion, and deepest love for as long as I live. I'll also love Haley, and be the very best father I can be to her." His heart was banging against his rib cage so hard it was bordering on painful. He paused. Swallowed. "So

Claire . . . will you give me the greatest gift I could ever receive and agree to marry me?"

She didn't hesitate.

"Yes." Her reply came out in a choked whisper, but there wasn't a shred of doubt on her face or in her voice.

The tension evaporated from his body so quickly he was glad he was sitting down. Otherwise, he had a feeling his legs would collapse beneath him.

He wasn't alone, however. Her hand didn't feel any too steady when he lifted it to slip on the ring.

Once it was secure, he slid his fingers into her silky hair and cupped the back of her head. "Before I seal this with a kiss, tell me how long I have to wait to say I do."

"I'd like to say next week."

"I'm good with that."

"But I'd also love to have a small, elegant wedding, like Maureen did."

"How long would that take to pull together?"

"Maureen and David began making plans the day after he proposed, but getting it done in four months was tough."

"So what date did you have in mind?"

When she traced the line of his jaw with her fingertip, it took every ounce of his willpower not to capture her hand and press a kiss to her palm. "Why don't we say our 'I do's' when the lilacs bloom again?"

"Around the end of April, right?" He considered the idea. "That might work. Paris is supposed to be beautiful in April—or so the old song says."

She blinked. "Paris?"

"Can you think of a more romantic place for a honeymoon?"

She stared at him. "A Paris honeymoon? Wow. I've never set foot outside the US."

"If there's somewhere else you'd rather go . . ."

"No. To be honest, anywhere alone with you would be wonderful."

"So I could take you to Branson?"

She chuckled. "Well, now that Paris has been put on the table . . ."

"Then Paris it is. And I'm pretty certain I can talk my mom into babysitting—unless you want to bring Haley along."

"On our honeymoon?" A look of mock horror spread across her face. "Forget it!" Eyes glinting with mischief, she gripped the lapels of his jacket and pulled him close. "That, my love, is going to be rated adults only."

Her breath was warm on his cheek, and the faint floral scent that was all Claire enveloped him as he guided her mouth toward his. "I like the sound of that. In the meantime, why don't we start with a preview that's rated for general audiences?"

"At the very least."

Her sweet lips welcomed his, eager and ardent, and as they both gave expression to their love in a kiss filled with passion and promise, joy overflowed within him.

For here, in the arms of this incredible woman, he'd found hope . . . home . . . and his own happy ending.

And for as long as he lived, he would give thanks for the gift of her love—and for a little girl's letter that had brightened so many lives.

Author's Note

A few years ago, I was asked in an interview if being a writer is a lonely profession. The question took me aback—because even though I spend most of my work week alone in front of my computer, I have never, ever been lonely. Yes, writing is a solitary occupation—but my days are filled with the fascinating characters who people my novels. How could I be lonely?

One Perfect Spring is a great example of this. Keith and Claire and David and Maureen (as well as many of the other characters) all had interesting stories to tell. Watching their relationships evolve, walking with them as they dealt with the fallout from old choices and the challenges of new ones, kept me intrigued—and anxious to find out what happened next. I hope you felt the same as you turned the pages!

While my fictional characters are great company, many real people also play an important role in my career. For this book, I owe a deep debt of gratitude to the following:

#1 *New York Times* bestselling author Debbie Macomber. With warmth, graciousness, and generosity, she took time out of her busy schedule to read this manuscript and offer me the stellar endorsement you see on the front and back covers. May your star continue to shine!

The amazing team at Revell. From editing to cover design, from marketing and publicity to sales and distribution, you are the best!

All the readers who seek out my books. You make it possible for me to give life to the characters who ask me to tell their stories—and I give thanks for you every day.

And finally, dearest Tom—my husband and hero. Since our very first date, you, too, have been the wind beneath my wings. Three dot . . . for always.

Irene Hannon is a bestselling, award-winning author who took the publishing world by storm at the tender age of ten with a sparkling piece of fiction that received national attention.

Okay . . . maybe that's a slight exaggeration. But she *was* one of the honorees in a complete-the-story contest conducted by a national children's magazine. And she likes to think of that as her "official" fiction-writing debut!

Since then, she has written more than forty-five contemporary romance and romantic suspense novels. Irene has twice won the RITA award—the "Oscar" of romantic fiction—from Romance Writers of America, and her books have also been honored with a National Readers' Choice award, two HOLT medallions, a Daphne du Maurier award, a Carol award, a Retailers Choice award, and two Reviewers' Choice awards from *RT Book Reviews* magazine. In 2011, *Booklist* included one of her novels in its Top 10 Inspirational Fiction list for the year. She is also a Christy award finalist.

Irene, who holds a BA in psychology and an MA in journalism, juggled two careers for many years until she gave up her executive corporate communications position with a Fortune 500 company to write full time. She is happy to say she has no regrets! As she points out, leaving behind the rush-hour commute, corporate politics, and a relentless BlackBerry that never slept was no sacrifice.

A trained vocalist, Irene has sung the leading role in numerous community theater productions and is also a soloist at her church.

When not otherwise occupied, she and her husband enjoy traveling, Saturday mornings at their favorite coffee shop, and spending time with family. They make their home in Missouri.

To learn more about Irene and her books, visit www.irenehannon.com.

Read an excerpt from
DECEIVED

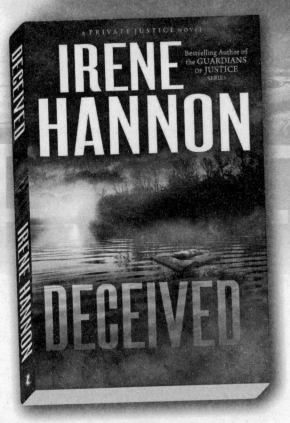

The next romantic suspense novel from
IRENE HANNON,
book 3 in the PRIVATE JUSTICE series
• • •
Coming
OCTOBER 2014

A stranger was coming up her driveway.

Decorative tube of icing poised over the cake, Kate Marshall froze as the crunch of gravel outside the open windows at the front of the house stopped by the porch.

Definitely not John. He would have headed straight to the detached garage in back, as usual. Besides, he and Kevin never cut their Wednesday fishing outings short. And none of their friends would make a social call at this hour of the morning.

A car door slammed, and she finished the last swirl of red icing on the *y* in *birthday*, frowning as a tingle of apprehension skittered through her. How silly was that? This was Hilton, New York, not New York City. A peaceful village of six thousand people. Just because she was a big-city girl who'd never quite acclimated to the solitude of their five-acre spread on the outskirts of town didn't mean it was unsafe.

Still, as the doorbell rang, she grabbed her cell out of her purse and slipped it in the pocket of her jeans—just in case.

But as she entered the living room and caught a glimpse of the dark-colored cruiser through the front window, her step faltered.

There would be no need for a 911 call.

The police were already here.

A sudden swirl of memories kaleidoscoped through her mind, catapulting her back sixteen years, to her eighteenth summer. A porch swing . . . a tall glass of tangy lemonade . . . a heart-melting romance novel. All the makings of a perfect June day.

Until a police car pulled up and a grim-faced officer emerged.

Two minutes later, as the man informed her and her mother that a faulty construction elevator at a job site had plunged her architect father three stories to his death, the perfect day had ended.

But history didn't repeat itself.

God wouldn't do that to her.

Would he?

Reining in her burgeoning panic, she breathed in, then out, and forced her feet to carry her across the living room.

Through the art-glass sidelight next to the front door, she had a distorted view of the uniformed man on the other side. He appeared to be young . . . and his expression was serious.

Her heart lurched.

Fingers fumbling the lock, she opened the door. "May I help you?" Her rote words seemed to come from a distance, leaving a hollow echo in her ears.

"Mrs. Marshall?"

"Yes."

The man clasped his hands behind his back and planted his feet a shoulder-width apart, in military at-ease position.

But he didn't look at ease.

His posture was rigid, his features taut.

"I'm Trooper Peyton, New York State Police. Did your husband go fishing in Braddock Bay this morning?"

"Yes."

He cleared his throat, and his Adam's apple bobbed. "I'm afraid there's been an accident."

No!

The denial screamed through her mind as she clutched the edge of the door, her slippery fingers leaving a smear of icing on the shiny white woodwork.

It looked like blood.

She tore her gaze away from the crimson smudge, her stomach

clenching as she forced her brain to process the man's statement
. . . and came to the only possible conclusion.

John was hurt.

Badly.

Otherwise, he would have called her himself.

Cold fingers squeezed her heart as she choked out the question she didn't want to ask. "My son . . . is he . . . is Kevin hurt too?"

The uniformed man frowned. "Your son?"

She blinked, furrowing her own brow. "Yes. My husband and son were together. Kevin's almost f-four." Her voice hitched on the last word.

The officer reached for his radio. "Let me call that in. The last I heard, they were only looking for a man."

Looking for?

The room began to spin, and she grabbed the door frame with her free hand. Darkness licked at her soul, snuffing out the light like storm clouds advancing on the sun. "What do you mean, looking for?"

His features softened as his radio crackled to life. "I'm sorry, ma'am. All we have so far is an overturned boat and an adult life jacket."

Adult life jacket.

As the words reverberated in her mind, she shook her head, trying to clear the muddle from her brain.

No.

That couldn't be right.

"Wait." She plucked at the man's sleeve. "You shouldn't have found a loose life jacket. My husband and son always wore their vests."

He held up a finger and angled away to speak into the radio, conveying the news about Kevin in a crisp, official tone before he turned back to her.

"If you could give me a description of what your husband

and son were wearing, ma'am, it would be very helpful to the search and rescue team."

He wasn't listening to her.

She stepped closer. In-your-face close. "Did you hear what I said? They always wore their life jackets. Always! John promised me they would, and he never broke his promises. There shouldn't be a loose life jacket. And where are they?" Her pitch rose as hysteria nipped at the edges of her voice.

"I don't know the answer to that question, ma'am, but we're doing everything we can to find them." The officer's reassuring tone did nothing to soothe her. "May I come in while I ask you a few more questions?"

She stared at him as an insulating numbness began to shroud her, weighing down her arms and legs, dulling her senses. "You expect me to just sit here while my husband and son are missing?"

"Professionals are handling the search, Mrs. Marshall. The most useful thing you can do is give us a description and answer some questions."

It wasn't enough.

But how else could she contribute? With her fear of the water, she'd hinder more than help if she showed up at the bay.

Closing her eyes, she sucked in a breath—and sent a silent, desperate plea to the almighty.

Stay with me, Lord. Please! I need your strength.

The officer took her arm. Wondering, perhaps, if she was going to cave?

Not yet.

But soon.

Because even as he guided her toward the couch, even as she prepared to answer his questions, she knew with soul-searing certainty that nothing she told him was going to change the outcome on this day intended to celebrate the beginning of her husband's thirty-sixth year.

And she also knew there would be no more happy birthdays in this house.

───Three Years Later───

Kate sniffed the enticing aromas wafting her way from the food court, transferred her shopping bag from one hand to the other, and checked her watch. Nope. She was already behind schedule, and being late for her one-thirty client wasn't an option. No lunch today.

So what else was new?

On the plus side, maybe she could swing by Starbucks after dinner and apply those saved calories to the ultimate summer indulgence—a double chocolaty chip Frappuccino, heavy on the whip.

A wry grin tugged at her lips as she lengthened her stride. Like that was going to happen. If this day followed her typical pattern, she'd be so exhausted by the time she got home she'd opt for a quick omelet or nuke a frozen dinner, then fall into bed—and the oblivion of sleep. But that was okay. Better catatonic slumber than nights spent watching the LED display on her bedside digital clock mark the slow-motion passing of middle-of-the-night minutes.

Cutting a path straight toward the escalator that led down to the first level of the mall, she averted her head as she passed the Mrs. Fields shop. Tempting, but not healthy.

But her pace slowed when her stomach rumbled, and somehow her course drifted to the right.

Okay. One cookie.

Two minutes later, cookie in hand, she took a large bite and closed her eyes as the warm chocolate melted on her tongue.

Nirvana.

Far tastier than the turkey sandwich in the fridge at work—the lunch she would have been eating if she hadn't volunteered last night to exchange her neighbor's defective heating pad during her lunch hour. But with the older woman's arthritis acting up . . . with the sweltering heat of a St. Louis July taking a toll on seniors who ventured out . . . with West County Center just ten minutes away from her office . . . how could she ignore the prodding of her conscience to do a good deed?

Besides, she might not be as old as her neighbor, but she knew what it was like to be hurting, and alone, and in desperate need of a respite from pain.

The chocolate lost some of its sweetness, but she shoved the last bite of cookie in her mouth anyway and picked up her pace toward the escalator. She was *not* going to let melancholy thoughts ruin this moment of pleasure. She'd done that far too often over the past few years—as her mother never hesitated to remind her during her occasional calls from the West Coast. Take what life hands you and get on with it, that was Angela Stewart's motto. And truth be told, it had served her well as she'd forged her executive career. Unlike her daughter, she hadn't needed valium to get through her first year of widowhood.

Then again, she hadn't lost a child too.

Kate shoved the chocolate-smeared paper napkin in a trash can, blinked away the moisture in her eyes, and straightened her shoulders. So she wasn't made of the same tough cloth as her mother. So she had a softer heart. But she'd survived the hard times and gotten her act together eventually, hadn't she? And that soft heart had turned out to be an asset in her counseling work.

A horde of Friday lunchtime shoppers jostled her as she approached the escalator, and she tightened her grip on the shopping bag. Good heavens, you'd think it was the day-after-Christmas sale.

Leading with her shoulder, she inserted herself in the middle of the surging throng, then maneuvered through the clusters of chattering women to claim a riser and began her descent. And to think some people found shopping fun.

Her errand had gone smoothly, though. Assuming she got out of the parking garage without delay, she should be back at the office in time to grab a bottle of water, touch up her lipstick, and run a comb through her hair before . . .

". . . a poppysicle?"

As the eager, childish voice carried over the background hum of mall noise, the air whooshed out of her lungs and she grabbed the railing.

Poppysicle?

The only child she'd ever heard use that term was Kevin.

And that voice—it sounded like his.

How could that be?

Whipping toward the adjacent ascending escalator, she scanned the crowd. Several risers above her, moving farther away by the second, she caught a glimpse of a youngster about seven or eight with hair the hue of ripening wheat.

The same color as hers.

The same color as her son's.

"Kevin?" Her incredulous whisper was lost in the cavernous echo of the mall.

She tried again, raising her voice. "Kevin!"

The boy angled her way. She caught a profile. Then a full face. As they made eye contact, as he frowned and cocked his head, her heart stalled.

He looked just how she would have expected Kevin to look when he was seven.

As they stared at each other, the noise in the mall receded. Movement slowed. Everything faded from her peripheral vision. Only the little boy's face registered.

Dear God, is that . . . ?

No. Impossible.

Wasn't it?

Two very different sisters . . .
an unexpected homecoming . . .
one unforgettable summer

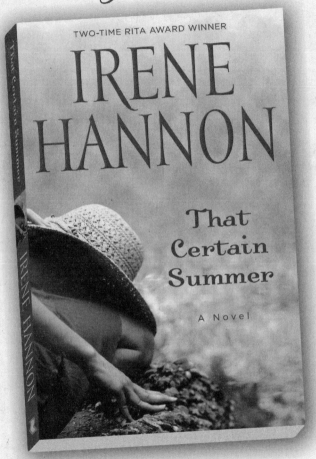

"Whether it's a fast-paced suspense or a contemporary
[romance], fans can't get enough of Hannon's uplifting stories."
—*RT Book Reviews*

Revell
a division of Baker Publishing Group
www.RevellBooks.com

Do you enjoy some SUSPENSE with your ROMANCE?
Check out IRENE'S latest bestselling romantic suspense novels!

"An excellent suggestion for readers who enjoy Mary Higgins Clark's subtly chilling brand of suspense."
—*Booklist*